CRUCIBLE OF FEAR

D.W. Whitlock

For my wife, who has always supported my forays
into the creative unknown

Excerpt from TechBeat.com article:

Beast in the Machine:
The New Face of Digital Harassment

By Ian Weller

Cases of cyber-harassment are on the rise, ranging from negative comments on social media to cyberstalking, the most insidious form of electronic harassment. Cyberstalking typically involves a bad actor attempting to damage their target's online reputation through negative social media posts, accusations of professional incompetence on networking sites, occasionally escalating to physical threats to their person and/or loved ones. Sometimes money is demanded to cease the harassment, but usually the perpetrator wishes to harm their target as an act of revenge for a perceived injury to themselves...

CHAPTER 1

Spider

Dante Ellis gazed down, eyes narrowing as a harsh blade of light raked the office interior revealing desiccated corpses under the tattered remains of web.

How long had a spider been there? he thought.

Kneeling, Dante peered closer and spied the predator's remains dangling from a few dusty strands where the windows joined at his corner office. It surprised him. He'd been here many late nights as the cleaning crew made their sweep. They were very thorough, but somehow, they'd missed this.

In the dim light straining up from the city below, Dante saw the spider's legs were kinked inward, its final act before dying. Gossamer remnants of web clung to the glass, fluttering in micro currents above the twenty or so confirmed kills.

Dante smirked. *Little guy had been busy.*

He pictured it floating above the busy mail room on a strand of silk before being sucked into an elevator shaft. It continued sailing on the updraft, legs splayed as it swirled all the way to the thirty-second floor of the Monolith tower. How it had negotiated the busy studio floor all the way down to Dante's corner office, he couldn't fathom, lying in wait to ambush unsuspecting prey.

Light swept the office again as a helicopter outside slowed

to a hover, appearing no larger than one of the spider's kills. Its spotlight continued over the tops of low-slung buildings to reveal an overturned car on the 134 freeway. Flames licked at the underside as smoke boiled up in a black smudge. Brake lights bloomed in a crimson smear as Friday evening traffic slowed to crawl.

A muffled cheer rose up from the party in the studio kitchen and Dante checked his watch.

Almost time.

He rose to his feet and looked down at the elephant pendant in his right palm. It gleamed in the dull light like a drop of mercury. "For when you get scared," Abigail had told him. He closed his hand around it.

The inner office door opened with a snick and he turned, head swimming. The wine he'd drunk earlier lay tart on the back of his tongue. The doorway was a black void, but Dante knew who it was. Only one other person had that code.

"Naomi," he said.

There was no sound, no movement. Dante peered into the darkness.

"Who's there?"

A dark figure emerged from the doorway, one arm thrust forward. Dante stumbled back, slipping a hand into his suit jacket to grab his phone. The figure's arm twitched. Sharp pain flared in Dante's chest as his mouth went dry. A delirious thought occurred to him as the phone slipped through his fingers.

The spider bit me.

Blinding white pain radiated out to encapsulate his whole body in a spasm of agony. The room tilted and something hard crashed into his face. Stars skittered off like electric cockroaches as everything went black.

Blood displaced the taste of wine in his mouth.

Ragged jolts of pain rippled through him, making his limbs kick as his entire body went numb. His vision returned, distorted, the office etched in shifting streaks of gray and black.

He lay on his right side, arm stretched out—hand clenched in a tight fist. Dante hoped Abigail's pendant was still there because right now, he needed it.

A light flared near his shoulder and hummed three times, more felt than heard. His phone. Dante tried to squeeze his eyes shut but he could only manage a weak flutter. The light died and his vision sharpened for a moment. The dark figure stood over him, the outline of the person's body razor-sharp against a starless sky. A ghost of its reflection shone in the glass behind.

The helicopter's light brushed past again, dimmer, revealing the figure to be a man dressed in black, face hidden behind a mask. A small object rose up over his shoulder, its delicate, greenish body reflecting brake lights from the traffic choked freeway far below. The orange wings flitted in a blur as it hovered.

It was a dragonfly.

A drone, much larger than the insect it had been built to mimic, its body at least eight inches long. The bulbous head bristled with miniature lenses and antennae that ticked with tiny movements as a red eye winked on its underside.

Dante's phone flared again and he heard the buzzing this time. A text appeared on the screen. The words smeared into dark streaks as he tried to read the small letters trapped inside the text bubble.

The man knelt beside Dante, gazing down at him for a moment, eyes glittering. Then he turned and hefted an object from a messenger bag slung over one shoulder. It was a rectangular black box with an elliptical hole at one end, about the size of a laptop but thicker by a few inches. He removed the top section and set it down, then slid the bottom of the box underneath Dante's clenched fist. His breath came out in a raspy hiss as he tried to protest. The dragonfly hovered closer, its flinty eyes adjusting with the faint hum of gears.

The dark figure sat back on his heels and pulled the mask up, head hung low. There was something strange about his face. Dante narrowed his eyes, face muscles twitching with the effort.

The man was crying.

"Sorry," he said, wiping his face with the back of one arm. "They were just never going to stop."

The dragonfly vibrated its wings with an impatient jitter and the man pulled the mask back down. He picked up the top of the box and placed it over Dante's right hand. The two halves sealed shut with a series of harsh clicks. The low throb of distant music filled the silence.

Pain lanced deep into Dante's wrist followed by a cold heaviness in his hand. He struggled to move, gasping as a wave of cramps rippled through him.

"Don't fight it," his attacker said, voice thick. "It'll only make it worse."

For a moment, Dante hoped this was a joke gone too far and everyone from the party would come pouring in, laughing, slapping him on the back.

From inside the box came a high metallic squeal, like screws being tightened down. The sound stopped and the room became silent again save for the whisper of the drone's four wings.

The party had gone strangely quiet.

The masked man turned his face away and a muffled thump discharged from deep within the box, followed by a slight tug at Dante's wrist. His body went icy cold.

This was no joke.

With trembling fingers, the man reached down and picked up the box before rising unsteadily to his feet. The box slipped from his grasp and fell, one corner striking the carpet with a thud. The two halves split open and the contents of the box spilled out and spun to a stop.

"Oh, Jesus," the man said.

Dante peered at the pale thing that lay there, eyes straining to pierce the gloom. Whatever it was, it had legs.

The legs twitched.

A hysterical laugh bubbled up in Dante's throat. *It's the fucking spider.*

The hum of the dragonfly's wings pitched down as it dropped lower then hovered again, a few feet from the floor. A bright pinpoint of light speared out from its underside, the beam flicking across the floor before coming to a halt.

The legs of the spider twitched again. But it wasn't a spider. It was a hand.

His hand.

The sickly, sweet odor of cauterized flesh stung the air as dark fluids oozed from the blackened stump. Dante's stomach hitched and bile rose in his throat, the sour taste scorching his tongue.

The man picked up the severed hand with a thumb and forefinger. A bead of silver slipped out of the palm, dropping to the carpet. Dante's fear-poisoned brain tried to remember what it was.

The hand dropped into the messenger bag. The man shuddered as it disappeared inside. Then he scooped up both halves of the box and fled, disappearing back through the inner office door, the hum of the drone close behind.

The room fell silent again.

Spasms wracked his body as Dante rolled onto his stomach, right arm heavy and unresponsive. He winced as his phone lit up, the touch of his face bringing the screen to life.

Need to call somebody.

He tried to speak but all he could muster was a low groan. It was a struggle to lift his head, neck joints popping under the strain. As the screen came into focus, the text he'd received earlier resolved, tack sharp. The words struck him like a hammer blow.

*And if your right hand causes you to sin,
cut it off and cast it from you.*

His heart thudded as pain lanced up his arm. He clutched

at the stump with his other hand, the seared flesh slick with warm blood. He tried to call out again but his throat closed up, the cords of his neck taut. With a grunt he rolled onto his back, the ceiling tiles spinning above him.

Dante Ellis was finally able to find his voice, and he screamed.

CHAPTER 2

Perfect Things

Two weeks earlier...

"C'mon, sleepy head. Time to get up," Dante said, throwing open the curtains.

Bright morning sun filtered in through the oak trees outside. The bedroom window was only open an inch, but he could already hear the hiss of the 101 freeway under the incessant bleat of car horns. Dante peered past the shifting leaves down into the valley and saw that West Hollywood was already wide awake.

Through the morning heat, glittering windshields shimmered along the narrow streets between low slung buildings, a byproduct of a city built among active fault lines. Further south, taller buildings of glass and steel jutted up along Miracle Mile as if daring nature to do its worst.

Abigail stirred, bright green eyes blinking in the harsh light before she made a face and pulled the blanket over her head. Dante sat on the edge of his daughter's bed and pulled the blanket down. Nine years old and she already looked so much like her mother. Strong jawline, reddish brown hair. Same button nose. Pale, olive skin but still with the ruddy glow of youth in her cheeks. He reached down and smoothed the hair away from her face and tucked it over one ear.

"Daddy?" Abigail said, opening her eyes. "I had that dream about mommy again."

Dante felt his throat tighten. "Abigail..."

"She's underwater, her hair is all floating around and she's trying to say something but she can't." Tears appeared at the corners of her eyes, threatening to break loose.

"It was just a dream," Dante had said those words many times before, but Abigail remained unconvinced. "It just means she's watching over you and always will be." Dante sighed. "You were all she ever wanted. You know? A perfect, beautiful little girl. You look so much like her."

Abigail nodded, blinking back tears. "Yeah?"

"When you were in her tummy, she ate all the best foods and took special vitamins. For a treat, she'd have ice cream. Mint chocolate chip. You'd kick up a storm," Dante said, tugging one of her feet. She didn't giggle like she usually did. Just held his gaze and frowned.

"I know where babies come from, Dad. I wasn't in her tummy. I was in her..."

"Hey, how about I take you to school today?"

"What about your video meetings?"

"No meetings today. Let's give Kelly the morning off. Just me and you. Okay?"

Abigail squinted at him, then smiled.

"Okay."

Abigail dashed through the dining room, dressed in the navy-blue jacket and skirt of her school uniform. Kelly Shepherd sat with her legs tucked beneath her at the breakfast nook, bemused smile on her face. Her black hair shimmered in the morning light, stark against the pale skin of her face. The purple track suit she wore hugged every curve but the zipper was pulled up to her throat, Dante noted with disappointment. A tall silver carafe and a matching bowl of sugar cubes stood before her. The slender fingers of one hand encircled a thick, porcelain mug, filled to the brim with fresh coffee. Her eyebrows inched up with surprise as she spread her arms.

"What, no kiss?"

Abigail ran back to her and kissed her cheek. "Daddy's taking me to school," she said in a whisper.

"I know," she said, grinning.

Abigail hurried off, shoes ticking across the tile floors. The door leading to the garage opened with a bang and Abigail disappeared inside the darkness.

"Turn on the light!" Kelly called out to her. "Don't just run into a dark room."

Dante strolled in, gazing after Abigail with a grin.

"Just like you," Kelly said. "Running headlong into things."

Dante poured some coffee into an insulated travel cup Kelly had set out. "More fun that way," he said. The lid went on crooked and he struggled to push it on straight.

"Give it here," Kelly said as she reached over and pulled it from his grasp. She slammed her hand down on the lid, locking it in place before handing it back over.

Dante laughed. "When it doubt, pummel it into submission."

"More fun that way," Kelly said. "She misses you."

"I know," Dante said. "I really appreciate you helping out."

She opened her mouth then closed it again, eyes distant. "Of course."

Dante sat across from her and watched as she sipped her coffee, full lips pursing at the bitter taste. She grabbed a sugar cube and plopped it in her cup, giving it a quick stir with a spoon.

About a year ago, they'd shared a bottle of wine and watched episodes of a show she'd starred in about models by day, hackers by night. They'd kissed, but since then, she'd kept it strictly platonic, at her insistence. *Catwalk* had been a hit, run for nine seasons and was in syndication in several markets. It kept Kelly flush with royalty checks and in the contacts of casting directors, netting her the occasional part. She always smelled faintly of lilac and Dante had formed a Pavlovian response to that scent in spite of his better judgment.

She caught him staring.

"What?" she said, gazing across the table with deep blue eyes. The morning sun touched the green around her pupils and his breath caught.

"Uh," he said, "I was just wondering how the audition went."

"Didn't get it. I guess they don't need another has-been clutching at her script in desperation." She shook her head. "I didn't really prepare for it anyways."

"That doesn't sound like you. 'Prep is paramount'."

"Yeah, I know. I just...feel like I've been prepping my whole life. And for what? I'm just tired of it, I guess."

"I hope it wasn't because you were taking care of Abigail," Dante said. "I've just got so much going on right now."

"Warren always had so much going on. I hardly ever saw him. Always buried in his projects. It was like quicksand, what he did. He could never escape. Just long enough to catch his breath then down he'd go again."

"That's not me."

"Friends warned me about getting involved with a producer, but whom else can you meet in the biz except other self-centered obsessives? Warren promised when we got married that he'd slow down, take it easy, not make the same mistakes that he'd made with his first wife. You know I only met his kids once? That was at his funeral."

"Kelly..."

"I know, I know. I'm just the next-door neighbor. Not my place," she said taking another sip. She grimaced and put her cup down. "Your coffee sucks, you know."

Dante slid his hand over hers. "It's not like that," he said giving her hand a squeeze. "Those first few years after Michelle died...I don't know what we would have done without you."

Her eyes found his again. "That little girl loves you, Dante. She needs you."

"I'll take time off in a few months. After I get the new media building up and going. I promise."

"After. That's how it was with Warren. Always after."

"Was the audition for an overbearing mother? Cause you would've killed it."

Kelly leaned toward him. Her eyes serious. "When are you going to find a nice girl and settle down?"

Dante held his hands up in surrender. "And...scene." He stood and kissed the top of her head. "Thanks, Mom. I'll see you tonight."

Kelly watched Dante stroll out through the kitchen door into the dark garage, raising a hand as he turned to give her a wave.

She shook her head. Neither one of them had bothered to turn on the garage light.

CHAPTER 3

Old and New

The garage door rose with a hum, allowing bright morning light to flood in. Dante sighed and took a moment to appreciate his latest tax write-off. All electric, ready to pounce, shiny as a shark's eye, according to the brochure. A bit over the top but he had to admit, the Mako looked damn nice sitting there.

Abigail peeked under the thick, canvas tarp that covered the other car in the garage, head tilted to one side. She kicked at one of the tires.

"Why can't we take grandpa's car?"

"Hey, don't. It's a classic." Dante pulled the tarp back down over the cream-colored hood and shooed her inside the Mako.

He slid into the driver's side and the eagle-wing doors hissed shut with a spongy kiss. Still had that new car smell too. He breathed in deep. *How could it be poisonous when it smelled so good?* he thought. Dante gazed down at his phone, finger flicking across the screen to check through what appeared to be countless emails waiting for him.

"Dad, do you have to? I want to tell you something," Abigail said.

"Just a few. Go ahead, I'm listening."

Abigail frowned and turned away, folding her arms across her chest. Dante scanned the emails until the car chimed, offering to drive. He punched the auto-drive cancel on the dash screen. Slipping his phone into the charging cradle, Dante eased the Mako out into the street.

After hugging the tight confines of Torreyson Drive, Dante turned onto the winding curves of Mulholland that led out of the Hollywood Hills. It was the long way to Cahuenga Boulevard but he loved carving those tight turns, relishing the feeling of control the car gave him.

Dante turned off the street and slid in behind the long line of other vehicles queued up in front of Abigail's school, Gilroy private academy. Parents barely glanced up from their phones as children leapt out and scampered up the concrete walkway. Dante sat with a vacant stare of his own as he skimmed over the hundreds of emails he received every day. Expense reports, contract offers, updates from his lawyers, dozens of junk emails begging him to fill out a survey. They always seemed to slip past the filters.

He kept skimming until one caught his eye. It was just a blank line, out of place among the dense list. As he peered closer, it flickered, gibberish filling the subject line.

Dante frowned and checked the sender. Robert J. Bainbridge. It must be important. Bob was a phone guy, loved the sound of his own voice too much to waste it in written form.

With a fingertip Dante tapped on the email. An indecipherable wall of gibberish flashed on screen before disappearing.

He felt a tug at his elbow.

"Dad."

"Abigail, what?" Dante said, then sighed. "Sorry, what were you saying?"

"I didn't say anything." Abigail opened the door and stepped out. "Love you," she said, shutting the door before hurrying off into a swarm of school uniforms.

"Love you," Dante said to the empty car.

A pang of regret prickled inside him as he watched Abigail trudge through the chaotic swirl of children rushing inside. The red in her dark hair shone amongst the blue uniformed throng of shuffling bodies until she disappeared inside the front doors.

The phone buzzed.

He sighed again, eyes tightening as he read the text on the screen. Lifting the phone closer he checked the sender.

Unknown.

The image of Abigail's hair faded from his mind as his read the text again.

The more a thing is perfect,
the more it feels pleasure and pain.

CHAPTER 4

Monolith

The Mako slid smoothly down Alameda Avenue, sun shimmering in the rearview mirror. Dante took his hands off the wheel and let the auto-drive take over. The phone sat in the charging cradle mounted on the dash, but still he felt the phantom twitch of it against his outer thigh. Something about that text had bothered him but he couldn't quite say what it was.

The more a thing is perfect,
the more it feels pleasure or pain.

The text disappeared as he'd sat there staring at it. Spam email and robocalls used to be a major problem, but the latest offender was sales texts. Most were filtered out but sometimes one or two slipped through.

Is that what this was?

Maybe the rest of the message had been cut off. The words seemed vaguely threatening but for all he knew, it was just a coupon for a massage parlor.

Dante lowered the window and let the cool morning air fill the car, clearing his head as the Monolith Media tower came into view. The glass and steel structure stood high above the surrounding buildings, dominating the skyline like a multifaceted black mirror. Dante squinted, but couldn't see his new Ellis Media building going up further down through the glare.

As the Monolith loomed large overhead, the security gate sensed his car and rose with just enough clearance to enter. The Mako slid into the underground parking without a sound. He'd chosen this building for many reasons but the feature that clinched it was a private stairwell and elevator that led to the inner offices of the upper suites.

Dante took the stairs.

Taking them two at a time, he ran all the way up to the thirty-second floor. A sheen of sweat covered his face as he input his code into a keypad next to the door. The lock popped with a clunk and the lights rose as he entered, illuminating dark wall panels of walnut and a beech wood changing bench. He stripped off his shorts and t-shirt, dropping them on the black slate tile as he strolled barefoot to the shower.

He winced and lifted his left foot, peering down at the hard, white growth that had formed on the ball of his foot. More annoying than painful, he was glad this Friday morning it would be surgically removed.

The shower hissed to life as he stepped in. Closing his eyes, he placed his palms flat against the wall and let the warm water run over him, releasing knots that had formed in his shoulders.

The more perfect a thing is perfect, the more it feels pleasure or-

He punched the shiny chrome button under the shower head and the water ceased.

Drying off, he walked back out and tossed the towel on the bench. One wall slid open revealing dress shirts and tailored suits along with a selection of Italian leather shoes. He selected a crisp blue shirt with a white collar and cuffs along with dark slacks and shoes. He combed his thick, dark hair back from his forehead and tugged at the few grays that had begun to show at his temples before smoothing them down. He touched the scar that crept up his forehead into his hairline then checked his teeth in the mirror.

His clothes still lay on the floor where he'd left them and he glanced around. The PUP 1.0 sat mutely in one corner, charging light blinking on the back of its rounded, rectangular orange body. Its four mechanical legs were tucked underneath and the arm attached to its back was folded up tight. It was a beta unit, and upon delivery it had operated flawlessly, emptying waste baskets and putting clothes in the hamper. Lately though, it had begun to act erratically, tossing clothes into the waste basket and ignoring trash altogether. The rest of the time it sat motionless, connected to its charger as if in protest. Dante kicked the clothes into a hamper against the wall and pumped a fist as they disappeared inside.

He pushed down on the brushed aluminum handle and entered his outer office. A workstation sat along one wall, sporting large monitors mounted on metal arms. The opposite wall was floor to ceiling windows with a view of Studio City, Bel air, and the hills of Topanga State Park. Beyond that was the Pacific Ocean, visible on the rare, smog free day.

His desk was a modest glass and steel structure devoid of any decoration. The high-backed leather chair was tucked in, rarely used. It seemed like when he sat behind that desk something bad happened. A serious talk with an employee about their future. Cancelled contracts. When he had to fire someone. He'd been sitting in that expensive, comfortable chair when he'd got the call about Michelle.

He sat on the front edge of the desk and a large screen on the wall in front of him sprang to life. His calendar appeared, highlighting upcoming meetings as Naomi walked in, a tablet tucked under one arm.

She swept past without looking at him, heels ticking as she walked over and sat on the couch, one leg crossing over the other. Her blonde hair was pulled back into a severe bun and a pair of thick-framed glasses sat upon the bridge of her nose. Her deep brown eyes scanned over her tablet before she flicked her hand and the calendar updated.

"Uh, good morning?" Dante said.

"After your little speech to the team you have that meeting with Megan Zhou and Raj Vikal from Hinds & Younger Foods."

"Right. I'm ready."

"And Skylar Westfall of Spearhead Data called," Naomi said.

"Several times. I thought we were done with him."

"We are," Dante said. "The contract is dead after that stunt he pulled. Building access revoked months ago. It's in the lawyer's hands now."

"Some whiz kid he turned out to be."

"Well, he looks younger than he actually is. Some kind of growth issues when he was a kid. He's brilliant, could've worked anywhere. Microsoft, Google, Amazon. Thought sure there was something there."

"Another young Dante in the rough?" she said, one eyebrow raised.

"Anything else, Naomi?"

"Bob is going to call sometime after eleven. Tomorrow, you have a lunch interview with Ian Weller of Techbeat.com at the new building and the summer party is next Friday night, but I got that covered. And Dante?"

"Yes?"

"Hinds & Younger Foods is huge. You need to land this one."

Dante bristled. "I got this. I know Megan. We used to work together over at the Bliss Group. That's how this works, Naomi. Connections."

"Yes, but Vikal is the one you have to impress."

"I. Got. This."

"That's what I want to talk about, actually," Naomi said. "I'm on all of our accounts as a senior producer. My fingerprints are all over them, each and every one."

"Agreed. You're a huge asset to Ellis Media."

"I'm more involved than you these days, what with the new building and lawyers and permits."

"Naomi," Dante said, an edge creeping into his voice.

"Give me Hinds & Younger. I already know who I want to direct the spots for us. Milos Kazan. Remember him? He did our Veritas Insurance ads. He'd be perfect for this. I already pinged his agent and he said Milos has a gap in his schedule coming up."

"We don't even have the account yet."

"But you got this," she said with smirk.

"You're not ready."

She looked at him, eyes hard. "More like you're not ready. Just can't let go, can you? I break my ass then you swoop in at the end, making all your little changes. I'm not the only one who feels this way...," she stopped herself and took a deep breath. "I'm ready to move up, Dante, and you know it."

"Not yet."

"When will I be ready? After I let you fuck me again?"

Dante glanced up sharply. "Is that what it was? Just a fuck?"

"No, it wasn't like that, but it's...complicated." She shook her head. "I like you, Dante, you know that and I adore Abigail but my whole life is tied up in this job and I'm good at it. I just can't be with you. Not while I work here. If anything happened with us..."

"I'm used to it," Dante said, hating the words as soon as he'd uttered them.

"What was that?"

Dante walked around his desk, pulled out the chair and sat down. It creaked in the silence. "You're right. I just...anything else?" he said with a tight smile.

Naomi eyed him before peering back down at her tablet. "Just one other thing."

"Yeah?" Dante said, staring at the green hills of Topanga Park through the haze. No ocean today. Not even a glimmer. The Pacific could be a stubborn bitch.

"Someone named Colin Murray is here to see you."

Dante's eyes narrowed.

"You know him? He's in the lobby. Says he's an old friend."

It had been a long time since Dante had heard that name. He swallowed hard.

"You alright?" Naomi said.

Dante checked his watch then got to his feet. "Tell him to wait."

CHAPTER 5

Dear Baby

Dante walked down a long, gray carpeted hallway with doors placed at regular intervals on either side. Edit bays, recording booths, sound editorial, even a Foley room for performing and recording sounds were all housed here and he'd overseen the installation of each one. From his first tiny studio above a hardware store to the top floor of the Monolith Tower, they had come a long way. And they were still growing. He felt a thrill of excitement as he thought of their new home being built right down the street where Alameda and Riverside met.

He heard the murmur of his staff conversing in low tones, awaiting his arrival at the small stage set up directly behind the wall separating reception from the studio floor. A smattering of applause broke out as he strode up through the maze of cubicles then through a gap in the crowd.

Some wore loose body suits with the hoods pulled down, bleached a stark white with angular black stripes marching across at varying angles. Called dazzle camo, the pattern was supposed to confuse AI tracking software used by police, CIA, NSA or whatever "Big Brother" boogeyman was currently in vogue. People who wore them were dubbed "Maskcreants" by the news media but they weren't illegal. Yet. Dante didn't mind if people wore them at work as long as they kept the hoods off.

It seemed more of a fashion trend than anything.

He thought they were just being paranoid.

Along the far wall, a string of longtime employees clapped perfunctorily or stood with arms across their chests, annoyed at having their work interrupted for a speech they'd all heard before.

Lights dimmed as Dante clipped a small microphone on his lapel. He went over the presentation in his head, even though he knew it well. The first time he'd given it was at NAB, almost ten years ago. The video had racked up half million views, and sparked no shortage of debate in the comments over his "willful manipulation of consumer anxiety". At first, he thought he'd sunk his career with his insight but the exact opposite had occurred.

A spotlight flared on overhead, tracking him as climbed up and strode center stage. He looked out over the shadowed faces of artists, designers, editors, writers and producers with pride swelling in his chest. Ellis Media had grown to over two hundred employees in the last few years and their ledger was full. So full, they'd begun outsourcing smaller accounts to other firms. He stepped forward and held his hands up for silence before he spoke.

"Fear. It drives so much of our behavior and what we consume. Fear that you can't run fast enough if you don't have *those* shoes. Fear that life will outpace you without the fastest car with the latest technology. Fear that someone won't love the real you if you don't smell like those beautiful people in commercials who dive off glaciers into an icy blue sea. Fear, ladies and gentlemen. The most primal, powerful force in our lives, outpacing anger, hate. Even love.

"If you think about it, all those other emotional responses are mere extensions of fear. And lucky for us, that's where advertising comes in to play. I've been accused of selling fear, but it's not as simple as that. You can't point to a man-eating shark then offer to sell a shark cage. The art to advertising is much more subtle than that."

Dante paused for a moment. The studio was silent, all eyes on him.

"As advertisers, we create the illusion of what life would be like with the specific advantage that our clients' product offers. It's about identifying, then evoking a specific emotional response, then offering a lifeline. If we do our job right, people will create their own fears, their own sharks, if you will.

"But people are smart. Remember that. Always respect the consumer. It's not their fault if they don't understand the message. It's *our* fault. We control the narrative and I can't stress this enough. Subtlety is key. Allow me to share a story with you."

Dante paused, gazing over the crowd before continuing.

"Before my daughter was born, my late wife and I went shopping for cribs at Babies First, back when they still had brick and mortar stores. I was struck by what I saw, or rather, didn't see. Diapers, clothes, formula, strollers, cribs. Where were they? All the things you really need for a newborn, nowhere to be seen. So, what did I see? Safety products. The front half of the entire store was devoted to the safety of your newborn son or daughter.

"Soft edging for sharp furniture. Special, hypoallergenic mats and blankets of all kinds, shapes and colors. On the packaging of every single one of those products was a magnified view of all the horrid creatures hiding in the carpet. God forbid your fragile little creation be allowed near such evil."

Dante walked along the stage, counting off with his fingers.

"Cabinet locks. Baby gates. Motion sensors. Monitoring systems supplying around the clock video feeds of your precious little captive, all of them with infrared night vision built right in. Federal prisons, take note. You'll find nothing so secure as a modern nursery."

A few people chuckled.

"No subtlety at all. No finesse. You'll get the new parents that way, but after your first kid you realize all of that safety stuff is for the parent. Not for the child."

Dante looked down a moment, collecting his thoughts.

"Picture with me now, a newborn baby, sleeping peacefully in their crib. We truck back slowly, revealing the infant tucked into a Smart Swaddle with built in heart monitor, their tiny body held in place by a gently vibrating Tranquil Tuck. A gentle shushing rises and falls, emanating from a Soft Sounds on the changing table, mimicking the natural audio-scape of the womb. We pull back even more, revealing a multi-camera setup tucked inconspicuously inside a series Teddy Cams placed around the room, all with built in night vision.

"Still with me? Cross dissolve to the parents sitting comfortably downstairs at the dining room table, a live feed from the Teddy Cams displayed on their smart TV and on their phone app. But they're doing something a bit strange in this day and age. They're writing a letter. A handwritten letter with actual paper and ink. A *Dear Baby* letter.

"The scene dissolves to a laughing toddler running through the morning sun, then a young boy dressed in his baseball uniform, the winning trophy held high overhead as his parents congratulate him with hugs and teary kisses. The scene changes again. It's nighttime and the parents are sitting at that very same table with a young man in a cap and gown. He looks up from the letter his parents wrote all those years ago and smiles. An overlay appears that reads: Dear Baby. Products, for life."

Applause broke out and Dante let it wash over him. All these years later, he was still very proud of the campaign that had made his career. The applause waned and he spoke again.

"So where were the sharks in that scenario? There were no sharks. The parents made sure there were none. But the take-away is the same. The sharks are implied to exist outside the protective bubble and the lifeline was the entire Dear Baby product line. So here at Ellis media, we don't sell fear. You can't sell something that already exists at the very core of the human psyche. We identify the fear, but sell the lifeline.

"So, what about fear in our own lives? Well, allow me to

leave you with this. It has served me well, and hopefully it'll serve you as well when you're afraid of taking that irreversible leap."

Dante cleared his throat before he spoke again. "Beware; for I am fearless, and therefore powerful."

CHAPTER 6

Ghosts

Dante punched his code into the keypad next to his office door and the lock opened. He twisted the knob and pushed inside, feeling a little smugger than he cared to admit.

He stopped short, his grin fading.

"Nice speech," said a slender man standing in the middle of his office.

Colin Murray was still as tall Dante remembered, but he was even thinner now, almost skeletal. He grinned and blinked, causing his whole face to twitch as if the simple act caused him pain. Since Dante had known him, he'd had that facial tic and it had earned Colin the most obvious nickname when they were kids: Twitch.

Dante extended his hand and they shook. Colin's grip was firm, but when Dante pulled him into a half embrace and patted his back, he could feel his sharp shoulder blade through the thin fabric of his suit.

Dante motioned for him to sit on the couch. Colin sat as far as he could at one end, eyes on the floor, barely making a dent in the cushion. He pushed a lock of pale blond hair away from his forehead as Dante joined him, the couch leather creaking as he sat. The silence stretched as neither man spoke.

"Well, it's good to see you, Colin. How long has it been?

Three, four years?"

"Five," Colin said with a full-face blink. He turned and looked at Dante, eyes flicking upward. "Still got it I see."

Dante touched the scar at his hairline. "It helps me remember how hard things can get."

Colin's face tightened and he looked away. "I don't have any problems remembering how hard it can get."

"What can I do for you, Colin?" Dante said, an edge creeping into his voice.

Colin shook his head and smiled. "Ah, shit, Dante, I'm sorry. I thought about what I was going to say for a long time, but I'm blowing it, aren't I?" The thin man stood and trudged over to the corner where the floor to ceiling glass met. "Fuck," he said under his breath, gazing out over the city below, muscles bunching in his jaw. He turned, eyes bright. "How's Abigail?"

"Smart and kind, like her mother," Dante said. "Impatient, like me."

Colin shook his head and looked back down at the city. "Things didn't go exactly how we planned, did they?"

Dante sighed, got to his feet and stood next to Colin. "What happened to you?"

"Just couldn't get past it. Not like you anyway." Colin turned and gazed at Dante. His eyes haunted. "After what happened, you know. At the Place," he swallowed, motioning to Dante's head.

The Place was an old pumping station where they'd hung out during the summer as kids. It was much cooler out of the sun inside its cinderblock walls among the rusty, dripping pipes. Until that day when both their lives had changed there.

Colin's face brightened. "Hey, remember when we borrowed your dad's car and T-boned that VW Bug?"

Dante smiled at the memory. "I didn't even know he was capable of that much passion. 'That Porsche's a classic! Now the bonnet's all fucked up!'" Dante shook his head. "The bonnet. I tried to tell him that German cars don't have bonnets, but he insisted." Dante checked his watch. "Listen Colin, I'm swamped. I want to catch up, but can we get together some other time?"

"This'll be quick. I came with an offer. You deal with raw, uncompressed 24 K video streams, right?"

Dante was taken aback by this sudden left turn into shop talk. "Uh, no. Nobody does. 24 K TV's are barely on the horizon. I want to get ahead of the curve, sure, but it's just too much data to deal with."

"Right," Colin said. "I'm still at Kellerman Digital, of course, and I head up some of their big data compression projects. We're looking into video streams too, on the fly compression and decompression but at data rates unheard of. We use machine learning software and it's getting faster all the time. Video is much easier as the software can make educated predictions of the final image. It's not perfect but to the human eye it won't look any different."

"Sounds intriguing," Dante said, a little disappointed. All these years without a word, then he suddenly shows up and it's all business. "Your timing is perfect actually. The boy genius we contracted a while ago to do exactly that turned out to be a bust."

"Huh," Colin said as he took out his phone, finger hovering over the screen. "Can I send you the deck? It has all the info."

Dante nodded but Colin just stood there, a muscle twitching at the corner of one eye.

"Go ahead," Dante said. "It's okay."

Colin's finger flicked across the screen. "You got it. Take a look and if you're interested, let me know." The thin man hurried over and pushed against the door, causing it to rattle.

"There's a knob," Dante said.

Colin glanced over his bony shoulder, face scrunching up with a nervous grin. "Oh yeah, I forgot." He turned the knob and slipped out.

Dante stared at the open doorway for a moment before he walked over and pulled the door shut again. A spiky slew of emotion swelled inside his chest, things he hadn't felt in a long time. Guilt crossed with a sense of responsibility? Not exactly. More like a debt unpaid.

One he could never repay.

I don't really owe Colin though, do I? He made a choice that day at The Place. I've learned to live with my own wounds, Dante thought as he touched the scar at his hairline. He sighed. Colin was just another one of those fractured, personal complications that he seemed to accumulate as he grew older, dropped in a box and filed on a shelf for another time. Sometimes forever.

Until today.

After sitting at his workstation, Dante wiggled the mouse to wake it up, then typed in his passcode. Scanning through his emails, he found the deck Colin had just sent him and opened the attached file. All the screens flashed and went dark. He reached out and moved the mouse again. An image appeared of a widescreen television with the caption: Machine learning aided compression for Large Data Sets.

Dante sat a moment, brows knitted before he hit ESC on the keyboard, causing the image to vanish.

CHAPTER 7

Westfall

A chime rang out and Dante glanced at the notice that popped up on the monitor. Half an hour until his meeting with Hinds & Younger.

Naomi was right. He had to nail this one.

Dante slipped a hand into his pocket. *Shit, must have left my phone in the car again.*

Dante rode the elevator down to the parking garage and pushed open the double doors. The August heat had picked up and he tugged at his collar. Stark morning light shone through the barred windows that ran along the top edge of a concrete wall to his right. He hurried past the cars parked below to his assigned space.

"Fuck!" Dante said, swatting at a large dragonfly that zoomed past his face. Its green body glittered as it swooped up and landed on a bundle of pipes. The orange wings flitted twice as it rested.

Michelle loved dragonflies, Dante thought. *Don't think she'd like this one.*

Suppressing a shudder, he jogged over to the Mako and reached inside as the door eased open, retrieving his phone. He stood back as the door eased shut again. Someone was standing near the front of his car, silhouetted against the light.

"Mr. Ellis."

It was Skylar Westfall. His boyish face was pinched with worry under meticulously parted hair. He wore flip flops, cargo shorts and a t-shirt with a cartoon image of a dog sitting in a burning kitchen saying: This is fine.

"You shouldn't be here," Dante said. "If you have anything more to say, talk to my lawyer."

"Wait, just hear me out."

"You screwed me, Skylar. I invested in your company for exclusive access to Cruncher then you go and upload it for free?" Dante turned to go. "We're done."

"Mr. Ellis," Skylar called after him. "Dante," he said louder, holding up a sliver square about the size and thickness of a dime.

Dante stopped and glanced over his shoulder.

"This is better," Skylar said, high voice dropping to a conspiratorial croak. "It's called Bothrops Asper. Blows Cruncher out of the water. Install it and you'll see what I mean."

"Bothrops what? Jesus, Skylar." He shook his head and continued walking. "What the hell happened to you?" Dante noted that it was the second time he'd said that today.

Skylar followed close behind. "I'm trying to help you. Please, you *need* to take this."

"Listen, it's business, not personal," Dante said over his shoulder, voice echoing off the concrete. He stopped in front of the glass doors leading to the elevators.

Skylar stood behind him, reflected in the glass. His small hand was outstretched, the tiny silver square gleaming in his palm. He looked every inch of his five and half feet. Childlike. There was something about his eyes though. They were hard, like the eyes of a much older person who'd been changed by what they'd seen.

Dante sighed. "Give it here," he said, holding his hand out.

Skylar put the tiny chip in his palm. "Plug this into any USB on your network and it'll take care of the rest."

"Now get out of here," Dante said, "you're trespassing."

Sweat trickled down his back as he walked inside the air-conditioned lobby and stabbed the up arrow. A chime rang out and Dante stepped into the elevator.

As the elevator hummed upward, he held the USB chip up to the light between a thumb and forefinger as if he could tell what was stored there. The elevator chimed and he stepped out, flicking the tiny chip into a trash can as he strode back to his office.

CHAPTER 8

Security

Dante dropped into his office chair and checked his watch. Ten minutes until the meeting. He lifted the office phone and punched in a number.

"Security, Officer Boyd speaking," replied a bored voice.

"My name is Dante Ellis and I was just in the parking structure downstairs. One of my ex-contractors was just down there but his security should've been revoked a long time ago."

"What was the name?"

"Skylar Westfall," Dante said.

A moment went by. The faint clack of a keyboard could be heard. "Yeah, revoked on March 7th, no further entry detected. You said he was in the parking structure?"

"Yeah. Which is strange because he's never parked here."

"Huh. That is strange."

The silence grew and Dante cleared his throat.

"Was there anything else, uh, sir?" Boyd said.

"Yes. Check the video feeds from ten minutes ago. Maybe you can see how he got in."

Boyd sighed and typed some more. It sounded like a baby elephant pounding on the keys.

"Take your time, Officer Boyd," Dante said.

The typing stopped and the silence stretched before Boyd

spoke again. "That's weird."

"What?"

"Well, I see you. Blue shirt, white collar?"

"Yeah, that's me."

Boyd chuckled. "That big bug scared you."

"More like a pterodactyl," Dante said defensively.

"Oh, shit, you got a Mako? That thing must move."

"Focus, Boyd."

"Sorry. So, yeah, I see you. Looks like you're talking to somebody."

"Any audio?"

"No. Privacy reasons."

"You see Westfall?"

"Who? Oh, the other guy. Nope, just you."

"What? How can that be?"

"Dunno," Boyd said. "You walk over to your car, looks like you're talking to somebody, you walk back to the lobby doors, you stand there, holding your hand out, then you go back inside. All by yourself."

"That's it?"

"That's it."

"I don't understand," Dante said. "You don't see anyone else at all?"

"You sure this guy was down there?"

Dante sat for a moment, staring at the desktop. "Can you send me a copy of that video? From all the cameras you have down there?"

"Yeah, you swatting at that bug was funny as shit."

"No, not that. I want to have a look for myself."

"I'll have to ask my supervisor, but he already left for the day. I can ask him tomorrow, maybe."

"Do it. And get an exterminator down there before that pterodactyl takes somebody's head off."

"I'll let facilities know." The phone went dead.

Dante leaned back and gazed up at the ceiling. Skylar Westfall was not in the video. *What the hell?*

His phone chimed. Five minutes.

Dante went into the bathroom and splashed cold water on his face, going over the pitch in his head. Toweling off, he grinned at his reflection with a confidence he didn't quite feel.

CHAPTER 9

Fishbowl

Naomi had set the meeting up in their largest conference room, the fishbowl. It was situated at the southwest corner so clients could see the busy studio floor through the glass panels and the valley outside the floor to ceiling windows. A large oak table dominated the center with high backed leather chairs.

A highlight reel from Ellis Media's most successful campaigns played out on a drop-down screen from the ceiling. Dante watched Raj Vikal of Hinds & Younger Foods across the table out of the corner of his eye. Megan Zhou sat next to the older man, fingers clutching her phone. She shot Dante a quick glance, biting at her lip. He winked at her then glanced back at Vikal. The old man's lips twitched as images from the Dear Baby campaign played across the screen. Dante saw his in. He pressed a button on the table and the screen went dark.

"I could quote ROI numbers, click throughs, percentages watched of all our ad campaigns. We have all that data available and it speaks for itself. But I think the most important thing to point out is the core of what makes our approach successful. Emotion. We feel that's the most important part of any campaign," Dante said.

Vikal's lips tightened before he spoke. "My grandson was two weeks old when I first saw one of your commercials. It had a great effect on me, even though it was a manipulation."

Dante opened his mouth to speak but Vikal held up a hand.

"I mean that as a compliment." He dropped his hand then turned to Megan. "They have our updated logo, specs on the new product lines?"

Megan nodded. "They've already begun ideation on a few pitches, right Dante?"

"That's right."

Megan's phone erupted with a blast of screeching guitar riffs and she silenced it as Vikal glared at her. "Sorry," she said, eyes wide.

The older man's phone rang as well and he pulled out the device, silenced it, then dropped it on the table with a clatter. "I apologize. My people know better than to interrupt while I'm in a meeting."

"Not a problem. I can send over what we've come up with so far..." Dante's voice trailed off.

Something was happening out on the studio floor.

People were clustered together in tight groups, hunched over their phones while others sat in their cubicles, faces slack. Some leered, lopsided grins on their faces. An intern ran past the conference room to the restrooms in the lobby, hands clamped over her mouth. Then, as if on cue, everyone on the studio floor turned to peer through the transparent walls of the fishbowl.

They were staring at Dante.

He rose slowly to his feet, a knot forming in the pit of his stomach.

"Oh my god," Megan said, eyes locked on the phone clutched in her hand.

Vikal snatched it from her and glared down at the screen. Dante could see the flicker of video reflected in his eyes, something that made the man's dark complexion go pale. He pushed the phone back at Megan and turned away.

Naomi rushed in, the door ringing as it struck the floor stopper. She hurried over and spoke in hushed tones into

Dante's ear. "They sent it to all our clients."

"Sent what?" Dante said, gazing around.

A few people had returned to their workstations but most still stood in shock, staring, or looking away as Dante's eyes scanned over them. He turned his attention back to the conference room. Vikal glowered at him. Megan bit her lip, refusing to meet his gaze.

"What the hell is going on here?" Dante asked, voice strained.

"This," Naomi said. She held up her phone.

Dante's mouth went dry as he stared at the video playing on the small screen. "Is that...me?

CHAPTER 10

Hollywood

Briana Warren stepped out of the taxi and tucked her short, honey blond hair back over her ears. Her bright green eyes sparkled as she peered down Sunset Boulevard with a thrill. Traffic tore by at dizzying speeds, causing her long skirt to flutter up around her legs. She tugged her skirt back down, smile faltering as an unpleasant blend of exhaust and scorched asphalt caused her nose to wrinkle.

A trunk slammed shut and the driver carried her suitcase over, cowboy boots clunking. The old man was tall and lanky with a cloud white hair parted on one side. He set the case down on the sidewalk with a thunk. The concrete was dotted with years of discarded gum, baked hard by the sun. He wiped a forearm across his brow.

"In town for a visit?" he asked, pale gray eyes flicking to the messenger bag at her shoulder.

"Uh, no. Well, something like that," Briana said.

The old man gazed at her a moment from under bushy brows, wrinkled face tightening. "Well, if you want my advice-"

"I don't." Briana reached into her bag, clamping her teeth down on the apology that threatened to break loose. "How much do I owe you?"

He squinted down at her, eyes glinting in the flash of wind-shields sweeping past. "First rides' free if you tell your friends." He clunked back over and yanked open the driver door. "Uber is killing the taxi industry."

The old man eased himself into the taxi with a groan then cut back into traffic to a chorus of shrill horns. Briana hefted her messenger bag and gripped the handle of her suitcase and stared, mouth slightly open.

I'm really here.

She peered westward and frowned. Not a palm tree in sight. *No corn stalks either, thank God.*

The buildings were all drab and boxy and short, except for one down the street up on the left. Its shiny glass and steel looked out of place among the stubby little structures that crouched along Sunset Boulevard. It reminded her of Disney-land in a way. Main Street had felt so big, so ripe with magic and possibilities when she'd visited as a girl. But when she'd returned years later with her high school graduating class, it'd felt small and fake, a polished, sanitized version of reality. But there was nothing polished or sanitized about Hollywood, at least from where she stood.

I must look like a husker, standing here gaping, she thought as she pulled out her phone and typed.

I'm here Dad.

A moment passed before her phone chimed.

Good. You're doing the right thing.

Her thumbs went to work again.

How's mom taking it?

Don't worry about her.

Just take care of yourself.
I love you.

She began typing in a response when another text appeared.

You left your bible here.

That gave her a jolt. Thumbs hovering, Briana didn't quite know how to respond.

"Hey, baby doll," said a deep voice from behind.

A shiny black Mustang sat at the curb with two men seated inside. The engine rumbled as it idled, a low, throaty growl. The passenger grinned at her, teeth a pearly white. His icy blue eyes bored into hers, pinning her there like an insect. He looked to be in his early thirties or so, his strong jaw covered in carefully cultivated stubble. He looked familiar, but she couldn't place from where. Dark, curly hair fell to the shoulders of his leather jacket. Briana wondered how he could stand it in this heat.

Must be a Hollywood image thing, she thought.

The driver was younger and stared out the windshield, eyes hidden behind mirrored glasses. Bleach blond hair swept back from his forehead.

"I'm Mel. You look lost." That smile again.

She'd heard all about the pretty boys in Cali but seeing some up close sent butterflies swirling inside.

"No, I'm fine. I...just stepped out for a smoke," Briana said as she turned and walked to a glass door tucked underneath a black canvas awning. She gave the handle a tug.

"They don't open 'til tonight," Mel said. "I know the owner. I could introduce you."

Briana held onto the door handle a moment. She could see him watching her, reflected in the glass. "No thanks. I'm fine," she said over her shoulder.

"Says she fine," Mel said. "Okay then, see you around. Baby

doll."

Her eyes followed the car as it drove away, her stomach fluttering with relief and a tinge of regret.

Real smooth, Briana. A smoke? Ugh.

She walked to the corner, disappointment blooming inside her again as she gazed upward. The world-famous Whiskey a Go Go stood over her but barely, its cramped two stories patterned with sun tortured red and black paint. Gazing at the marquee, she read off the upcoming acts listed there: Silent but Violent. Intellectual Death Puppets. Cassie McMillian.

Briana Warren.

Even though the place was a letdown in the stark light of day, she still hoped to sing there someday. So many great artists had come through this place. The Doors, No Doubt, Avril Lavigne. A few blocks south down on Santa Monica Boulevard was the Troubadour where Linda Ronstadt had first sung.

Heat rose to her cheeks. *I should be so lucky.*

A blue street sign jutted from the side of a light pole on the corner. "Clark Street", printed in blocky white letters. Checking the address on her phone, Briana hoisted her suitcase and strode up the hill leaving Sunset Boulevard behind.

She stopped short.

There, rising high into the pale blue sky above a cluster of shabby apartments was a single, perfect palm tree.

Briana smiled.

Excerpt from TechBeat.com article:

Online Giant Wins Bid to Unleash Drone Army

By Ian Weller

Early this morning, online delivery giant Minovo.com was awarded the coveted exemption from the FAA's Part 107 rules that restrict the use of drones for Beyond Visual Line of Sight (BVLOS) flight, delivery, flying over people, and night flying. This exemption allows Minovo to use their army of drones to deliver small packages all throughout greater Los Angeles as well as Orange County...

CHAPTER 11

Vegan Spaghetti

Gary Wexler followed close behind his wife Gail to the front door. Their two-and-a-half-year-old twins, Terry and Jerry, were in their playpen, screaming as if hot coals had been loaded into their diapers. Gail checked her reflection in the mirror next to the door, smoothing down her wrinkled business suit.

"That home steamer doesn't work at all," she said. "Or you don't know how to use it."

"A/C is on the fritz, remember? It's like a meat freezer in here so it didn't work."

"I can't go to work like this," she said, turning to look at the back of her navy-blue slacks.

"Here you go," Gary said, handing her a sealed plastic container. "Last night's vegan spaghetti."

She ignored him, continuing her incessant smoothing.

"You look fine. Really," Gary said.

With a sneer, she looked him up and down. "Like you'd know."

He stiffened, cinching the belt of his robe. Her lunch almost fell from his grasp. "It's not my fault."

"I know, I know." Gail looked at her reflection again and sighed, angling her head up to check her makeup. "You look terrible. The twins keep you up last night?"

"Not at all," Gary said, trying not to hate her. He'd spent most of the night soothing their teething children as Gail slept, droning like a Skilsaw. He allowed himself a moment to hate her. It felt good. She caught his eye in the mirror.

"Why are you smiling like that?"

"I'm just happy to see you looking so smart and sexy in your business suit."

"Yeah, well, I wish I had something to leer about."

Gary said nothing. He lacked the energy to play "what's wrong now" with his wife, especially when he knew only too well. As if she'd let him forget. Two months ago, he was riding high on his promotion then bam. Out on his ass. It made no sense. Downsizing, his boss had said, with a confused look on his face, like he hadn't known it was coming.

For a moment, he'd been relieved. After years behind the IT counter, Gary wondered what could be worse. No walk ups were allowed, but goddamn it if one of those dorks didn't stroll up every day with a five-alarm fire, mashing the buzzer about something usually fixed with a reboot. The only cool thing about his job was his position on the emergency response team. He qualified due to his three whole years in the Army, even though he'd never seen combat. Not only had it come with a decent increase in pay, but he'd been trained and certified in the use of non-lethal takedowns via Taser gun. The Tasers were locked away in a safe, so the chances of him actually being able to use one in an emergency were close to zero.

Don't have to worry about that now.

Because now he knew exactly what *was* worse. And boy fucking howdy he longed for those days, plopped on his stool in the back, ignoring the buzzer while some ham-handed butterball leaned on it until Gary trudged out to tell the dope to reboot his computer. Again.

The twins renewed their bid for attention with their favorite acapella, agony in D minor. Their voices united to form a white-hot spike of aural anguish that had no equal. He was convinced that someday the neighbors would call the cops and a SWAT team would storm in, followed by a well-placed sniper's bullet putting Gary out of his misery.

He looked down at his two little darlings, their wild hair sticking up at all angles, mucus streaming down their faces as they wailed. The phrase, kill your darlings, popped into his head and he snorted.

Where'd that come from?

They were struggling over a dragonfly plushie, even though they had two of everything. The toy slipped free and one fell back. Gary couldn't tell which one. Maybe Jerry. Whichever one it was, he screeched loud enough to peel paint.

He stood there, numbly holding out Gail's vegan spaghetti as she patted and smoothed and fretted. The world began to shudder and press in closer and he squeezed his eyes shut.

"Gary!"

"Muh?"

She snatched the container from his hand.

"I was talking to you. You're technical. Do something about the air conditioner. And get dressed for god's sake. That stupid robe. This isn't the Playboy Mansion."

"Yes, dear," he said as she left, closing the door with a slam that rattled the bay windows.

He shivered, trudging over to the thermostat. It was one of those smart ones, the little readout telling him it was ninety-nine degrees inside even though it felt cold enough to hang turkeys. He slipped his phone out of his pocket and tapped on the Thermo Think app. It refused to sync with the thermostat and Gary cursed under his breath. He moved the phone this way and that, trying to improve the signal. He backed up a step and his foot slipped on a Dear Baby tummy-time mat. With a yelp, arms wind milling, he fell flat on his back, groaning.

The twins stopped screaming.

Gary peered up from the floor and saw them peeking over the edge of the playpen, eyes wide and curious. A grin spread on his face. Throwing himself on the carpet again, he groaned louder. The two of them giggled. He kicked his legs in the air, sending his slippers flying. The boys laughed again and he felt his exhaustion melting away.

He crawled over to the playpen and scooped them into his arms, twirling them around as they squealed with delight. Shuffling down the hall with one under each arm, he jogged into the master bedroom. After he placed them on the bed, they began jumping up and down.

If Gail found out, she'd tear me a new one, Gary thought. *Screw it. Let 'em play.*

His grin broadened as he slid open the closet door. Inside, behind his vast array of black hoodies was a gray metal panel. He yanked it open, exposing columns of white breaker switches. As the boys bounced and squealed behind him, he scanned with a finger down to the HVAC breaker and flipped it off. The hiss from a vent above shuddered to a halt and he sighed with relief.

"Should warm up pretty soon," he said, gazing out the window at the morning light. "Gonna be another hot one." Something flickered up in the sky and he tilted his head. "Hey, guys, look!"

The twins stopped bouncing and gazed outside as a flock of white drones drew closer, visible through a screen of trees. They flew up and out of sight over the house, but their irate buzzing could be heard through the ceiling as they passed over. Gary went down the hall to the back door, his sons waddling close behind.

A large shadow was building in the back yard as the drones gathered together somewhere beyond the edge of the roof. Gary opened the back door and shivered in the heat that bled through the screen door. The deafening sound of miniature propellers set his teeth on edge and he looked back at his little boys, concerned for their hearing. They gazed up at him, wide-eyed, hands clamped over their ears. Gary smiled at them then knelt down, peering through the screen door up at the sky.

There were hundreds of drones up there.

The twins crept forward and pushed themselves past his legs, pressing their faces up against the screen.

"Airplane, Daddy," Jerry said.

"Yeah," Gary said. "I don't know…"

The drones lifted straight up into the sky and disappeared.

"All gone," Terry said.

But they weren't all gone. One remained behind, hovering above the overgrown backyard. It was different from the others, smaller, its metallic body glinting in the sun. Orange wings twitched as it swept down and placed a small object on the concrete slab of the back patio. It was a box about the size of a golf ball, made of wood.

"Dagonfye," said the twins in unison.

They'd just started doing that and usually, it made him smile, but right then, it gave him gooseflesh. The dragonfly drone lifted off, hovered a moment before sailing over the unpainted wooden fence surrounding the back yard.

Gary stared at the box, wondering what could be inside. He couldn't recall ordering anything that small. He'd heard on the news that drone deliveries had been recently legalized, but a group that large seemed like overkill just to drop off one tiny little box. He reached up and put his fingers on the screen door handle when the house alarm went off.

Red lights triple strobed as ear piercing beeps rang out. The twins clutched at him, eyes going wide.

"It's okay," he said. They jumped at the harsh tone of his voice. He picked them up again, one in each aching arm as he trudged back down the hall. The boys began to cry as he placed them back in the playpen and jogged over to the alarm panel.

What was the code? Gary jabbed at the little keypad. He gritted his teeth so hard he could hear them squeak over the combined din of screaming children and blaring alarms. He squeezed his eyes shut, trying to think, when a loud pounding came at the door, causing him to jump.

"Who's there?" Gary called out.

"Police. Open the door. You have three seconds to comply."

Gary yanked the door open and an officer decked out in full riot gear aimed a gun at his face.

"Hands where I can see them!"

Gary's hands shot up as he peeked over the policeman's shoulder. A boxy black truck was parked across the driveway, SWAT emblazoned across the side. The twins screamed as the alarm continued to peal. It was the single, most excruciating thing he'd ever heard in his life.

"Oh, thank god," Gary said. "Tell your sniper to aim for the head."

CHAPTER 12

Hyenas

The apartment building was four stories tall with wraparound balconies jutting out from its beige exterior, hemmed in by a thin metal railing. Each door was a rich mahogany, stark against the pale walls. Beyond a low brick wall topped with squared off shrubs grew leafy palms and the clean smell of cool water. One palm brushed the face of a balcony, its fronds reaching deep inside.

Briana sighed with relief.

On the way up, she'd passed more than a few places that were either rundown or reeked of sour garbage. One of the apartment buildings was famous for a wild rock band that lived there during the eighties. Motley Dudes or something. But the white paint was a dingy gray and there was stucco crumbling along the bottom edges, revealing rusty chicken wire.

A buzz rattled the nearby security door and the lock popped like a gunshot, startling her. The door eased open a crack and Briana gazed around before grasping the knob, warmed by the morning sun. It opened with a rattle of springs as she walked through.

Climbing the pebbled concrete steps, she made her way to the fourth floor, the metal framework jittering under her feet.

She wondered how this place had survived all the earthquakes. Briana had never experienced one and the thought terrified her.

There're scarier things than earthquakes back home, girl.

Warm air flowed down the enclosed hallway as she walked, ruffling her clothes. The last door on the right had three brass numbers on it: 402. She raised her hand to knock when it swung inward.

"Oh my god, you're here!"

A young woman leapt out and threw her arms around Briana. She stood back, her hazel eyes gazing out from under a cascade of blue hair. A single lock of shimmering purple fell from over her right ear as her grin widened.

"Briana, right? I'm Leish. Nice to finally meet you in person!"

A flush rose to Briana's face. The young woman was naked, or nearly so. She wore a white pair of men's briefs and a glowing red light on each nipple, and nothing else. Briana glanced away and found her voice.

"Did I come at a bad time?"

"Of course not. Come in, come in, come in!" Leish grabbed her hand and tugged her inside.

A large room with dark hardwood floors and crisp, white walls opened up before her. An elaborate computer setup pulsed with light nearby, the screens of multiple monitors dancing with lights. Along the far wall to her left was a white tiled kitchen and dining area, filled with tripods and lights and cameras, poised and ready for someone's close-up. A sliding glass door stood open to a large rooftop balcony, turfed with green and populated with deck chairs and a large hammock. Two plush velvet couches sat in an L shape in the center with a short coffee table stacked high with photography books and fashion magazines.

Briana went to the workstation and knelt down, staring in awe. The case was matte black with a red flame pattern emblazoned across the surface. Lights shone behind a clear panel, pulsing blues and purples. A small cylinder filled with orange coolant swirled as the fluid flowed through clear pipes that fed a heat exchanger installed over the CPU.

"Liquid cooled? This thing must really scream," Briana said.

"Have no idea. Somebody else set it up for me. You know computers?"

"Yes. Well I did. I didn't have a lot of money growing up so I saved up my allowance for parts and I'd build my own. I wanted to be a software engineer when I was younger."

"That's so cool!" Leish said. "What happened?"

"Boys don't like nerdy girls. Well, not real, *real* nerdy girls."

"It's a guy thing. They love to know more about this type of stuff. The dude who set it up mansplained the whole process to me like I could give a shit. Come on."

Leish pulled her past a wall sized flat screen down a long hallway, painted black. "Your room's down here."

They swept by a closed door on the left. Briana slowed. "Is that your room?"

"The whole apartment is my room."

Leish tugged her hand to the end of the hall and motioned to a door on the right. "Bathroom's in there," she said before opening a door on the left. "You're in here."

A twin bed sat against one wall, covered with plush hyenas of all shapes and sizes. Some had fallen on the floor. Briana almost jumped as she noticed a big one at least four feet tall next to the door. It sat on its haunches facing the bed, its orange eyes glassy and bright.

A nightstand was tucked next to the bed with a small lamp on top. A pink scarf lay draped over the shade. Leish bent and turned it on, bathing the small room in a rosy glow. She swept some of the plushies onto the floor then took Briana's bags from her and tossed them onto the bed.

The pasties began to flash. Leish cupped her breasts and looked down, brows knitted together. "Uh oh. Make yourself at home. I'll be right back," she said before disappearing back down the hall.

Briana sat on the bed and blinked for the first time since entering Leish's apartment. This place was nothing like back home.

On the floor lay a loose pile of fabric covered in zigzagging black stripes. She picked it up, holding it between her spread hands. It was a bodysuit of some kind, with a hood. A zipper ran all the way up the back.

A soft flutter whooshed by her ear and she recoiled as a large insect wheeled around and hovered above her, just out of reach. Glittering in the dim light, its wings were an orange blur, shiny eyes twitching back and forth.

Not eyes, Briana saw. Cameras.

She eased onto the bed and lifted a hand. The drone hovered closer. Tiny motors whirred as the cameras on its head adjusted, ticking back and forth.

"It's okay," she said, extending an index finger. "I won't hurt you."

The drone came closer, hovered for a moment before lowering onto her finger. She let out a soft "oh" and smiled. It barely weighed anything. Its body was a silvery green, about the size of her pinky. The wings were about six inches long, made from a thin gossamer film that looked very much like real dragonfly wings. Instead of shot through with veins though, small, interlocking diamonds were etched across the translucent orange surface.

Pulling her hand closer, the eyes followed hers and she could see her face reflected in the tiny lenses. The legs tightened and the hairs on her neck stood up as she stared into the glassy depths of those shiny, little eyes.

Not eyes, Briana thought. Cameras.

"I think it likes you," Leish said from the doorway. She'd slipped on a pale silk robe patterned with graphic style koi fish. The drone lifted from Briana's finger and hovered for a moment, cameras scanning in all directions before it flitted up to a corner. It rested upside down on the ceiling, legs twitching before it fell still.

"Amazing," Briana said. "Where did you get it?"

"Just came in the mail one day. It's a beta unit. I get stuff all the time," Leish said, waving a hand over the boxes stacked against the far wall. She sauntered over and flopped on the bed next to Briana. More stuffed hyenas fell on the floor.

"Why?" Briana asked.

"I'm an influencer. Companies send me their stuff to try out."

"Like this?" Briana said, holding up the stripped bodysuit.

"Sure. It's not very sexy so I only tried it on once." She nodded to the large hyena next to the door. "That big fella over there showed up the other day with a card that said 'from a secret admirer'. I mostly get workout clothes or skin care products, energy drinks. If I can find an angle on how to sell it, I will. Depends on the product and the contract. I was in the middle of a shoot when you showed up."

"A shoot?"

"Yeah, I have a whole automated camera rig and lights that can be set up based on preprogrammed styles. It's in the dining area. I prefer natural light though. I take a lot of pictures out there on the patio. Didn't you check out my Instagram?"

"I'm...not on Instagram."

"Oh my God, girl. If you're going to make it out here, you got to be on social," Leish said as she flashed a devilish grin. "We've got so much work to do."

Briana's gaze flicked away and she fidgeted with her skirt. "That's what you we're doing when I got here? Taking pictures?"

"Trying out a new product. The pasties are trackers, so when you take pictures or video the software puts different shapes over your nipples in Realtime, like stars or emojis. They were running low so I had to go charge them. I recently started streaming games too. Mostly League and Fortnite. I do unboxing and tech reviews too, dressed to entice likes. Nothing beats a pushup bra to get a bump in followers."

Briana looked up. "That's how you make money?"

"Yep. I get paid based on how many followers I have and the number of likes I get while promoting. Some of the stuff I get, I just sell online. I keep all that junk in here. One of my biggest sources of income though, is exclusive content. Only Fans."

"Only Fans?"

"Nudes," Leish said. She leaned in and brushed her fingertips across Briana's cheeks. "You're so adorable when you blush, baby doll!"

"Shut up," Briana said with a laugh, pushing Leish's hands away. "My gosh, what don't you do?"

"*My gosh?*" Leish said, shaking her head with a grin. "Well, country girl. I can't sing like you."

Briana blushed again and glanced away.

"I remember when I first discovered you on YouTube. Your voice, so clean and raw with emotion." Leish lifted Briana's chin with a finger. "It's who you are. The real you. That's when it hit me. Leish, I said, you bish. You want, no, you *need* to help this girl realize her dreams." She smiled, her eyes sparkling. "And you're so pretty. Way too pretty to waste on corn fields. And now here you are. Meant to be."

Briana smiled and bit her lip before glancing away.

"You should take down those videos on YouTube of you shooting shotguns and stuff with your dad, though," Leish said. "Especially the hunting ones."

"Okay," Briana said, face falling. "Why?"

"Makes you look like a redneck. That's a bad thing out here."

"Oh."

"By the way," Leish said as she slipped a clipboard and pen out from under the bed. "I need you to sign this release form."

"Yeah, okay," Briana said, her smile fading even further. She took the pen and scribbled her name on the line at the bottom. "What's this for?"

"No big deal. Standard form. It just means you understand that while living here, your image may appear on various social platforms in some form or another, but only after your express permission, which you just gave. I stream a lot so if you're here, you're going to be online. Understood?"

"Okay," Briana said, bending down to pick up one of the plush toys from the floor. "What's with all the hyenas? You got a whole pack."

"It's called a cackle, not a pack. And the hyena is my spirit animal. What's yours, do you think?"

Briana stared into the shiny eyes of the stuffed hyena. Its head hung down at the end of a long slender neck. She tugged at the scruffy orange mane that sprouted along its back.

"I don't know..." she trailed off. Then she sat up straighter and spoke with a voice stronger than she'd intended. "A lioness. Part of a sisterhood. Self-sufficient hunters at the top of the food chain."

Leish raised her eyebrows, a smile turning up the corners of her mouth. "Very good." Then her expression darkened. "But did you ever think that as strong as she is, a lioness still serves an alpha male? Hunting for him, fucking whenever *he* wants, killing her babies if she dares mate with another male. Is that what you want to be?"

"No," Briana said, her voice going soft.

Leish's phone rang and she slipped it from a pocket. "Tell me what I want to hear, Melvin." She listened for a moment before rolling her eyes. "That's not good enough and you know it. Call me back when they agree to everything in my rider."

She dropped the phone on the bed and lay back again, head resting on the spotted hide of a plushie. She reached up and traced her long, delicate fingers along its snout. "I'm telling you, girl. Hyenas got it all figured out."

"Yeah?"

"The cackle is run by the females, led by a queen. And they're not just scavengers like most people think. They're hunters. All kills go to the females and the males take what's left, fighting over scraps with the vultures." She sat up and took Briana's hands in hers. "As women, that's what we should always strive to be. Amazons of the animal world. *Hyenas.* And we take whatever the fuck we want."

CHAPTER 13

Rooftop

Dante placed his hands on the parapet and exhaled as sounds of the city drifted up from far below. A horn blared out followed by squealing brakes as someone almost got themselves killed on an electric scooter. The sun winked out as a swarm of delivery drones whizzed by before splitting off in various directions. Heat from the metal trim bled into his palms but he barely felt it.

Who would come at him like this? Colin?

For years not a word then out of nowhere, the guy just happens to drop in the same day Dante's career is torpedoed by a thirty second video. And what a video it was.

Disgusting, he thought as he swallowed, wondering if he'd ever scrub it from his brain. *Could Colin have done this though?* He was a talented coder for sure, but the poor guy looked worse than the last time Dante had seen him. He never was the vindictive type. More of a lifelong victim. Always had been. You don't get the nickname "Twitch" for nothing.

Skylar Westfall though, was brilliant, had the motive and the means, but he was just a punk-ass. *Wasn't he?* He also said he'd wanted to help Dante, and it looked like he meant it.

This didn't really fit either one of them. They were both wicked smart and could probably just hack Dante's accounts and steal from him.

Why come at me like this? Dante thought. *And show up on the same day?* It didn't make sense.

It was definitely personal though.

Dante thought back over his career. He'd rubbed some people the wrong way over the years. Fired people, canceled contracts. He was in the middle of a few lawsuits right now. He'd walked away from bad deals and been burned by a few himself, but it had always been business, not personal. Most people understood that, but some couldn't separate the two. It could be anybody though.

The comments on YouTube following his NAB presentation years ago on the psychology of selling had devolved quickly. In ran the gamut from ravings about the government trying to control people's minds, specifically by the CIA and their MK Ultra operation in the sixties, to subliminal mind control by greedy mega corporations.

What seemed to be most agreed upon, though, was that Dante and people like him perpetuated a never-ending campaign of disinformation that defrauded people every day. Defrauded them of what, exactly, no one seemed to be able to articulate. In reality, the Internet was a big place full of angry people with nothing better to do then to pursue a cause, no matter how misguided.

Someone was trying to smear him, discredit him. Another firm going after the Hind's & Younger deal maybe, trying to take Ellis Media out of the running. It was a big win, for whomever got it. Years of work across several campaigns.

Character assassination, then. Had to be. Cancel culture taken to the extreme. It was fucked up no matter how you looked at it. Worse than that.

It was criminal.

He turned and strode across the roof and back downstairs to his office.

CHAPTER 14

House Calls

Gary sat on the couch in a daze. A tech from Home Safe stood near the front door, interfacing with the alarm system via USB cable and tablet. He was a small man dressed in blue coveralls with thinning black hair and a thick, bushy mustache. Sweat beaded his forehead even though the AC was back on, full blast. The little man shook his head and poked at the tablet, causing the screen to flash.

Ms. Elamin, a rep from Think Thermo, sat at the dining room table bent over a laptop. She hadn't offered a first name. Young, in early twenties, she was dressed in dark blue slacks and a white blouse. A matching blazer hung over the back of the chair. A hijab kept her hair back from her face, revealing a pair of meticulously kept eyebrows above large, dark eyes.

The boys were wrestling with Sergeant Chavez on the floor, squealing with delight. It just so happened that Chavez and his wife were pregnant with twins as well and they couldn't be more delighted.

Talk to me again in a year, Gary thought.

As soon as Chavez realized a false call had been made, he'd shut off the main breaker, plunging the house into glorious silence. As the rest of the SWAT officers left, he'd helped calm the kids down and personally called the alarm and thermostat companies, threatening large fines if they didn't send some-body out right away. This had all transpired well after Gary had been handcuffed while a heavily armored knee crushed his kidneys.

Chavez placed the twins in the playpen with a juice box for each and came over and joined Gary on the couch. Gary rubbed his lower back with a grimace.

"Sorry about that," Chavez said. "I knew you'd been swatted as soon as we busted in but we have to secure the scene first."

"Swatted?"

"Yeah, it's a form of criminal harassment. It's when some-body calls in a false report of erratic behavior of a person or persons at a residence, most likely armed. Then we show up in all our gear and bust the door down."

"This happens a lot?"

"Didn't used to, but it's becoming a real problem. Internet streamers do it to each other so it'll occur live on stream to get a laugh or for revenge. Guys do it to ex-girlfriends and vice versa. A young guy was recently shot and killed in Kansas dur-ing one of these incidents. It's expensive, too."

"I'm going to get charged for all this?"

"No, not you. We find you who did it though, you better believe they get this tacked onto the bill. I didn't mind this one too much though, right guys?" Chavez said to the boys who lay happily in the playpen. He turned back to Gary. "You have any idea who'd do this? An estranged family member, somebody at work? Ex-girlfriend or boyfriend?" Chavez glanced at the twins then back at Gary. "Someone else maybe?"

"Well, if my wife is stepping out then she's got more energy than me. I just got let go from my job so if anybody's got a beef it's me."

"Do you?" Chavez asked.

"Do I what?"

"Have a beef? With somebody at work I mean."

"No, I was just saying," Gary said. "I can't think of anybody, really."

Chavez grunted. "Well, if you remember anything, give me a call." He passed his card to Gary as he rose. "Listen, sorry again and have a nice day."

Gary followed him to the door.

"And take care of those little rascals, okay?" Chavez said.

"Thanks again," Gary said as he closed the door.

"Well, everything looks good," said the tech from Home Safe. He unplugged the cable from the alarm system, whipped it around the tablet and dropped it inside a tool bag at his shoulder.

"What was wrong with it?" Gary said.

"Don't know. Just a glitch. Won't happen again. One of those things, you know?"

"I do. I work in IT."

"God bless you, buddy." He saluted with two fingers and left.

Ms. Elamin still sat at the dining room table, squinting down her laptop. She typed for a bit, the keys clacking under her fingertips. Gary checked on his sons before sitting down across from her.

"Weird," Elamin said.

"What's that?"

"You had a virus, but it's gone now."

"Gone?"

"You're in IT, right? Sorry, I heard you tell that tech."

"Yeah, we run virus checks all the time," Gary said.

"When the software finds the virus, what does it do with it?"

"Quarantine, then adds it to the database."

"Right," Elamin said. "So, my anti-virus found it, then it just disappeared. I mean it was a blip, blink and you miss it. Fortunately, I was watching when it happened. The virus count read zero, jumped to one then back to zero, but nothing made it to quarantine. You ever see that before?"

"Can't say that I have," Gary said. He didn't add that he wouldn't have noticed anyways, let alone cared. It was easier to just wipe a drive and re-image. "What kind of antivirus are you running?"

"Proprietary. Very secure. The whole system is. It's one of our selling points. I've never seen the problem you're having on any of our systems. Ever."

"How do you know?"

"I'm lead engineer," Elamin said. "I architectured most of it. That's why I came out. I usually don't do house calls."

A sudden thought occurred to Gary. "Hey, you aren't looking for any IT people, are you?"

The doorbell rang.

"Excuse me," Gary said and jogged to the door. He grabbed the knob then paused. "Who is it?"

"Delivery for Wexler."

Gary put his eye to the peephole and saw the distorted image of a middle-aged man staring back at him with sleepy eyes under a blue cap. A large panel van was parked in the drive behind him. Sleepy Eyes held up a pen.

"Okay, hold on," Gary said and the opened door.

He took the pen and was about to scribble his name on the electronic clipboard when another truck pulled to a stop. A muscular, deeply tanned woman leapt out with a package tucked under one arm. As she jogged up the path to the front door, more delivery trucks pulled up outside, brakes squealing, filling up the cul-de-sac. Drivers piled out, some balancing multiple packages in their arms.

"Here ya go," said the tan woman before placing the box down and hustling back to her truck. She had to hop to one side to make way for the other deliveries.

"Sir, if you'll just sign," said Sleepy Eyes.

"Wait," Gary said, "I didn't order all this stuff." His eyes went wide as the drivers crowded forward and placed their deliveries on the ground in front of him.

What the hell is going on?

CHAPTER 15

Brown Mustard

Dante sat at his workstation and the monitors sprang to life. He opened a browser and searched for cybercrime. Scrolling past the links for security companies and lists of cyberpunk movies he found what he was looking for. He clicked on the link for fbi.gov.

An image of a hooded figure appeared in front of a map of the world, their fingers hovering over a ghostly keyboard, the requisite rainfall of 0s and 1s trailing down behind him. Dante scrolled down through the blocky bold headings and bullet points of the most commonly perpetrated cybercrimes. Network intrusions, ransomware, identity theft. Scanning the page, he kept scrolling past an image of a silhouetted online predator, then down to brightly colored cartoon animals smiling and waving from inside a grid of squares. At the bottom of the page under an FBI seal were links to everything from the Ten Most Wanted to a guided tour.

How the fuck do you get in touch with the FBI?

The door opened and Naomi stepped in. Her mouth was compressed in a thin line and she stood stiffly, hands clenched at her sides. "Dante..."

"Hold on," he said without looking at her.

Scrolling back to the top, he clicked on the little home icon.

A list of headings appeared, including icons to social media. Next to the Facebook logo was an email icon and he clicked on it. A subscription page for FBI updates opened.

No contact info.

He pounded the desk in frustration. "Goddamn it all!"

"Dante."

"What?" he said, turning to glare at her.

"It's going to be okay. We'll figure this out, alright?"

"How? How could *we* figure this out? It's my face and... everything else in that video, not yours."

She held his gaze, eyes flashing briefly. "I'm already on top of it. I've crafted an email about the incident."

"The incident? The fucking incident?"

"Dante," Naomi said, her voice firm. "I know you're upset but you need to keep it together."

He turned away and stared back at the screen. Breathing deep, he tried to slow his racing heart. "The thought of so many people seeing it, the employees, our clients." He glanced at her again. "Abigail."

Her hands slipped up to his shoulders and began kneading the knots that had tightened there.

"I know," Naomi said. "We just need to get out in front of it as best we can and move on. This is going to be a thing for a while, though."

"It'll probably go viral."

"It's on Twitter and Instagram, Facebook. I've already informed them all. The links will be removed soon. I released a statement on all our social platforms. Something else will come up soon and it'll be gone."

"But not forgotten," Dante said. "Not for a long time."

He could handle the inevitable jeers from some of his staff and business partners, but the thought of Abigail possibly seeing this someday made his stomach clench. Not for the first time he was glad she'd never wanted a phone. All her friends had them of course, but Abigail said she didn't need one as long as there was paper for her to draw and songs to sing. She was like her mother that way, quiet, more comfortable out of the way, observing.

An old argument with Michelle charged into his head. Once the baby came, she said, he needed to slow down, be home more. He accused her not understanding what constant pressure he was under to deliver. She smiled at him in a sad, knowing way, as if she had a secret. The old memory infuriated him and exhaled, the air coming out in a hiss. Naomi felt the tension jump back into his shoulders and her hands fell away. She walked to the door and turned, hand on the knob.

"Read over the email I wrote and let me know if you approve so I can send it out to our clients."

"I'm sure its fine," Dante said. "Send it out. We should probably get in touch with certain people personally, as well."

"Already on it. As soon as the email goes out, I'm on the phone along with the producers for each account to handle any questions personally."

"Thanks, Naomi," Dante said with a thin smile.

"You're welcome," she said, closing the door behind her.

Dante turned his attention back to the screen and saw what he hoped was a way to contact somebody with a badge. He moused over to the words "submit a tip" and clicked. Underneath, another bold heading were links to forms and finally what he was looking for: a phone number. He knew the chances of talking to an actual human being were slim, but he hated the thought of filling out an online form.

Dante pulled out his phone, punched in the number and waited. It rang twice before connecting. A prerecorded female voice thanked him for calling the FBI and began to list menu items. A series of clicks interrupted and he pressed the phone tighter to his ear, trying to make out what the voice was saying when it cut out.

Dante sighed and considered pounding the desk again.

A series of strange sounds chittered and he pulled the phone away from his ear. The sounds ceased and the phone rang again before connecting.

"Tell me you didn't forget the brown mustard," said a gravelly, female voice.

"Excuse me?" Dante said.

"Who's this?"

"Dante Ellis. I called to make a harassment report."

"Oh, I thought you were one of the interns. I can't eat pastrami without brown mustard. You? Never mind. How'd you get this number?"

"I called the number on the website and was connected to you," Dante said.

"That's strange. This is my private phone. Try the main number again."

"Hold on, do you deal with cybercrime?"

"Well, yes. Special Agent Boucher, Cybercrimes Division. But you'll have to make a formal complaint before your case can be evaluated. If there is merit to the claim then it is assigned to an agent who'll then schedule an interview. Listen, just call back. I can't connect you from here."

"Someone sent a video of me having sex with a donkey to all of my contacts."

There was a long pause on the other end. "Safe to assume it wasn't you?"

"Of course not."

"Sounds like a deep fake then," Boucher said.

"A deep fake?"

"Yeah. A piece of software developed several years ago, clearly for the good of all humanity. Somebody named Goodson or Longfellow or something. It uses machine learning to create a map of a face from a series of images and video, then applies it to another person. They use it in movies, phony political messages, fake celebrity porn. Some are really bad but others can be quite convincing. When this whole deep fake thing started, there was one of president Obama you'd swear was real."

"Somebody put Obama in a porno?"

"God, no!" Boucher laughed. "Just him giving a statement or

something."

"Yeah, I think I remember seeing that."

"They're all over the place now. Do a search on YouTube. Celebrity face swap videos with people doing voices. Swapping one actor with another. There's at least a dozen phone apps, too."

"So, can you help me?" Dante said.

"You said you're being harassed. What else has happened besides the video?"

"I got a threatening text when I dropped my daughter off at school this morning." Dante repeated the quote to agent Boucher. "Then the video was sent out a few hours later."

"So, here's the thing," Boucher said. "Criminal cyber harassment has gone way up over the last few years. We got a backlog a mile long. It's started to get pretty bad for some folks. There's a retired lady out in San Bernardino that gets deliveries she never ordered, calls all day and night, and her car has been towed several times. She's been swatted by the police at least twice."

"Swatted? You mean when the cops smash down the door and rush in?"

"Exactly. Cops get a call about somebody armed and barricaded in their home they're legally required to respond."

"What can I do?" Dante said.

"Let me put you in touch with a guy who specializes in cyber security, Dmitry Molchalin. He's got a company called Shadow Trace that deals with this sort of thing."

"You said criminal cyber harassment. My case isn't criminal?"

"You know who's harassing you? Or have a suspicion of who it might be?" Boucher asked.

"Well, no, not really."

"What does 'not really' mean? Do you have any estranged family members, ex-lovers, disgruntled workers, business associates that may consider you an enemy...?"

"No one in particular," Dante said. He wasn't ready to name

names to an FBI agent quite yet.

"I see."

"It's a tough industry, but it's business, not personal."

"What do you do?"

"Advertising."

"Right. Well, in my experience, Mr. Ellis, business is very personal. But without a suspect, directs threats, identity theft or stolen money then it's not criminal."

"A donkey sex video isn't a crime?"

"Depends on the state. But deep fakes aren't illegal, Mr. Ellis. At least not yet."

"Great."

"Get in touch with my guy Dmitry," Boucher said. "Let him dig around. It'll cost you, but he can get you some answers or at least halt any further intrusions. Or wait six months to get your case assigned."

"If cyber harassment is way up then why does it take so long?" Dante asked.

"Cyber terrorism. So much easier to get funding for that particular boogeyman than deep fake donkey shows."

CHAPTER 16

Fresh Fish

Briana let the warm water wash over her, letting it ease the tightness in her neck. She tilted her head back, sweeping her hair away from her face and sighed. Looking up at the water drops collecting on the shower ceiling, she let her mind drift.

What am I doing here?

This place was so different from home. Mom had already been right, in a sense. Briana had barely stepped out of a taxi before those two guys pegged her as new in town. Briana recalled her mother's lecture over dinner the night before she left.

"Everyplace has a heartbeat," Virginia said. "The heart of our home beats slow, not exciting enough for you as I well know. But it's steady and strong. Always will be. This place you're going, it has a heart too."

"Mom, please," Briana said.

"You're going to hear what I have to say!" she said, slamming the table. Silverware clinked.

Briana went stiff, unblinking.

"Virginia," her father warned.

"*Leland,*" Virginia said, glaring at him until he glanced away. Briana was proud of him. He lasted almost a second.

"Briana," her mother continued, softer now. "The heart of

this place you're going, it's not well. Oh, it beats fast and hot and makes everything fresh and exciting. But it's sick. So very, very sick. It attracts the weak and corrupts them. It's like cancer of the soul."

"There's...other reasons why I'm going," Briana said, looking at her father. The muscles in his jaw tensed, but he stayed silent.

Virginia went on, undeterred. "They have cameras everywhere. And I do mean everywhere. Places you wouldn't expect. Inside toilets."

"*Mom.*"

"I saw it on the news. Everyone livestreams everything. All people out there think of is themselves, and they use naïve, young girls for all sorts of terrible things. Use them up and throw them away like trash. Girls like you, far from home. Fresh fish, they call them."

Briana shook her head. "That's me. A fresh fish with soul cancer."

"You're a whore in training," Virginia said. "You just don't know it yet."

"Virginia," her father said again, voice firmer. He waited until Virginia focused on him, meeting her gaze with a quiet intensity of his own. "The lord has a plan for all of us. You're no different. When we first met you were young, confused. Estranged from your family. Your father. Looking for-"

"Oh, save it for your flock, Reverend," Virginia said, reaching for her wine. "We ain't in church." She emphasized her words with an exaggerated southern drawl, sipping noisily before setting the glass down again with a thud. Her hands shook as she smoothed down the table cloth. Leland looked like he'd been slapped across the face.

"Mom," Briana said, sliding her hand over to grasp her mother's. "I need to do this. For me."

Virginia withdrew her hand, avoiding her daughter's eyes. Her lips were pressed tight into a bloodless line as she blinked away tears. Briana looked to her father again but he sat silent and withdrawn, eyes locked on his hands.

Briana watched the inner turmoil play out over her mother's face, hoping for a break in the storm. But the older woman stared at the table cloth, refusing to meet her gaze.

"I can't do this anymore," Briana said, her voice caught as she left the table.

Virginia's shrill cry called after her. "Run away, Briana. That's what you do. Just run away."

The pipes squealed and the water went cold, pulling Briana out of her reverie. She squeezed her hands into tight fists, focusing on the pain as her nails dug into her palms.

What's wrong with me? I did it. I'm here. I'm really here!

Another thought intruded. *What about Mark?*

She'd always love him. How could she not? He'd been her first everything. First kiss. First love.

A low, ragged voice intruded her thoughts.

You cheating bitch!

She placed a hand to her cheek and squeezed her eyes shut. He'd been so different that last time he'd come back from deployment. Thinner, meaner. Eyes hard, like black marbles. Mark had been back for two weeks before he'd even called her, then he'd shown up drunk to her apartment, raving, tearing at her clothes in a frenzy before dropping her with a blow to the jaw. She'd awoken in the middle of him thrusting and moaning, eyes wild, sweat dripping off his face. A drop fell into her eye.

It burned like battery acid.

He'd been the one to cry afterward, sobbing against her like a child as she smoothed a hand over his coarse hair, whispering that everything would be alright.

Her hands had been so cold.

Briana pressed her clenched fists against her head. She was just another one of *those* girls now. One day, you think you're in love, and the next you're Googling how to cover up bruises.

Pipes shrieked as she spun the knobs and the water pattered to a stop. Pulling the shower curtain aside, she stepped out and shivered. She wrapped a towel tight around her body, gazing around the room. Nothing seemed out of the ordinary. White tiles, sink, toilet. Foggy mirror. Something just didn't feel right though.

Were there cameras in here, like Mom had said? Would Leish really do something like that?

Briana took a quick peek in the toilet. If there was a camera there, she couldn't see it. She thought of that release she'd signed and cinched the towel tighter. Hadn't there been a news story about landlord who'd spied on his tenant? A beam of light from where he'd scratched the silver off the backside of a bathroom mirror gave him away.

Leaning over, Briana flicked the light switch off with a finger. The room plunged into darkness. Light from under the door shimmered in the mist but there was no beam from the mirror, no staring eyeballs.

God, Briana. Get a grip, she thought. *Mom's right. You really are a fresh fish.*

She heard a soft skittering and flicked the switch on again. The little dragonfly drone was perched on the sink, its beady eyes twitching. Briana took a step back as it lifted off and hovered, coming close to her face. It swooped low and disappeared through the gap underneath the door. Briana swallowed, her throat tight.

She didn't want a dragonfly drone anymore.

Opening the door a crack, she peered down the hallway. No sign of the drone. She started to ease the door shut when she saw it. It was a tiny blotch on the ceiling out in the main room, too far away to see if it was still watching her. Slipping into her room, she closed the door behind her. She grabbed a pair of jeans and an oversized sports jersey from her suitcase and pulled them on under the watchful eyes of a cackle of plush hyenas.

CHAPTER 17

Clandestine Cubes

Dante threaded his way through midday traffic. His hands gripped the steering wheel as he merged onto the 134 freeway, fingers aching. The Mako chimed, a message on the screen offering to drive. Stabbing a finger on the center console screen, he killed the display. He had to do something to keep himself busy.

A garbage truck cut him off and skidded to a stop in front of him, but he barely noticed. The events of that morning played out through his head, drowning everything else out.

For the second time that day, he'd stood on the studio's small stage and spoken to the staff, this time apologizing for a "deep fake donkey show" as Special Agent Boucher had called it. As he approached the stage through the crowded studio floor, Dante could feel the eyes of all his employees on him, watching his every move. Silence hung heavy in the air. His feet thudded hollowly as he climbed onstage and began to speak, face burning as he realized he'd forgotten to clip the microphone to his lapel.

Tires squealed up ahead as the garbage truck lurched to a halt once more. Dante stomped the brake pedal to the floor and roared with frustration until his throat hurt. Horns blared behind him as traffic up ahead began to flow but he ignored the commotion. The Mako chimed, offering to drive again.

"No, goddamn it!"

An engine revved as a car screeched past him, the driver screaming something unintelligible. Dante gripped the steering wheel until the faux leather creaked. Blood pounded in his ears as he goosed the accelerator and cut left. The side-view mirror disappeared with a shriek of tortured plastic as a lane splitting motorcycle flashed by. The mirror spun into the air, sunlight flashing as it fell down among the tightly packed cars ahead. The rider didn't even slow down.

A cold sweat broke out over him as the Mako chimed, alerting him to the damage with a top-down schematic diagram of the car. Then it did something it had never done before.

"Would you like me to drive, sir?" the car said with a refined English accent, the voice silky and feminine.

"Uh," Dante said slowly. "I guess?"

"It would be my pleasure," the voice said as the auto drive alert appeared. Dante frowned and he lifted his hands from the wheel as it spun on its own, the car nosing its way back into traffic.

"It…can talk now?" Dante said to himself.

The current software version flashed on the screen, as if that meant anything to him. His phone rang and he lifted it to his ear.

"Yeah," Dante said, his voice slightly hoarse.

"I hear Mexico is lovely this time of year."

"Bob, I swear to god."

Dante pictured Bob Bainbridge's handsome, square jawed face leering on the other end and he gripped the phone until it squeaked in protest.

"Yeah, sorry kid. I can only imagine the morning you've had," Bainbridge said.

"Something I can do for you?" Dante said.

"Naomi wanted me to check the accounts for anything that looked suspicious. Everything's kosher, so we're okay there."

"Well there's that. Did you send me an email this morning?"

"Fucking hate email," Bob said. "Somebody's cyber harassing you?"

"Looks like. I'm on my way to talk to a security specialist right now."

"Sounds like it's going to cost."

"Doesn't everything?" Dante said. "Either way, this shit needs to stop. I'll let you know if I decide to hire them."

"Gotcha. Hoops on Friday? You need to work on that jump shot."

"Can't."

"That's what I thought. Later."

As Dante pulled the phone away Bainbridge called out, voice tinny and faraway.

"Bob?" Dante said, pressing the phone back to his ear. "You still there?"

"What did that mean? What you said."

"I don't know. What did I say?"

"At the end of the video. You looked right at the camera and said something about being fearless or powerful or something. It sounded just like you, too. Hold on lemme play it again," Bainbridge said, voice laced with glee.

"Thanks for the update, *Bob*," Dante said and disconnected.

He squeezed his eyes shut and rubbed his forehead. *The deep fake spoke in the video as well? How did they do that? And who were they?*

Hopefully Shadow Trace could get him some answers.

The Mako eased over and exited the freeway at Victory Boulevard. Used car lots and liquor stores rushed by outside, followed by strip malls, giving way to neighborhoods of shabby, single-story homes. The center median was filled with red gravel and dotted with the occasional palm tree, yellowed fronds unruffled by wind.

The houses gave way to cash preferred businesses again, marked by a billboard reminding everyone that suicide was never an option. The Mako turned right on Van Nuys Boulevard, then cut left through a gap in traffic before gliding into a lot marked "Shadow Trace Parking only."

Dante stepped out into the valley heat. The bitter tang of pollution was strong here, biting and caustic. Stepping aside as two kids on electric scooters zoomed by, Dante strode to the front of the building.

Square columns held up a roof that stretched out over the front of a square, white tiled building, reminiscent of a bank. A black iron fence formed a courtyard of sorts around the front. The glass entrance was completely blacked out. A voice, tinny and hollow, burst out from a box mounted next to an entrance gate.

"Mr. Ellis. Please come in."

The gate buzzed and Dante stepped inside. It closed behind him with a clang. The front doors parted with a hiss as he approached. Arctic air blasted out and he felt a chill ripple through him as a tall man came forward from the darkness. He had long black hair with a streak of gray running through, swept into a tight bun at the nape of his neck. Dante thought he'd make a great movie vampire. The man stuck out a slender hand.

"I am Dmitry Molchalin of Shadow Trace," he said with a clipped, Russian accent.

Dante took the hand and Molchalin gave one solid pump before letting go.

"We spoke on the phone earlier, right?" Dante said.

"We did. Come with me."

Dante followed the man into a dimly lit room up through two large black cubes that dominated the space, each at least sixteen feet tall. There were two doors in the face of each one, the corners curved like those on a battleship. The upper doors were offset from the lower ones, each accessible by a thin, black ladder. The cubes hummed as they walked by and Dante resisted the urge to reach out and touch one.

Molchalin turned left at a wall of computers kept in slim racks inside a glass fronted enclosure. A multitude of tiny lights winked inside, flashing with rapid pulses.

"This way," he said over his shoulder as he turned and disappeared behind the enclosure.

Light bloomed as Dante followed and saw Molchalin enter an office with a plain metal desk and two faux leather chairs, one on either side. The tall man sat behind the desk, his dark eyes tracking Dante's every move as he eased down into the empty chair.

Dante jerked a thumb over one shoulder. "What are those things?"

"Ah, the cubes. Each contains eight private cubicles, completely secure," Molchalin said.

"You got people in there?"

"Yes. Software engineers on several different security projects. They only communicate if working on the same project and only through secure encrypted connection. The large enclosure along the back wall houses our private servers. Very secure."

"Isn't that a little extreme? People in boxes?" Dante said.

"I can assure you, Mr. Ellis, we take security very seriously."

"I see. So, about my problem." Dante told him about the deep fake video and the strange text he'd received that morning.

The more a thing is perfect,
the more it feels pleasure and pain.

Molchalin gave a terse nod. "First, we need to secure your network. My team and I will visit your studio and install our suite of Shadow Trace software. It is like a digital immune system, seeking out malware of all types before isolating each one. Shadow Trace also actively monitors all data flow through your network by passing it through one of our private secure servers here on site. You'll be back up in a day, two at the most, completely secured."

"That's it?" Dante said.

"No. There are sites on the dark web with lists of targets to harass for money, usually paid with crypto currency. My team will perform a search for any mentions of your name."

"Dark web, huh?"

"Not as exciting as it sounds," Molchalin said. "The dark web is just a collection of servers accessible through an encrypted browser known as TOR. Makes it much easier to hide your digital tracks. There are the lists I mentioned, plus illegal markets like the Silk Road and AlphaBay for drugs and weapons."

"You think I'm on one of these lists?"

"It is possible. Some are for jilted ex-lovers posting revenge porn along with a request to smear the target in online forums and social networks. I suspect you're on one or more of the professional lists. It would explain the multiple methods used so far. Most likely perpetrated by different people, makes it harder to track down. And the simple fact that you have not been directly threatened or blackmailed. Are you involved in any lawsuits?"

"A breach of contract and a zoning dispute with the city."

"We will look in to this. It is possible this is an attempt to smear you by lawyers but not very likely. My instincts tell me this is simple harassment designed to defame and discredit you, possibly by a disgruntled employee or professional rival. It is a growing problem. If it makes you feel any better, you're not alone."

"Can't say that it does. The fallout from that deep fake video alone is going to follow me for a long time." Dante leaned back and rubbed his forehead. "What a mess."

"Why a donkey? Are you a democrat, Mr. Ellis?"

"There's an urban myth about something called a donkey show, supposed to take place somewhere in Mexico, where a woman has sex with a donkey on stage. I think it's supposed to be something like that. I don't know what that would have to do with me though."

"Maybe it's a metaphor. A narcissistic jackass having intercourse with a bestial analog of himself."

Dante laughed without humor. "You think?"

"Just a theory. There is a similar story in Russia about Catherine the Great having sexual intercourse with a horse, but stories like these were circulated during her reign to disparage her. Your video could be as simple as that. We can help you there as well. Our services include online reputation restoration."

"How does that work?" Dante asked.

"My team will track down any sites where the deep fake video has been uploaded and have our legal team send a cease and desist. Then we outsmart search algorithms by seeding the Internet with positive posts designed to rank high with search engines. Most people don't click past the first page of results, rendering anything negative virtually invisible."

"Let's cross that bridge when we come to it. I can't believe it's all that easy, though," Dante said. "What else could be going on here?"

Molchalin held his gaze for a moment before he spoke. "Someone with the talent, means and sheer force of will has specifically targeted you and this is just the beginning."

CHAPTER 18

The Package

Boxes were piled up at least four feet or so, most of them about the size of a toaster. He'd checked his accounts but there were no outstanding charges. Gary brought some of the boxes in and the twins were having a ball stacking them up and knocking them down like they were miniature kaiju.

His phone rang. He knew it was Gail before he even connected.

"So, Amex just got in touch."

"Gail, something crazy is going on."

"Uh huh. You maxxed out your own card so you had to use mine?"

"What are you talking about?" Gary asked in shock.

"All the charges are from Adult Flair DVD. Not really my style."

"Hold on," Gary said as he dropped the phone in one of the loose pockets on his robe.

He tore open one of the boxes and a stack of DVDs spilled out. They were all pornography. He scooped them up and stuffed them back in the box. One of the twins got a hold of one and took off, screaming with frustration as Gary chased him down and took it away. Curious, he scanned the cover. It was an image of two Asian women, naked bodies entwined with that of a muscular blond man. He scanned the title as a very frustrated toddler punched him in the testicles.

Two Wongs make a White.

With a groan, he jammed the porno back in the box and tucked it under an arm as he lifted his phone and pressed it to his ear.

"Listen, I didn't have anything to do with this. Somebody got your card info and for some reason used it to buy all this stuff and mail it here."

"Do you really expect me to believe that?"

"Gail, darling, it's been a real shit day and I don't need your little insinuations right now. My back is still killing me from when that cop pinned me down."

"What are you're saying? You got arrested?"

"Would you shut up and listen to me for once?"

The twins stopped pushing boxes around and gaped at Gary, eyes wide.

"Someone is harassing us and I don't know why. The cop said something about a jilted boyfriend. Anything you'd like to tell me? Something about your little lunch buddy, Ted?"

"No," she said, her voice low. "Of course not."

"The thermostat had a virus, that's what caused it to go on the fritz. Then the alarm went off and the cops showed up," Gary said. "The SWAT team, Gail."

"Oh my god! Are the babies okay? Why didn't you call me?"

"They're fine. I'm alive too, thanks for asking. Somebody called the cops with a false report. It's called swatting. Then all these packages started showing up. I looked it up online. The swatting, the messing with smart devices, the packages. This type of thing has been reported before, just not all at the same time. We've been targeted by a hacker or some script kiddie that wants to mess with us. And no, I have no idea why."

"Well, I'm coming home. Right away."

"Good idea. When you get here, call Visa and straighten this mess out."

"What are you going to do?" Gail said.

"As soon as you get home, I'm going back to bed."

Still clad in his robe, Gary used a sledge hammer to pound a wooden post into the ground. Nailed to the post was large piece of cardboard with a message scrawled across it with fat black marker: WE DIDN'T ORDER ANYTHING. NO MORE PACKAGES PLEASE.

He'd only slept an hour or so and the ache in his lower back had ascended his spine with a prickly vengeance. During that time the pile had grown, extending down their short driveway almost to the street. Gail had to park her Audi a few cars up when she'd come home.

He couldn't wait to hear all about it.

A young woman jogged by in a tight black running suit, her pony tail bouncing as she gazed down at the packages with interest.

"Got a lot of packages there," she said, jogging in place. "What's in them?"

"Porn mostly," Gary said. "Some sex toys."

She laughed, her face becoming a frown as Gary remained impassive. She bounced off and Gary turned back to the house, wishing he had that much energy to waste.

Something buzzed his face and he ducked, dropping the hammer with a thump. It came at him again and he karate-chopped as it swooped in low, his hand missing it by a mile. It hovered low to the ground about five feet away, orange wings a blur.

It was the dragonfly drone.

The little wooden box it had left at the back door earlier was suspended below its metallic green body by its legs. He'd forgotten all about it. Gary peered around, but the street was empty of people. He wondered if this little gift was from the hackers.

Had to be.

Gary stepped toward it and the box dropped to the street. The dragonfly hovered back a few feet as he came closer and knelt down. Picking up the box, he held it up and inspected it closely. It was made from balsa wood and appeared to be carved from one piece, except for a small door inset in the top. There were no markings. He held it to his ear and shook it. The dragonfly emitted a loud buzz that made him jump.

"Okay, okay," he said. "No shaky."

He tried to slide the small door back but it clicked instead. He hooked a fingernail under the edge and eased it open, half expecting it to explode in his face. Inside was a flat, smooth object, like a large coin, pearlescent gray in color. Turning the box over in his palm, the object fell out and he held it up close.

His body went stiff.

On the face of the object were the twins, their soft features perfectly captured, wild hair sticking up from their heads. Their arms were intertwined, bodies overlapping to form the shape of a heart with their heads creating the dual curves of the top. He peered closer, rubbing his thumb across the surface. If it was a 3D print it was a damn good one.

He turned it over.

It was a mirror image of the obverse, different in subtle but terrifying ways. The boy's mouths were thrown open in silent screams of agony, their delicate little fingers curled like claws. Their bellies were slit open down the front, bulbous coils of intestines spilling out. The dragonfly flitted its wings and flew off.

"What the fuck is going on?" Gary said, his breath coming quick and shallow.

In a daze, he withdrew the card Sergeant Chavez had given him earlier. His phone chittered with a harsh, insectile sound. As Gary read the text displayed on the screen, the card slipped from his fingers.

CHAPTER 19

Voices

Her parents were arguing in the next room again, their voices muffled through the walls. First, Mom's reedy shrill followed by Dad's gravelly rumble. Briana hugged her baby doll close, small hands pressed over her ears. Then her mother laughed, her voice swelling, becoming sweet and gleeful.

Briana awoke, confused for a moment. Then she saw the hyenas staring back at her and remembered where she was. Rubbing her eyes, she scooped up her phone from where it had fallen on the floor and checked the time. 3:36 PM. Her stomach rumbled. She hadn't eaten since this morning at the airport. The voices started up again next door. It was Leish, talking fast, her voice confident and strong. Briana lay back and curled on her side. She couldn't hear what Leish was saying but she knew the tone.

Listen to me. Damn it.

She smiled. It was awesome to hear another young woman be so confident, so sure of herself.

A lower voice boomed out, rattling the door. Briana jerked upright. She knew that tone only too well. Mark's voice was laced with it every time he spoke.

Listen to me. Bitch.

Briana waited for a moment, but the voices had fallen silent. A door opened, harsh in the lull, followed by a slam. Footsteps creaked across the wood floor as Leish hummed to herself, growing softer as she moved away. Briana's stomach cramped again. She couldn't hide in here all day. Steeling herself, she got up and turned the doorknob.

Briana walked down the hall, then across the main room to the kitchen. Leish was bent over one of her cameras, fiddling with the controls. She wore chunky high heels and a long black jacket that hung mid-thigh. She turned and her face lit up. "Hey, baby doll. Hungry?"

"Starving,"

"Good. I ordered some food. Should be here soon. Go relax on the patio and I'll meet you out there."

Briana turned to go when Leish stopped her. "Wait, take a look at this. What do you think?"

Briana peered down at the small screen on the back of the camera cradled in Leish's hands. It was an image of Leish, lips parted and pouty, flipping the bird. Over each nipple were yellow emoji hands, middle fingers extended as well.

"Subtle," Briana said.

"It's supposed to be sexy sassy. Too bitchy, do you think?"

"Leish, can we talk about something?"

"Already? That's like a new record for me. What's wrong?"

"Who else lives here? I heard a man's voice."

"Nobody else lives here. That was Melvin, my manager, over vidcon."

"It sounded like he was in the room."

"Listen, Briana. It's just you and me. Okay?"

"And that contract..."

"It's not a contract, just a release form."

"Yeah, I know, but it doesn't feel right."

"I know what you're thinking. THOT attention grabbing instahoe. There must be cams all over. Listen to me. There's no cameras in your room." Leish glanced down the hall. "Or your bathroom. Is that what you're worried about?"

"Well, yeah. I mean I know it's your thing but I'm kinda

private."

Leish took Briana's hands in hers and gazed into her eyes. "Listen, Briana. You're a beautiful girl but that's not why you're out here. You're here because of your voice. I can't do this forever. I know that. I'm using what I have while I have it, but I know by the time I'm thirty or so, ass shots are going to be much less of a reality." She twisted her neck and looked at her backside. "Maybe sooner than that. I want to find and develop talent. It's part of my larger plan and that starts with you. Understand?"

"I don't know."

"What can I do to ease your mind?"

"That dragonfly drone," Briana said. "It was in the bathroom while I was taking a shower."

Leish's eyes narrowed as she scanned the room. She stalked over to her computer and turned, her jaw set. "You mean this drone?" she said, pointing to where it sat perched on the corner of the desk. The wings twitched.

Briana nodded.

Leish brought her fist down. Hard. She held the drone up between thumb and forefinger, her face tight. The little orange wings hung at odd angles, one looking as if it was about to fall off. The legs twitched and she dropped it on the floor, crunching it under her heel. She gave her foot a twist then strolled back over to Briana, hands on hips.

"We good?"

Briana gazed down at the tiny mangled drone, then back up at Leish.

"Yeah," Briana said with a soft smile. Lingering doubt still swirled inside and she pushed it away.

Leish licked her lips and smirked. "Let's talk about tonight then, shall we?"

CHAPTER 20

Lumetri Scopes

Dante rode the private elevator back up to his office. Dropping onto the couch, he kicked off his shoes. His chest felt tight and he undid the top buttons of his shirt and took a deep breath.

I'm supposed to feel better, Dante thought. *Especially for how much this is going to cost.*

But something Dmitry Molchalin said at the end of their meeting stayed with him, grating on his frayed nerves.

…this is just beginning.

"How's it going?" Naomi said.

Dante jumped. He hadn't heard her come in. Gazing up at her, he smiled tightly. "Great."

"You don't look too great."

"I'm fine. I need you to write an email for me."

"What about?"

"Tell everyone to take the next two days off. Paid of course."

"Two days? We have so many things in flight right now, Dante. Two days is going to hurt."

"It'll hurt worse if we don't do it. Shadow Trace is coming by tomorrow to setup their security software."

"You're going with these guys after one visit? Maybe you should talk to some other companies first. Shop around a bit."

"Well, they came highly recommended by the FBI for one,

and you should have seen this place. Very high tech. Totally secure. The guy who runs the place, Dmitry Molchalin, calm and cool. A total pro. I felt better just talking to the guy and what they could do for us. Not to mention they're close, right over in Van Nuys."

"Van Nuys?" she said, one eyebrow going up.

He'd felt the same way when he'd looked up the address. A world class cyber security firm in the armpit of the valley? Dante ignored her. "Can I rely on you to be here? I need your backup on this."

A slight smile turned up the corners of her mouth. "Of course."

"Good, because I'm bringing Abigail in tomorrow and I need somebody to watch her while I'm busy with Shadow Trace. I don't feel safe having her at school."

"What about your friend. Kelly."

"I just need you to do this, okay?"

Naomi's eyes hardened. "Understood."

She turned on her heel and left, leaving the door wide open. Dante sighed, got to his feet and eased the door shut. He understood why she was angry. They'd have to talk about it, and soon, but he couldn't worry about that right now.

He opened a browser and googled deep fakes. Video links along the top showed the highest viewed videos, most of which seemed to be replacing someone's face with the Internet's darling boy, actor Nicolas Cage. Other videos described what the technology was and how dangerous it was going to be in the very near future.

Dante had experienced firsthand just how true that was.

He clicked on the Wikipedia article and scanned through it. It was like Boucher had said, the software was developed by academia within a field called computer vision, using deep learning and neural networks. The software analyzed hundreds of source pictures to create a 3D model of the actor's face. It also used something called a GAN, or generative adversarial network to determine the best way to map the model onto another person's body. The technology was then furthered by amateurs with the best intentions for all humanity clearly in mind.

Pornography.

Celebrity porn made up most of the deep fakes with entire sites and message boards devoted to sharing the final results. There were commercial options available as well as an open source alternative that could be updated by anyone with adequate programming skills. It meant that this technology was accessible to anyone with a PC and time to kill.

Scrolling down, Dante stopped on the heading: Concerns. The first article described a CEO being fooled into transferring funds by someone using audio deep fake technology to impersonate the voice of a chief executive over the phone. Bainbridge said Dante had spoken at the end of the video.

The next article was called effects on credibility and authenticity. Dante didn't bother reading any further. Closing the browser, he leaned back in his chair and considered getting the bottle of bourbon from his desk drawer before doing what had to be done. Taking a deep breath, he moused over to the email icon and double clicked.

He scrolled down past the hundreds of shocked and angry return emails before giving up. Naomi could handle all of that. He switched over to sent emails, found the deep fake video and saved it to the desktop. It unnerved him that someone could use his private email to send something like this without him even knowing. Steeling himself, he opened the file and clenched his jaw as it filled the screen.

Raucous voices leapt out from the speakers and Dante dialed down the volume. The video was dark, shot in crowded room with a round stage at the center. Drunken faces of men jeered in and out of the shadows, ties loosened, all of them dressed in black suits. The view moved to the right then whipped down, jostled by the crowd. The camera swung back up and panned over, closer now, pushing past a man's bald head. Two blurry shapes filled the screen, overexposed by what appeared to be a bright clutch of bare bulbs overhead. The camera's digital iris adjusted, rendering the leering faces encircling the stage almost invisible. The center of the room came into sharp focus and Dante held his breath, heart thudding in his chest.

A rail thin, naked man stood onstage, directly behind a donkey. He was thrusting his hips back and forth while the animal chewed, its dark eyes glazed over. The man turned and peered at the camera with a lopsided grin as the camera zoomed in closer. Dante hit the pause button.

Deep fake Dante, he thought with dark humor.

The whole thing was fake, he realized. A collection of videos artfully stitched together from different sources. To his trained eye, it had all the earmarks of being post processed, well beyond the deep fake part of it. The lighting on the man looked a bit odd and the overall image had a dreamy, smeary quality to it. That made it no less disturbing though.

Acid bubbled up, burning the back of this tongue. He'd heard of such things of course. There was always that guy in every group of college buddies who swore that donkey shows were real, hand to god, they had a cousin in the navy who'd been to one. But seeing one, especially with him as the star made him feel violated in a way he'd never thought possible. His face burned as he thought of everyone on his contact list seeing this disgusting farce.

This is bad, he thought.

The glee in Bainbridge's voice rang through his head and he was glad the smug fuck wasn't here right now. He'd probably break his face. Dante shook his head. Watching the whole video was almost too much but it had to be done. He hit play again and the video stuttered back to life.

Deep fake Dante continued to leer at the camera before licking his lips and speaking.

"Beware; for I am fearless, and therefore powerful."

The screen went black.

Dante sat for a moment, stunned. The voice sounded like

him but was clipped and scratchy. He's said those words a hundred times or more, but couldn't recall where they were from.

Didn't matter, he thought. *Time for a closer look.*

At the beginning of his career, Dante had done rough cuts of commercials before passing them onto the senior editing team. He wasn't sure what he would discover but it was worth a shot.

Dante opened up Reel View video editing software. Reel View consisted of a time line window where video and audio clips could be assembled and edited along with two video windows above: Source and Output. He dragged the video from the desktop onto the time line and the source window lit up with a still image from the video, as did the output window. The two images looked the same, but the output window would update based on any changes Dante made.

Zooming into the image, he scrubbed his mouse pointer along the time line, causing the video to shuttle back and forth. He could see the telltale shimmer of pixels along the edge of the man's body. The shadows didn't really match the rest of the scene as well. The man had been cut out of another video using what was called a traveling matte and composited into this one. Dante breathed a sigh of relief. Whoever the guy was in the video was definitely up to something sexual, just not with an animal.

He panned over to the donkey and the matte lines were more obvious. It was much harder to pull a matte on fur or hair, the pixels being so small. To Dante, it looked like the video was shot in a shitty strip club and the man and donkey were composited in later.

Dante clicked on a small dial icon and opened up the "scopes." Lumetri scopes were a set of five tools that displayed the color information of a video signal. He selected a waveform scope and a window opened, displaying a white, jagged mountain range against black. Numbers ranging from –20 to 120 ran along the side, going from bottom to top. The waveform for standard videos lay somewhere between 0 and 100, but the peaks in this video reached far below and above what he'd expect. This wasn't standard video, but an HDR or high dynamic range video. He looked at those spiking peaks again and a sudden thought occurred to him.

There's something hidden in the white levels of this video.

Dante adjusted a slider on the panel and the output window changed, the video becoming pale and bleached out. Dante scrubbed along the time line, watching as the video updated frame by frame. There in the background, beyond the group of leering men, was something that turned his blood to ice.

It was Michelle.

Her dark hair drifted slowly as if underwater, sad eyes watchful. A sudden thought struck him and the room tilted, his breath coming in ragged gasps.

It was Michelle from Abigail's dream.

Whoever was harassing him, they had eyes and ears in his house.

CHAPTER 21

Long Game

Abigail stared out the window as Dante drove. There had been no other texts from unknown, but those words from the earlier text still rattled in his head.

The more a thing is perfect...

He'd spent the rest of the day calling up future tenants of the Ellis Media building as well as high-profile clients he knew personally. He assured them something like this would never happen again, security was going to be tighter than ever. Most were very understanding but cautious. He had no doubt he'd lost a few of them over this.

"Dad," Abigail said.

"Yeah?"

"Some of the kids were talking about you at school."

Dante's heart sank. "What about?"

"Your video."

Oh shit. "What did they say?"

"It was Joe Haley. He saw your NAB talk on YouTube. He wants to be a YouTuber. I said the real money was in producing the videos like you. It's the long game."

"You said that?" Dante said as relief flooded through him. "Good for you."

CHAPTER 22

Part of the Cackle

The city coursed by outside the convertible limo, intermingled lights and darks easing by. The driver glanced into the rearview mirror, checking on the two young women in the back seat. He made sure to keep his speed under forty miles an hour, otherwise a relaxing nighttime ride would become the eye of a hurricane.

The air was warm, thick with odors of a long day drenched in the late August sun. A hint of metal on the back of the tongue. Wet concrete with a hue of old coffee and cigarette ash. Street dogs with fried onions, gyros and the oily stench of food trucks. Very different from the natural scents of fresh cut corn and recently tilled earth.

Briana loved it.

She twirled a single lock of hair from over her ear as the breeze washed over her, dyed purple earlier that afternoon. It stood stark against the natural blonde of the rest of her hair.

Leish was watching her, hazel eyes glittering in the dance of lights, blue hair shifting in the wind. She reached up and pulled a matching purple lock straight out and grinned.

"Part of the pack now," Leish said.

"Cackle, don't you mean," said Briana.

"Very good." She tucked the lock back over her ear and tilted a silver flask to her lips. Her long, slender throat pulsed as she swallowed. With a grimace, she passed it over to Briana.

Briana took the flask but hesitated. Her mother's dire warnings seemed so very far away now. Putting the flask to her lips, she took a tentative sip, then slugged it back.

"There you go!" Leish said, clapping.

Briana shivered and stuck her tongue out, almost dropping the flask on the floor.

Leish pulled a small pipe from her purse and stuck it between her lips. The sound of glass against teeth made Briana wince. The tip of the pipe was a bright shiny eye, the iris an icy blue. With a snap of her fingers, she flicked open a shiny silver lighter. The flame guttered as she puffed, the thick gray smoke swirling on the breeze. Briana wrinkled her nose, but took the proffered pipe and lighter. She tried to flick the lighter as she'd seen Leish do but the small wheel bit into her thumb, the flame refusing to catch.

"Ouch!"

"Here, gimme," Leish said, scooting over close. She snapped her fingers and held the flame over the bowl of the pipe as Briana inhaled deeply. Her eyes watered as she held her breath, lungs crawling with flaming green gnats. It wasn't the first time she'd smoked weed, but whatever this stuff was, it was strong. She exhaled with a wheezing cough as Leish rubbed her back.

With a tickle in her throat, Briana tilted her head against the leather seat and stared up into the night sky. No stars, just a layer of soft, pinkish-orange clouds, ignited by blue–white spears of searchlight beams that swept over the haze in a cloverleaf pattern. Briana blinked, the afterimage of those intersecting beams flashing against a field of black. It made her feel like the luckiest girl in the world.

"Good?" Leish said.

Briana nodded, her head swimming. "Oh yeah," she said, gazing around as she slid her fingers along the car door. "Where did you get this thing?"

"Connections. It's all who you know out here. This, my dear, is a 1964 Lincoln Continental, limo conversion. Black on black, similar to the one Kennedy was shot in."

Briana gazed at her in fascination. "How do you know all that?"

Leish pointed a bare foot at the back of the driver's seat. "It's on a silver plaque right there."

Briana giggled. "You're still one of the coolest people I've ever met."

"Likewise," Leish said. "I'm glad that little black dress fit you."

Briana tugged at the hem. "It's a little shorter than what I'm used to."

"You got the body for it, that's for sure." She reached out for one of the silver buttons done up all the way to Briana's throat. "Undo a few of those. Let the girls breathe!"

Briana swatted her hand away. "Get away!" She smoothed her hands along the top of her thighs. "It's beautiful. I've never worn anything like this."

"It's yours."

"No, I can't."

Leish squeezed her arm, leaning in close. "Please. I want you to have it."

"Thank you," Briana said. "Sorry about earlier. Guess my mom really got into my head with stories of cameras and predators looking to use me."

Leish glanced away. "Yeah, there's some real creeps out here." She gazed back again, eyes somewhere far away. "Just stick with me, baby doll. I got you."

Brakes squealed as the Lincoln eased to a stop in front of a multistory brick building, all the widows painted black. A line of expectant club-goers stretched down the block, curving around the corner and out of sight. A V-shaped bouncer dressed in black stood at the door, grim faced, an ear piece tucked in one ear.

People in line stirred, curious about the new arrivals in the shiny black car. Leish patted Briana's leg.

"Watch this."

She sat on the door's edge then swept her legs over to the other side and stood up, whipping her hair back in a flourish. Her leather pants gleamed in the flash of lights from the several phones held up high. Catcalls and whistles broke out and she blew kisses before stripping off her shirt, revealing a lacy black bra.

The crowd roared.

With one hand on her hip, she twirled the thin fabric overhead before tossing it in a high arc toward the crowd. A girl with a shaved head leapt up and caught it, shoving a guy next to her that tried to take it away. People clapped and hooted while others shook their heads, one mouthing the words "attention whore." Leish spun and opened the car door, extending a hand to Briana.

"My lady," she said.

Briana took her hand and stepped onto the sidewalk as more flashes fired off. "Smile, this is the first moment of many," Leish whispered into her ear.

Several small drones drifted down from above, propellers whining like angry bees. One stayed higher up, away from the light. It looked a bit like a dragonfly.

Leish gave Briana's hand a tug. "C'mon."

The two young women hustled through the door as the bouncer stepped aside, waving them in as boos from the line fell away behind them.

Bars edged with colorful neon bordered a large dance area. Bodies shifted in time to music with barely enough room to move. Scantily clad wait staff weaved through, deftly maneuvering drink trays held high overhead. Off to the right was a raised DJ booth. The records were spun by a topless woman painted with glowing white stripes. Dancers, both male and female, gyrated on platforms dotted throughout the club as strawberry scented fog drifted down from above.

The ceiling faded high into darkness, four stories above. A

drone swarm hovered up there, lights flashing and changing color, aligning and realigning to form various shapes. A yellow star, burning bright before fading out. A pair of lips opening to reveal three white Xs. A pink heart, pulsing softly before breaking with a jagged crack down the center.

A VIP mezzanine stood against the far wall, enclosed in glass. It was accessed by a circular staircase that twisted up through the center, guarded by a velvet rope and two beefy security guards. The raised platform was crowded with girls and somber-faced men in sports jerseys or dark suits, holding court with their entourage from the confines of plush couches. Briana peered closer, rising up on her tiptoes to see.

Her mouth fell open. "Is that who I think it is?"

Leish craned her neck and nodded. "Harold Weintraub, that's him. He's going to put me in a movie, you know."

"No, not him," Briana pointed to a tall man with dark ginger hair. His head was shaved on either side, accentuating the curly mop above. Wire-rim glasses with red lenses sat on his nose and he wore a gray stripped shirt and dark pants. On his feet were ruby red sneakers, bejeweled and glinting. He was laughing, arm thrown over another man's shoulder.

Leish pulled Briana's hand down. "Don't do that. And yeah, that's him alright."

"He just discovered Chantilly. They're working on her album now," Briana said.

"You want to meet him?"

"Wait." Briana said, clutching Leish's arm. "You know Dillon Travis."

"Shots first," Leish said, scanning the crowded room before waving with her hand. A muscular Asian man appeared, dressed in loose fitting jeans with a bandoleer over one shoulder holding shot glasses. He grinned as Leish jumped into his arms and he almost dropped his vodka bottle.

"Tony!" she said. "Meet Briana."

Tony pulled Briana in close with his free hand and hugged both girls tight. The two of them squealed and Leish spanked his ass until he let go and poured two shots. The two young women clinked glasses and knocked them back as Tony shuffled to the beat.

"More, more," Leish said, holding her glass up. Tony refilled their glasses and they drank again. He held up the bottle and waggled it.

"One more?"

Leish took their empty glasses and shoved them toward his chest, waving him off. Tony backed away, mock injury on his face.

"So, here's the plan," Leish said, looping an arm through Briana's. "We're going to work our way up to the VIP area. There're some music producers up there I want you to meet. Real heavy hitters looking for new talent."

"What about-"

"Yes, yes, Dillon Travis. But first..."

"Yeah?" Briana said.

"Ready for the time of your life?"

CHAPTER 23

It Just Is

They danced and drank and Briana had never felt so alive. It was as if a bright, cleansing light burned inside her, chasing away all the fear and sadness she'd ever felt. It would sound stupid if she said it out loud, she knew, but it's how she felt. She wanted to savor this feeling forever.

Mom and all her dire warnings seemed like the ravings of an overprotective crazy woman now. Hollywood was nothing like she'd said. The people here were so friendly and Leish was like watching poetry, so effortlessly alive and in her element, bathed in flashing light and pounding rhythm.

Leish was taking selfies with a couple of girls when she caught Briana staring. She cocked her head then swept in close, tracing a finger over her lips. Briana's heart began to pound. Leish stepped back, a smirk on her face as she slipped into the crowd. Briana lost sight of her and hurried to catch up.

Leish introduced Briana to everyone they met as a singer, her latest discovery. It made her feel special, out here for a real purpose. Most smiled and congratulated her. Some rolled their eyes and one girl in a silver dress and smeared lipstick threw her head back and cackled. "You and everybody else," she said before shuffling away.

The dance floor was filled with women in groups of two or

three, holding their phones up to capture themselves dancing or duck-facing for the camera. A few men danced as well, but most of them held their phones up to record someone else, usually a girl.

One of Dillon Travis's songs came on and a roar went up from the dancefloor. Briana gazed up to the VIP area and saw him peering downward. He raised a glass as the beat thundered out.

"I wanna dance," Briana said to nobody in particular.

She pushed into a group nearby and grabbed the hand of a young guy dressed in a purple suit patterned with fleur-de-lis. His boyish face lit up as she pulled him into the mass of gyrating bodies. Briana danced and spun, letting the rhythm take her away. They moved closer, and she didn't stop him as he put his hands on her waist.

A few songs later, Leish came over and pushed the young man away. The guy glanced backward as he slunk off and Briana shrugged and blew him a kiss.

"I feel like a princess," she said in Leish's ear.

"More like a queen. C'mon, let's go."

They weaved their way over to the VIP stairs, taking a few more vodka shots along the way. The velvet rope dropped and they were waved through. Briana's head was swimming and she held on tight to the rail as it curved around in a tight corkscrew to the upper level. Her stomach fluttered. She'd never met any industry people before and she didn't want to make a fool of herself.

They emerged from the stairs, found the bar and ordered more shots. The music was quieter up here, but the voices were louder, everyone shouting over each other to be heard.

A security guard stepped forward and held up a hand. He was muscular and tall, well over six feet, dressed in a black t-shirt and pants. He flashed a light in their eyes and told them to open their purses.

The light stabbed inside Leish's clutch before she was waved on. She stood nearby, twisting her purple lock around one finger. The guard motioned for Briana to come forward. She opened her purse and he pointed the light in. She moved to pass. Another man appeared, his face stern. He was older, balding, chubby face beaded with sweat above a rumpled suit.

"Hold it, Johnson," he said to the muscular guard, yanking the flashlight from his grasp. "I got this."

Johnson raised his hands and backed up a step. "Yes, Mr. Newton."

"Arms up," Newton told her, flicking the flashlight up and down. "Straight out from your sides."

"What? Why?" Briana said.

Newton glared at her as the people behind him went silent, eyes watching. He gripped her arm above the elbow. "Please exit the VIP area."

"Hey!" Leish said, stepping forward. Newton held up a finger and she stopped, face tight.

"Wait, it's okay," Briana said and raised her arms. The noise died down as others in the VIP area turned to watch. He eyed her up and down before sticking the flashlight between his teeth. Reaching out he began to pat her down, having her turn halfway through. His hands lingered as he touched the sides of her breasts and again on the swell of each buttock. Trying not to flinch at his touch, she could feel the eyes of the others crawling over her. The thought of someone like Dillon Travis seeing her like this made her face flush with heat. Shrill voices of Mark and his friends cawed in her head and her stomach turned sour. Leish stood nearby, swiping at her phone screen.

Briana felt a flash of anger.

"Alright, get the hell outta here," the security guard said, swiping his flashlight back. He raised it overhead as Newton ducked and shuffled away with a devilish grin. "And my name is Williams, you fat fuck," he called to Newton's retreating backside.

Newton leapt over the back of a couch and bounced once before falling to the floor, spilling drinks. He lay sprawling, kicking his short legs as everyone laughed.

Tears burned in Briana's eyes as she looked away.

Leish took her arm. "Sorry about that."

"I'd like to go now," Briana said, searching through her purse for nothing in particular.

"Briana-"

"It's okay, I just want to go."

"Listen, it's part of it, okay?" Leish said. "It just *is*."

"Easy for you to say."

"He's a lawyer in the biz for everybody that matters. Powerful. Connected. You're new here and he knows it. It's just a test. You only pass if you stay. Leave now, you're never getting back up here. *Ever*."

Briana wiped her eyes and nodded. "Okay."

Leish glanced around. "I don't see Dillon. I'm sure he'll be back soon. Let's go meet Harold Weintraub. The movie he's putting me in? It's called *Inner Bitch*. It's about a female merc squad. Guns for hire. C'mon, he's sitting right over there."

They weaved through the crowd to where a large man sat on a green velvet couch. His bald head gleamed in the flashing light. A thin line of whiskers traced the edge of his chin. Gold rimmed sunglasses hid his eyes. A blue suit barely held in the pressure of his bulk, with a crisp collared shirt underneath unbuttoned to reveal several thick ropes of gold chains resting on a thatch of dark chest hair. One meaty arm was thrown over the back of the couch. His other paw held the base of a champagne flute balanced on the upper swell of his stomach.

"Wait here," Leish said.

Leish weaved through shifting bodies before placing her hands on the arm of the couch, leaning down to speak into Weintraub's ear. He inclined his head slightly, then turned to gaze up at her. He put a large hand on hers and spoke into her ear, silver teeth flashing. Leish yanked her hands back as if from a hot stove. The large man laughed and shook his head. She stood for a moment, her eyes turning fierce before coming back over.

"Now's not a good time," Leish said.

Briana nodded and folded her arms across her chest. She couldn't imagine what would cause Leish to react like that and she didn't want to know. Dillon Travis was nowhere to be found. Everyone else was drinking and laughing and it felt like they were outsiders with no way in.

Leish gazed around, her jaw set. She turned to Briana.

"Let's get the fuck out of here."

CHAPTER 24

Squirrel Suicide

They emerged into the night air, still stuffy and warm even though it was well past midnight. Knots of people stood in groups along the sidewalk, smoking and waiting for rides. A girl sat on the sidewalk, skirt hiked up, vomiting loudly into the gutter as another held her hair back. Two men nearby stood chest to chest, screaming at each other while their buddies egged them on. Their girlfriends tried to pull them apart, faces slack with boredom.

Phone cameras caught it all.

A silver Prius pulled up to the curb and Leish broke into a run, Briana struggling to keep up in her heels. Yanking the rear door open, she pushed Briana inside then leapt in after her. The driver turned around, eyes glowering from under thick eyebrows. "Careful please, ladies," he said in clipped English.

"Hey!" said a blond girl in heavy makeup and shiny gold dress, clomping over in chunky heels. "That's ours!"

"Go, go, go!" Leish said and the driver accelerated away.

They watched through the rear window as the girl ran after them and stumbled, ankles folding up as she fought to right herself in a bizarre pop and lock. She crashed to her knees, causing her blond wig to tumble into the other lane before disappearing under the tires of a passing truck.

Briana and Leish looked at each other then broke into gales of wild laughter.

"Did you see that? That squirrel on her head just committed suicide!" Leish said and they screamed.

"Oh my God, you're crazy!"

They fell against each other, trying to catch their breath. Leish turned and gazed at Briana before she reached out and brushed her fingers over her lips.

"God, you're pretty," she said, leaning in close.

"Yeah?" Briana said, heart thudding. She could smell Leish, her perfume—feel her warm breath on her face. They kissed lightly at first. Briana flinched as Leish's tongue slid into her mouth.

"No girls, no," the driver said. "I take my kids to school in this car."

"Eyes on the road, pervert!" Leish said and they laughed again. Briana laid her head on Leish's shoulder and they watched the city outside drift by.

Perched on the rear window outside was a small dragonfly drone, its beady eyes locked on the two young women inside.

CHAPTER 25

Ersatz Adirondacks

Gary sat in one of the two plastic Adirondacks he'd insisted on buying a few months ago. He did his best thinking while slouched in one, cold beer in hand, breathing the night air. Gail hated them. Said they were tacky. It's probably why he loved them so much.

Not tonight though.

Tonight, he agreed with her. Fucking things sucked. And it wasn't a beer he held, either, but the small gift delivered by a counterfeit dragonfly. His thumb traced over the surface of the little heart shaped object in the darkness. He could feel his son's smooth faces, then the sharp edge where their mouths were thrown open wide in agony. It wasn't a gift.

It was a threat.

He'd heard somewhere that dragonflies were good luck, so it stood to reason that a mechanical mockery of one brought the exact opposite. Nature out of balance, or something.

"Gary?" Gail called from behind the screen door. "The twins are asleep."

"I'll be in in a minute."

The screen door opened and Gary groaned internally. Gail came out and sat on the other Adirondack, readjusting herself to find a comfortable place on the edge.

For Christ sake, just sit, Gary screamed in his head.

Then she said something he'd only heard her say once before. It was after the twins were born prematurely and were in the NICU, all covered in tubes and wires.

"I'm scared, Gary. Really scared. What's going on?"

His anger bled away, tempered by shame. He looked down at himself. He'd never even changed out of his robe. Cold seeped into him even though the heat of the day had barely begun to die down.

"It's going to be alright. Really. I'll take care of it. Okay?" he told her.

She nodded, barely visible in the darkness. Sliding back into the chair, she tilted her head up, looking into the sky. "Hey, a shooting star." She sighed. "These chairs aren't too bad, are they?"

"Yeah," Gary said. He lifted his phone and reread the anonymous text he'd received earlier that evening.

This is only a taste of what's to come.
Do as instructed. For the sake of your family.

Gary's finger hovered over the screen a moment before he sent back a single word.

Anything.

CHAPTER 26

A Little Wiser

They stumbled into the apartment after struggling to get the key into the lock, giggling the whole time. As the door swung open and banged against the wall, music swelled from the speakers tucked throughout the room. Leish waved her hand downward, causing the volume to lower before flumping onto one of the couches. Briana joined her, falling back against the cushions. The ceiling spun and she leaned forward, blinking. Leish poked her with a bare foot and Briana almost fell over. They laughed.

"Oh my god, you do this all the time?" Briana said.

"Pretty much. See and be seen. It's a big part of the game. You have stay in people's minds or you disappear. All about content too. Constant updates. It's gotten easier though. I'm down to updating social media twice a day instead of eight or nine times, so that's good."

"Sounds exhausting."

Leish sighed, lying back against a cushion. "It never ends. I tell you what I'd really like to do someday is just travel. Not to post on social. Just for me. Travel all around the world. Start down in Mexico and climb El Castillo at Chichen Itza. Visit Palenque and Tikal. But first, Tulum. Have you seen it? They have a Maya pyramid overlooking to the ocean."

"Sounds beautiful. You'll do it someday," Briana said.

"Yeah," Leish said, staring up at the ceiling. She sat up. "Let's talk about what's next."

"What's next?"

"We record a demo."

Briana frowned. "What about my videos?"

"That's a start but you have to record a demo in an actual studio, not just a vid shot in your bedroom."

"I have a little money but I need that to pay my share of the rent until I get a job. I didn't really think about that."

"We'll figure it out. I'm your manager, right?"

"How much?"

"I have a friend with a recording studio. I'll make it happen. Okay?"

"Okay," Briana said grinning.

They fell silent. Leish closed her eyes, nodding to the music.

"Can I ask you something?" Briana said.

"Of course."

"What did he say to you?"

"What, Harold? He just likes to joke around a little."

"You seemed pretty upset about it."

"Briana...just leave it. Okay?"

"Okay."

Leish's face flushed and she blinked, one tear escaping down her cheek. She wiped it away with a flick of her hand, causing her blue hair to shimmer in the dim light. "Don't ever cry," she said. "Lubricates your dreams. Sends them that much faster down the drain." Leish leapt to her feet, fists shaking as she screamed "Fuck you, dreams!"

Briana opened her mouth to speak then closed it again.

"He said...," Leish shut her eyes tight. She sighed, breath shuddering. "It doesn't matter what he said."

Leish dropped back to the couch and took a cigarette out from a silver case on the coffee table and lit it with shaking hands. Then she laid back, eyes on the ceiling, the cherry glowing bright as she inhaled with a crackling hiss.

"I'm still in the movie he's making. Just got a sick sense of humor, that's all," she said, exhaling blue smoke into the air. "All part of the shit show."

Briana stood up, wavering. "I need to go to bed. Still on Central Time."

"Oh god, I'm sorry. Forget about my shit. It just…"

"*Is*," Briana said. "I know."

Leish frowned, stubbing out her cigarette. "Here, let me help you," she said, sliding an arm around Briana's waist.

They stumbled down the hallway, Briana kicking off her shoes on the way. Light shot out from underneath the closed door on the left, a pale blue glow reaching out across the hall.

"Somebody else here?" Briana said.

"Just us."

As they entered her room, Briana slipped out of Leish's arms and fell back across the bed. She opened her eyes and frowned, pushing hyenas out of the way. Leish stood near the door, one foot tucked behind the other, hand on top of the big hyena's head.

"Can I ask you something?"

"Yeah, sure," Briana said.

"No, it's stupid."

"Leish, anything. Really."

"Do you like me?"

"What?"

"I mean, we got along so good on the phone that first time and we've been texting a lot since, but…it's hard to tell sometimes who your real friends are. You know?"

Briana sat up. "Leish, come here," she said, patting the bed next to her.

Leish's eyes dropped to the floor before she came over and sat down. Her eyes lifted and found Briana's.

"You are seriously the coolest, most bad-ass chick I've ever met," Briana said. "So confident and strong. But also, the sweetest, most generous person. I wish I could be like you."

Leish blinked away tears and bit her lip. "Yeah?"

Briana nodded, smiling softly. "Yeah."

They sat for moment until Briana looked away. "Don't look at me like that."

"Like what?"

"Like...we're going to finish what we started."

Leish leaned in and gave Briana a quick kiss. Her eyes searched Briana's, darting back and forth, waiting. Briana's lips parted, heart jackhammering in her chest, their breathing loud in the small room. A warm flush swept through her as she put a hand on Leish's thigh and kissed her back.

It was so different from kissing Mark, or any of the other boys she kissed. Leish tasted sweet, her lips were so soft, her probing tongue gentle. And yet....

Leish stood and grasped the bra closure between her breasts.

"Wait, I don't know if I can do this," Briana said.

"It's just us. Nobody will ever know." She unclipped the bra and dropped it to the floor.

Briana clamped a hand over her mouth, stifling a laugh.

Leish planted her hands on her hips glowered. "What?" She looked down and saw the light up pasties, blinking on and off. Leish covered her face.

"Oh, god. I forgot I put those stupid things back on."

After Leish left, Briana lay in bed, staring at the ceiling, watching it drift back and forth. She could barely keep her eyes open. But when she closed them the world threatened to spin out of control. How many shots had she had?

Not nearly enough.

Disappointment bloomed inside her as she recalled what happened in the VIP area. She could still feel those pudgy hands on her body and her stomach clenched. Earlier that evening she'd felt special, accepted and so happy that her mother had been wrong.

Until she wasn't wrong.

Briana shook her head as Leish's words rang in her ears.

It's part of it, Briana. It just is.

Hot tears threatened to flow and she swallowed, blinking them away. She pulled a stuffed hyena close, hugging it tight to her chest as her eyes slid closed. The spinning wasn't so bad anymore and she drifted off to sleep.

Mark's voice thundered out.

Briana jerked upright, the room threatening to tilt and spill her onto the floor. Music was playing in the room next door, the low rhythmic pounding causing the walls to vibrate. She crept to the door and eased it open an inch and peered down the hall.

It was empty.

The door down the hall stood ajar. Light speared out along its edge, waxing and waning in time with the music. Briana sneaked across the wood floor, feeling it pop under her bare feet. Leaning forward, fingers gripping the doorframe, she peered inside.

The walls were lined with floor to ceiling mirrors, like a dance studio. A workstation bristling with monitors sat in the far corner, blue wash from the screens eking out a soft glow.

Clothing racks lined one wall, weighed down with everything from leather jackets and skinny jeans to feathery costumes and lingerie. Lights flashed along racks set in the ceiling, causing bright shafts to drift as a disco ball spun overheard. Cameras were mounted throughout the room aimed at a small stage. A brass stripper pole jutted up from the center.

Leish eased down the pole, wearing only a crown of black feathers. Her eyes were dark hollows, shadowed a smoky black. Her pale skin shimmered as she strutted and spun, dusted with blue glitter.

This must be the exclusive content, Briana thought.

She was struck again by how confident Leish was. So secure in her own skin. *And where did she get her energy?* Briana envied that, but she also wondered what she'd gone through to become so strong.

It's part of it, Briana. It just is.

She watched as Leish swung around the pole from one hand, then kicked up and hooked one leg behind the other. She drifted slowly to the stage, hair cascading down, shiny and blue as a Steller's Jay wing. The purple lock shone in the wash of a black light and Briana lifted a hand to touch her own.

Movement at the corner of the room caught her eye. Someone was at the workstation. She shifted to the left, but she couldn't see through the veil of a transparent shift hanging down from the clothing rack. Squinting, Briana peered closer.

A man leaned back, barely visible beyond the edge of an over-sized monitor. Dark, shoulder length curly hair, a hint of stubble along the jaw, the dull shine of a leather jacket. She crept forward and her arm touched the door, causing it to open a bit. The man stiffened and peered around the edge of the monitor. His icy blue eyes fixed on hers.

He smiled.

A chill ran through her as she stared at those perfect rows of teeth, gleaming to match the sparkle in his eyes. It was Mel, the pretty boy in the black car.

There were no butterflies this time.

Briana crept back to her room and closed the door. She sat on the edge of the bed and hugged one of the hyenas tight. *What was he doing here?* But she already knew the answer.

Mel was Melvin of course, Leish's manager. Probably her boyfriend as well.

And that was *his* room.

CHAPTER 27

Homemade Faraday Cage

They had dinner with Kelly. She gave Dante concerned glances over the rim of her wine glass and he finally shook his head at her. She nodded with understanding and he loved her for it. She helped him with the dishes before laying a hand on his shoulder and walking back home next door.

As Abigail sat at the dinner table doing her homework, Dante went through the house and checked every smart device he could think of. TVs, thermostats, even the smart fridge he'd bought a year ago. He had no idea why he needed a smart fridge, but it seemed like a good idea at the time. He made sure Bluetooth and Wi-Fi were turned off on each one, then changed the password on the Wi-Fi router.

He gathered up all the tablets, chrome books and any other handheld devices they had in the house, including the old ones Dante kept in a bottom dresser drawer. He made sure they were all turned off and piled them up on the kitchen table. His phone was on but face down out on the coffee table, close enough to hear it ring but far enough to keep away prying eyes and ears.

He hoped.

Another thought occurred to him. He grabbed a roll of aluminum foil from the kitchen, a file box from his home office and a roll of duct tape. He lined the box and lid with foil and taped it into place, then put all the devices stacked on the table inside. Sliding the lid over the top, he stood back, satisfied.

Homemade Faraday cage.

After saying goodnight to Abigail, Dante took a shower then collapsed on the couch, surfing through channels before shutting the TV off. Exhaustion fogged his brain but sleep was a long way off. His frayed nerves jittered as he thought of Michelle's sad eyes watching him from the background of the deep fake video. Judging him. He knew she'd disapprove of the way he was raising Abigail. Him spending so much time at work. Naomi.

He recalled when they'd become pregnant. She'd changed so much after holding up that white stick with a plus in the tiny window, eyes brimming. They'd talked of having kids, but Dante wasn't quite sure how he felt about the reality of it now that it was here. Children never had quite fit into his business plan.

Michelle made him promise to come home every night for dinner, no matter what. He'd made it almost a full week before pulling an all-nighter that stretched into a month. In the first few years of their marriage, she'd been a supportive, and for the most part, silent partner. But as motherhood loomed closer, she'd put the baby first in every conversation. Refused to speak of anything else. Now she was gone and he had to do the best he could, no matter what she would've thought.

You didn't leave me much choice now, did you Michelle? he thought.

Dante's phone buzzed, dancing across the coffee table. He scooped it up, the screen blinding him in the dark. It was a text from Dmitry at Shadow Trace. It seemed odd he would text this late, but he did say they took security seriously.

We are still on for tomorrow Mr. Ellis?

Dante thought about all the apologies and promises he'd

made to his employees and clients earlier that day. Thought about his future in light of this attack on his image. Bainbridge was right. It was going to be expensive. But it would cost so much more to fix the damage later, if that was even possible. He tapped in a response.

Definitely.

Excerpt from TechBeat.com article:

Light-Duty Autonomous Vehicles Authorized for use on California Roadways

By Ian Weller

As of Dec. 17, 4-wheeled autonomous vehicles will be allowed to operate on the streets of southern California provided that all permit requirements have been met. They'll be easily recognizable, requisite bright white with an orange stripe down the side, alerting the public to their presence through this exclusive color combination. Other color variations have been proposed and may be adopted in the future...

CHAPTER 28

Shadow Trace

Dante opened the door to his office and Abigail ran ahead, dumping her backpack on the floor.

"You got schoolwork today. Don't forget," Dante said.

"Hey Dad, something's wrong with pup," Abigail said, kneeling down over the inert robot.

"It just stopped working the other day."

"He, Dad. Not an 'it'."

"Right."

The phone on his desk rang and he walked to the outer office and lifted it to his ear. "This is Ellis."

"Mr. Ellis, this is Officer Boyd, building security. I talked with my boss. He says you can have the video."

"Great. Can you email me a link? Or I can come down with a thumb drive."

"Yes. I mean, no. The only problem is, after forty-eight hours all video is deleted."

"Officer Boyd, it's only been twelve hours or so."

"Oh. Well, I just checked and the video's gone. Folder's empty for the whole day on every feed."

"Has this happened before?"

Silence.

"Boyd?"

"I don't know."

"You don't know? Who would?" Dante asked.

"Oh wait, one more thing," Boyd said over the sound of shuffling papers. When he spoke again, his voice was robotic and stilted. "Sir, would you mind filling out a quick survey of your experience with our security services? I would really appreciate it."

Dante disconnected as Naomi walked in.

"Where's Abigail?"

He jerked a thumb over his shoulder. "Inner office messing with pup. Is Shadow Trace here yet?"

"Not yet," Naomi said, eyes flat. "Remember, interview today with Ian Weller from Techbeat."

"Right. And thanks for coming in today." He called for Abigail and she came in, backpack over one shoulder, eyes on the floor.

"Hey kiddo," Naomi said.

"Why can't I go with you?" Abigail said.

Dante shook his head. "I have too much to do."

"I could be your assistant or something," Abigail said, eyes searching Dante's.

"I'd like that. I really would. But..."

"Come on, let's go," Naomi said, opening the door. "Your Daddy doesn't need any help. From anyone."

Abigail's face fell and she trudged out of the office. Naomi flashed him a stiff smile before following his daughter out and closing the door.

Dante sighed and sat on the edge of his desk, thumping his fist on the wood. Pup walked in, four legs pumping with electronic shushing sounds as its rounded feet clunked on the floor. It crossed through the room and batted against the closed door repeatedly, making it rattle in the frame.

"You don't like me either, huh?" Dante said before tapping the shutoff switch on pup's back. It eased to the floor onto its belly and lay still. He hefted the robot under one arm and carried it back to the charger when his phone chimed.

Shadow Trace was here.

Dante met Dmitry Molchalin in the foyer. He was dressed as he was the other day, black suit and tie, skin pale as milk. They shook hands and Molchalin nodded to his team. Two men and one woman, as pale and humorless as their boss, dressed in black button-up shirts with the company logo over the breast pocket. Each had a hard-case on wheels and stood poised and ready, hands on the T handles.

"What do you need from me?" Dante said.

"Access."

Dante led them up through the rows of cubicles. All the monitors were dark, the seats empty. "I had everyone leave their machines on, I figured you'd want to scan them."

"Yes. We'll start with the servers, then work our way through making sure each system is clean. Have you thought of a server-based system?"

"The new building we're moving to will be like that. Each desk will only have a monitor, mouse and keyboard. Way more secure and I don't have to deal with upgrading the machines every three years."

"What security plan do you have in place?" asked Molchalin.

"I'll let you know." Dante wanted to see how this went first.

"Of course."

Dante punched in a code on the keypad next to the server room door and pushed inside. The blast of air conditioning blew his hair back as he stepped aside and let Dmitry and his crew in. They disappeared among the racks as Molchalin sat at a workstation next to the door. He moved the mouse to wake the computer up then glanced at Dante.

"Password?" he said, voice raised over the noise of cooling fans.

Dante hesitated, the vague notion of letting a vampire across his threshold tugged at him before scribbling the admin password across a Post-It pad on the desk. Dmitry input the code and the screen came to life.

"One other thing," Dante said.

"Sorry?" Molchalin said, pointing to his ear.

Dante leaned closer. "I have reason to believe that whoever is doing this is listening to me at home."

"We could install Shadow Trace on your home network and your phone as well."

"I'm not ready to do that just yet. I shut down all my smart devices and put them in a foil lined box and I changed the wireless router password. Anything else you can think of to do?"

"Short of installing my software, it sounds like you've done all that you can." Molchalin opened a command prompt window and began to type. "Give us a few hours, I'll let you know what we find."

"One other thing," Dante said. "It's probably nothing, but a guy I hired a few years ago, Skylar Westfall, got onto the property. I'd revoked his security pass but he was in the parking structure on Monday morning, the same day the deep fake video went out. Said he wanted to help me and gave me a USB chip. I threw it away. What's strange though, he wasn't on the security video."

Dmitry stopped typing. "You saw this?"

"Well, no. A security guard did. I asked for the video but it'd been deleted."

Molchalin nodded. "Anyone else I should know about?"

Colin Murray, Dante thought. "No. Can't think of anyone."

"I'll look into it," Dmitry said and turned back to the monitor and began typing again.

Dante left them to their work. As he walked back through the studio, he glanced into Naomi's office and spied Abigail curled up on a chair against the wall, bent over her sketchbook. Naomi sat behind her desk, fingers moving rapidly across her keyboard, lips set in a grim line. There might as well be a million miles between the two.

He got a call from Colin and he stopped to answer. Dante felt a twinge of guilt at almost giving his name up to Molchalin. He had no real reason to believe Colin was involved. A feeling maybe. But the timing of his visit was...concerning.

"Just wanted to see how you are doing," Colin said. "That video. Nasty stuff."

"Yeah, I'm still trying to process it all. I've heard of deep fakes but nothing like this."

"Nobody has. The voice even sounded like you. I didn't know you'd actually read that book back in high school. Thought you just cheated off my paper for the test. Ms. Barnes English class, third period. Remember how hot she was?"

"I do remember. Ms. Barnes and that quote. I use it in my rah-rah speeches all the time. Just can't remember where it's from."

"It's from Shelley's Frankenstein. You must've really pissed someone off," Colin said.

The entire passage seeped into his brain a bit at a time, the memory clawing up through the mist like the monster himself. "Beware; for I am fearless, and therefore powerful," Dante said. "I will watch with the wiliness of a snake, that I may sting with its venom. Man, you shall repent the injuries you inflict."

"Damn," Colin said. "What's going on?"

"Somebody's harassing me. It started with a text on Monday morning. 'The more a thing is perfect, the more it feels pleasure and pain.' I looked it up. It's from Dante's *Inferno*. Then later that same morning, the deep fake went out."

"Is there anything I can do? Want me to talk to some of the security guys here at work?" Colin asked.

"No, I got this. It's being taken care of as we speak. Somebody's just trying to discredit me. A disgruntled employee or competitor. Maybe some Internet wacko. It's a good reminder how important cyber security is these days, that's for sure."

"Our security over here is like a steel trap. We're doing mobile authentication as well as hardware keys when we sign in. It's a major pain in the ass, but necessary these days."

"Listen, Colin, I haven't had a chance to look at your deck, yet."

"Understandable. How 'bout lunch today?"

"I can't today, but yeah, let's get together soon. It's been too long."

They said their goodbyes and disconnected. Dante continued on back to his office, emotions churning inside. They had been best friends growing up, like brothers. No matter how much their friendship had eroded, they still shared a bond. Forged by trauma, yes, but that shared bond made Dante's feelings toward Colin complex and difficult to parse through. He had to be careful and take it slow. Colin had disappeared on Dante before when things got tough and his instincts told him things were only going to get tougher in the near future. Dante was sure of one thing, though.

He missed the guy.

CHAPTER 29

Mel Rose

"Good morning, Briana."

She halted, staring for a moment before continuing into the kitchen.

Mel sat at the table cluttered with camera gear, an unlit cigarette perched on his lower lip. His starched button up shirt was open at the throat, the lapels embroidered with black roses. He smiled, revealing those perfect white teeth as he flicked open a lighter, the flame illuminating his face.

"Uh, hey," Briana said, opening the fridge. She found bottled water inside and unscrewed the cap, taking long swallows before wiping her mouth. She put the cold bottle to her head, letting the cool air from the fridge wash over her.

"Wild night?"

"Huh?" she said, turning. "Oh, yeah it was pretty crazy, at least for me."

"It's a good thing I'm here, then. This town can be like that. Chews up little girls and spits them out." He smiled again, full wattage.

He was downright beautiful, Briana decided. But something about his eyes was off, predatory in the way they tracked her every move. He hadn't blinked once. "We met before. Remember? I'm Mel Rose. Call me Mel."

He didn't bother to shake hands and his eyes never left hers. "Hi, Mel...Rose. I'm Briana."

"I know, I know," he said his voice silky. "I see she's already let you into the pack." He reached up and pulled a lock of hair down from over his left ear and stroked it between his thumb and forefinger. It was purple, out of place against the dark black of his mane.

Briana pursed her lips. *Not a pack*, she thought. *A cackle.*

"So. You're Leish's latest discovery," Mel said. "And what a discovery you are."

His eyes crept over her body through a haze of blue smoke. Briana wished she'd worn more than a long t-shirt to bed. Her skin crawled under his gaze.

"Love your music, by the way," Mel said, clapping his hands. "Hot stuff."

"Thanks," Briana said, trying to keep the disgust off her face.

"I remember the day I first heard your voice. Told Leish about you right away. I said, 'Leish, this is the one.'"

Briana's stomach tightened. Leish had neglected to mention that.

"Great. Nice to meet you." She turned to go.

"I see you caught the show last night."

"The show?" Briana paused before turning back to face him. "The show, right." She nodded. "Wait. The *show*. You were on Mulholland Hills. That reality show about rich kids trying to make it in Hollywood?"

His eyes narrowed. "That was a long time ago. I'm a businessman now. People are my business."

"How do you mean?"

His gaze slid to her bare legs and she resisted the urge to tug the hem of her shirt down.

"Talent management. Leish is a client. My only client," he said. "Until now."

"She told me her manager was somebody name Melvin."

He grinned. "She's a good girl and knows I like to keep my

D.W. WHITLOCK

private affairs private. Being on that little show was fun, but it was a bit too much exposure. I had to lay low for a while. You understand."

Briana did. She cringed, recalling his behavior on the show. After Mulholland Hills was cancelled, various Hollywood interviews of fellow cast members and victims of his predatory behavior had exposed him for the misogynist shithead that he was. *Looks like he hasn't changed much. Except now he prefers lurking in the background.*

Or the shadows.

"See you," Briana said, turning away. The cigarette smoke was making her eyes water.

"Yes, you go now," Mel said with a flick of his fingers.

She strode down the hall, teeth gritted against the torrent of curses she longed to hurl at Mel Rose as she shattered that smug, toothy grin with her fist. But she didn't even slow down.

Run away, her mother's voice said. *That's what you do. Run away.*

A sob escaped her lips as she closed the door behind her. She glared at the ugly stuffed hyenas, biting her lip.

Her mother was right.

CHAPTER 30

Stun Gun

The last of the boxes sat lined up on the edge of the driveway, no more than ten or twelve left. Gary watched through the window as they were picked up by a barrel shaped man one by one and tossed into the open door of a panel van.

The twins were wrestling on the carpet behind him, grunting and giggling. He knew it was only a matter of time before one or both would start screeching, but he enjoyed the moment of relative calm while he could.

Or tried to.

Gail was happy. The thermostat kept the house at an even seventy-eight degrees now and the alarm had not made a peep. She had her spot on the driveway back as well. She'd sang to herself before leaving for work that morning. He couldn't remember the last time she'd done that.

Last night, she'd shocked him by putting one of the porno movies from the box he'd opened in the DVD player. It wasn't very good though, lots of thick makeup and heavily shellacked hairdos and Gary had turned it off. Gail fell asleep almost immediately, but Gary lay awake next to her, anxiety making his body ache. He dreaded hearing his phone vibrate, expecting it to be *them*. They'd promised to contact him soon, but so far, nothing. Things seemed to be back normal but that gnawing sensation of waiting for the other boot to come crashing down frayed his nerves.

A crash startled him back to now.

The driver kicked the latch closed on the truck door then sauntered over and got behind the wheel. The beep, beep, beep of the truck backing up made Gary's head pound, but at least the last of the boxes were gone. He watched the truck drive up the street and disappear. It was so quiet in the house. Too quiet. He gazed around the room as a chill coursed through him.

The twins were gone.

"Boys?" he said. Ears straining, he listened to the dead silence.

Gary ran through the house, calling out for them, checking their usual hiding spots, under beds, behind doors, a million horrible scenarios playing out in his head. He heard one of them, his small voice calling out from the back of the house.

Gary dashed down the hall and through the laundry room, eyes scanning to see if they'd climbed on the machines again and gotten to those delicious looking detergent pods. Then he saw them, small bodies limned in sunlight as they stood, noses and hands pressed against the sliding glass door to the backyard.

"Dagonfye," they said in unison.

Gary crept slowly over and knelt behind them, gazing outside through the double paned glass.

It was indeed a dragonfly. A drone similar in appearance to the one that had dropped off that ugly little sculpture of the twins screaming in agony. Gary felt the pressure of it against his leg. It hadn't left his robe pocket.

The dragonfly drone was perched on the arm of one of his beloved plastic Adirondacks, its four orange wings oscillating up and down in series. First the front wings, then the back, pulsating over and over.

He would never sit on that chair again.

It was metallic green like the others, but what made this one so striking was its size. It was big, the body at least four feet long, the wings stretching out far over the lawn. The tail curled up like a scorpion's then relaxed again. Gary shivered as the twins cooed in surprise.

The head was bristling with sensors and cameras and sharp little instruments that rotated and twitched in rhythmic patterns, causing Gary's exhausted eyes to shudder. A long metallic stalk turned and focused on them, telescoping out to gaze at them through a crystalline lens that winked in the morning sun.

"C'mon, guys," Gary said. He stood, pulling at the twins. They protested, little fists battering his knees.

The dragonfly's many instruments spread with a series of harsh clicks then stopped, sharp points fanning out around its head. It sat stock still, as if it were dead. Gary watched, holding his breath. The boys had gone still as well, grasping onto his arms.

The wings snapped to point at the sky as all the instruments tucked inside its bulbous head. Gary's spine stiffened as he knelt and pulled the boys close to him, encircling them with his arms.

The dragonfly twitched its wings downward and shot straight up, the Adirondack flipping over as it disappeared high above in a smear of green and orange. Lying on the patchy grass below was an L-shaped, black object, the tip encased in yellow plastic. A silver lightning bolt was embossed on the grips, gleaming in the sun.

It was a Taser gun. Just like the one he'd been trained to use.

Gary swallowed, heart thudding, stars shooting across his eyes with each thunderous pulse, thoughts frantic. *What the fuck do they want me to do with a Taser gun?*

The twins gazed up at him, their eyes wide. They'd never seen their father look so frightened before. His phone buzzed in his pocket and he yelped, causing the boys jerk back as he looked at the screen.

Friday night. Be ready.

Gary dropped the phone, pulled his sons close and hugged them, vision blurring with tears. They hugged him back, small arms wrapping around his neck and he knew he would do whatever it took to keep them safe.

CHAPTER 31

Dazzle Camo

It was strange to see the studio so dark and quiet on a work-day. It was warmer than usual as well, the smart thermostat sensing fewer bodies to keep cool. Dante strode up through the cubicles to the kitchen to get a Coke from the fridge. With a flash of irritation, he saw that someone had left their dazzle camo lying on the granite counter top. He set the can down and pinched the garment at the shoulders, letting it hang to the floor. It looked like children's footed pajamas with a zipper that ran up the back from the crotch, all the way to the top of the hood. A mesh screen covered the eyes and mouth areas. The fabric was smooth and white with thick, black stripes zig-zag-ging from top to bottom. Dante wondered if it really worked as advertised, confusing pattern recognition software. Maybe the Maskcreants were on to something. He slung it over a shoul-der and went back to his office, waving goodbye to Abigail and Naomi where they sat ignoring each other in her office.

CHAPTER 32

Ellis Media Building

The construction elevator gate rattled shut and Dante punched the up button. Ian Weller staggered, throwing his arms out as the rusty cage began to ascend. His horn-rimmed glasses had slid down the bridge of his slender nose and he pushed them back into place and blinked.

"Sorry about that," Dante said with a grin.

"Yeah, right. Lemme guess, you played high school football," Ian said, tugging at the bottom of his tweed vest. He whipped out a silk handkerchief and knelt, wiping dust off his square toed shoes.

"And you were in all the school plays. Hey, Ian. I really appreciate it. Thanks for doing this."

The slender man stood back up. "Yeah, great. Another fluff piece for my old buddy, Dante."

"Tech beat not sexy enough for you?"

"Autonomous vehicles and drone deliveries. Absolutely thrilling."

Ian craned his neck to peer out of the elevator cage. His eyes scanned the floors as they rattled upward on a track that stretched up through a square gap in the center of the building. Hoses and cables snaked around stacks of building materials crowding each floor. All the tool boxes were shut tight, work lights off. He turned back to Dante and pushed his glasses up again.

"Where's all the workers?" Ian said.

"Little issue with the city permits right now. It'll be resolved soon. Shall we get started?"

Ian pressed the red button on a digital recorder in his hand. "So, tell me what makes the Ellis Media Building so special."

Dante cleared his throat and shifted into pitch mode. "Exposed steel construction for the framing. And if you look closely, you can see a copper filament mesh embedded in every window. The whole building is one giant Faraday cage."

"What's a Faraday cage?"

"You don't know?"

"For the readers."

"Right. At its simplest, it's an enclosure designed to shield the interior from electromagnetic fields. It can be anything from a large, specifically designed structure such as this building to a metallic snack sack. I remember a story of a guy who put his work phone in a chip bag to block the GPS while he was out golfing during work hours so his boss couldn't track where he was. Got away with it for years before he got caught."

"I'll have to remember that one. What else?" Ian said.

"All power and signal cables are shielded to eliminate electromagnetic noise. Heating and air conditioning are triple baffled to minimize white noise throughout the building, plus recording rooms use a new kind of air conditioning that removes heat from the room as opposed to blasting in cold air. The process is completely silent. Every workstation is just a mouse, keyboard and two monitors. All processing is done via shared server network. The machines are kept in a super cooled, clean room with limited access. And no wireless Internet anywhere in the building."

"That's gotta be a no go for some people. Why is that important?" Ian said.

"Clean sources and complete security. It's the holy grail."

"Explain that."

"All media goes through a process of initial capture, compression, decompression, post-processing and final output. Even film is transferred to digital. Something is always lost. Along the way, many different digital hands touch the source, adding to it, but ultimately taking away from it as well. It's a balance of how much you can tweak an image, even in these days of high dynamic range. Not to mention final output which is compressed, further degrading the image quality."

"Do regular folks really notice this?"

"Consumers don't, at least not yet, but industry people most definitely do. But as 8 K becomes 16 K and so on, people will become savvier to quality or the lack thereof. They may not be able to say why something looks bad, but they can tell. Most people could tell you which looks better in a side-by-side comparison, an old VHS tape or high-definition video," Dante said.

"So how does the construction of this building help with that?"

"You get enough electromagnetic frequencies bouncing around, from lights, computers, laptops, it can throw off the calibration of monitors and can affect the human brain..." Dante trailed off. A large flying insect was hovering just outside the windows, keeping pace with the elevator as they ascended. Its metallic green body gleamed in the sun. "That's weird."

"What?" Ian said following Dante's gaze. "I don't see anything."

"It looked like a big dragonfly out there." *Like the one from the parking garage*, Dante thought.

"Hey, dragonflies are good luck," Ian said. "Up this high, probably a drone. They're making them that look like all kinds of things now. Why not insects?"

"Right. Well, when you've worked around computers as long as I have...shit. Lost my place."

"The whole building is one giant Faraday cage. No radio waves in or out."

"Exactly," Dante said. "It makes security that much simpler as well. Everything is hard-wired and routed through a secure, on-site server farm, including the Internet."

"It sounds like overkill. Do you think others will feel this way?"

The elevator came to a stop at the top floor and they stepped out. There was no ceiling in place yet, just metal beams and a temporary office in the far corner.

"I know they do. The building is completely leased out. Like I said, you do this long enough and minimizing anything that will affect your product, even if it seems like voodoo, becomes a very precious thing. And don't forget about security. Piracy is a huge issue and knowing that employees can't just plug in a phone and upload your unreleased movie or TV show to the dark web is a major selling point."

"Great," Ian said. "Listen, I have to ask about it or my editor will kill me."

"The deep fake," Dante said.

The office door opened and a young man stepped out. He halted, squinting at them from under a white hard hat.

"This is private property," he said, his voice wavering a bit. "You shouldn't be here."

Dante strode over with Ian hurrying behind him and the young man backed up a step.

"Who are you?" Dante said.

The young man swallowed. "Andrew Dean of Itinerant Server Systems. We're sub-contracted through Adler–Darrow construction."

"To do what exactly?"

"This," he said, pointing at a silver pole that began to rise up from the office roof. It extended high up into the air, the tip rotating at a forty-five-degree angle as metal screen dish opened up. The dish was about two feet across, made of a thin, wire mesh. It rotated a few times, the dish angling before it came to a rest.

"Oh, I know who you are. Of course, Mr. Ellis," Dean said

putting his hand out. They shook. "Sorry, didn't recognize you at first."

"That's okay," Dante said. "I didn't expect anyone to be here. You said you're a sub-contractor?"

"I came out to set up the mobile server. Here let me show you."

Dante and Ian followed Dean up a short set of metal stairs into the office. A bank of fluorescents bloomed on overhead as they entered. The air conditioner unit was on full blast, the interior a welcome chill.

Standing along the far wall was a large black case with a thin pullout drawer, mouse and keyboard inside. The image on the built-in monitor was a purple and orange gradient with the simple outline of a beaver seen from the side. The case was etched with a faint pattern, but it was hard to make out exactly what it was. Possibly a set of wings.

"The dish on the roof communicates directly with a satellite. As long as it has line of sight, we can put this baby anywhere, even inside a giant Faraday cage like this. The dish goes up when it's needed, talks to the satellite, goes down when it's not. Pretty cool, huh?" He eyed the case, running his hand along the side. "I've never even seen a system like this before. We don't do a lot of Ubuntu. But if it boots up, then I hook it up." He laughed, an awkward snort.

"What is it for exactly? I mean the building isn't even close to being finished," Dante said.

"Don't know. I'm just the delivery boy. Guess they just wanted it ready to go." Dean leaned over and typed on the keyboard. A motor hummed on the ceiling. "Retracting dish now." The young man stood upright and his hardhat slipped down over his eyes. He pushed it up with a fingertip. "So that's it for me. I need to lock up now."

"Sure. We'll get out of your way," Dante said.

Dante followed Ian back outside and watched as Dean locked the door and strode over to the elevator. The gate rattled as he stepped inside and pulled the gate shut. The motor hummed and it chattered downward, out of sight.

"So, where were we?" Dante said.

"The deep fake video. We can go off record if you want," Ian said.

"Right. No, if this is a sign of things to come and I can help anyone avoid or alleviate the pain it has caused me, then I'd like to talk about it. I don't know if I can help but I'd like to try,."

"Was it just the video or was there any other harassment?"

Dante hesitated. "Actually, let's hold off. I want to make sure this thing is over before I talk about it publicly."

"Don't want to poke the bear, huh. I get it. As long as I get the exclusive."

"You got it," Dante said.

"I need it. The tech beat is stale, baby. You should have seen CES this year. Smart toilets? Really?" Ian shook his head, then pushed his glasses up and leered. "Think they might hit you with a deep fake again?"

"Don't sound so excited. I hope to hell not. I dread the day when my daughter finds out about Deep fake Dante."

"Oh, that's great. I'm going to use that," Ian said with glee, typing a note on his phone.

"Not until it's over. Okay?"

"Right. When the fat lady sings."

CHAPTER 33

Ruins

Briana leaned in close to the bathroom mirror and applied a light shade of green to her eyelid. Her phone rang. She gazed at the screen, hesitating before scooping it off the counter and connecting.

"Hi Mom," Briana said.

"Hey beautiful," came a man's voice.

She froze, mouth going dry.

It was Mark.

How could she do this to her? Mom loved Mark, had from day one. Briana couldn't ever figure out why.

"Before you hang up just listen," Mark said. "I'm sorry about what…happened. You just make me crazy sometimes. But I'm glad you left. Really, I am. It's given me time to think and understand that you need this. *We* need this. I just wanted to say that I'm happy for you and I hope you find what you're looking for out there."

Stunned, Briana didn't know what to say. *Could Mark really mean it this time?* She wanted to believe he could change but he'd talked this way before.

No, she decided. He wanted something.

"I gotta go," Briana said, sounding smaller than she'd hoped to.

"Briana wait."

She could hear another voice in the background and her face grew hot. It was her mother.

"I'm doing much better," Mark said. "Remember that group of vets I work with?"

How could she forget. Mark and some friends he knew from the military got together every month or so to stay frosty, whatever that meant. He told her it was mock training missions, but she only saw him after he'd come back, shit-faced drunk. She recalled the last time he'd come to her apartment right after one of these missions. He stumbled in and collapsed on the bed, out cold, rucksack falling to the floor. She looked inside and found a Glock 19 pistol, several magazines of ammunition, black military style clothes and a walkie-talkie with a wireless earpiece. At the bottom was a large manila envelope, fat and heavy with whatever was inside. She pinched the metal clasp and lifted the flap. Inside were stacks of cash, held tight with rubber bands. Ten thousand dollars to be exact.

Mark mumbled something and she tucked the envelope back inside his ruck. When she pulled off his boots, her hands came away sticky, dark with mud. The mud washed off as a brownish pink swirl and smelled sweet, a bit like raw ham. With a start she realized what it was.

Blood.

"Mark, I can't really talk right now," Briana said.

There was a silence on the other end of the phone—a calm before the storm.

"I just wanted to tell you," Mark said with careful restraint, "that I'll be in California sometime next week on a job. Maybe I could come see you. As a friend, that's all."

"Got to go." Her voice sounded like someone else's, lifeless and flat. "Really. I have some job interviews."

"I'll call you when I get in town now that I have your new number. See you soon."

The phone went dead.

Briana lifted the eye shadow applicator then let her shaking hand fall again. Hot tears stung her eyes. She didn't know what hurt worse. Her mother's betrayal or the fact that her escape plan was now in ruins.

CHAPTER 34

Inside Job

Dmitry Molchalin was waiting in Dante's office.

"Mr. Ellis," he said rising from the couch. "Our scan is complete."

"How'd you get in here?"

"Naomi let me in."

"Find anything?"

"Yes," Molchalin said. "And no."

"What does that mean exactly?" Dante said as he sat behind his desk.

Molchalin remained standing. "We installed Shadow Trace and scanned all your drives. It found the usual malware, some of it already quarantined, some not. Nothing really serious. Your security software has registered a three percent increase in attempts at gaining access from encrypted sources over the last month. All of them were successfully blocked."

"What are you saying?"

"A hacker can hide their tracks but there's always a trace. Always. You just need to find it and Shadow Trace was designed to do exactly that. But there is no evidence of intrusion. Your network security software is actually quite robust. Shadow Trace is better of course, but there have been no unauthorized intrusions recorded. No hacking. My compliments to your information security team."

"They'll be glad to hear that. What does all this mean?"

"Most likely, whoever gained access did so with a passcode. My opinion is that someone you know is harassing you."

A cold weight settled in Dante's chest. His mind scanned through some of his employees but none really stood out. The few that were openly gruff with him were editors or colorists, people that worked sixty-plus hour weeks but made crazy money. A lot of Ellis Media's operating budget went to these specialists. Most of them were divas to boot, requiring catered lunches, specific temperature requirements, sparkling water imported from Denmark. Dante was glad to do it, talent like that was worth every penny, every hassle. But they were artists, not engineers. Why bite the hand that feeds? It was a small world too, advertising. If they were to get caught...it just didn't make sense.

"What about Skylar Westfall?" Dante said.

"I put my best researcher on it. She couldn't find him. Unless he's a fifteen-year-old girl in Missouri, an eight-year-old boy in Oregon or a fashion model living in Paris then he doesn't exist."

"Great. Does the fact that he can make himself invisible to security cams pique your interest?"

"It does."

"Okay. So, besides Skylar Westfall or a rogue employee, what else is a possibility?"

"There is no other possibility."

"Bullshit," Dante said.

Molchalin nodded. "You could question your employees. Employ voice stress analysis to register microtremors indicating deception."

Dante stared at him a moment before speaking to make sure he was joking. "Taking all my employees into a dark room one by one and sweating them under harsh lights is not an option. This isn't the KGB."

Molchalin seemed unfazed by the barb, but Dante could tell

the comment had rankled him. *Good,* he thought. *Shadow Trace is expensive.*

"You mentioned chat rooms as well when we first met," Dante said. "Anything?"

"There are thousands of chat rooms that hackers use."

"That isn't what I asked."

"Our software monitors several chat rooms at all times for chatter. We keep records going back ninety days. Nothing."

Dante nodded. "I signed your contract Mr. Molchalin. I read it as well. I have thirty days to cancel, without cause, and I'm not feeling too confident in my investment right now. I need to know you and your team are doing all they can to find out who is doing this and deliver them to the proper authorities. Do we understand each other?"

"Yes, Mr. Ellis."

"Glad to hear it. What did you find on the Dark Web? Anything?"

"No. Your name does not appear on any sites involved with soliciting harassment."

Dante exhaled loudly. "What's next then?"

"We install Shadow Trace on your cell phone. The one constant in all of this has been the texts."

"Not an option. My whole life is inside that phone. For all we know, Shadow Trace could allow another point of entry. What else?"

"We monitor and wait for another intrusion," Molchalin said.

"I was afraid you were going to say that."

CHAPTER 35

Flagged

Sweat seeped into Briana's eye and she blinked, wiping it away with the back of her hand. It only made it worse. Her feet ached and she wished she'd worn flats instead of heels.

Squinting through the glare on the front window of a coffee bar, she peered at the 'Help Wanted' sign before pushing the door open. A bell rang merrily overhead. She made her way around a line of people engrossed with their phones to the far end of a long bar topped with glass cases lined with pastries. Light jazz played from speakers hidden overhead as the fingers of young screenwriters chattered on laptop keyboards below. A slender young woman with bleach blond hair smiled at Briana from behind the counter as she came over.

"Hi, I'm Tracy, assistant manager. Do you have a resume?" she said.

Briana slipped one out of her purse and handed it over. "How'd you know?"

"You got the look." Her eyes scanned the resume before looking up. "Says here you worked at a coffee bar before?"

"Yes. A Charlie's back in Neb...back home."

"No shame. Nobody's from around here. Shit, I'm from Minnesota." Tracy's eyes skimmed the resume again, lips pursing. "Wait here. I'll be right back."

Briana's heart sank as she watched the young woman go. She'd lost count at how many places had turned her down today. She'd spent most of the morning tromping up and down Sunset Boulevard under the hot sun from one rejection to another.

There was a tap on her shoulder and she turned.

"Sorry, honey," Tracy said. "We're not looking right now. Just filled our last spot. Try again next month."

"I have experience," Briana said, her voice rising. She waved a hand over the room. "You're telling me you don't need help?" She bit her lip, holding back an exasperated sigh. "Please."

Tracy took Briana by the arm and walked her to the front. When they reached the door, she gave Briana a hug and spoke low into her ear.

"You've been flagged. Do not hire. I don't know why. Sorry." She stood back, hands on Briana's shoulders. "Good luck out there, okay?"

Briana went back outside, the bell ringing overhead again. It sounded more like a taunt this time. The midday sun blazed down on her, but she felt cold. It made sense now why the same thing had played out over and over again, all morning long. She thought back over the places she'd worked since high school and couldn't recall any major issues. One boss had come on to her, but he'd been understanding when she told him she had a boyfriend. Or so she thought.

How do you get flagged with a 'Do not hire' anyway?

It seemed illegal but everything unfair feels that way. She trudged back up Sunset past more help wanted signs then turned at the Whiskey A Go Go, toward the apartment.

As she stepped through the front door, she was almost knocked down by the booming sound of explosions and gunfire. Leish sat cross-legged in front of her computer screen wearing a scooped tank top, eyes wide and glassy, right arm twitching as she played a game.

"Be right with you, baby girl," she called out without looking up.

Briana bristled at the pet name before she dropped onto the couch and lay back, staring at the ceiling. Mel had called her baby girl, too. Should've seen the connection. She was sweaty and thirsty, but too depressed to get up again.

Do not hire, she thought. *What am I going to do?*

"Oh, fuck that!" Leish said, slamming her desk with a fist. "Eat a dick, Hammerhedge73! You suck bleached ass."

She yanked off her headphones and tossed them on the desk. "Oh hey," she said to the camera perched atop a monitor. "You guys wanna meet my new friend?" She turned and waved Briana over.

"No," Briana mouthed as she sat up.

"Oh, c'mon."

She came over and grabbed Briana by the hands and tugged her over. "Say hi to Briana, guys."

On the screen was a large window displaying the game Leish had been playing, some cartoony looking shooter game. To the right was a chat window suddenly alive with comments, scrolling up faster than Briana could read.

"What are they saying?" Briana said.

Leish peered closer. "They want us to make out. C'mere, momma!"

Briana pushed her away and with a frown and went back to the couch.

"Signing off, bitches," said Leish as she closed the window and the game disappeared. She came over and flopped on the couch across from Briana.

"I was just teasing," Leish said. "Hey, what's wrong?"

"No one will hire me. I spent all morning going up and down Hollywood Boulevard, then Sunset. 'Help Wanted' signs everywhere. Everyone turned me down. Finally, somebody told me I'd been flagged with a 'Do not hire.'"

"Sounds illegal."

"That's what I thought."

"What are you going to do?"

Briana sighed. "I don't know."

"Well, there's other ways to make money."

"I'm not like you, Leish," Briana said, sounding more exasperated than she intended.

"Oh, you mean a THOT." She gazed down at herself, nodding. "Titty streamer." She snapped her fingers and pointed. "Camwhore!"

"I didn't mean it like that. More like, comfortable in your own skin."

"I know what you meant," Leish said with a sly grin. "And you're right. But I'm just using what I got while I got it. Girls got a shelf life and I don't plan on being a MILF in my thirties. Even though the money is good, I hear."

"Sounds like something Mel would say."

Leish ignored her. "Oh shit, I almost forgot!" she said, jumping up and hurrying back to her computer. She scooped up her phone and typed, her thumbs a blur. Briana's phone chimed and she slipped it from her purse. There was new email. She tapped with a finger and opened it up.

Yo Leish,

That girl is fire! Once you get a demo recorded, send it my way. I'll make sure it gets to the right ears.

Dillon Travis

Briana stared up at Leish. She stood there, arms crossed over her chest, nodding slowly.

"Dillon Travis heard *me* sing?" Briana said.

"Oh, yeah," Leish said. "Didn't I tell you?"

Briana leapt to her feet and threw her arms around Leish, crushing her close. "Oh my god! Thank you, thank you, thank you!"

"It's all you, girl. Of course, it takes money to record a demo."

Briana pulled back from her with frown. "You said you'd take care of that."

"And I will. But my finances are complicated, what with all my varied income streams. I don't know shit about it. Mel takes care of all that stuff. He told me I could pay for it next month, but we really need to move on this now. This is like, a once in a lifetime thing."

Briana sank down to the couch, staring at the floor. She had maybe four hundred left in the bank, besides two hundred or so in cash. The dream of recording a demo that could be heard by Dillon Travis seemed to shrink away from her and fade, drifting to the floor like ash.

She looked up at Leish. "You said there were other ways to make money. What did you mean exactly?"

CHAPTER 36

Trapped

Dante eased the Mako into the driveway and waited as the garage door rose. His eyes fell on the shield-shaped sign jutting up from the front lawn that read: This home protected by Dome Defense Smart Security.

Smart security, which meant it was connected to the Internet. He hadn't thought of that last night as he'd raced around, shutting off devices before dumping them into a foil-lined box.

He eased the car into the garage and stopped when the windshield touched a tennis ball hanging from the ceiling. Abigail hopped out, opened the door and ran into the kitchen to get her afternoon snack, right past the security keypad. Dante couldn't even remember the last time he turned it on and he felt a flash of anger at himself. He entered at least half a dozen codes at work every day.

A company rep had come out a few years ago and installed the security system. Motion and heat sensors had been placed at strategic positions throughout the house. Then came the cameras. A fisheye lens housed inside a plastic half-dome about the size of a softball. One was perched outside above the front door and another inside, covering the living room. Completely wireless, software updated regularly through the internet and easy to use.

Maybe too easy.

Dante touched the driver side door and watched it tighten into place. Everything was automatic now, motorized, monitored by smart software, electronic eyes and ears listening at all times. For the first time he could recall, it bothered him. The slow but inevitable takeover had happened in the background as daily life prattled on, operating under the premise of ease of use and increased security. Taking root like a worldwide Virginia creeper vine.

Dante frowned at the thought.

Some grew along the front of the house. It had been there when he and Michelle had first visited years ago while out house hunting.

Michelle had loved it.

He recalled how she reached out and plucked one of the small, blue berries and held it up close. The Realtor warned her they were poisonous and she'd thrown it at Dante, laughing, her voice like silver.

He smiled at the memory.

What had really sold her were the security features of the house itself. The previous owner had installed steel shutters over every door and window, turning the whole house into one giant panic room at the press of a button. Just inside the front door was a glass panel. A large push button was mounted inside, a glowing red eye dull and watchful at its center. A wicked looking fireman's axe hung next to the button on hooks, all black except a silvery edge along the blade. Stenciled across the glass was the requisite: In case of emergency, break glass. Dante hadn't really been sure they needed something like this but Michelle insisted, reminding him how much time he spent away.

The corner had been pulled up again on Dad's car cover and he went to tug it back down. Abigail loved to look at it. He didn't quite know why. Maybe because she wasn't supposed to. It had been a while since he'd seen it himself. He lifted the corner and flung the cover back to get a better look.

His eyes swept over the 1975 Porsche 911 turbo in Sahara Beige. He'd always hated the color but the thing could move. Dad had spun out the first time the turbo had kicked in. It was the one extravagance he'd allowed himself after the divorce. He said it was a write off, good for taking clients out for cocktails. He could even fit his golf clubs in the bonnet, he'd told Dante in a hokey British accent that dads the world over excelled at. Dad was an insurance salesman and had been good at it, enough to buy a classic Porsche post-divorce in California. Then again, mom hadn't wanted much.

Just to get away.

But Dad had never been a car guy and when it showed, it was painful to witness. He told everyone about the bonnet, like it was a deep, dark secret of the car world. But he sure loved his 911. He'd talk Dante's ear off about the simplicity and elegance of its design, the analog gages and hand crank windows, none of that digital or electronic crap. His favorite feature was the ignition on the left-hand side, so you could start the car while engaging first gear.

Extremely handy in the high-stakes world of life insurance, Dante thought.

Dante had considered many times of getting rid of it, but Dad had said not to sell it. Ever. He'd insisted on it in those last painful days at the assisted living facility confined to a bed, eyes staring, fingers curled into claws.

Dante rarely drove it anymore. The lack of power steering and the sticky clutch made it hard to drive. Yet, he still kept the key on his keyring. He used that key now to open the passenger door and sit inside. The smell of old leather and dust filled his nostrils, along with a sour smell that had survived countless shampooing. One of Dad's clients had puked in here after a night of cocktails at the Hoff's Hut bar.

There was another scent too. The faint odor of something sweet with a chemical undertone, but he couldn't quite place it. It came to him as he breathed in deep. Hair spray. Covert or Convert or something. Dad used to shellac his hair with it every morning.

The smell triggered a memory.

It was what Dad had said to him as he lay dying, his hand clutching Dante's, thinning hair combed back and held down with that damn hairspray.

"Bomb it," Dad said, nodding as if it was the most important secret in the world. It was funny in a way and so terribly sad too, that his last thoughts and words were about his beloved 911's trunk, what he thought was the bonnet. Dante had stayed through the night, holding his father's hand as the life left his eyes and he slipped away. All his father had left him was the car, his beloved 911. Dante's mother had insisted through her lawyer that dad had money socked away somewhere, hiding it from her. It was the last time he heard anything from her until she died a few years later.

So, he'd kept the car for Dad, but also for Abigail. If she liked it that much, she could have it when she got old enough to drive.

Pausing just inside the kitchen door, he hit the arm button on the alarm console. The crack of bolts shooting home on every window and door reverberated throughout the house.

"Daddy?" Abigail called out from her room.

"It's okay. Just the security system."

It had been a long time since he'd heard that sound. The sound that said everything was secure. That's how it used to make him feel. But in that moment of silence that hung heavy in the air, another word came to mind.

Trapped.

CHAPTER 37

Silver Elephants

Dante knocked on the door frame and entered Abigail's room. Her back was propped up on pillows and she was scribbling in her sketchbook, face tight with concentration. She looked up as Dante came in and sat on the edge of the bed.

"What are you drawing?"

"Robots versus skeletons," she said as she turned her sketchbook around and held it up for him to see.

Grinning, his eyes followed a streak of rocket smoke that trailed from the boxy arm of a purple robot before ending in an explosion of fire and skulls.

"You should come work with me someday," Dante said.

"How about tomorrow?"

"Yeah, sorry kid. School tomorrow. Everything seems to be back to normal."

He took the sketchbook and her pencil box and placed them on the dresser. "Time to sleep," he said, wincing as he placed his bare foot on the wooden floor. He lifted his foot up and gazed down at the hard growth that clung there. He saw Abigail staring at it, face serious. He wiggled his toes.

"Are you scared about going to the doctor's tomorrow?" she said.

"A little nervous maybe."

Abigail reached under her pillow and withdrew her hand, clenched in a tight fist. "Close your eyes and put out your hand."

Dante did as she asked.

Something small and cool dropped onto his palm. He opened his eyes and looked down. It was a tiny, silver elephant pendant. Dante smiled, remembering when he'd bought it for Michelle. It was the day she'd called and said they were going to have a baby.

"Where did you get this?" Dante said.

Abigail pointed to the ornate wooden box on her dresser. "I found it in mom's jewelry box."

Dante fingered the small, shiny trunk, curved upward in the shape of an S. He peered closer at the tail and saw the small cleft etched there.

"You're missing the baby."

"There's a baby?"

"The trunk snaps here, into the mamma's tail," Dante said as he held it closer to her and pointed. "See?"

She sat up but Dante placed a hand on her shoulder. He didn't relish a walk down memory lane right then, digging through Michelle's old jewelry box.

"It's late. Tomorrow."

"But I need to find the baby. It needs its mother!" Tears welled up in her eyes.

"No," Dante said, louder than he intended. "It's been a long day."

Abigail's lips trembled as she rolled over, hiding her face from him.

Dante sighed and walked over, rummaged in the jewelry box for a moment before closing the lid. Michelle's engagement ring sat in a velvet tray to one side, and the sight of it caused an ache in his chest.

"We'll look for it tomorrow," Dante said. "I'll leave the mommy right here."

Abigail shot bolt upright. "No! You take it. If you get scared or nervous, you'll have it with you. Okay?"

Dante nodded, not trusting his voice. This seemed to put her at ease. She blinked her sleepy eyes and lay back down once more. He turned off the light and sat on her bed again, staring at the little elephant under light that bled in from the hall. He waited until her breathing became slow and steady before slipping the pendant into his pocket and closing the door behind him.

CHAPTER 38

A Slight Pinch

"Now just lie still, Mr. Ellis. You're going to feel a slight pinch," came the soft voice of Dr. Benoit from the monitor suspended above him. Her large, brown eyes stared out from the screen as greenish orange light filtered in from outside. She wore surgical scrubs and cap, but the mask was pulled down from her face.

"Where are you right now?" Dante said.

"I'm in the Philippines helping with Operation Smile."

"That's wonderful," Dante said, voice a bit slurred. "Pretty cool you can be there, but take care of me here."

He heard the soft shushing of motors then the promised pinch as a needle eased into his foot. His sole went numb and all sensation became slight tugs and pressure as the Caduceus surgical robot went to work. He heard another sound, a harsh flitting that reminded him of something but he couldn't recall what it was.

"Used properly, technology can be a wonderful thing. Just relax, Mr. Ellis. You're doing fine," Dr. Benoit said. "Would you like some music?"

"No thanks," Dante said, closing his eyes. "Might just take a nap."

"That'd be the sedative we gave you. Should be fine as long

as you hold very still."

That wasn't going to be a problem. They'd strapped his left leg to the table and held his foot in place with a plastic brace on either side. He'd eyed the Caduceus robot somewhat suspiciously as they prepped him, a mechanical hybrid of octopus and praying mantis painted medical white. It was one thing signing a release form to allow a robot to perform routine surgery, quite another to see it hulking silently in the corner as you were strapped down nearby. Dr. Benoit had assured him it was completely safe as he'd signed a release form. She just happened to be halfway around the world right now, Dante had noted with unease.

The soft sounds of the robot shushing back and forth were very soothing and he felt as if he might actually fall-

A gunshot jerked him awake.

A nurse appeared in the square window set in the door and jerked frantically on the handle, eyes wide, ponytail snapping back and forth. Not a gunshot, Dante realized. A door bolt racking home.

Why was the door locked?

Dr. Benoit's eyes went wide and frantic before the screen went black. The robot sounded different now, higher pitched. The soft tugging at his foot had become rapid, insistent jerks, like a voracious animal was tearing at a kill.

Pushing himself up on his elbows, Dante froze. A metallic green dragonfly drone hovered above the robot, a red light blinking on its underside. The robotic limbs of the medical robot were flailing in a wild blur, all manner of instruments bristling at the tip of each one. One arm swung out and struck a light bar on the wall and it shattered in a hail of glass.

The room plunged into darkness.

Light bloomed at the tip of one snakelike appendage, throwing crazy shadows as it whipped through the air. Another arm lowered and rapidly flicked its tip in a tight pattern at his foot with a single-minded intensity.

Adrenalin shot into his blood.

What the hell is it doing? Dante thought as he tried to peer through the shifting gloom.

Muffled shouts came from outside the door, shaking Dante out of his fugue. He tugged at his leg, pulling frantically at the straps that held it in place. His leg came free with a rip of Velcro and he fell off the table with a thud.

The door exploded inward as he dragged his numb leg across the floor, crawling away from the nightmarish thing that hitched and jittered on the far side of the room. Personnel flooded past him as someone helped Dante out into the hallway to rest against the wall, lungs hitching as he gasped for breath.

Loud voices spilled out of the medical suite as people dodged the flailing arms, screaming instructions at one another, trying to shut the thing off. A loud shriek rose up and the nurse with the pony tail ran out, blood trailing from her arm.

A husky security guard appeared, walkie-talkie bouncing against his hip. He raised a bright red fire axe as he bounded into the room and hacked at the robot, blade rising and falling in a shower of sparks until the thing lay dead and twitching. Fire spewed from the broken chassis as oily smoke boiled out. Alarms trilled and emergency lights flashed along the ceiling.

The big man threw the axe to the floor with a clang. He pushed his way back into the hall through the milling throng of teal scrubs and shocked faces, mopping his brow with a forearm. Dante gazed up at him with dumbstruck awe. They shared a lopsided grin.

"Tell me you got that dragonfly too," Dante said.

The guard's eyebrows rose before his eyes went to Dante's foot, his brow tightening a fraction.

"This man needs medical attention," he called out in a loud voice.

Dante looked down, vision going gray. The pale flesh of his

foot ended abruptly in a deep, meaty red. His heart began to kick inside his chest, causing blood to jet in five ragged streams and spill out onto the floor as the dragonfly disappeared down the hallway.

CHAPTER 39

Non-Disclosure

"Daddy," Abigail said, "the doctor's here."

Dante opened his eyes.

A gray-haired doctor in scrubs stood at the foot of the bed. He was talking, but the words were muffled, coming from far away. Dante's left leg was elevated, foot disappearing into a plastic boot suspended from a rack over the bed. Blue light seeped out through small gaps along the outer edge.

It felt like it was clamped under a truck.

He gazed around the hospital room and saw Abigail standing to his left, eyes bright. Kelly sat in a chair behind her, face creased with concern. She gave him a strained smile.

"Thirsty," Dante said.

Kelly held a straw to his lips and he drank.

The doctor cleared his throat. "As I was saying, I'm chief of surgical medicine, Dr. Resnick. The surgery went very well and with our advanced healing therapies you should be up on your feet in a few days. Physical therapy is vital early on in your recovery. With a little work, you should be able to walk without crutches or a cane in a few weeks."

"How many toes?" Dante said.

"Excuse me?" Resnick said.

"How many toes were you able to save?"

"None, I'm sorry to say. They were too damaged in the incident."

Dante frowned. This was no incident. The memory of the attack charged into his head, the surgical robot's arms flailing in wild arcs.

Every arm except one.

That arm moved with calm indifference, oscillating in short, rapid strokes like it was mincing raw bratwurst. That one was *slicing*. In his shock he hadn't seen it, just felt the tug thrumming up through his bones. But as the memory flooded back, he knew the doctor was right.

His toes were gone.

Not in one fell swoop, but in multiple passes as the scalpel hummed through flesh and bone in a blur. His stomach lurched as he recalled the thin slices of toe flying off and dropping to the floor, severed too fast for blood to flow.

"If you need anything, please let us know." The doctor left as a woman and a man entered, both dressed in business attire, faces stern.

"Mr. Ellis? My name is Trish Pike and this is Ed Westcott. We represent Caduceus Medical robots."

Pike was in her early thirties, dressed in a dark blue suit and crisp white shirt. Her dark hair was pulled back into a severe ponytail from a sharp featured face that jutted like an ax blade. Wescott was in his late fifties, pepper gray crew cut, charcoal suit and tie. From the creases around his eyes and his thin, bloodless lips, Dante guessed he'd been raked over the coals in the very recent past over this little incident.

"If you guys are here to ask if I have insurance, I'm going to be pissed," Dante said, speech slurring a bit.

"We'd like to talk to you if that would be alright," Pike said.

"I assume you're going to cover all this," Dante said, motioning to his foot.

"Of course," Pike said. "We want to express our deepest sympathies for this accident."

"This was no accident. Somebody hacked your robot, then it

hacked my foot."

A small cry came from Abigail's throat and tears welled in her eyes. "Daddy."

"Oh, god, Abigail. I'm sorry. I'll be okay."

Kelly took Abigail's hand and led her from the room.

Pike stepped forward, slender briefcase in one hand. "I speak for everyone at CMR when I say that I'm very sorry for the dismemberment of your foot, Mr. Ellis. Really, I am."

"Okay," Dante said, staring at his booted foot. Panic flared in his chest. *My toes are really gone.* He swallowed, forcing the anxiety away. But it didn't go far.

Pike glanced over her shoulder at Westcott. He nodded, face grave. She spoke again. "We're prepared to cover all medical costs, including any follow up surgeries, physical therapy, prostheses. We'd also like to offer you a settlement that I'm sure you'll find generous."

"As long as I sign whatever's in that briefcase."

"Let her finish, Mr. Ellis," Westcott said.

Dante didn't like the way the older man hissed his name. "Alright, go ahead."

"Two hundred and fifty thousand dollars."

Dante glared at Westcott, anger scalding his insides. The older man returned his gaze, but his mouth twitched.

"Mr. Ellis?" Pike said.

"I'm still waiting for her to finish," Dante said to Westcott.

Pike looked over her shoulder. "Ed..."

"First and final offer."

Dante snorted. He didn't know what pissed him off more. The fact that they were trying to buy his silence while he was high on painkillers mere hours after their robot maimed him, or that Westcott thought he could stroll in here and low ball him for what would definitely fetch a hell of a lot more in court. But Dante wanted something much more valuable than money.

"I was just wondering what the going rate for a pound of human flesh is these days," Dante said.

Westcott clenched his jaw before speaking. "One million."

"Listen, you've got a much bigger problem here than my silence. You've got a major security breach on your hands."

Wescott and Pike listened as Dante detailed what had happened from texts to video to him sitting here now, five little piggies lighter. "I'm telling you. Your machine was hacked."

"Impossible," Westcott said.

"How's that?" Dante said.

"We believe it was a simple malfunction,"

"A simple malfunction."

Westcott nodded. "Our machines are secure. Our decryption bullet proof."

"It sliced my toes into kibble and you call it a simple malfunction?"

"What is it that you want, Mr. Ellis?" Westcott said, his voice edged like a knife.

"I want you to find out who did this."

Westcott nodded—a clipped motion. "We'll look into it." He snapped his fingers at Pike.

"Hold on," Dante said. "Then, tell me who's responsible so I can report them to the FBI."

"Out of the question. It was just a glitch."

"The fuck it was!"

"Five million dollars says it was," Westcott said.

That sucked the air out of the room. Pike glanced over her shoulder. Wescott ignored her, pale gray eyes boring into Dante's as the silence stretched.

"Look," Dante said, "this isn't an isolated incident. I'm being harassed and now I've been attacked by one of *your* robots. If your machines have been compromised then you got a potential health crisis here."

"We're not in the business of tracking down hackers, Mr. Ellis," Pike said.

"I appreciate that, but I need evidence to bring to the FBI." Dante hated the strained pleading in his voice. "Listen to me. There was a drone in the room when it happened. It looked like a dragonfly. I've seen it before. That's how they got in to your machine."

The two suits shared a look, Westcott's eyes narrowing before he spoke. "We're going to take a hard look at our encryption but I need your discretion on this. It's business, not personal. You understand."

The phrase left a slimy film in Dante's mind. How many times had he uttered those exact words before letting the axe fall? Dante decided he didn't like being on the shit end of this particular stick.

"We're making a very generous offer here," Pike said. "Please."

She snapped open her briefcase and placed a stack of papers, dense with text, onto the table that spanned the bed. She flipped to the last page and stepped back. Westcott came forward and placed a gold Mont Blanc pen next to the non-disclosure agreement and tapped it with a finger.

"Sign," he said.

Dante sat for a moment, thinking. Five million dollars. This was money he just didn't have right now. Any extra money the business had was tied up in the new media building's cost overruns while he waited for the permits to clear. Asking his fellow investors for help was a no go. If he was going find out who was behind these attacks, Dante would have to figure out another way. There'd be no help from Caduceus Medical Robots. He'd ask Molchalin what all those people in their clandestine cubes at the Shadow Trace office could do, legal or otherwise.

How does a cool five mil sound, Dmitry?

He glanced up at Pike and Westcott. Boucher would have to be told about this. It didn't really matter if he signed this thing or not once the FBI got involved.

He hoped.

It's business, not personal, he thought as he picked up the pen. The pressure on Dante's leg increased as he signed his name. He hooked the pen in the collar of his hospital gown and winked at Westcott.

It was petty, but fuck that guy.

A buzzing sound came from the nightstand next to the bed. Dante's phone glided along with each vibration.

"Can I get that for you?" Pike said.

"Would you mind, Ed?" Dante said to Westcott.

The older man's face darkened and he left without a word.

"Sweet guy."

Pike sighed as she picked up Dante's phone and handed it to him. "You have no idea."

As Dante looked at the screen, a hard knot settled low in his stomach. It was another text from unknown.

"Mr. Ellis?" Pike said, her voice faraway, sounding like it came through a rusty drain pipe. "Are you alright?"

Dante scanned the text, throat tightening as he read.

If thy foot offends thee, cut it off:
it is better to enter into life maimed,
rather than to have two feet and be cast
into the lake of everlasting fire.

CHAPTER 40

Exclusive Content

Leish grabbed the stripper pole and leapt, the blood red of her stiletto heels seared crimson arcs through the air as she spun. Mel hunched behind the workstation in the corner, eyes locked on the screen. Lights flashed from the rack along the ceiling, causing stars to drift by as a disco ball spun overhead. The cameras mounted all around the stage captured every move, their shiny, silent eyes watching.

A pale porcelain mask stared up at Briana from where it rested on her jittering knee, its face clean and smooth with just a hint of features. A line of pink ran vertically down the lips as if someone had shushed a lover, according to the sticker inside the mask. Above the eye holes arched a pair of thin eyebrows etched with a rapid flick of the wrist.

Briana thought over what she'd learned earlier that afternoon, preparing herself to earn the money she needed for her demo. She followed Leish to the "studio," as she called it, and stood nearby as she pawed through the various costumes that hung from racks along the wall. Mumbling to herself, she lifted various articles and held them up before tossing them on a chair, dismissing them with a shake of her head. A table nearby was piled high with masks of all kinds, from translucent plastic to clowns with kinky fake hair. Briana was drawn to the porcelain mask, its elegant hints at the wearer underneath, feminine yet androgynous at the same time. It was lighter than it looked, made from very thin ceramic with an elastic band to hold it in place. Briana slipped it over her face and glanced over at Leish.

"Oh, that's all you, baby girl," Leish said. "And this." She held up a pleated skirt with a black and white tartan pattern.

"Why do you have all these masks?"

"I wear them sometimes when my face isn't quite right."

Briana gave her a questioning look, but Leish shooed her toward a black velvet curtain hanging from a rack bolted to the ceiling. After sliding the curtain closed, Briana put on the skirt along with a button up shirt tied to expose her belly and stiletto heels taller than she'd ever worn before. Leish had to show her how to sexy walk in the stilettos, placing heel well past toe to knock her hips as she strode forward. After a few attempts, she couldn't stop laughing, so Leish turned the lights low and put on some music with a slow, grinding beat.

But it was the mask that made all the difference.

The thought of being watched while doing something she'd never thought of in her wildest fantasies made her flush and feel as if she was burning with light that could be seen for miles. She leaned against the pole and stared at herself in the mirror, feeling beautiful in a way she'd never felt before. Alluring yet untouchable.

Powerful.

And nobody would ever know it was her.

"That's it," Leish said, nodding. "You've got it. It's all about confidence."

After the lesson, alone in her room, Briana had touched herself, riding a wave of wild, reckless pleasure, biting down hard on the leg of a stuffed hyena to keep from crying out.

Leish crept across the stage toward her, bringing Briana back to the moment. Her eyes were alight with an inner flame as she crawled forward on her hands and knees, slender fingers slinking over the edge of the stage into a cloth sack below. Her back arched as she flung her arms into the air, sending a cloud of money to flutter down from above.

That was Briana's cue.

Briana pulled the mask down and stood, wobbling a bit before taking a deep breath. The vodka shots she'd had earlier made her vision swim in time with the music that thundered through the room. The lights brightened, rotating to focus on Leish as the music sank low. Leish smiled at a drone camera that rose up from the edge of the stage, red light blinking on top.

"Allow me to introduce a new dancer to the stage," Leish said. "The mysterious and alluring, Silhouette."

The lights extinguished and Leish led Briana onstage, the edge outlined by small orange light strips. She stiffened as Leish put her arms around her neck and whispered words of encouragement before disappearing, leaving her alone.

The music began to thump like an electronic heart as the lights rose once more, revealing Briana, no, *Silhouette*, her arms stretched above her head, grasping the brass pole. Briana felt stupid and exposed standing there like that, but Leish had insisted that the first pose set the tone. She strode around the stage in time with the beat, trying to keep her ankles from snapping with each step. Grabbing the pole up high, she swung around but she hadn't leapt hard enough. She was rotating too slow, hand chaffing with a squeak, hip banging against the pole.

This is stupid, Briana thought, her conviction wavering.

She came to a stop and stepped wide, back arched with arms down at her sides, hands balled into fists as she stared off into the distance, chin dipped low. Alpha pose, Leish had called it. Briana saw herself in the mirrored walls and stared in disbelief. Whoever was gazing back at her from behind the mask wasn't Briana anymore. Her body flushed with that feeling again, that hot glow of power and she grabbed the pole and swung around again, this time slicing a smooth arc through the air. Coming to a sudden halt, she grasped the pole high with both hands, arching her back as she gazed upward and lowered to her knees. Her vision pulsed and the ceiling disappeared, colors swirling together in a heady maelstrom of light and shadow.

She snapped her head down and saw Leish standing next to Mel behind the bank of monitors, playing with the curl of purple hair at his temple. They stared at her, enraptured, Mel's dark eyes gleaming. There was a flitter of movement and Briana gazed upward to the where the wall met the ceiling.

A dragonfly drone clung there.

Hadn't Leish smashed it with her fist? Briana thought.

Its green body glinted, orange wings shuddering as air currents shifted over it. Briana understood. This was a new one.

Her flesh crawled as an icy wave extinguished the heat inside her. Clutching her hands to her chest, she backed up a few steps before leaping off the stage then down the hall to her room. The door slammed behind her and she huddled on the bed, arms wrapped around her legs.

"Fuck!" she heard Leish's voice echo down the hall followed by footsteps. A knock sounded at the door. "Baby, you okay? What happened?" A moment passed. "Come on, honey, you don't get paid unless you do the full half hour."

Briana pressed her hands over her ears, heart thumping in her chest.

"Don't worry about it," Mel said, his voice muted through the door. "We got what we need."

Leish shooshed him and spoke again. "Take your time, Briana. Come out when you're ready. We're here for you. Okay?"

The footsteps receded and the door slammed shut, subduing the thunder of music as Briana pulled the mask off and flung it against the wall, shattering it into a thousand shards. Her phone chittered on the nightstand. It had never made that sound before. She picked it up and looked at the text on the screen.

Daddy never has to know.

With a chill she unlocked her phone and checked the sender.

Unknown.

The tiny word pulsed along with the pounding of her heart. The phone chittered again and a link appeared below the text. With a shaky finger she reached out and tapped it. Her mouth went dry, a ragged scream threatening to break loose from her throat as she watched the small screen.

Briana and Leish were sitting on the bed, kissing. It cut to Leish, standing and removing her bra, the pasties blinking red. The video then showed Briana dancing on the stage in her mask before the scene changed to her throwing the mask against the wall, porcelain shattering in slow motion.

The screen went black.

She rose to her feet and gazed wildly around the room, trying to guess where the hidden camera could be. Scanning the boxes stacked along the wall, her eyes flickered over the dark spaces in between before locking on the large hyena that stood next to the door. Creeping closer, phone clutched in one hand, she peered into its left eye. It was darker than the right one. She jumped as a small iris snapped open inside.

The phone chittered again.

A video appeared. It was a fisheye view, distorted. She was looking at herself, kneeling on the floor in that stupid schoolgirl costume. With a cry she swiped at the hyena and it tumbled across the room, coming to rest with its face peering up at her.

The phone chittered and buzzed in her hand like a trapped fly, the screen filling with the same words over and over again:

Daddy never has to know.
Daddy never has to know.
Daddy never has to know.

CHAPTER 41

Don't

Gary Wexler hunched at the table in his robe, munching on a banana, head aching. The twins were having breakfast, which meant they were smashing bananas of their own when they weren't tossing cereal on the floor. Gail was drinking a diet fruit drink as she thumbed upward on her phone. Gary felt a buzz in his pocket and jumped, causing the twins to giggle. Smiling shakily at them, he pulled his phone out, anxiety spiking.

It was a text from *them*, a list of instructions that became more bizarre as he scrolled down.

"At the table, Gary? Really?"

He started at Gail's voice and the twins giggled again.

"Uh, sorry. It's from a Jim Hodge at Tech Check. He wants to get drinks this Friday night, talk about my potential future there."

"Gary, that's great!" Gail stood and leaned in to kiss him on the cheek before frowning. "You don't look very good. Are you feeling alright?"

"You better go. Don't want to be late."

"Okay. Bye, babies," Gail said, kissing the twins before hefting her briefcase and moving to the door. She didn't bother to check her reflection in the mirror before she left.

Glancing at the text again, Gary's bleary eyes scanned over the numbered list. He tossed the phone onto the table then pulled out the business card officer Chavez had given him. Tilting the card back and forth, he watched morning light play off the shiny gold badge printed next to the name.

He reached for his phone.

The house alarm blipped once, causing Gary to jerk upright in his chair. The twin's eyes went wide. No laughing at him this time. His phone lit up, one simple word filling the screen.

Don't.

CHAPTER 42

Probable Cause

Dante walked through the living room, turned, then went back to the kitchen. The boot had been removed after three days and he was glad to be rid of the clunky thing. The blue light it emitted had kept him awake. The pain was almost gone, except for when he put his weight too far forward. Abigail watched him from the couch as he went by, clutching an aluminum cane across her lap.

"How am I doing?" he said.

"Good. You're still limping though. Does it hurt?" she asked.

Dante stumbled as he put his left foot down, trying to stop too fast. "Only when I do that," he hissed.

Abigail hopped to her feet but Dante held up a hand. "No, I got it." He stepped carefully over to the couch and sat down. Abigail stood there watching him, hand on one hip, concern etched on her face. She looked so much like her mother right then.

"Your mom would be so proud of you," Dante said. "You know that?"

Abigail smiled and helped him lift his bandaged foot onto the coffee table. Dante sighed, waiting for the dull throb to ebb away. At least there were no phantom pains. Those only came at night.

Dr. Resnick's bedside manners sucked, but he'd been right. Whatever advanced healing they'd used worked really well. He'd described the process as a combination of several techniques including focused hyperbaric oxygen therapy, stem cell therapy and 3D printed skin grafts.

Dante checked his watch. "Abigail, do you want to go to your room and draw? I have somebody dropping by soon that I need to talk to."

"No, but I'll go anyway. Do you need this?" she said holding up the cane.

"All yours."

She ran to her room, aiming the cane like a gun at unseen foes as she went.

Dante's phone rang. It was Boucher.

"You got my email, I assume," Dante said.

"I did."

"So, what do you think?"

"We're just not there yet."

Dante sat in stunned silence. "With all that's happened we're not there yet? What if they go after my daughter next?"

"Well, what do we got? We got some vaguely threatening biblical texts. Oh, and one from Frankenstein of all people. We got a deep fake donkey show, offensive yes, but only that. Not slanderous or libelous, you haven't been injured."

"Haven't been injured?"

"I'm getting to that. There is no evidence connecting any of this. We don't know where the texts came from. We don't know who did the deep fake. Shadow Trace found nothing on your network, and no one has claimed responsibility or asked for money. There's no chatter on IRC or the Dark Web and the medical robot thing is a no go. You signed that away."

"What about the dragonfly drone in the room when the robot went nuts?"

"What about it? I'm guessing you were doped up during the procedure, right?" She huffed. "Dragonflies. Mr. Ellis, it might be better if you don't mention that again."

"I don't understand. Don't you have probable cause at this point?"

"Probable cause. I swear to god, movies and cop shows have made my job so annoying sometimes. I can't just open an investigation. There has to be a clear link between everything that's happened. It's all about building a case based on provable evidence, defining a pattern. As far as the robot incident, it's your word against theirs, and I can guarantee you whatever's left of that thing was destroyed by Caduceus Medical. I could possibly get evidence by monitoring their network and hope for another attack, but I need a court order to do that. For big companies like Caduceus Medical, it's a nonstarter. And my one potential witness, you, just signed a gag order that keeps him from saying anything. I hope whatever they paid you was worth it."

"I'm sorry you find all this so annoying."

Boucher sighed wearily. "I want to help you, Mr. Ellis, but I'm going be honest with you. We are understaffed and overbooked. You should see my office. I'm in the basement for Chrissakes."

Abigail hopped up from behind the couch and pointed the cane at Dante, making a pew-pew noise. He shook his head no and waved her back to her room. He waited until she was out of sight again.

"Do you have any children?" Dante said.

Boucher hesitated a moment. "I do. A daughter."

"What's her name?"

"Mr. Ellis..."

"Dante, please. What's her name?"

Boucher sighed again. "Patricia. She's at Pepperdine. Premed."

"You and your husband must be very proud."

"I am. My ex-husband decided years ago that Italy suited his lifestyle better than L.A. Been a deadbeat ever since."

Dante sat for a moment, trying to calm the pulse pounding at his temples. "What can I do?"

"Have Dmitry continue to monitor everything. If there's another intrusion, he should be able to trace it. And no promises, but I'll talk to my supervisor. My instincts tell me this isn't over."

A knock came at the front door. Dante disconnected with Boucher and peered through the peephole. It was Molchalin. He wore his usual black suit, but the tie was loosened, his collar open. Dante unlocked the door and led him through the living room outside to the deck. He slid the door shut and gazed around. No dragonflies. He thought about mentioning it to Molchalin then remembered Boucher's warning. Maybe he was just imagining things.

"I just got off the phone with Agent Boucher," Dante said.

"What did she say?"

"That I don't have a case, but this probably isn't over."

Molchalin leaned against the railing and stared down through the oaks that grew green and thick on the hillside. Glass on the buildings sprinkled across the valley floor sparkled like a collection of semi-precious stones in the setting sun. The dark rectangle of the Monolith tower stood tall and watchful. Further up was the unfinished Ellis Media Building, the copper mesh infused glass glowing a reddish orange.

"I can't do anything illegal," Molchalin said.

"Well, they've changed tactics, haven't they? You need to adapt. The question is, how much?"

The tall man turned and looked at him. "I can't. I have a reputation to maintain."

"Then who can?" Dante pointed to his bandaged foot. "This has to stop. I can't wait for their next move and hope we get something. What's next, my left testicle? And what if they decide they're done with me and go after Abigail? Shadow Trace is not cheap, Dmitry, along with the monthly you're gouging me for. And so far, you haven't been able to tell me a damn thing."

Molchalin looked down into the valley again. "There are channels..." he said before clamping his mouth shut. "You don't really know what you are asking me to do."

"I can pay. More than what I'm giving you. Way more. I just need something concrete to hand over to Boucher."

Molchalin laughed. "These people I'm thinking of don't do it for money. If they want money, they take it. It's all just numbers anyways. For them, it's about information and influence. They probably know about this already. They might be behind it. If not, they're going to view this as a challenge on their turf."

"Their turf?"

"America."

"Jesus. Who are these guys?"

Dmitry ignored him. "Keep your money. As soon as I tell them, they'll eliminate the problem. But you'll be trading one form of harassment for another. You'll owe *them*. And someday they'll collect on that debt."

Dante slammed his fist onto the railing. "Why is this happening to me? I'm not a politician, I'm not rich. I don't have any influential friends. Hell, I only met the mayor once and that was when I was a plus one at a charity dinner. What the fuck is going on here?"

Molchalin held his gaze before speaking. "Nothing about what's happening here makes any sense. But if I do this, if I contact these people—make no mistake—it's a deal with the devil himself."

"Listen Dmitry, I'm getting five million dollars from Caduceus Medical. Five million. It's yours. Tell me there's something you can do with your people in those black cubes first before I throw in with the lord of darkness."

"Perhaps." Molchalin straightened and cinched his tie. "I'll be in touch." He turned to go.

Dante felt his stomach clench as he called out to him. "One other thing."

Molchalin glanced over his shoulder. "Yes?"

"I have another name to give you."

He raised an eyebrow. "Tell me."

Dante clenched his jaw before he spoke. "Colin Murray."

Dmitry left without another word, leaving Dante standing alone in the pale light of early evening. There was a flitting sound from the trees below and he scanned the gently swaying oaks before backing inside and sliding the glass door shut. He pressed a button on the wall and the blinds slammed shut, throwing the house into darkness.

CHAPTER 43

Home

Briana opened the bedroom door and peeked around the edge. The apartment appeared empty. She'd barely left her room in the last few days, only to grab food and visit the bathroom, and only when it was dead quiet. Leish had come to the door a few times, pleading, before finally giving up.

She crept to the bathroom and slipped inside. The room was dark, just a hint of morning light beginning to blush through the small frosted glass window above the shower. She kept the lights off. Just because she couldn't see them, didn't mean there weren't cameras in here.

Waiting for the water to warm up, Briana wondered how involved Leish was. There was no doubt Mel Rose was part of this in some way, whatever "this" was exactly. He just happened to be there as soon as she'd arrived in Hollywood. *He's just a pretty boy, has-been, isn't he?*

The guy just didn't seem smart enough to pull any of this off. So far, being creepy and pressing record on a web cam appeared to be the extent of his talents. *Who was really behind this and what did they want? And why her?*

Fresh fish, her mother's voice said. *Catch of the day.*

She checked her texts again. Nothing besides the last one from unknown, reminding her to tell no one and wait for further instructions. She wondered how much Leish knew what was going on. It didn't really matter. Briana couldn't trust her anymore. She tugged off her t-shirt and stepped out of her shorts into the shower.

The warm water did little to ease the hot, prickly feeling inside. It seemed like everyone in her life had lied to her, treated her like a thing to be used. Except her father. The thought of him seeing that video made her sick. It would destroy him. There had always been that long-standing belief that preacher's daughters were natural born whores, not out in the open exactly. Just implied. This would make it true, at least for her.

It's part of it, okay? It just is.

They were Leish's words, but the voice was her mother's, laced with that knowing tone of hers. She turned the knobs off and toweled dry, hurrying as it grew brighter from the rising sun. Her phone chittered with that foreign, insect-like sound and she knew.

It was them.

She pulled the towel tight around her and wiped the condensation off the phone screen.

Friday night. Be ready.

A list of numbered instructions filled the screen as she slumped on the edge of the tub, face hidden in her hands. Briana wanted to go home.

She just wasn't quite sure where that was anymore.

CHAPTER 44

Two Bunnies

Take-out cartons sat in a cluster at the center of the table, the flaps open. The heady aroma of deep-fried foods hung in the air. Colin stabbed a pair of chopsticks into a plate of steaming noodles then lifted them high into the air, the noodles dangling above his open mouth. He slurped them down as Abigail made a face then giggled. Dante smiled, swallowed a mouthful of broccoli beef chased down with a swig of Tsingtao. Two empty bottles already sat next to Colin and he was on already well into his third.

Colin burped. "Did your dad ever tell you about the time when we made a skateboard ramp?"

"Dad? On a skateboard?"

"Hey, I was actually pretty good," Dante said. "I could rail grind. Sort of."

"We found these old pieces of plywood…wait, you tell it, Dante. You were always the better storyteller."

"Well, like Colin said, we found this big pile of old wood, plywood and stuff, and we didn't want to waste it."

"It's a rule," Colin said. "You can't waste old wood. Gotta make a fort or something."

"So true. We nailed a couple of palettes together in the shape of an L, then we used two-by-fours to create a kind of curved frame to nail the plywood to, for the ramp. It was a thing of beauty."

"It was deathtrap."

Dante laughed. "It really was. The wood was old and splintered, there were bent nails hammered down all over the place. I convinced Colin that I should go first, being the better skateboarder and all."

"What happened?" Abigail asked.

"We built it at the bottom of a hill, the idea being you'd get a good head of steam going then rocket into the air, do an edge grab and shoot back down. It was going to be epic."

"Wait a minute," Colin said, face serious. "Probably shouldn't tell this one. She could get ideas."

"Well, maybe you're right," Dante said, nodding.

"No, I want to hear it," Abigail said.

"I don't know..." Colin trailed off, shaking his head.

"Dad!"

"Okay, okay," Dante said. "So, I jog to the top of the hill, board tucked under one arm, and who's standing there? Matty Markham. He was an older kid, classic neighborhood bully type. Twelve feet tall. Long hair. Held back a year in school. He'd been watching us and asked if he could go next. I told him he should do the honors. I felt so lucky that he wanted to try out our skate ramp and not pound us for once. I mean, the kid actually smiled at me. All fangs, but still, a smile."

"So?" Abigail asked.

"So, he jogs up the hill, gets a running start and comes down perfect, knees bent, hair blowing back."

"He was really bookin'" Colin said.

"God, don't remind me," Dante said. "Matty comes to the bottom of the hill, really moving at this point. He dips low to the ground and hits the ramp dead center." Dante smacked the table with a hand. "And the whole thing rips apart, right down the middle with a huge crackling explosion."

Abigail laughed, her eyes sparkling.

"Matty kept going, arms wobbling, hits the gravel and flies

into an oak bush. Two bunnies popped out, trying to escape whatever had demolished their house."

"Two bunnies!" Abigail screamed.

"I don't remember the bunnies," Colin said, laughing.

"Did the bully get hurt?" Abigail said.

"Not a scratch. Very, very cross though. Like a bear in the woods cross. Colin was on the ground cracking up, so he was no help. I got cut on a branch trying to pull Matty out of the bushes, but he was stuck. I gave up and we took off, Matty screaming bloody revenge. Later, the cut got really infected. That's how I got this scar," Dante said, pointing to the ragged line of white skin on his elbow.

"What about that one on your forehead?" Abigail said.

Dante's grin faded.

"You never told me how you got that one. Did the bunnies come back for revenge?"

"Yeah, something like that," Dante said and stood, beginning to close the take-out cartons. "Time to get ready for bed, Abigail."

Colin poked at his food with a chopstick. He flashed a nervous smile before looking down at his plate again.

"Okay," she said and got up, looking back and forth between them. "You got your elephant, Daddy?"

Dante shook his head. "My room, I think. In my wallet."

"I haven't found the baby yet," she said. "Can I look for it before I go to bed?"

"Tomorrow, Abigail."

"Okay," she said, drawing out the word. "G'night Colin."

"Night."

They sat in silence as Abigail's footsteps echoed across the floor and faded down the hall. They sipped beer in silence until they heard the muffled hiss of the shower.

"She's a little Michelle, isn't she?" Colin said. "I'm sorry I missed so much."

"Yeah," Dante said. "About that. I need to be careful, here. Okay? She lost her mom and I can't take a chance that you're going to be in her life again then...not. Understand?"

"Of course. I don't want to rush things. I just miss you, man. You know?"

Kelly walked in from the back, wearing jeans and black tank top, the airy scent of lilac in her wake.

Colin's eyes lit up. "Oh my god, you're..."

"That's me," Kelly said smiling brightly. She put out her hand and Colin grasped it in slow motion.

"Hi," Colin said. "Katrina Steel was my favorite character. You kicked ass on that show."

"Thanks," Kelly said. "Did all my own stunts."

"That's amazing," Colin said, still shaking her hand.

"Kelly Sheppard," Dante said. "Meet Colin Murray. An old friend."

"Nice to meet you, old friend," she said as she withdrew her hand and glanced at Dante. "Thanks for letting me use your computer. Something's wrong with my Internet again."

"Anytime. You're still good to watch Abigail tomorrow night?"

"Wouldn't miss girls' night for anything. We're going to stay up way past ten and talk about boys. Or maybe I'll show her some more kick boxing moves." She jabbed at the air a few times. "Nice to meet you Colin," Kelly said as she left. Colin watched her go.

"That's your babysitter?"

"Neighbor actually. Well, a friend. But, yes, she watches Abigail for me."

"Jesus, Danny boy," Colin said, shaking his head.

Dante finished putting the cartons in the fridge and sat back down with two fresh bottles of beer. "I had a look at your deck."

"You did? When?" Colin asked.

"When I took a break from clunking around the house."

"What did you think?"

"I think...maybe it's what we've been looking for. Could give us an edge."

"That's great, Dante. Really."

"I'll call Bob Bainbridge and set up a meeting so you two can go over the financials. If everything looks good, we can sign the contracts and get started. How does Kellerman figure into this exactly?"

"Oh, I won't be doing this through Kellerman Digital," said Colin as he rubbed his hands together and grinned. "This will be my little side hustle."

"They're okay with that?"

"What they don't know..."

"Colin. I want this to be above board."

"It will be. It *is*. Don't worry about them."

They fell into silence again. Dante rotated his beer bottle, trying to read the small print on the label. Colin tapped his plate with a chopstick.

Tink. Tink. Tink.

"You ever think about it?"

"No," Dante said. "It's been what, twenty years?"

"Twenty-one. Twenty-one years. I think about it all the time." He tapped his chopstick on the plate again, little discordant notes until he dropped it on the table. "I tried to bury it, but it was always there. In the shadows," Colin said wiggling his fingers. His face fell and he stared at the table. "Nobody blamed me, for what...I did. Which made it worse in a way. Like it didn't matter. But it *did* matter. To me it did, anyway." Colin's eyes went glassy as he stared somewhere faraway. "I was just so scared all the time after that. Remember? Therapists couldn't do shit. Meds helped a little, but the fear was always just...there, no matter what."

Colin finished off his beer and set the bottle down a bit too hard. He twitch-blinked, eyes catching Dante's. "It sure helped *you* though. After you got out of the hospital, you shot up almost three inches while I seemed to shrink. You started playing basketball, got girls. You were a totally different person and I was still just 'Twitch'."

"You did what you had to do. The cops agreed. I don't remember much, but I'll always remember that. I just wish you just didn't take is so hard," Dante said.

"Yeah, me too."

"After three days in a coma, I just figured life couldn't get much worse than that."

"Yeah, you were fearless after that. You wanted to do something, you just did it. Didn't have quite the same effect on me," Colin added.

"Well, you weren't the one in a coma," Dante said.

"Sometimes I wish I was."

"You just hid in your house all the time. I couldn't get you to do anything. Well, anything outside."

"I had my computers. My coding. We just found a different way to deal with what happened, I guess. I mean we went into business together later, didn't we?"

"Yeah, we did. I hate to lay more guilt on you, but you left at the worst time. Business was really picking up and your pipelines made everything run like clockwork. Then Michelle died, I had to raise a toddler, run a company. And you skated. We had plans, Colin."

"*You* had plans. I had loans. My folks didn't have money like your dad did. Hell, I'm *still* paying off my loans. When that job offer from Kellerman came along, I couldn't pass it up. The money was just too good and it was all R and D. Neural nets, artificial intelligence, machine learning. Cutting edge. It's what I'd always wanted to do. Not pipelines and batch processes."

"I'm not talking about that. I'm talking about how we were working together, everything was going fine, then you just became a ghost."

Colin clenched his jaw again before exhaling loudly. "I didn't mean to just...disappear. You were the 'what if' in my life, and it was just too hard to be around."

"The what if?"

"Yeah. The what if I weren't a loser," Colin said, flashing a lopsided grin. "I mean, look at you. You got this crazy shit going on in your life, just got your toes hacked off for chrissakes and you just, handle it, you know? I was just tired of seeing you win all the time. And when *didn't* you have girls chasing you? From when we were teenagers, up through college. Even now." Colin blinked, whole face twitching. "The few times I did go out with you and your college brosefs, well, let's just say that pussy shrapnel theory was bullshit."

"Pussy shrapnel?"

"Yeah, any girls who didn't want you, or them, would be left over for me. Pussy shrapnel."

The bathroom door opened at the end of the hall and Abigail crossed over to her room dressed in a thick robe. After a moment the light in her room went out.

"As the father of a young girl," Dante said, voice low, "I don't ever want to hear those words in this house again."

Colin drank some more beer and continued. "If you hadn't sent that hooker to the dorms that one time, I would've never gotten laid."

"You knew?"

"Not until later when I thought about it some more. Figured she was working off one of your scripts. I mean she was way, way outta my league, there to meet her boyfriend but got stood up again, tears in her eyes. Good stuff. Very convincing. Like I said, you always were the better storyteller."

"Sorry."

Colin took Dante's beer from his hand and drank long deep swallows before setting the bottle down with a thunk. The other three bottles near him wobbled. When he spoke again, his voice was louder, more brittle. "Don't be. Shit, your heart was in the right place. Then you got your first cherry job right after school and I was barely scraping by writing banking software. Fast forward a few years, my good ol' buddy Dante is striking out on his own. 'Hey Twitch, wanna come work for me?'"

He was almost shouting now.

"Colin..."

"Oh, sorry." He held a finger to his lips. "Shhhhh. School day tomorrow." He downed the remaining beer and held up the bottle to one eye like a telescope. "Got any more?"

Dante shook his head. He hadn't taken one sip before Colin had snatched it away.

"Then I got the call from Kellerman," Colin said. "It was great, man. I was with others of my own kind. None of us had lives. So, I buried myself in my work, wouldn't leave the office for days at a time. Shit, sometimes weeks. We made some real breakthroughs, but...all that repressed shit wormed its way back to the top and I just cracked."

"I didn't know," Dante said as a tinge of anger flared up inside.

"That's okay. Oscar-worthy hookers weren't going to fix this one. I moved back home for a while. Got some help and got better. I am better. Sorry I waited so long to get in touch, but the longer I waited, the harder it was to call."

"Then you just show up one day," Dante said, "the same day my life goes to shit."

Colin stared for a moment before he blinked, face twitching. "What are you saying?"

"I think you know."

"Do you think I'd be begging you for a contract if I was pulling this other shit?"

"I really don't know."

Colin stared back, eyes glassy. "After what I *did* for you all those years ago? I've had to live with that every day since, man, not you. How can you even think that?"

"I don't know what to think."

"I'm bored outta my skull at Kellerman, okay? I was demoted after my medical leave. 'Light Duty' they called it, but it's a fucking demotion. Better than getting fired, but I don't get to work on the cool stuff anymore. Listen, I'm trying to get my life back together. I thought if I...ah, fuck it," he said, swiping the beer bottles off the table. One shattered against the cupboard causing shards of green glass to rain down. "Besides, look at you," Colin screamed as he rose to his feet, glass crunching underfoot. "Cool as a cucumber. Nothing ever gets to ol' Dante!"

"Keep your fucking voice down," Dante hissed through his teeth as he reached across the table and grabbed Colin's shirt front. He glanced down the hallway but the light under Abigail's door stayed dark. "I'm scared to death, Colin. Understand? I've never been so scared in my life. Somebody is fucking with me and I don't know who or why. I saw my toes hacked to pieces. *Pieces.* I can still feel them, but I look down and they're not there. So, listen to me you wormy little shit, I have a daughter to take care of and a few hundred people who rely on me to keep it together. Whatever happens to me, they come first." He pounded the table with each word that followed. "They come first."

Dante let go and Colin fell back into his chair, shoulders slumped.

"I keep it together because I have to. Can't just lose my shit and drop off the face of the earth, then show up again like everything's peachy."

Colin stared at the table, not moving. "I'm gonna go now." He rose, the chair making a rude sound as it slid back. Tears slid down his face as he trudged through the living room. "I told myself it'd been too long."

"Colin, hold on a minute," Dante said, following him.

The thin man kept moving to the front door in a daze. Dante grabbed Colin's arm and spun him around. His eyes were dark orbs buried in purple hollows.

"Look at me, Colin. I know it isn't you. Okay? It's just some punk ass hackers. It isn't you. Alright?"

Colin nodded and wiped his face with the back of hand. "Got a little crazy, didn't I?"

"We both did."

Dante's phone buzzed and he slipped it from his pocket. "Hold on a minute, Naomi." He placed a palm over the bottom of the phone. "I got to take this. Are we good?"

"Yeah, we're good," Colin said, turning to go. He trudged to the front door and turned the knob.

"Hey," Dante called out to him. "Ellis Media summer bash this Friday night. You coming?"

Colin glanced back at him, a slight smile turning up the corners of his mouth. "Wouldn't miss it." He pulled the door closed behind him and Dante heard the alarm beep as it armed for the night.

"Hey," Dante said into the phone as he went back to kitchen. Glass shards glittered on the floor as he turned on the overhead lights. "Shit."

"Everything okay?"

"Yeah, fine. Just got a little mess to clean up here. How's things at the office?"

"Everything's good," Naomi said. "And don't worry, I covered like you asked. You pulled a hammy playing racket ball with a potential client. Everyone bought it."

"Perfect. You're a godsend, Naomi."

"I am, aren't I?" They fell silent for a long time. "Want some company tonight?"

Dante squeezed his eyes shut. *More than anything.* "Everything ready for Friday night?"

"Yep. Good to go."

"Okay. See you tomorrow," Dante said and disconnected.

Careful to sidestep the glass on the floor, he slid the Faraday cage out from under the table. The various devices slid around inside, plastic and glass ticking.

His phone vibrated. It was Naomi again. If he picked up, he knew he wouldn't be able to say no.

Dante placed his phone in with the other devices and closed the lid. The phone fell silent. He retrieved a broom and dustpan from the closet, left foot thudding on the floor as he swept up the shattered glass.

CHAPTER 45

Naomi

Dante strolled through the busy studio floor, nodding to those who noticed him or came over to ask how he was doing. Most ignored him, ear buds tucked in their ears, working on the various projects Ellis Media currently had on their slate.

Dante was impressed.

There were no silly cat videos playing on second monitors, no online shopping windows open. Naomi had really kept the place in order while he was out and ran a tight ship. Tighter than him.

Her cover story worked as well. Nobody looked at him twice. Attacked by killer robot was something he wanted to keep out of the rumor mill for a while. He wouldn't mind telling people that each toe was worth a million bucks, though.

He went into the fishbowl and dialed Dmitry Molchalin. It had been several days without a word. The call went to voice mail again.

What the hell? Had Dmitry found out who was doing this to him and...what?

The phone on the conference table blipped. "Mr. Ellis? Megan Zhou on line three for you."

Dante picked up. "Hi, Megan. Tell me something good."

"Mr. Vikal has made a decision," Megan said. "He wants to

go with you. This is huge, Dante. Print *and* broadcast. That donkey thing really disgusted him but when Naomi called and explained what was going on, he was angry that it happened to you. I asked him if he was sure and he really doubled down. He said it was wrong and it could've happened to anyone."

"That's great news," Dante said. "Listen, don't tell Naomi just yet alright? I'm going to bump her up to executive producer and I want her first account to be you. I'll announce it tonight at the summer bash."

"Awesome! I love Naomi. See you then."

They said goodbye and Dante hung up. It *was* great news. Really great. This was a huge account. Just the shot in the arm they needed.

He couldn't have cared less right then.

Dante dialed Molchalin once more then disconnected as it went to voice mail.

Time to pay Shadow Trace another visit.

CHAPTER 46

Vacancy

Dante stood at the center of the Shadow Trace office, watching as dust motes crawled through shafts of light that shot through boarded-up windows. Nothing remained of what he'd seen on his first visit. Not the crisp chill in the air, the large, black cubes that dominated the space or the server farm enclosure at the rear. Everything had been swept clean. The heat was close and still, as if the room was holding a stale breath.

"Over the phone, you said something about an office move. What's your time line look like?" said a paunchy man in tan slacks and blue button up shirt. Keys jangled as he came over to join Dante. A small lock box was clenched in one hand. Beads of perspiration dotted his balding head and dark sweat stained both underarms. Pinned on his left breast was a shiny name tag that read: Sunset Realty, Charlie Melton.

"Next month or so. How long ago did you say the previous tenants moved out?" Dante said.

"Two, three days. Ten years they've done business here then up and left. We'd just signed a new lease with them too. There's an early termination fee but we can go over all of that. Good timing for you, though, eh?"

"Yeah," Dante said. *What the hell happened to Shadow Trace?* Not everything had been removed. Molchalin's office was still tucked in the far corner, door open a crack. Dante made his way over through the dim space, past where the server racks used to stand and placed his palm against the door. It eased open without a sound. There was a faint smell of something sweet, coconut or almond, a soapy smell.

Dante stepped inside the small room and peered into the darkness, trying make out anything that might have been left behind but it was too dark. He stepped over to flick the light switch when his foot came down on something and he slipped, throwing his arm out for balance. His arm hit the wall with a rattling thud.

"Everything okay back there?" Melton said, his voice echoing across the bare concrete.

Dante ignored him and slipped out his phone. He knelt down and turned on the phone's flashlight. The bright beam threw the small rectangular object into sharp relief. It was a bar of soap, mangled from where he'd stepped on it. The top was mushroomed, streaked with gray. The strong smell of coconut wafted upward.

Dante stood and panned the phone around the room, illuminating the walls. Something was scrawled there in big letters, but it was difficult to make out against the gleaming white of the walls.

Swinging the phone light over to a corner, he saw a small pile of dust and debris left over from the hasty clear out. Striding over, he knelt and grabbed a handful, then flung it into a high arc over the wall. As the dust rained down, it collected on the soap smudges, darkening the pearlescent streaks into something legible.

Dante stood back and raked his light over the wall. He snorted in disbelief at this cloak and dagger turn of events. A strange feeling stole through him, like he was being watched. His phantom toes twitched. He jerked at the knock on the door frame from behind and turned.

Charlie Melton stood in the doorway, squinting as Dante's light shone onto his face. He motioned to the words etched onto the wall in coconut scented soap. "What's that supposed to mean?"

Dante shook his head and read the words again.

DARK MESSIAH IS COMING FOR YOU.

Excerpt from TechBeat.com article:

Technological Breakthrough: Scientists create "Synapse Map" of human brain

By Ian Weller

A Synapse map, or Synaptome, has been created from a human brain for the very first time by researchers at BaselMek Medical Industries. Using high-speed spinning disk confocal microscopy (SDM), Diffusion-weighted Magnetic Resonance Imaging (DW-MRI) along with special machine learning software, a team of scientists, neurologists and engineers have completed an eight-year-long study to create a three-dimensional map of the human brain at the synaptic level.

"The real game changer was the SDM microsopy," says Dr. Patricia Shimizu. "Our imager, an Andor Dragonfly 500, allowed us to capture super resolution down to the molecular level, essentially where thoughts occur."

When asked what's next on the horizon, Dr. Shimizu replied, "Now that we have a synaptome map, a Connectome, the complete electrochemical architecture of the human brain, can be created. The next logical step would be 3-D printing of biological tissues to create an actual, organic brain. It's very exciting!"

CHAPTER 47

Retrocam

The phone chittered, causing Briana's hand to tighten on the refrigerator door handle. She hadn't eaten all day and her head swam as she read the text. The list of instructions appeared again, her frown deepening as she scanned the bizarre steps that lay ahead of her that night. None of it made any sense, but if it would keep that video out of her father's inbox then she'd do whatever it took.

Leish glanced over from where she streamed the latest gaming craze, trying to catch Briana's eye. After a moment, she gave up. With a war whoop she dove back into the fray but it lacked her usual verve.

The chair legs screeched as Briana slumped into a chair at the kitchen table. All the cameras had been removed. In their place was a bowl of red apples and she grabbed one, biting with large, frantic bites.

"You okay?" Leish said. She was standing across from her, hand gripping the top a chair. Briana hadn't seen her come over.

Briana swallowed, large chunks of apple sticking in her throat before sliding slowly down. Rising to her feet she said, "Busy night. I got to go."

"Briana," Leish said, tears in her eyes. "I don't know exactly what's going on, but I'm sorry."

"Don't." Briana brushed past Leish down the hall to her room. She closed the door behind her and kept the light off. As instructed, she changed into long black slacks and black button up shirt, the unofficial uniform of baristas everywhere. She wouldn't be slinging coffee tonight though.

With nothing to do all week except worry and wait, Briana had gone through the boxes of Leish's swag stacked along the back wall. *After* she'd turned the large hyena to face the wall. The thing creeped her out. It had been tricky to do in the dim light that leaked in around the blinds, but she didn't trust having the lights on in here ever again.

In among a box of other electronic odds and ends, she found a small video camera that used mini DV tapes, the word RETROCAM stenciled along one side in red. Somebody's poor attempt at rebranding.

Briana liked it.

There was a pullout touch screen on one side and a viewfinder along the top. It was older tech, made before anything was smart or connected to the Internet. Her dad had one like it back home, the tapes full of Briana singing at school talent shows or church functions.

When Leish said people sent her all kinds of stuff, she wasn't kidding. Another thing Briana had been shocked to find was a gun along with a box of shells. It was a Hatfield single shot twelve gauge—the kind they sold at Walmart for about a hundred bucks—still in the box. Her father had one, given to him by a member of his church. They had taken it out to the range only once. The trigger pull was at least eight or nine pounds and it was a light gun so it kicked like a mule. She preferred her Remington 870 anyways. She'd gotten pretty decent at trap shooting before giving it up for more girly things.

She'd hefted the gun and broke the barrel, making sure it was safe. Then she snapped it closed and swung it high, imagining a clay pigeon with Mel Rose's face on it exploding in the sky. The smell of gun oil made her miss home. She leaned it back in the corner and draped the dazzle camo over the gun again to hide it.

After tucking the black shirt into her slacks, she slipped the strap of her messenger bag over one shoulder and patted the corner to make sure the low-tech camera was still inside. She wasn't quite sure what she was going to do with it, but it gave her a sense of control, something they couldn't reach. Maybe she would make a little video of her own, get some proof of what, exactly, she didn't know. She bit her lip and almost plucked the camera out of the bag and flung it across the room.

If *they* caught her with it...she shuddered.

She resisted flipping the bird at the large hyena's back and checked her phone.

Time to go.

CHAPTER 48

Trapped

Gary stood on the corner down the street from where his family was safe at home, tucked in at the end of the cul-de-sac.

Trapped, more like it, he thought.

The occasional car passed by, the people inside giving him strange looks. Gail had told him to change, said he looked like an out-of-work preacher as he'd walked out the front door. He didn't dare tell her that the very first instruction in the text was to wear all black.

Another car drove near and he made like he was checking his watch, even though he didn't wear one. The vehicle slowed down, the hum of its motor dissipating. Gary glanced up and saw it was one of those new autonomous vehicles. Boxy with rounded edges, white with an orange stripe down the side. A translucent dome was perched on top. Dim lights blinked inside. There was no cabin at the front, just a horizontal strip of LEDs cleaving the early evening air with a bright blade of light. The rear door whispered up, exposing the interior cargo bay.

It was empty.

Gary hesitated and the horn blew, a one second blast that seemed to go on forever. If the twins had been there, they would have laughed to see him jump before he hurried inside the truck. The door slid shut and the truck sped off, throwing him onto his ass. Gary grimaced as a light strip came on overhead. He switched the Taser to his other pocket and rubbed his sore butt cheek as he crawled away from the door. Sitting with his back against the wall, he listened to the hum of tires on pavement as the autonomous vehicle sped off into the night.

CHAPTER 49

Autonomous

The autonomous truck rounded another corner and dropped with a thump before continuing along at a much slower pace. Briana crouched down against the wall and hooked her fingers into a lip that ran along the inside where the upper and lower halves fit together.

Where are they taking me? she wondered.

The truck eased to a halt and the door rose up. It had been such a strange experience to climb into the back when it had appeared in front of the apartment, rear door hanging open.

She scooted across the floor and stepped out.

The reek of rotting garbage wafted over and she pressed the back of a hand to her nose. A dark alley stretched away from her, lit by the occasional naked bulb. Low buildings were tucked along the left, some with roll up metal loading doors shuttered tight.

To her right, a cinder block wall hemmed in the back of the alley, standing ten feet tall or more, topped with a chain-link fence. Spiky tufts of yellowed grass peeked out along the top of the wall against a deepening sky. Briana pictured an empty lot up there with junk cars and burning barrels, homeless folks huddled around them.

Large dumpsters lined the alley, like the ones used at construction sites. A smaller dumpster sat nearby, painted green with a black plastic lid. New odors drifted over her, burnt plastic and chemicals, more tasted than smelled. Briana was about to check the instructions again when a dragonfly drone swept down from above and hovered in front of a plain, metal door painted a flat gray. Industrial Printers LLC was stenciled across the door in black paint. A sign next to the door read: Night Pick up. Below it was a rectangular metal hatch, about one foot by two, sealed tight.

Briana walked over, eying the dragonfly with suspicion before kneeling down. A harsh clang rang out as bolts retracted and the door lifted up with a screech. The dark opening yawned like a toothless mouth, the sharp metal frame around it scaled with rust. Her nose wrinkled as a sharp odor wafted out. She didn't want to put her hand in there.

The drone made a harsh clacking sound with its wings. Briana braced one hand against the wall and slid her other hand inside. She felt nothing at first, so she stretched her arm down a little more. It was deeper than it looked. Still nothing. She pulled her hand out and the drone objected again.

"There's nothing in there," Briana hissed. The drone dove at her face, causing her to flinch. Then it hovered back, waiting. Gazing back at the dark opening, she slid her hand inside once more, past her elbow, then further still, her cheek almost touching the frame around the edge. The harsh tang of metal stung her nostrils.

Still nothing.

She was about to pull her hand out when her fingertips brushed against the smooth surface of something inside. Pushing her body tight against the wall, she stretched her arm down as far as she could. Her fingers clamped around the edge of a rectangular object, still hot to the touch. Dropping it in alarm, she grasped it once more and slowly pulled the object out, holding it in her hands.

It was a box, like a laptop but thicker, flat black in color with an elliptical hole at one end. The box cooled rapidly in the night air and she slipped a finger under the lip, lifting it open.

A pair of sharp metal blades glinted inside.

The drone protested and she let the lid drop with a clack. After stuffing the box into her messenger bag, Briana walked back over to the waiting truck. The drone didn't follow. Her eyes followed as it rose straight up, almost disappearing high above. It hovered there, glinting like a little green star. A small red light began to blink on its underside.

It's now or never, she thought. A thrill coursed through her. *Am I really going to do this?*

She stepped inside the truck's cargo bay and tucked her phone in the small lip that curved along the inside wall. That was most likely how they'd been tracking her, through the GPS in her phone. Dropping to her knees, she opened the messenger bag, reached past the strange box and pulled out the mini DV camera before jamming it into her pocket. Leaving the bag in the center of the cargo area, she turned and hopped out.

The door slid closed with a shush. The instructions clearly stated that she was to return to the truck, pass the bag to the occupant then take the same truck back home. She felt exposed, standing out there in the open as she glanced up. The red light on the underside of the drone began to flash faster and Briana's heart skipped.

Uploading data or something? she thought. *It must be almost done. If it sees me out here…*

She dashed to the green dumpster she'd spied earlier, hoping it was a recycling bin. With her fingers she tried to lift the lid, but it held tight. A metal bar lay across the top, locked at one end with a padlock. Her eyes darted to the drone again.

The light blinked faster, almost a solid glow now.

Heaving up on a cover, she was able to force the stiff but flexible lid open but it closed as soon as she let go. A square wooden post leaned against a wall nearby. She tucked it under one arm and dragged it over to the dumpster. With the heels of her hands she pried the plastic lid up again, then wrestled the post up under the edge. Shifting it back and forth, she wedged it in to allow the lid to stay open. The gap was only about a foot or so, but it would have to do. She checked the drone.

The red light stopped and the dragonfly began descending with alarming speed.

Briana dove in through the opening, causing the post to fall inside after her. Her hands slid into a spiky bed of plastic scrap as the lid snapped shut, trapping her left foot.

With a grunt, she yanked her foot free, plunging the interior into darkness. Her shoe fell on the stained asphalt outside with a rubbery, muted plunk and her heart almost stopped as she heard the angry flutter of wings.

The dragonfly drone was coming closer.

CHAPTER 50

Messenger Bag

The truck dropped suddenly and then drove slow and steady before easing to a stop. The door rose up and Gary blinked at what he saw.

It was the inside of another truck, identical to his except for one thing. A black messenger bag was in the center, the wide, flat strap lay in loose tangle.

Gary went over the instructions in his head. *Wasn't there supposed to be someone in the other truck? Guess the plan changed.*

It made him nervous.

He scuttled over and slipped the strap of the bag onto his shoulder. A phone sat on the small ledge that ran along the interior. He reached out to take it, then hesitated.

Where the fuck was the other guy? he thought. Licking his lips, Gary grabbed the phone.

He scooted back into his truck and sat against the wall, the bag held protectively on his lap, and waited. He'd let *them* know the other guy wasn't there and he had their phone. Gary wasn't going to let someone else screw this up. He was going to follow the plan to the letter, for his family.

The doors slid shut and the truck began to move.

Almost over, Gary said to himself. *Almost over.*

CHAPTER 51

Dumpster

The heat was stifling in the dumpster as she held her breath. The drone was still hovering just outside. She strained to listen for the flit of its wings, imagining it dropping low to scan her shoe and realize she wasn't where she was supposed to be. Sweat beaded on her forehead, threatening to seep into her eyes and she squeezed them shut.

An image of her father appeared behind closed lids, eyes bleary as he gazed in shock at the video of her daughter engaged in something that made him sick to his soul.

Maybe this wasn't such a good idea.

A vehicle approached from the far end of the alley and Briana heard the chatter of wings as the drone flew off. Wiping her forehead with the back of her arm, she removed the mini DV camera from her pocket and pushed the power button. It sprang to life with a soft, electric whine.

Creeping forward, Briana pushed the lid up just a crack, resting the camera on the edge to capture what was happening outside. She peered at the small pullout screen, eyes glinting in the dim light as she watched.

Two identical autonomous trucks sat end to end in the alley as if performing some strange mating ritual. The trucks separated and the one she'd arrived in eased past the dumpster and out of sight, her phone with it. The other truck drove further down the alley, then sped across a four-lane street before disappearing into the darkness below a taller building that towered high above.

Peering closer at the screen, she saw a small W and T at the top right corner. She tapped on the W. Nothing happened. Pressing a fingertip on T caused the image to expand, zooming in on the darkness. A few cars drove by, their headlights left streaks across the screen.

Squinting, she looked for any sign of the other truck but the gloom remained impenetrable. The heat was near unbearable now. Sweat trickled freely down her back. *Time to get out,* she thought. She placed a palm against the lid to pry it up again.

Then she saw it.

A quick flash of taillights as the truck came to a halt. It was barely visible on the screen, the image fuzzy, shaky from her hand. The rear door rose, dim blue light revealing a dark figure crouched inside. The figure emerged and jogged out to the street, partially light by a streetlight. It was a man, dressed in black, same as her.

He stood for a moment, gazing upward. Briana tilted the camera up and saw a shiny glass building, stretching high above. It was the tallest building around here by far, the windows a smoky black. She panned back down and watched as the man climbed the steps past a large sign that read: Monolith Media Tower. The double-doors at the front opened and he disappeared inside. A faint smudge followed him in.

Must be the drone.

She withdrew the camera and snapped the screen shut before pushing it back into her pocket. Forcing the lid open with a shoulder, she wriggled out, rolling onto the pavement. It was much easier going out, than in. From the opposite end of the alley came the faint sound of music.

A plan began to form in her head. She'd catch a taxi back to the apartment in time to meet up with the autonomous truck that had brought her here. The instructions stated that she'd be brought directly home after the hand off had been made. There might have been more, but she couldn't remember. Briana sighed with frustration. It didn't matter now. The dragonfly drone probably had more important things to do than make sure she made it back. With how slow that truck drove, it should be easy to grab a ride, beat it back to the apartment, wait for it to show up, then grab her phone when the door opened.

Right. Easy.

Getting some evidence had seemed like a good idea back in the safety of her room, swinging back and forth between anger and fear. She touched the camera in her pocket. It wasn't much, but at least it was something *they* couldn't control. She hoped it was worth the risk.

Briana threw one last glance over her shoulder then headed down the alley toward the deep bass rumble of dance music.

CHAPTER 52

Burning Oil

Gary strode past the unmanned front desk through a set of glass security barriers as they slid open, then down a long hallway past a bank of elevators and glass enclosed offices to a plain gray door. There were no locks or handles, just a key card reader that glowed red. The reader flashed three times before turning green and he pushed the door open. The drone shot through the doorway ahead of him.

Three elevator doors stood before him. The first one on the left was open and waiting. The drone clung to one of the panels inside. Gary walked in and knelt down as the doors closed.

The messenger bag dropped with a clunk and he threw back the flap. He removed the black box and placed it on the tile floor, then lifted the lid with a finger, grimacing at the array of electronics and wires tucked inside. He leaned back, allowing the drone an unimpeded view.

Mounted at equal points just inside were four hypodermic needles, their reservoirs empty. Gary removed four small glass bottles from his pocket. They'd been delivered last night by the large drone, left behind on one of his Adirondacks. The thing had been even creepier glinting under the moonlight.

He inserted a bottle behind each of the four hypos. Clear liquid emptied from the bottles with a hiss as each of the hypos filled to the three ml mark.

A few inches in from the hole at the end were a pair of curved blades, held in place by sturdy levers and small hydraulic rams. The blades brightened and the smell of burning oil filled the air before they snapped shut with a metallic clink. They reset with the sound of scissor blades scraping. It put his teeth on edge. Gary closed the lid and slid the box back into the bag with a shiver.

As he stood, he withdrew the Taser and held it down at his side. The elevator doors opened and he went to a flight of stairs that led to the roof. He crept to the top and sat on the top step to wait. His face lit up in the dark as he flipped through pictures on his phone of the twins playing on the carpet, running in the park, sleeping in their cribs. He stopped on an image of Gail holding the babies when they were just days old, a look of pure joy in her eyes. A text appeared, vibrating the phone like a fly trapped under a glass.

It was time.

Gary stood and removed a balaclava from his pocket and slipped it over his head. He tried to swallow but his throat was dry and prickly.

C'mon, he urged himself, breathing in slow and deep. *You can do this.*

He hefted the bag with its strange contents, held the Taser up like he'd seen on a million cop shows, and descended the stairs, slipping inside the first open door on the right.

Almost over, Gary said to himself as he approached the lone man standing in the dark office.

Almost over.

CHAPTER 53

Summer Bash

Electronic dance music thundered out from speakers placed throughout the kitchen area of Ellis Media. Orange globes sat intermittently along the outer walls providing the crowded space with small pools of warm illumination. Knots of people clung together, shouting to be heard, drink in one hand, over-loaded plate of food in the other. Some of them wore dazzle camo. A full bar at the far end of the room was doing brisk business. Two younger employees had already been escorted out and shoved into Ubers, barely able to stand.

Naomi sipped her Manhattan and scowled. Maybe the free bar had been a bad idea this year. It was barely past ten and everybody was already smashed. After checking her phone for the third time, she scanned the room.

Where is Dante? she thought.

He had the yearly announcement coming up at 10:30 PM and she wanted it to happen before everybody got too wasted to remember what he'd said. Tonight's the night. Promotion time.

It'd better be or I walk.

Her eyes flicked across the room again. *Where is he?*

Colin Murray stood next to one of the globe lights. Drink in one hand, plate piled high with fruit in the other. Orange light was supposed to be forgiving, making people appear softer, more appealing. Colin lifted his bony arm and took a sip, throat bobbing up and down. To Naomi, he looked just like a skeleton.

Or the grim reaper, she thought.

He must've sensed her gaze because he looked at her and grinned, raising his glass.

Naomi groaned.

Colin lifted his arms higher as he made his way through the jostling crowd, doing a little jig as he swerved around a girl that stepped backward into his path. The plate slipped from his hand and she watched as grapes and strawberries rolled across the floor, as if escaping a predator.

Dante must've been a real dork if this was his best friend as a kid. She liked Dante. Liked him more than she cared to admit. He was funny and sweet. Very handsome. But dating the boss had been a bad idea, especially when he was a widower with a nine-year-old girl. Naomi had never even been married. Barely knew her nephew. It was just too much too soon. Convenient because they worked together, but complicated just the same. She shook her head.

What was I thinking?

She was thinking about how he looked stepping out of the shower early one morning at work some months ago. Right after, he'd given her his office code. That probably wasn't why he'd done it though. Or had he? Then again, she'd been the one to peek into the inner office when the shower went silent.

Early bird gets the worm, she thought. *And sees the boss naked.*

Now his skeletal friend was undoubtedly coming over to make his move, fill the void left in her life by the very recent departure of Dante Ellis. He must have told him they'd broken up or maybe Colin suspected. He had that look in his eye.

Colin jerked to a stop, grin wilting on his face. Something across the main studio floor caught his eye. Naomi followed his gaze, peering into the darkness.

A shadow weaved up through the cubicles, back lit by green exit signs. The arms were pulled in tight, one hand holding the other. It bumped against a desk, causing a bank of monitors to spring to life. Pale blue light bloomed from the screens, illuminating the person struggling to stay upright.

It was Dante.

Naomi rushed forward, pushing past people as they turned and watched Dante shove his way drunkenly toward the kitchen.

"Somebody get the lights!"

She was almost to Dante when he fell to his knees, hunched over, his whole body wracked with spasms. Naomi fought against the tide of bodies that backed away as she felt a scream rise up to her throat.

The lights came on and everyone squinted in the sudden glare as the music died. Dante looked up and stared straight through her, eyes glassy and wide. Naomi finally made her way to him and knelt down, grabbing his shoulders.

"Dante!" she screamed.

His eyes found hers and he stared, uncomprehending. His left arm fell away and he held his right arm up between them.

Where his hand should've been was a charred stump of oozing flesh, wet blacks and deep reds with pale pink peeking through. The air was thick with the reek of seared pork and she felt her gorge rise. Naomi skittered back, hands flying to her mouth.

Dante's eyes fluttered as the stump puckered and split. Jets of bright red blood gushed onto Naomi as Dante collapsed onto his face, forehead striking the white tile with a harsh clack.

Naomi fell to her knees and vomited, Dante's hot blood still bitter on her tongue.

CHAPTER 54

The Big Tip

The autonomous truck was just easing to the curb as Briana's taxi turned off Sunset toward the apartment.

"Hurry! Go to that truck up there!" Briana said, swatting the headrest.

The taxi driver glared at her before speeding up the hill and screeching to a stop behind the truck. Briana leapt out, eyes scanning for a drone.

There were none in sight.

The gate on the truck slid up and she leapt inside, sliding her hand into the ledge where she'd left her phone.

It wasn't there.

Leaning out of the truck, Briana gazed around before turning back to search the interior with frantic intensity. Her phone was gone. She stepped down from the truck and the door slid shut. It made a tight U-turn and drove back down toward Sunset and out of sight.

The taxi was still there, the driver staring at her through the window. He waved at her and she trudged over in a daze as the driver side window slid down.

"You're Briana, right?" said the driver.

She nodded.

"So, I just got this really weird text."

"A text?"

"And a hundred-dollar tip, or else I would've just drove off. It's kind of creepy, if you ask me."

"I don't understand."

"It's from Dark Messiah. It says, 'Tell Briana, Daddy knows'."

CHAPTER 55

Rotten Starfish

Light seeped in through his eyelids, along with the sounds of soft hissing and that unmistakable hospital smell. His first thoughts were for Abigail, but he knew she was okay. She was with Kelly, and he knew she'd give her life before—

My hand is gone.

There was no shock or surprise, just awareness of that simple fact. He remembered every moment of it as well, viewed through a dispassionate layer with painless, preternatural crystal clarity, one moment after another bleeding together.

Someone coming in.

Naomi?

No. A man.

White-hot pain and the taste of blood.

The cloying stench of scorched flesh.

Twitching spider legs.

Twitching fingers.

My fingers.

Abigail's elephant pendant falling, a flash of silver streaking down. The man picking up Dante's hand like it was a rotting starfish, his body stiff with revulsion as the dragonfly watched with its beady little eyes.

Not eyes. Cameras.

He wondered if this video was already on line, racking up views.

Harsh whispers crowded in, the comments section below coming to life.

Got what he deserved.

Not so fearless now, is he?

Purveyors of lies pay with a pound of flesh.

His throat tightened, the sinews of his neck going taut. *Just a bunch of online ogres, hiding behind fake names, right? Sad, fucking joke, all of them.*

We're not a joke anymore.

That gave Dante pause, the whirling sludge of his thoughts congealing around an idea. Had those comments, or the anger that fueled them, created a monster that found its way into the real world to take a chunk out of him?

Two chunks, to be exact.

But hadn't the man said sorry? Dante pondered this. *Yeah, right before he let that nightmare box take my hand off.*

Someone was in the hospital room with him. He could smell the coconut scented soap they'd used to wash their hands. Those coconut scented streaks on the wall back at the abandoned Shadow Trace office leapt into his brain.

Dark Messiah is coming for you.

Is that what Dark Messiah was? Dante wondered. *Some avenging angel for the trolls?*

"Dante? I'm Tricia. Can you hear me? Give my fingers a squeeze. Hard as you can."

The voices spoke again.

And if your right hand causes you to sin, cut it off and cast if from you.

Dante squeezed and his hand locked into a frozen claw that shook as needles danced over his skin. His face contorted and Tricia spoke again.

"No, your left hand, hon. Squeeze your left hand."

Tears of frustration streamed down his face as Dante closed his left hand around her thumb, weak as a baby.

"That's good. Very good. There's a little girl out there who's very worried about her daddy."

Dante's throat was dry and his body felt like a million pounds of wet cement. Whatever drugs he was on this time were a hell of a lot stronger than his last visit. *Guess you get the good stuff when you lose something really meaty.* He worked his jaw.

"Sh'okay?" he managed.

"She's fine. Kelly is here as well, and your friend Colin. He saved your life from what I heard. You owe him a new shirt."

"Sh'okay," he said, opening his eyes.

Dante was inside a fishbowl, the whole world distorted and shifting. Colin leaned against the far wall, face twitching as he blinked. He flashed a weak smile then looked away. Abigail was next to the bed, eyes brimming with tears. Kelly stood behind her, face pale and drawn, her hands on Abigail's shoulders.

Dante blinked, trying to focus. Kelly wiped away tears and smiled, putting on a brave face. His eyes fell to Abigail. The steady beep of his heart monitor filled the empty space that stretched as he mustered the strength to utter the inevitable phrase that followed every human trauma, both great and small.

"Everything's going to be okay."

A cry rose in Abigail's throat as tears spilled down her cheeks. His right arm jerked up to reach out to her, but it was held down by tubes and straps, so he let it fall. Her face blurred and he had to look away, just not there.

Not *there.*

Not where his hand used to be. Somewhere safe. Down at his feet maybe, little hills under the sheets, left one lower than the other.

Not a whole lot of me left, is there? His eyes slid shut again.

CHAPTER 56

Those Goddamn Machines

A hand touched his forehead, then his cheek, the skin soft and cool. Lilac filled his nostrils and her warmth pushed away the chill that hadn't even registered, until it was gone.

Reaching up, he took the hand and squeezed it.

"I know it's too much to ask, but if anything happens to me," he said, opening his eyes.

Kelly looked down at him, holding his gaze. "Oh god, Dante." She nodded. "I'll take care of her. Nothing bad will ever happen while she's with me. I promise."

He squeezed her hand again and she leaned in close, eyes holding his before she kissed his forehead.

"Sleep," she said.

Kelly and Abigail were gone. No Colin either. Too bad. He wanted to apologize for ruining his shirt. There was only the beep and hiss of machines to keep him company. Dante scanned the various monitors and pumps, no doubt connected to the network via cable or wireless. Everything was smart these days.

It felt more like a curse.

A computer monitor was mounted to the wall via mechanical arm, folded up like a cobra, ready to strike. Countless fingerprints smudged the darkened screen. His eyes moved to a webcam perched on top of the monitor.

Am I being watched by Dark Messiah right now?

Dante looked around for a cloth or towel to toss over its glossy eye, but there was nothing. He sighed. It didn't matter. He wasn't in any condition for a round of ICU Cornhole anyway.

The beeping continued, unabated.

Those goddamn machines, he thought. They put his teeth on edge. He'd had enough of hospitals and networked smart machines to last a lifetime.

The lock snicked and the door opened, revealing a long hallway lit intermittently by harsh fluorescents. At the far end, just outside the light stood a Caduceus Medical robot, its pale arms splayed out, stock still and spiderlike. Dante stared at the thing in the shadows, icy fear stiffening his spine.

The robot leapt to life and skittered down the hallway with terrifying speed, its bladed feet leaving deep gouges in the tile. Dante began to shudder, every muscle in his body cramping as it sped closer, time crawling as it leapt into the room, fingernails sprouting at the tips of its legs as it became an over-sized, human hand.

The hand closed around his chest and tightened.

Dante jerked awake, heart hammering. Gulping air, he shuddered as cold sweat dripped down his ribs under the hospital gown. Grimacing, he shut his eyes as his right hand began to throb. He could feel the weight of it, the presence—even though he knew it was gone. He resisted the urge to wiggle his fingers, some gesture to convince himself otherwise. Squeezing his eyes tighter, he watched as faint gold and green patterns appeared, swaying like beaded curtains.

You're going to have to look sometime.

A dull ache settled into his chest as he thought of all the things he'd done with his hand, mind drifting from one memory to the next.

Silly faces on a fogged-up bus window on the way to kindergarten. That rare occasion when he raised his hand in

Ms. Gordon's second grade math class. Pictures in crayon and watercolor and, then later in colored pencil. Games of catch and jump shots. Punching Geoff Melnor in the nose, that little prick. The time he slammed his hand in a car door and it swelled up with painful throbs, like a heart had leapt up his arm to live there.

High fives with friends and Colin, even though he hated them.

The simple pleasure of itching his scrotum. Well not itching really, everybody said that. It was more of a pinch and roll.

Touching a breast in seventh grade on a dare while Anne-Marie Traynor slid a hand up his shorts. They'd both squealed as the other kids counted down from five, Dante's voice higher than hers until she pulled her hand away like she'd touched hot coals.

"His thingy jumped!"

He smiled at the memory.

All the countless handshakes, deals made, pats on the back during hugs. The rhythmic thuds of his taped hand in a tight fist, striking a speed bag in concert with the other.

Michelle's engagement ring had been put on with that hand. Her wedding ring as well, one dovetailing neatly with the other. Surprised himself when he'd eagerly cut Abigail's umbilical cord when she was born, even though he swore he never would. That hand held the phone when a faceless doctor called about Michelle. "Better that you come to the hospital, Mr. Ellis."

Better for whom?

Balled that same hand up and punched a hole in the wall when they'd told him she'd just slipped away. Enlarged heart. It was a cruel joke, that someone like Michelle would die from having too big a heart.

Rose petals.

Opening his fingers and letting them drift down on a perfect spring morning through the fragrant odor of fresh tilled earth, the sun on his face. On any other day, he might have felt blessed.

Bitter tears slid down his face but he made no move to wipe them away. He hated those tears and swore he'd never cry again—show his daughter what it meant to be strong, fearless, no matter what life threw at you. A cold fire burned out the ache inside and he shook as heat flushed his face, mouth twisted up in a scowl, the faint gold and green behind his eyes becoming a deep red.

Strange. It was like his brain needed to say goodbye to his hand so his body could accept it. That it was gone, but it was going to be okay. It was just a hand.

But it wasn't just a hand, he raged back.

It was his contact with the world. And he didn't lose it in an accident, some unforeseeable occurrence. It had been taken from him.

Stolen.

It was time.

Dante gritted his teeth, trying to maintain the swell of emotions as his right hand closed into a fist, squared off and powerful. Maybe he hadn't lost it after all.

Dante opened his eyes.

A groan escaped his lips as he saw the plastic sleeve cinched tight around his wrist. Blue light emanated from slits along the sleeve. Hoses snaked out and curved down under the bed, one draining fluid the color of liver pâté.

The phantom hand erupted with agony as it locked into a useless, gnarled claw. The heart monitor was blipping fast, but Dante barely heard it as something hissed and the pain bled away. The hand turned to warm jelly as the drugs went to work.

Footsteps echoed down the hall and Dante prepared tell the nurse that everything was fine and to kindly leave him the fuck alone. This particular misery did not love company, but thanks just the same.

The door opened and an older woman came in, dark curly hair clipped close to her skull. She wore a charcoal suit over her stocky frame with a powder blue blouse underneath. The expression on her puggish face was flat but her eyes burned with a fierce light.

"Special Agent Boucher," Dante slurred, raising the stump of his right arm. "Think I got a case now?"

CHAPTER 57

BOLO

Boucher listened as Dante recounted the chain of events leading up to now. From the first text in front of Abigail's school, up to the words scrawled in soap at Shadow Trace, to the man gaining access to his office and the amputation. The dragonfly drones. She made notes with a small pencil nub in a memo pad cupped in one hand.

Gazing around, Boucher saw the wheeled table at the end of the bed. "Do you mind?" she said as she moved the table into place. Putting the pad down, she began to write again, the letters small and blocky.

Dante liked that. No way to hack a pencil and paper.

Boucher read through her notes, made a scribble or two before fixing him with her gaze.

"The quotes are chosen for the message, not the source," Boucher said.

"Seems so. They're just using whatever serves their purpose." Dante cleared his throat. "Whatever *that* is."

"Terrorism," Boucher said. "They want to make your life hell, put your head on a swivel at all times. Create a cloud of fear that follows you everywhere you go. I use the word terrorism, Mr. Ellis, because that specific classification unlocks a lot more resources at the bureau. The question is," Boucher said.

"Why you?"

"Your boy Dmitry was supposed to help with that, but he's flown the coop."

"We'll find him. He's gone to ground, but he's still local. No record of him leaving the country yet. Got a nationwide BOLO out for him."

"BOLO?"

"Be on the lookout. He pokes his head out, we'll get him."

"He's part of this then?"

"Not likely."

"What does that mean exactly?"

"It means he's a CI, so we give him the benefit of the doubt until we find out otherwise."

"CI?" Dante said with a sigh. "Sorry, I'm not up on all my feebee lingo."

"Feebee. God, I hate that one. Confidential informant. He works with us, but not for us. That's all I can really say at this time."

"Female Body Inspector," Dante said. "Always liked that one too."

"Yeah, it's a classic."

"There's this kid, too..."

"Skylar Westfall. There's a very strong possibility he's involved."

"Dark Messiah."

Boucher held his gaze. "Yes."

"Ever heard of them?"

"No, but that's not uncommon. New groups pop up all the time, usually formed with black hats from other orgs as ideals and alliances change."

"I know that one. Hackers. Black hats and White hats, bad guys and good guys."

"Right. Speaking of good guys, you got a protection detail now. Two officers are with your daughter as we speak and I got one standing right outside this door. You don't go anywhere without them, understood?"

"Yes," Dante said. "Thanks, Agent Boucher. Really. I can't keep Abigail safe anymore like this..." Dante said motioning down at himself.

"Sorry it had to get to this point," Boucher said. "I have a daughter too."

"I remember. Patricia. Pre-med. Pepperdine."

Boucher's eyes lit up. "It ain't cheap. Especially on my salary. But it's worth it." She smiled wistfully. "She's my baby."

Dante grinned back and they sat for a moment, thinking of their girls.

"What's next?" Dante said.

Boucher's face hardened again. "Forensic examination of all your devices, security systems, professional and personal. We monitor your phone as well, so the next time they get in touch we can trace it. I assume that's okay with you?"

"At this point, yes."

"Good, because I have a court order that says I can do whatever I want anyway. I apologize now for this invasion of privacy but it must be done. We're way past deep fake donkey shows. This is an act of terrorism, Mr. Ellis. And we're going to take these fuckers down,"

Boucher slipped a hand in her coat pocket. "We found this in your office. Thought you'd want it back," she said, her voice soft as she placed a small object on the table. "I'll be in touch."

Boucher left.

The elephant pendant lay on the table, blinking lights from the machines reflecting in its shiny surface. Dante reached out to pick it up. The hoses restrained his arm, the phantom hand prickling as he let it fall back to the bed.

"Fuck," he said.

CHAPTER 58

Marionette

Red neon crept in below the curtains from outside, shifting to a soft purple every time the blue vacancy sign blinked on. Briana had asked for a room in the back, but the only one available was above the office, overlooking the parking lot. The old man behind the counter looked harmless enough. There could still be tiny cameras hidden in clocks and toilets though. She'd keep the lights off.

Sitting on the edge of the twin mattress, hands worried together in knots, Briana wondered what she was going to do. Her laptop sat beside her, closed up tight. She wasn't ready to face the onslaught of shocked and angry responses that likely filled her inbox. Hopefully things wouldn't seem so bleak in the light of morning. Her exhausted mind flitted through the evening's events before seizing on the moment she heard those terrible words.

Daddy knows.

The bewildered taxi driver sat there, staring, as she pushed in through the front security gate, panic flaring up inside as she dashed up the stairs and down the hall to the apartment door. Hesitating, her hand gripped the doorknob. Leish had to have known about the camera in the hyena's eye. She'd also convinced Briana to dance for the webcam show. Her face flushed.

Had her father watched the video yet?

Briana had to get out of here. She turned the knob and pushed the door open, letting it swing wide until it rested against the stopper.

The apartment was dark except for a blue wash from the television. It was a reality show, the volume low, voices barely a murmur. Leish lay curled up on the couch wearing only a long t-shirt, her back to the door. She remained still as Briana strode down the hallway to her room.

Tearing open drawers, she stuffed everything into her suitcase then went back down the hall to the studio door. It was dark inside, so she kept the door open to see. Grabbing a plastic bag full of shoes that hung on the clothing rack, she emptied them on the floor. Briana hopped on the stage and swept all the money that still lay there inside the bag as she crept backward. Her foot dropped off the edge and she stumbled back into the table piled with masks, causing some to fall.

Why did Leish have all these fucking masks? she wondered.

Briana shoved them off onto the floor. One of the brittle porcelain ones shattered, but it did little to quell her anger. Something dark lay among the bright shards and she knelt to get a closer look. It was a stack of crisp one hundred-dollar bills, held together by a thick rubber band. That went into the bag as well.

If it was stealing, she didn't care. Consider it asshole tax.

Back in her room, Briana stuffed the bag of cash in her suitcase and sat on the lid so she could snap the latches. On her way out, her hand closed around the barrel of the shotgun, still draped under the dazzle camo. She shoved the box of shells into her hip pocket and walked into the living room.

Leish was sitting up, knees pulled to her chest, arms wrapped around her legs. Her face was blank as Briana swept past. A dark bruise encircled each eye. Dried blood smeared from her nose across one cheek. Briana stopped, mouth falling open as she stared in shock.

"Oh my God, Leish."

The TV flashed, went dark then flashed again before the video of them together in the bedroom played in a loop. Leish stood, walked over and clutched the top of the screen. With a ragged scream she wrenched it off the wall with a shriek of rending plastic. She danced out of the way as the huge TV tilted over, the upper corner crashing into the floor. The screen shattered with a rippling crack. The whole thing laid askew, wires stretched taut from where they disappeared into the wall. Connections popped free with a twang as the weight of the huge screen slid all the way to the floor with a thud, sparks leaping from the rear as it crashed onto the floor.

Leish took one step back then collapsed to her knees. "We did what they wanted. But they still sent it to everybody," she said. "Every one of my contacts. My little brother saw it. All his friends saw it. He's only eleven years old."

Briana let the suitcase and gun fall from her grasp. Rushing over, she knelt down in front of Leish, grabbing her shoulders. The young woman blinked, the light in her eyes gone. Briana shook her roughly.

"Look at me, Leish. Who did this?"

"Wanna hear a joke?" Leish said, her voice far off. "What do you tell a bitch with two black eyes?"

Briana let out a shuddering sigh. She'd already heard this one. "Nothing," she said. "You've already told the bitch everything she needs to know."

Leish looked up at her, lips trembling, light dawning in her eyes.

"You too?" she said, eyes brimming with tears.

Briana nodded, then held the broken young woman as she sobbed. After a time when she'd quieted some, Briana took Leish's hands in hers.

"Come with me," Briana said.

"Where?"

"Away from Mel and scumbag movie producers and this whole, shitty, fake ass life."

"No," Leish said, pulling her hands free. "He didn't mean for it to be so bad. It just, got away from him."

"That first day, when you showed me the studio, I wondered why you had all those masks. He hits you, and you hide it. For him."

Leish opened her mouth to speak then closed it again. Her face darkened and she turned away. "You don't understand."

"You don't have to live like this," Briana said. "I ran away. You can too. Come with me now and we'll figure it out, together. Okay?"

"I love him," Leish said as she rolled on her side, face turned away. When she spoke again her voice was muffled. "Mel got into trouble with some people called Dark Messiah. Hackers or something, I don't know. Real trouble. They were going to dox him, ruin his life. They needed somebody to do something for them. I chose you. Nothing personal. Mel begged for my help. You should have seen him. He was so lost, like a little boy. I had to do it."

"So, you're like them." Briana's vision blurred. "You're *worse* than them. At least Mel and that fucking producer are honest about what they are. You're not a hyena, Leish. You hide behind this girl power charade but underneath it all, you're just another whore in training…"

Briana stopped, her mother's words tasting bitter as she heard them fall from her lips. Leish lay folded up on the floor, like a marionette who'd just had her strings cut. Her pale arms and legs looked so thin, lusterless blue hair fanned out over the floor in a ratty tangle. Sour heat erupted in Briana's stomach, nauseous and panicky.

She had to get away.

Backing up, she grabbed the suitcase and gun before rushing out the door and down to the elevator, the dazzle camo fluttering behind. She stumbled inside as the doors opened and sat down hard on her suitcase, biting back the scream she knew would break loose sooner or later.

Just not now.

She found herself down in front of the Whiskey a Go Go, this time with a crowd of people lined up to get inside. How excited she'd been to be on that very spot. It felt like a million years ago. Ignoring the drunken jeers behind her, Briana hopped in as a yellow taxi pulled up to the curb.

"Take me to a motel. Someplace cheap," she said, falling into the back seat. It was the same cabbie who'd dropped her off when she'd first arrived. Snowy white hair and pale gray eyes. With a nod, he lurched into traffic then cut a wide U turn, nosing the car east.

The bright lights fell away behind them. She felt his eyes on hers in the rear-view mirror.

"I remember you," he said.

"I think I'll take that advice now."

"Go home."

"I can't," Briana said, her voice small. She laid down across the seat and let herself sob. It was an ugly cry, but it helped take the edge off a little.

"Maybe it's time to find a new home," the cabbie said.

A horn bleated outside the hotel, startling her out of her reverie. Briana crept to the window and peered outside. Only one street lamp burned out of the five or so that dotted the lot, its greenish glow barely pushing back the night. A few cars and trucks were scattered throughout the motel parking lot, beat up and dingy. Most of the other rooms were dark. In the sky, the lights of a plane winked, shimmering, screened through the low, orange clouds trapped by the heat.

Briana crawled back to the bed and lay down, curling up on her side. She hadn't seen one drone since leaving the apartment. *And why would I?* she thought. They were done with her. She regretted that little trick she'd pulled with the retrocam. She was just so tired of being used and discarded, feeling completely out of control of her own life.

And now, her life was in ruins.

She fell into a fitful sleep and dreamed of dragonflies hunting her through a field of yellowed corn stalks as an icy wind shrieked a discordant hymn of loss overhead.

CHAPTER 59

Heavy Hand

The cat clock tick-tocked out in the kitchen, a reminder that life still marched on. Gary could picture its eyes looking back and forth, watching without seeing. He couldn't remember being able to hear it in their bedroom before.

It grated on his frayed nerves.

Gail lay next to him, her breathing soft and deep. He envied her. Behind closed eyes the hand lay waiting for him, twitching on the carpet. Along with the not entirely unpleasant odor of cauterized flesh thick in the air. Gary would never eat ham again.

His eyes slid shut.

The hand was still warm as he picked it up by its finger, heavier than he thought it would be. He couldn't remember running out of there, just found himself on a large red H in the middle of a helipad.

A rapid chopping sound from above caused his spine to ratchet up tight as he gazed skyward. The large dragonfly drone descended and Gary crouched, holding the black box up like it was a serving platter.

The hand shifted inside.

He squeezed his eyes shut, not wanting to see that horrible thing descend toward him with its shiny green body, the tail curling down as it hovered. The click of its thin legs tapping on the box made him cringe and he almost cried out when one touched his wrist.

The weight of the box disappeared and only then did he gaze upward. The dark silhouette of the drone shrank against the night sky before shooting off and out of sight.

Gary bent over and retched, placing his forehead against the warm surface of the landing pad. Sweat poured off him as he heaved, sliding down his face before dripping off. He couldn't seem to catch his breath but he had to go, escape before building security came back on. Only five minutes to get out. Lurching to his feet, he stumbled back inside.

The elevator ride down had been the longest of his life.

Throwing his legs over the edge of the bed, Gary peered into the dim rectangle of the open doorway yawning before him. Nightmarish images of that night danced across the darkness.

He stood and went to the bathroom, easing the door shut before flicking on the light. Gary wanted his wife to sleep, but he also hoped she'd wake up. Being alone with this terrible secret, one that could destroy all their lives if anyone else knew was crushing him. He couldn't tell her, of course, but at least he wouldn't be alone. Splashing cold water on his face did little to calm the knot in his stomach.

"Get it together," he said to the bleary-eyed man in the mirror. "You got a job interview tomorrow."

The house temperature remained at a solid seventy-eight. The twins were sleeping through the night. No more mystery deliveries, no more blips of the alarm.

No more texts.

Everything was back to normal, like it had never happened. Gary hadn't seen another drone since that night on the helipad. But the last text he'd received had run right through him like a cold knife.

Would that feeling ever go away? he wondered.

The light went off with a click and Gary sat on the edge of the bed again. Gail didn't even stir. He picked up his phone from the nightstand. Tapping on the screen, he brought up the final text from Dark Messiah. With a flick of his fingertip, he sorted through each of the images embedded within the body of the text.

Videos of the kids running at the park, wrestling on the carpet, sleeping in their cribs, the video tinted green by the baby monitor camera. Gail driving to work, sitting at her desk, having lunch with a man he didn't recognize. The last image was especially unnerving, him putting his cursed Adirondacks out at the curb next to the trash cans. The message was clear, but the following text at the very bottom drove the point home.

Dark Messiah is watching you.

CHAPTER 60

Digital Handshake

"Good morning, Dante. I'm Dr. Arellano, but you can call me Alexis. Ready to start your rehabilitation?"

Alexis was slender, about forty or so, short black hair pulled back into a pony tail. She wore a long white coat over teal scrubs.

"I guess so," Dante said.

The plastic cuff eased off into her gloved hands, the blue light winking off as she unplugged the cable. She placed the cuff on a tray, then wound up the cable with tight efficiency.

"Looking good. See?" She gently raised Dante's arm.

He glanced at the bright pink flesh along the suture lines before looking away.

"It gets easier," Alexis said, dark eyes smiling. She lifted a pant-leg cuff, revealing a prosthetic foot. Dante gazed down in surprise before she let it drop. She pulled her gloves off with a snap and dropped them into a trash can. "What would you say your pain level is?"

"Not bad. About a two, I guess." He grimaced, grabbing his wrist. "Just went up to a seven."

"Phantom pains? There's medication you can try. It's helped me."

Dante took a few deep breaths before shaking his head. "No

more meds. I'm going to be hooked on opiates as it is." He flexed his arm. "How has it healed so fast?"

"We used therapies similar to your toe amputation but with one a major difference."

"Oh yeah? How's that?" Dante asked.

"There are five main nerves in the arm. During surgery, I mapped each one to a spot on the flap used to cover the amputation. It's called sensory reinnervation. If you rub a finger over them, it'll feel pretty strange, but this will allow for a direct interface with the prosthetic you'll be receiving. We've partnered with a prosthetic company who specializes in hands. They're probably the best in the world and they're right here on site. If you agree, you're about to be fitted with their latest and greatest prototype. And let me tell you, this is no metal hook. I think you'll find the experience to be...interesting. Let's go take a look, okay?"

The stern looking police officer outside his room joined them as they walked down the hall to the elevator. Probably wondering what he'd done to pull this shit duty. As they ascended, Dante used his left hand to text Kelly with his thumb. It was slow going and he only dropped his phone once. Alexis either didn't notice, or pretended not to. The cop kept his eyes straight ahead.

Kelly texted him back and told him everything was fine and yes, Abigail was doing her homework. The policemen were fans—one knew every episode of *Catwalk*. She ended the text with a laugh emoji.

Dante felt a touch of jealousy.

They went down the hall to a door marked Rehabilitation Center and Alexis pushed it open. The officer stayed outside, mouth set in a grim line.

The rehab room was a large, open space with pale green walls and dark wood laminate flooring. There was a pair of wood walking rails, a set of steps, ramps, treadmills, mats, exercise balls and an above-ground hot tub. A table nearby had a mirror mounted down the center.

"What's with the table?" Dante said.

"Mirror therapy. Helps with phantom pains," Alexis said. "I'll show you how to use it later."

Along the left wall was a long table sporting prosthetic legs of various styles and builds. There were curved metal blades for running, others were metal tubes extending from a black plastic socket to an articulated foot inside a shoe. The selection of legs further down appeared very high tech, brushed metal tubes and carbon fiber with red metallic accents.

An older woman reclined in the tub, head barely visible above the bubbling surface of the water, pepper gray hair slicked back. She opened one brilliant green eye and gave Dante a quick glance before closing it again.

"Don't leave me in here too long Lexi," the woman said.

"You're supposed to be relaxing, Celia. Remember?"

"How can I relax with you two jaw jacking?" Celia said

"C'mon," Alexis said, laughing. "We're over here."

Dante followed her to the other side of the room. Along the entire wall was a frosted glass office, the gray panel next to the door glowing red. Etched on the door in silver letters were the words: Plexus Voltaic. Soft, dark shapes were visible inside.

Alexis badged in and stepped aside, following Dante as the door closed behind them. Soft light bloomed overhead. Along the back wall, an advanced looking 3D printer spanned the width of the room, various nozzles and arms visible through the clear panel on its face.

A table with two vertically mounted hand prostheses stood to the right. The first one was a typical metal hook type, the forearm socket made from age-stained wood. The claw was dull with patina and checked with rust. A tall glass dome enclosed it over a wooden base. "Break glass in case of Luddites" was engraved on a brass strip along the bottom.

"This... is the past," Alexis said as she walked ahead of him and turned, motioning to the other arm mounted there. "And this... is the future."

The other prosthetic was a hand and wrist mounted to an

arm socket. The bottom edge of the socket extended all the way to the elbow. The hand and fingers were a matte black. Rubber pads were on the tip of each finger with a larger pad across the palm. The finger joints gleamed brushed metal silver.

"What do you think?" Alexis said.

"Cool," Dante said. "Bionic?"

"Neuroprosthetic. The evolution of myoelectric prosthetics controlled by muscle contraction. Myoelectrics can only perform simple hand poses, usually open and close. This one is different. The secret is through its interaction. The reinnervation procedure will allow you to not only move this hand, but also feel temperature and pressure as well. You'll actually feel contact with objects. It also uses machine learning to improve its function based on how you interface with it. Like I said... the future."

"I'm guessing my insurance doesn't cover this."

"No, it's a prototype, worth about three million. Military grade, which means it's tough. And strong. We've been waiting for the right subject. We think that's you."

"Why not use someone in the military?" Dante said. "Must be plenty of...subjects."

"The government won't pay for this level of rehabilitation. Not even close. If this arm could be weaponized, though, I'm sure they'd be all for it."

"I see," Dante said.

"The only thing we ask in return is the data generated during use for application to future prosthetics."

Dante narrowed his eyes as he looked at the hand, its fingers slightly curved. "No way."

"This isn't like the Caduceus that maimed your foot," Alexis said. "Not even close."

"You know about that?"

"It can't be hacked, at least not remotely. No wireless. The only way to interface is behind this locked panel."

Alexis rotated the arm and pointed to a small panel on the back of the hand with a recessed lock.

"You don't even have the key. I visit once a week, hook it up to a secure laptop, download the data and apply any updates. This is about to become an extremely competitive market and we are very strict with security. At least try it first. It should help with those phantom pains as well. If you don't like it, no problem. You can go with ol' woody down there in the glass case."

Dante gazed at the hand, touching various parts, bent one of the fingers. He thumbed the panel but it stayed closed, the lock holding tight.

"Okay," he said. "Let's give it a shot."

Dante winced as Alexis slid the newly minted socket onto his arm, still warm from the printing process. After a laser scan and a fourteen-point tissue compliance measurement along his entire arm, the 3D printer began the process of layering a composite of materials together. The new socket was tailor-made, firm or flexible based on the soft or bony parts of his forearm. The stump was still tender, but the socket itself slipped on easily and fit well. Flexible straps crisscrossed his inner elbow and curved around the back. He flexed his arm to get a feel for it.

It felt good. Solid. Even without a hand on it yet.

Alexis brought a black box over and set it on the table between them. She lifted the lid and removed a small silver cylinder.

"The battery," she said. "It'll last a week and takes five minutes to charge. Graphene. Nobody has these yet. Going to change everything."

She bent his arm at the elbow and pressed a button on the underside. A hatch opened up and she snapped the battery into place and closed the hatch again with a click.

"Now comes the fun part."

Alexis reached into the box and withdrew a new hand similar to the one Dante had seen earlier. Dangling from the bottom was a clutch of small sensors, tipped in gold. There were five in all.

"This next part is going to feel a little weird. When I plug it in, the sensors will align to the nerve map, interface, then run a diagnostic. The hand will then enter a short learning phase. When I say, try and move your fingers, one at a time, starting with your thumb. Ready?"

Dante nodded. Alexis lifted the hand, inserted it into the socket and twisted it forty-five degrees until it snapped into place with a muffled clunk. It immediately jumped to life and began curling and flexing several times.

Dante flinched as the sensors found his nerves with a series of mild shocks. Each finger straightened and curled in turn before relaxing into a natural rest pose.

"Go ahead. Whenever you're ready," Alexis said.

Dante wiggled his thumb and the hand responded, but with a noticeable lag. He tried again and the thumb jerked to life much quicker, responding faster and smoother until it almost felt right. He wiggled his fingers and they went through the same adjustment until they rotated smoothly in turn, little motors whirring. He rotated his hand and the prosthetic rotated in kind.

Dante glanced at Alexis and grinned. "That weird phantom feeling. It's gone."

"Up top," she said, holding a palm up.

Dante raised his new hand and slapped it against Alexis' palm and he gasped.

"I felt that!" he said, running his left hand over the prosthetic.

"It only works on the finger and palm pads, but you'll be able to tell hot and cold, pressure and feedback when you touch something. Helps for picking up small objects. Speaking of which..."

Alexis reached into the box and removed a tray holding a series of small cubes and spheres of different sizes and materials. Some were shiny metal, others rough or smooth, some wood, and some were squishy. "For practicing. Try one," she said.

"I have another idea," Dante said, flexing the fingers again. There was a slight lag still, but it felt worlds better than a stump. He extended his hand, fingers splayed wide. She smiled and slipped her hand into his.

"Easy," she said. "Like I said, it's strong."

He eased the pressure and they shook.

"Thank you, Alexis," Dante said, eyes bright. "I never thought I'd shake someone's hand ever again."

"You're welcome," she said, blinking back tears of her own.

Loud splashing erupted from the rehab room and they hurried out of the small office. Celia was trying to climb out of the hot tub, slender arms thrashing about.

"Hey Lexi!" she called out. "Quit making eyes over there and get me out of this stupid tub!"

CHAPTER 61

Westfall

Abigail lay curled up next to Dante in the hospital bed, her breathing soft and even. He swept a lock of hair back from her face then gazed down at Kelly where she lay sleeping in a cot next to the bed. When she'd come in earlier with Abigail, Kelly was pushing the cot in on its wheels, no discussion. Was she here just for Abigail? She must be, but Dante was glad she was here.

The room was dark, lit only by the soft glow from mercury vapor lights that bled in through the slotted blinds. A traffic signal across the street rotated through its cycle, painting the walls in a faint green, then yellow, then red. Dante reached out and picked up the plastic cup holding his pain meds then tipped it to his lips. He swallowed the large, white pills with a chase of water, all using the prosthetic hand.

Dante smiled. He was getting the hang of it.

Laid out before him on the bed table were the training objects Alexis had given him. He squeezed one of the rubber cubes, the hand whirring, then placed it back on the table. He grasped a wooden block next and rubbed his finger over a series of grooves cut into the surface. It wasn't like feeling exactly, more like subtle vibrations. Alexis told him it would feel more natural as his brain adjusted to the sensory input. Neuroplasticity, she called it, the brain's ability to adjust to changes and remap parts to account for physical changes to the body or the brain itself.

His phone buzzed, sliding across the table before he lifted it to his ear.

"Dante Ellis," he said, voice low.

Silence.

"Hello?"

Clicks followed by a faint hiss, then a far-off voice, mechanical and distorted. Dante pressed the phone to his ear. The voice spoke again, louder this time.

"I need to talk to you but we don't have much time. In person if possible."

A fierce heat burned in Dante's gut and he gripped the phone tighter. "I'd love to meet you in person Skylar, so I can smash your fucking head in."

"I know who's doing this," Skylar said.

"Dark Messiah," Dante hissed. "That's you, right? Real cute."

Skylar sighed. It was a clipped, electronic sound. "I understand why you're angry but I can help you. I tried to before, in the parking garage remember? Bothrops Asper. If you'd just put that flash drive in." There were more clicks and a low boop. "Shit. Time's up. I'll try and contact you again soon."

Skylar disconnected and Dante lowered the phone. It vibrated again and he connected.

"Anything?" he said.

"Nothing," Bouchard said. "The call was encrypted and he wasn't on long enough. We'll get him next time."

"Who the hell is this guy?"

"We're working on it." Boucher hung up.

Dante tossed his phone on the table where it landed with a loud clack. He checked to see if he'd woken the girls, then slipped the prosthetic hand off, and laid it on the table. The oxycodone began kicking in as he curled up next to Abigail, glad this was his last night here.

Bothrops Asper. That was the second time Skylar had said that. Dante reminded himself to do a search on it as he drifted off to sleep.

CHAPTER 62

Spirit

Briana opened her eyes.

The early morning sun knifed in under the blinds and she rolled over and squeezed them shut again.

Dark Messiah.

That was what the taxi driver had said. It sounded like one of those cheesy hacker names from television but at least now they had a name. She found her laptop among the rumpled sheets and lifted the screen, mousing over to tap into the free Wi-Fi the motel provided. Even shit boxes like this place had wireless. A list of available connections popped up. First thing she wanted to do was use the Find My Phone app and track down her phone. She was about to double click on the Wi-Fi icon then stopped, slowly closing the screen. If she connected now, they'd find her.

Did that matter anymore? Maybe. After what I'd pulled, they were probably keeping an eye out. But how dangerous were they, really? They could ruin a life, that's for sure, but how much farther would they go?

She recalled of the black box with the shiny blades inside.

Better to stay hidden, she thought.

Briana emptied the contents of her suitcase out onto the bed. After changing into a clean T-shirt and shorts, she swept her hair back into a tight pony tail. It was going to be another hot day.

Dumping out the cash from the plastic bag, she separated the bills into even stacks by denomination before folding the wad in half and stuffing it into her hip pocket. She drew a finger down the stack of hundred dollar bills she'd found under the masks. There were eleven in all.

Briana went to the small rickety table next to the door and knelt down. There was a thin crevice where the metal legs of the table crisscrossed the underside. She tucked the stack of bills in there. Money wasn't going to be a problem, at least for a little while. The room was only sixty-nine bucks a night.

Sixty-nine, she thought. *Mom's right, this place is infected.*

The strange, zebra-striped garment lay draped over the gun where she placed it in the corner. Dazzle camo, Leish had called it. They looked like a kid's pajamas. She didn't understand how it worked exactly, but it was worth a try. It went on with a shooshing whisper as she zipped it closed. The air was stuffy, but she felt safe and hidden.

Invisible.

She plucked the key off the table and left, locking the door behind her. *Where to put the key?* Gazing down at the suit, she noticed a small slit stitched along one of the black lines near the waist. The key slid in and disappeared. Briana walked to the stairs and started down, slowing as she reached the first landing.

Am I really doing this?

A bell rang out from below, followed by a clatter as a bicycle dropped onto its side. A middle-aged woman with frizzy blond hair clumped up the stairs, a slender brown cigarette perched on her lips. She startled as she reached the landing, seeing Briana for the first time. The woman's yellowed eyes regarded her with contempt.

"Halloween's over, asshole," she said in a raspy croak as she pushed past and continued her way up. The rickety metal frame of the stairs shook with each heavy footfall.

The sun beat down on the dazzle camo, the heat inside building to an uncomfortable swelter. Briana clenched her jaw and stared up at the woman, hating her. She hated her halter top and jean shorts, the rank smell of her cigarette smoke, her chemical-damaged hair.

"You know what? Fuck you!" she screamed.

It felt good.

The feeling melted away as the woman jerked to a halt, but Briana held her ground. The older woman's head slowly rotated, eyes glaring down over one spotted shoulder, hooded under thick eye shadow. It was bright blue, like the belly of a lizard. For a strange, surreal moment Briana felt as if she were gazing at her future self, a version that *would* be if she didn't change her life right here and now.

The woman grinned, all gaps and yellow teeth. "That's the spirit," she said, clomped to the door at the top of the stairs and disappeared inside.

CHAPTER 63

Bait

Dante leaned against the rail and looked down at the tree-dotted slope that swept from the rear deck of his house. Crows cawed back and forth among the treetops, embroiled in a territorial dispute. Boucher sat on a deck chair sipping coffee as the sun crept up in the eastern sky.

"So, what do you think?" Boucher said.

"I don't like the thought of Abigail being away from me," Dante said, "but if you think it's the right thing to do."

"I do. It's just until we catch who's doing this. A week or two, tops."

"Where would you take her?"

"It's best if you don't know where, but it's close by. One of our secure locations along with two other agents I've selected. They're good people. I trust them. And Kelly of course. Don't think I could have stopped her if I wanted to."

"And I stay here as bait," Dante said.

"Yes. Once we get Abigail secure on the plane, I'll come back here. The techs are installing our equipment right now. Then we turn your home network back on and connect all your devices."

"Which airport?"

Boucher said nothing.

"Right. Better if I don't know. Then what?"

"We wait," Boucher said. "It's a big part of the job, unfortunately. Ninety percent boredom, ten percent terror. When they try another breach, we'll get 'em."

"Just like Skylar Westfall."

Boucher remained silent, sipping her coffee with a noisy slurp. "It's a shitty deal," she said. "But it's all we got right now. I have to ask. Do you have some sort of protection?"

"Protection?"

"A gun. Do you have a gun."

He raised his prosthetic hand. "And how exactly would I shoot it?"

"Doesn't answer my question."

Dante sighed. "Why can't Abigail just stay here?"

"She can."

"But..."

"Do you really want her to be here if something happens?" Boucher said.

Dante looked at the prosthetic hand before letting it drop. "No," he said. "Jesus, what a shit show." He glanced at Boucher. "I hate to ask..."

"Colin Murray. Age thirty-six. He's got a juvenile record, but it's sealed. Lives alone in Brentwood. Studio apartment at a place called Matisse, but he's rarely there. Spends most of his time at work. Software engineer for Kellerman Digital specializing in machine learning applications for big data management. They're flagged but that's not uncommon."

"What do you mean, flagged?"

"They have contracts with the government so it means they're hands-off for surveillance of any kind without express permission."

"Sounds ominous," Dante said.

"Not really. A lot of companies are flagged but that protection doesn't extend outside company property. When employees leave the grounds they're up for grabs."

"What else is he up to?"

"Eating takeout, a few hours online through an encrypted connection and sleeping. We took a peek. Chess and anime mostly."

"That's it?"

"He talks to you," Boucher said.

"What?"

"He talks to you, like you're right there. Whole conversations. We only get one half, of course."

"Jesus. What about?"

"Boring nerd stuff. Games, movies, stuff like that. He mentioned something about "a place" or "the place" one time. Mean anything to you?"

"No," Dante said. He could feel Boucher staring at him.

"You know he was in the hospital for almost six months? That's a helluva long time in a nut house."

Dante sighed. "What are you saying? Does he have something to do with this or not?"

"Well, he's infatuated with you, that much is sure. But listen, a stiff wind would knock this guy down. If anyone spoke harshly to him, he'd likely piss his pants. Maybe he's running a game on us. Mentally unstable software engineer by day, genius hacker terrorist by night. Profiling is not my thing, but he just doesn't fit. From where I sit, he wants to be your friend again, not ruin your life."

"Well, good," Dante said. "That's a relief, of sorts."

"You could do better, but it's funny what life gives you. Take Kelly, for example."

"I'm lucky to have her," Dante said. "She's a good friend."

"Oh, you don't have her," Boucher said with a snort. "When my husband left me, you know what I would have done to find someone who not only loved my daughter but wasn't a complete psychopath? I mean these things just don't happen."

"She doesn't feel that way about me."

"My god," Boucher said. "People are stupid sometimes."

"Don't remember asking you."

"Don't care. When you get to my age, made the mistakes I

have and you see somebody being colossally dumb, it's hard to let it alone."

"Great. *Anything* new on Skylar Westfall?"

Boucher set her coffee down on the table and leaned forward, hands clasped together in her lap. "It's simple, Dante. She just wants to know that you care. Really care," Boucher said. "And mean it."

Dante opened his mouth to retort then closed it. "That's good advice actually."

"Good boy. Agreeing with old people is the only way to shut them up."

"You're not that old." Dante said, waggling his eyebrows. "Maybe I need someone like you in my life."

Boucher shook her head. "Nah, I don't go for cripples, even at my age."

Dante glanced sharply at her and they both laughed.

It felt good to laugh.

They fell silent as Boucher lifted her coffee and sipped. Dante glanced back down the hill. The crows had quieted down, having found some sort of tacit agreement.

"Okay. Let's put Abigail somewhere safe," Dante said. "When?"

Boucher held his gaze a moment before speaking. "The plane leaves in two hours."

CHAPTER 64

Stay

Dante rapped his knuckles on the door frame. The prosthetic hand almost sounded normal to him. Abigail and Kelly looked up from where they were snuggled together in bed. They were reading Bunny My Honey. It was a little kid's book, but it was one of Abigail's favorites. Her mother used to read it all to her all the time.

"Mind if I come in?" Dante said.

"What's going on, Daddy?" Abigail said, clutching the book to her chest. Her eyes were large and watchful as if Dante might vanish any second. As he sat on the bed, Kelly slid her legs over the edge to leave.

"No, stay," he said.

Kelly nodded and sat cross-legged next to Abigail, sliding a comforting arm behind his daughter's back.

"So, you know some bad people have hurt me. We don't know who. Yet. But the FBI are going to catch whoever did this to me," Dante said. "Okay? They're going to get them."

Abigail nodded, waiting.

"But you're not safe here."

"No," she said, eyes widening.

"Abigail, honey, you're just going to go on a little trip with Kelly to a safe place for just a few days until this thing is over."

"Don't talk to me like I'm a baby. I need to stay here and take care of you," Abigail said, tears brimming. She flung the book aside and she squeezed her right hand with her left.

Kelly rubbed her back. "This is how we take care of your dad, Abby. By going somewhere safe so the bad guys can't hurt you. It'll be a little scary, but I'll be with you the whole time and trust me, nothing bad will happen when I'm with you." Kelly looked at Dante. "Nothing."

"We can stay in touch with these," Dante said. He pulled two phones out and gave one to Abigail. "Spy phones. Agent Boucher gave them to me. They're totally secure and we can talk whenever we want."

Abigail stared at the phone in her hands before setting it down. She looked up at Kelly, her lip trembling, then slid out of bed and went to the dresser. Lifting the lid of Michelle's jewelry box, Abigail reached inside before coming back over.

Wiping her face, she said, "Do you have the mommy elephant?"

Dante slid a hand into his pocket and pulled out his wallet. He opened it then shook the wallet over her open hand. The elephant pendant dropped into her palm. She took the baby and snapped its trunk into the larger elephant's tail and held them up with a teary smile.

"You found it," Dante said.

Abigail nodded and blinked, fresh tears sliding down her cheeks. Then she unsnapped the two and gave Dante the larger elephant back before wiping her face.

"Keep it safe. When this is all over and I come back home, we'll put them together and never take them apart again. Deal?" she said holding up her pinky.

Dante hooked his left pinky with hers. He raised his right hand up to Kelly, the motors whirring softly as the hand closed except for the smallest finger. "You're part of this too," he said.

Kelly gazed at Abigail, then swallowed before linking her pinky with his mechanical one, eyes locked on his.

"Deal."

CHAPTER 65

Safe Now

Dante sat on the couch, muscle bunching at his jaw. Letting Abigail go had been the hardest thing he'd ever done. If Kelly hadn't gone with her, there was no way he could have gone through with it. Colin sat nearby, here for moral support, but he looked worse off than Dante, foot twitching off time with his face. A soft knock came at the front door and Dante rose, putting an eye to the peephole before opening it.

"Thanks for stopping by, Naomi," Dante said.

She stood in the open doorway, limned in early morning light, dressed in a charcoal pencil skirt and blazer. He couldn't remember a time when she'd looked more beautiful. Her perfume wafted in, along with the pleasant odors of fresh cut grass and damp stone. A police officer shot him a quick salute from the end of the walkway and Dante waved back with his prosthetic hand. Naomi flinched before spitting a nervous laugh, staring at the hand before her eyes slid away. She flashed a quick smile at him, but it looked more like she'd smelled something foul. She moved past him, eyes scanning the room as if she'd never been here before.

"Hello," Colin called from the couch. He sat on the edge of a cushion, knee bouncing up and down.

She nodded toward him then turned back to Dante. Her face

was pale and she licked her lips, tongue darting in and out.

"You okay?" Dante said quietly.

"Fine," she said, eyes locked on the hand again. She reached out to touch it before pulling away. "Oh my god," she said, her eyes finding his. "Dante..."

"I'm fine," he said, hating the pity and disgust etched neatly on her face.

Glancing away, she blinked and smoothed down the front of her suit jacket. "I just can't stop seeing it. All that blood."

Dante hesitated. He wanted to reach out and hold her, tell her everything was fine, but the way she had looked at him made his face burn. *Can't say I blame her. She did catch a mouthful of blood.*

The prosthetic hand tightened.

"How are things at the studio?" he said, voice strained.

"Great," Naomi said, blinking. "Everything's great. A few people have quit since the summer bash, but we hired a few contractors to cover..." she trailed off, licking her lips again.

"Naomi?"

"Sorry. I'm just not good at this sort of thing." She exhaled a loud hiss as she swept past Dante toward the front door. "I can't do this right now."

"Can't do what right now?"

She opened the door then stopped for a moment before glancing over her shoulder. A tear slipped from her eye. "This is my last week with Ellis Media. I'm sorry."

The door stood open, her heels ticking on the flat stones of the walkway as Naomi made her escape. Dante went slowly over to the door and closed it again, twisting the deadbolt. Her perfume drifted through the heady scent of warm morning air. He walked back to the couch and dropped onto it, staring at the table.

"Sorry," Colin said.

"Figured a mouthful of blood would've brought us closer."

"Jesus, Dante," Colin said, shaking his head.

"You meet a lot of people in this business, you know?

You have drinks, get together at conferences, become friendly working on a projects together. Some you get to fuck." Dante shifted in his seat, frowning. "Play tennis or basketball with some, cards with others. Exchange cell numbers. Text witty little jabs. I got plenty of witty little jabs after that fucking deep fake video went out, I'll tell you that. You should have seen Bainbridge, eyes boggling at the thought of sticking it to me."

"Never liked that guy," Colin said.

"After my hand got cut off though, total silence. Not one of them so much as texted or called. Like I'm infected with losing and it's catchy. None of them are here now. Only you."

Colin looked back at him, the slight smile on his face melting. "Well, I got a lot to make up for," he said.

Dante turned and stared at his childhood best friend, heart thudding slow and painful in his chest like a kettle drum. "This really sucks, man."

Colin swallowed, throat bobbing up and down. "Everything'll be fine. Abigail is with Kelly and she's got ol' battle ax Boucher watching over her. Man, that is one tough lady. Five hours she questioned me," Colin said. "Gotta say though, it was pretty cool going to the FBI office. Boucher had Fat Burger delivered. Classy." Colin gazed at Dante. "Abigail's safe now. That's all that matters."

Safe now.

Dante nodded with a grimace, flexing his prosthetic hand.

"I didn't mean it like that," Colin said. "You could probably punch through a wall with that thing."

Dante raised the hand and tightened it into a fist. "Not really. It's tough but I was told not to overdo it." He rotated the wrist and extended the middle digit. "Hey, this finger works."

"Well, that might be good for the ladies," Colin said. "Just try jacking it with that thing."

Dante's spy phone rang and he scooped it out of his pocket. It was a video call from Abigail. He stabbed the connect button and Abigail's face filled the screen.

"Hi Daddy! We're here!"

"That's great," Dante said. "Where's Kelly?"

The view shifted over. "Right here. We have half an hour until our flight. We went right through, no screening or anything." Kelly leaned in closer and whispered. "This FBI stuff has its perks."

"We're not supposed to talk about that," Abigail said off screen.

"Oh, right," Kelly said, putting a finger to her lips. Abigail's face appeared again.

"I wish you were going with us. I miss you."

"I miss you too."

"And Daddy?"

"Yes?"

She opened her mouth to speak then stopped as her head turned away, revealing the terminal behind her.

"Abigail?" Dante said, pulling the phone closer.

Faint shouts rose up followed by shrill screams as people crowded away from a bank of windows. Dante rose, staring at the screen in shock. Abigail began running, the phone swinging wildly as Kelly urged her on. A massive flare of white erupted and Abigail screamed as the screen went black.

CHAPTER 66

Airport

Dante raced through the house toward the garage, frantic images from the spy phone replaying in his head. Through the surging panic of bodies, he saw an ugly red strip of carpet next to gray, white walls with large windows, blue stripe along the top.

He knew exactly where they were.

"Colin, come on!" Dante called over his shoulder, throwing a quick glance backward.

The thin man sat hunched over on the couch, eyes on the floor.

He didn't move.

The door slammed open with a bang as Dante dashed into the garage. He punched the garage door button as he sped by and it began to chatter upward, blinding light causing him to squint as he yanked the driver door up on the Mako and ducked inside. The garage door continued its upward climb, steady and slow.

Too slow.

Dante slammed into reverse and pinned the accelerator, hands clutching the wheel. The car surged backward and crashed through the garage door, hurtling ragged chunks of wood and glass across the street. Tires crunched over the debris as he shifted into drive, the explosive burst of torque sending him careening down the narrow street. A hard left put him on Mulholland with a crunch of metal and sparks that frightened a jogger and her labradoodle as he barreled by.

A slow-moving flatbed crowded the street ahead and Dante stomped the accelerator, juking into the opposite lane. A red Tesla appeared ahead, the driver's mouth thrown open wide.

Dante jerked the wheel left, sending the Mako up onto the steep sloping hill that bordered the street, the world tilting crazily as dual rooster tails of dust shot out from behind. The branches of an oak scrawled across the left side of the car with a hollow squeal as he skidded back onto asphalt. A yellow sign with a squiggly black arrow shot by but Dante barely registered it as he pushed further downhill. Only one thing mattered.

Abigail.

A speed bump caused the car the leap off the asphalt, clacking Dante's teeth together as he landed again with a chirp of rubber. He tasted blood as the curves kept coming, cramped hairpins and vicious hooks too tight even at low speeds.

Horns blared as he careened past Universal Liquors before a moment of silence underneath the 101 Freeway. His vision blurred as he shot back into the sun again, squinting in the sudden glare.

The city around Dante warped into a dangerous smear as he sped northward, slowing only to push through intersections before stomping the accelerator again. Peering up through the windshield, he saw the telltale glint of approaching aircraft in the sky.

Almost there, he thought. *Hold on, Abigail.*

The last mile slowed to a crawl even though he was pushing the car as fast as he could. Up ahead, a smudge of black smoke billowed and Dante's hands went cold. The car began to shudder and groan, the stench of burning plastic causing Dante's nasal passages to burn.

The Mako skidded around taxis and Ubers lined up in front

of a low-slung white and tan trimmed building. A short flight control tower bristling with antennae jutted above silver letters that read: Terminal A. Dante jammed both feet on the brake pedal, screeching to a halt as a tide of people surged out from the Hollywood Burbank Airport into the street.

The Mako continued to limp forward as Dante leapt out, plastic crunching as it came to rest against a metal pole. A veil of acrid smoke belched from the open doors of the terminal as he pushed his way inside.

"Abigail!" Dante screamed in the caustic air, sinuses crawling with needles as his eyes watered.

The last dregs of confused travelers stumbled by, coughing and retching, hands tight to their mouths. Dante kept low against the right wall as he raced deeper into the terminal. Fire leapt through a ragged hole up ahead where a jet had thrust its way inside, the crumpled aluminum nose poking through.

A door opened up, bright sunlight spearing inward. Boucher stepped into the terminal, eyes scanning, speaking rapidly into a radio. Dante spotted her and raced over. Her gun snapped up as Dante approached. Lowering the gun with relief, she glanced around before pulling him outside onto the tarmac as the door slammed shut behind them.

"Where's my daughter?" Dante said.

She held up a finger, radio pressed tight to her ear, listening to the tinny voice that spoke. Dante swung his gaze around as the peal of sirens rose nearby, coming closer.

Kelly was slumped against the wall, hands pressed to the side of her head. Bright red blood shone stark against the pale skin of her face and hands. Dante raced over and knelt down, grasping her shoulders. She winced as the prosthetic hand bit into her flesh. Gazing up at him, her eyelids fluttered as she fought to focus.

"They took her," Kelly said between sobs. "Oh my God."

"Who took her?" Dante said.

"Men. With guns," Kelly said, pulling her hands away to stare at her palms. A deep gash lay open at her temple. Fresh blood flowed down her face as her eyes found his.

"They took Abigail."

CHAPTER 67

Motel

Briana opened the door then locked it behind her before dropping into the rickety folding chair at the table. Sweat clung to her skin underneath the dazzle camo.

Why not just hide for a while? she thought. *I have money. I could wait for things to calm down a bit then go back home. Mother might never forgive me, but Dad would. Wouldn't he?*

But she knew that wouldn't be good enough. Not anymore.

Run away now, Briana, her mother's voice said. *That's what you do.*

"No," Briana said through gritted teeth.

She'd been used and discarded. Forgotten. *Again.* First Mark and now Leish and Mel and Dark Messiah, whoever that was.

Now she wanted to know why.

She gazed down at the pre-paid smart phone on the table top, still secure in its packaging. It'd lain there for the last day or so as she'd worked up the nerve. Reaching out, she grabbed the package and tore it open. The phone came on with a blip, an hourglass icon center screen slowly filling up as it booted.

A bead of sweat slipped into her eye. She rubbed at it through the dazzle camo but that only made it worse. The zipper went down with a zing and she was about to pull the hood off, then stopped. The phone had a camera in it, the buggy little lens wide open and staring. She tugged the zipper back up.

The phone came to life with a beep. Tapping and flicking her way around the settings, she turned off GPS. After signing in to the motel wireless, she downloaded the Find My Phone app. She began to tap in her information then hesitated, brows knitting together.

As soon as I sign in, they'll find me. Won't they?

She killed the app.

There hadn't been any dragonfly drones while she was out, but that didn't mean they hadn't been there, hidden somewhere, watching. She shivered, eyes flicking around the room. There had to be a way to find out something without arousing suspicion.

She opened a browser and did a search for "Monolith Media Tower." Ad links for realtors filled the screen and she scrolled down. There was a link for the building website along with info on how to lease office space there. The next link was a story on Techbeat.com about an incident that occurred there on Friday night. The same night she'd been there and delivered the strange black box. She tapped and scanned the story, her stomach sinking as she read.

A man named Dante Ellis had been attacked at a yearly party held on the top floor. The police provided no details, other than the victim had been severely injured but was expected to survive. There were no suspects and the alleged perpetrator or perpetrators were still at large.

Blood drained from her face.

With a shaky hand she did a search for Dante Ellis and opened the first link that appeared. It was a web page for his advertising company, Ellis Media. She tapped on "Team" and the page updated.

Dante Ellis, founder and CEO, smiled out from the picture above his name. He was in his mid-thirties or so, dark haired and handsome, his smile genuine. Briana read the text below.

Dante Ellis, founder and CEO of Ellis Media, has helped build some of the most recognizable brands in the business. Under his leadership, Ellis Media has garnered hundreds of industry awards...

She scrolled down to the bottom, frozen by what she read on the last line.

Dante lives in the Hollywood Hills with his daughter, Abigail.

Briana stood and backed up until her legs hit the bed. The mattress creaked as she sat down. *I'd been part of this...attack,* she thought.

There wasn't another word for it. Briana had helped hurt this man, no, severely injure this single father of a young girl. Tears stung her eyes and she blinked them away.

The rickety headboard creaked as she fell back against it. Grunting, she tried to lift the TV remote but it was attached to the nightstand with a metal bracket. After trying to wrench it free, she slammed a fist down and the TV blinked to life.

A weather bunny sashayed across the frame, pointing to a map of southern California dotted with grinning suns. A gray-haired anchor fake laughed at something she said, his dental implants glowing like fluorescent bricks. Breaking News, marched across the screen and his face turned mock serious as he spoke to a reporter in the field.

A woman with bright blond hair and a fuchsia blazer nodded as her image filled the screen. "Thanks, Phil," she said. "Details are sparse, but what we do know is that a plane crashed into the Hollywood Burbank Airport moments ago. We have cell phone video, but I have to warn our viewers, some of the images may be disturbing."

The screen changed to shaky cellphone video of people running and shrieking as a bright explosion lit up the screen. The shot cut to firetrucks racing past aircraft before showing firemen battling the churning flames that engulfed a large jet plane half-buried in the terminal wall. Other shots showed masked victims inhaling oxygen, faces streaked with soot, slumped on the curb or lying on blankets as paramedics hovered over them.

A group of dark-suited people stood together on the tarmac,

walkie-talkies and guns in their hands. They looked like federal agents of some kind. One person stood out from the group, a tall man with dark hair. Briana sat up and peered closer at the screen. He was stabbing a finger at one of the agents, talking fast. His arm was pitch-black and she thought he'd been hurt, maybe burned at first. It was a prosthetic hand. The man turned his head and glared, giving a clear view of his face before it cut back to the reporter.

It was Dante Ellis.

Briana sat bolt upright as the phone trilled three times on the bed. Scooping it up, her heart thudded as she read the message on the screen.

AMBER alert: Child abduction
Victim: Abigail Ellis, 9 Years Old
Suspects: Unknown/Military style clothing
Vehicle: Possible Black SUV
Last Seen: Hollywood Burbank Airport
If observed call 911

The reporter's voice boomed out from the television. "Police are asking for help finding a missing girl, Abigail Ellis, who was kidnapped by armed gunmen during the confusion earlier today...."

Briana shut the TV off, her thoughts a panicked jumble.

I should call the police, tell them what I know. Dark Messiah will find out, won't they? They've hurt people, ruined my life and now they've kidnapped a little girl. Had they also crashed that plane into the airport? They must have. What am I going to do?

Her mother's voice came to the rescue. *Run away now, Briana, that's what you do.*

"Shut the fuck up!" she screamed, her voice rattling off the yellowed walls.

"That's the spirit!" came a muffled shout through the wall.

Briana shook her head and got to her feet as an idea began to form, becoming a plan. She didn't want to use an Uber or taxi and take the chance of leaving a trail of some kind for Dark Messiah to pick up, even though she'd be wearing the dazzle camo. She needed to get across town in a low tech, untraceable way. A bicycle.

And she knew exactly where to get one.

CHAPTER 68

Dreaming

Oh, human race, born to fly upward,
wherefore at a little wind dost thou fall?

The reek of smoke still clung to Dante's clothes as he read the text again. He reached for the bottle of bourbon but a phantom hand was a poor substitute for flesh and blood. It cramped into a painful hook and he focused on the agony, hoping to chase away the panic that threatened to steal what self-control he had left. The phantom relaxed and Dante exhaled with relief as the cramp dissolved.

No escaping this, he thought, feeling the rage build inside.

So, he sat with it, let it run through him like a white-hot blade, sensed it extinguish any shred of hope he still clung to. With his left hand, he lifted the bottle to his lips and drank, adding fuel to the fire that burned inside.

The prosthetic hand was on the coffee table, charging light blinking, cord snaking off into the shadows. It lay on its back, fingers curved, like a dead spider.

The fingers twitched.

Alexis Arellano told him the hand did that during the charging cycle, some sort of diagnostic.

It twitched again. Like it was dreaming.

Dante slipped a Ziploc from his pocket and held it down with his stump. It throbbed as he struggled to open it. With a shaky hand, he removed two large, oblong pills, shoved them into his mouth and chased them with more alcohol. The Ziploc used to be full. Now it held less than half, about fifteen pills left.

Abigail is gone.

The shock of it scalded his insides with fresh agony as the events from earlier replayed in his mind, bursts of light and sound, more emotion than imagery.

The icy fear as he raced across town. The fiery panic that flared when he saw Boucher standing in a shaft of light. The terrible truth as Kelly uttered those words from behind a mask of blood.

They took her.

Kelly clutched at his arms, babbling over and over again how sorry she was as blood streamed down her face and spattered on the asphalt. He felt nothing, his mind numb with shock as an icy hollow swelled inside. She halted her pleas, face a mask of agony. The cold light in his eyes said it all.

You promised nothing would happen to her. This is your fault.

Kelly began to shudder, sobs wracking her body as paramedics swept in and took her away.

Boucher stood nearby in a clutch of uniformed men and women. She appeared older, the seams at the corners of her mouth and eyes deeper as she barked orders, sending them off in small groups to search.

As she saw Dante she began speaking, a torrent of words about four men dressed in black military garb, heads covered with black masks painted with stark white skulls. She stopped and listened, the radio squawking in her hand as the world around her sped by in the glare of whirling red lights.

Dante drank more bourbon, guzzling now. The pressure in his chest swelled to a shuddering crescendo, causing his eyes to water. The alcohol did little to quell the despair as it burned its way down. His stomach lurched as he let the empty bottle drop to the table with a loud clack.

Shadows clung to the furniture, making the usually warm space seem foreign and dangerous. Empty. Abigail's presence filled up the house in a way he'd never understood until now. She'd been gone before, of course. Sleepovers, summer camp. But she was safe, with people he trusted.

His vision blurred, the room around him becoming surreal and brittle, iced over with glass like it could shatter any moment. Warmth eased into his blood as the oxy kicked in, loosening the pressure inside a fraction. He pushed the disturbing thoughts away. Had to keep his shit together for what came next.

The follow up text from her kidnappers skittered through his mind.

Await further instructions.
Tell no one.

Colin had disappeared. Wasn't answering his phone, his apartment dark and empty. Boucher now considered him the lead suspect. A half empty glass of bourbon stood on the coffee table, ice clinking as it melted. Boucher hadn't taken one sip before a quick glance at her phone, the color draining from her face as she'd hurried out. That was over two hours ago.

The house creaked and Dante shot bolt upright, listening. "Abigail?"

Had she been hiding here the whole time?

Half running, half stumbling through the house Dante called her name, knowing she wasn't here but searching anyway. No one answered him. The house was empty.

He trudged down the hallway to his bedroom and dropped on the bed, cold sweat sliding down his ribs as he caught his breath. After a moment, he knelt down and swept back the throw rug, revealing a small panel set into the wood floor. Dante pushed a button on the panel and it popped open a crack.

Catching the edge with a finger, he lifted it open. Inside was a gray metal safe with a chrome plated dial and handle. With numb fingers, he rotated the dial, missing the combination twice before getting it right.

He'd never had to open it with his left hand before.

Slipping a hand inside, he pushed past documents and a bundle of cash before he found what he was looking for.

Back in the living room, he placed the gun next to his prosthetic hand, then pulled the charging cable out and slipped on the sleeve. The robotic fingers surged to life as he flexed, twitching and curling like metal snakes. He reached down and picked up the gun, staring at it in the dim light. It appeared to be a natural extension of the prosthetic, the black plastic and metal of the Glock 19 similar in texture and appearance.

With his thumb, he popped the catch and the empty magazine slid out. Extending his arm, Dante peered down the sights, nestling the front post into the rear, allowing his eye to focus on the front sight as he aimed at a lamp. He hadn't fired it in years, but he remembered that much. Motors whirred as he squeezed the trigger and the gun clicked, loud in the silent room. Dad had bought it years ago when Dante was still a teenager for something manly they could do together. He'd got it soon after pulling up in the Porsche.

They'd only gone to the range once. Dad was petrified of the thing. Dante admitted to himself that it had scared him a bit too. That first shot at the range was so much sharper and louder than he ever thought it would be. Right now, though, it felt good in his hand. The weight of it, the pressure sensors in the palm telling him it was there and solid.

Deadly.

His phone vibrated and he lifted it, the pale glow of the screen glinting in his eyes as he read the text.

The Place. 20 minutes.
Be there, or Abigail dies.

CHAPTER 69

The Place

The night was warm, heat shimmer causing the few visible stars to struggle like fireflies trapped in a spider's web. Dante slipped over the wooden rail that ran along the back of his patio and lowered himself to the ground, feet crunching on the dry grass. Shuffling down through the trees, he made his way to where Mulholland snaked along the hillside. Loose rocks crackled as he dropped to the empty street before crossing to a waiting car.

"Hollywood reservoir," he told the driver. He was a young guy, no more than twenty, with a shaved head and goatee. The kid glanced at him for a moment before putting the car in drive and speeding off.

The Place.

Dante hadn't thought of it in years. Blocked it out. He recalled when they found it as kids while exploring the fenced in areas around the northern end of the Hollywood reservoir. It was a small, concrete block building with vents along the bottom, capped with a pitched roof covered in tar paper.

They pried open the rust-eaten door with a metal pipe one sweltering summer afternoon, spinning wild theories as to what could be hidden inside. The entrance to an underground military facility, housing alien technology. More likely, the moldering remains of victims stashed here by a serial killer back in the eighties. Maybe someone had hidden gold here years ago and forgotten about it. The possibilities were endless and far too exciting to dismiss.

With a dry snap, the brass lock broke free and they slipped inside, hearts pounding as they entered the confined space.

Inside was a large, cast metal valve with a pipe running out of either side before curving into the ground. On the side of the valve was a large, spoked metal wheel, like on a ship. There were no aliens or dead bodies, but it was still pretty cool to a couple of twelve-year-olds. Their very own hidden hideout. Two rusty folding chairs along with a wire reel for a table finished off the place. More often than not, Dante and Colin would relax in the musty, cool interior, sheltering from the afternoon sun. It smelled of rust and standing water and rat dung.

They loved it.

As they grew older, talk shifted to girls they liked or how their lives would be different if they were cool. Dante had begun to grow weary of these chats and insisted they do something about it. Colin would shake his head vehemently. They weren't ready.

But Dante was.

During the summer before their junior year in high school, he'd filled out and shot up almost two inches while Colin stayed the same size, sallow chested and rail thin. He'd grown more anxious as the school year approached, suggesting they should home school or quit altogether and join the Army.

"Fuck that!" Dante said. "How the hell are you ever going to get laid out in the middle of a desert somewhere? Or dead?"

Dante laughed and playfully punched Colin's shoulder, causing him to wince and stare at the floor. Dante had noticed girls for a long time, and now, they'd started to notice him. Junior year, he decided, was going to be different.

With or without Colin.

No one knew of The Place, or so they thought. On a few occasions they'd find cigarette butts and empty beer cans not left there by them. Homeless, probably. They didn't give it much thought.

Two weeks before the start of their junior year, they met at The Place for one last time. Dante pulled open the door. Colin was already inside, back to the door, slumped on one of the metal folding chairs. He had a slender metal pipe in one hand about two feet long. Dull metallic notes rang out as he tapped it on the floor. Shutting the door behind him, Dante went to Colin and put a hand on his shoulder. Colin flinched at his touch, dropping the pipe with a clank. He looked up and stared at Dante, lower lip trembling. His eyes were a watery red, blond hair lay plastered to his skull.

"I have to tell you something," Colin said.

"What's going on?"

"Dante, I..."

The door opened with a squeal. Early evening light streamed in from outside. With a scuff of shoes, a slender shape blotted out the light.

"What is this? Some kind of ass pirate proposal?"

The voice was nasal and reedy, dripping with menace. A thin, teenage boy dressed in jeans and black t-shirt stepped inside. Dangling from one hand was a six-pack ring with one beer left, condensation dripping down the side. He was pushed aside by another boy who was pear-shaped and pimply, wearing a leather vest and thick, hobnailed boots that scraped as they thumped across the water-stained concrete. He blinked, piggy eyes wet and staring. He shuffled aside as a third boy entered, so tall he had to duck. Long, dark hair streamed down below his shoulders, angular features sharpened by a sneer. His leather jacket gleamed in the dim light as he leaned a skateboard against the wall with a bony clack.

It was Matty Markham.

They'd run that day after he'd crashed through the skateboard ramp, laughing. Left him lying in the bushes, screaming bloody revenge. But they hadn't seen him since, not once. He just disappeared. Lucky break, they figured. When did neighborhood bullies just vanish into thin air? That had been three years ago.

Maybe he'd forgotten.

Colin stood and wiped his face with the back of a hand, keeping behind Dante.

"We were just leaving," Dante said. "C'mon, Colin."

Matty stepped aside and extended his hand toward the open door, a toothy grin stretched on his face. Cool air drifted in from the reservoir, dry yet sweet. Dante took a step forward.

Matty gave a sharp nod.

The fat kid punched Dante hard in the stomach, doubling him over. Colin retreated behind the valve with a moan, hands clutching at the wheel. Dante stumbled back and leaned against the valve for support, gasping for air.

Matty glared at him, eyes hard under hooded lids. He jabbed a finger. "I owe you," he said. "You and 'Twitch' over there."

The skinny kid tittered, revealing teeth too large for his head. The fat kid licked his lips as Matty Markham slid the jacket from his shoulders in one swift move. A silver ring gleamed on the middle finger of his right fist.

Icy fear churned in Dante's stomach as they closed in. He'd never been in a fight before. Not a real one anyways. But this wasn't a fight.

It was a slaughter.

The chill in his body leached away as a prickly heat surged into his veins. His jaw clenched and he stood to his full height, eyes burrowing into Matty's.

Fuck it, he thought. *If I'm going to get my ass beat, they're going to have to work for it.*

The skinny kid dashed forward and Dante threw a punch but he ducked and slid away. It was a feint to allow Matty a clean blow. They'd done this before. Dante sensed the swing coming and flinched, causing Matty's fist to glance off his scalp, the ring leaving a deep gash at his hairline. He followed up with a hard left that caught Dante on the chin. His head snapped back and stars danced across his vision. They descended on him, raining blows as Colin screamed for them to stop, his voice shrill. Dante curled up on the dusty concrete as the fists and feet pummeled his body, the taste of blood thick in his mouth.

They stopped abruptly and backed off. Matty knelt and grabbed his jacket then slipped it on before slinging his skateboard over one shoulder. He nodded to the other two boys and they turned to go.

Dante spat blood as air hissed between broken teeth. A few lay in the dust. There was no pain, just a throbbing ache where they'd pummeled him, pulsing in time with his heart. Anger flared deep inside as he watched them leave through swollen eyes. They didn't even bother to look back. Dante began to shake with rage. Struggling to his feet, he gripped the valve's cool surface for support. His fingertips left bloody smears on the cast metal.

"What are you doing?" Colin hissed. "Stay down!"

Matty Markham stopped and glanced over his shoulder, one eyebrow shooting up.

"Fuck," Dante spat between gulps of air, "you."

Matty's eyes gleamed as he turned back around, letting his skateboard slide to the ground before stopping it with a foot. A wicked grin split his face as he dropped his jacket once more, the other boys crowding the doorway behind him.

Colin streaked passed Dante, a scream tearing loose from his throat. Matty's sneer became a shocked grimace as Colin thrust the metal pipe up under his chin. Colin skittered back with a reedy moan as Matty pawed at the pipe with jerky movements, a deep scarlet foam erupting from his mouth. Matty stumbled forward and the skateboard shot backward out from under his foot. He collapsed straight down onto the pipe, driving it up through the top his skull. His body jerked, blood pulsing from under his chin as he crumpled onto his side. His friends stood rooted to the spot, mouths slack before they bolted, leaving Matty behind as Colin wailed, his high-pitched voice ringing off the walls.

Dante didn't remember much after that. Just the sensation of floating in a dark, watery place where sound and light struggled to reach him as his lungs hitched, never quite able to capture enough air.

The squeal of brakes brought him out of his reverie as the car slowed and turned off the road. They rolled to a stop at the south end of the reservoir where the walking trail began, tires popping on gravel. A two-foot wall topped by a chain link fence surrounded the entire reservoir, the galvanized metal of the fence patchy with oxidation. Rusty-brown smears crept down the white painted wall like dried streaks of blood. A dense copse of pines beyond the fence stretched high above, seeming to poke the bellies of low clouds dusted a pinkish orange by the city lights.

"Here okay?" said the driver.

"No. Get back on Montlake and drive north. Keep going until I tell you to stop."

The young man shrugged and stared driving again.

Dante's thoughts returned to when he'd woken up in the hospital. He didn't know how long he'd been out after Matty and his buddies had given him the beat down of his life, but he'd awoken to pain. In a haze, his dad told him Matty Markham had died, but Colin's actions had been ruled as self-defense. Dante had felt guilt upon hearing of Matty's death for reasons he couldn't quite figure, but the feeling evaporated as crushing pain thrust in from all sides. What he hadn't felt during the attack had come alive to wreak its vengeance on every nerve in his body.

The next two weeks were the hardest of his life.

He'd emerged feeling lighter though, freer in a way that was hard to explain. Colors seemed more vibrant. The bland hospital food tasted glorious. He felt alive. Strong.

Fearless.

It was stupid, he knew, this feeling. But if he could survive something like that, coma and everything, well, then it couldn't get much worse than that.

Until someone kidnaps your daughter.

He shifted in the seat, adjusting the Glock at his spine to keep it from digging into his back. The car's headlights flashed over the fence that ran along the reservoir once more as they turned westward around the north end.

"Stop here," Dante said.

The driver eased to a halt and Dante pressed some cash into his hand. He stepped out and watched as the car's tail lights faded off into the night. A single street lamp burned nearby, throwing a pool of greenish light where Tahoe drive eased up the hill into a housing community tucked among squat palms and tall, furry pines.

Dante walked southward about a hundred feet until he found what he was looking for. It was a locked gate in the fence, the same one they'd climbed over as kids. He jammed the toe of his right shoe into a link in the fence and made his way up, the fence rattling with dull metallic notes as he climbed. It was awkward going with his prosthetic hand tucked protectively against his chest and toes missing from his left foot. When he reached the top, he threw a leg over and straddled the gate, the wire along the top digging into his crotch. He slipped his other foot over and dropped to the thick carpet of pine needles that extended to the shoreline. The Glock slipped from his waistband and thumped on the ground. Dante scooped it up with his prosthetic hand, the motors whirring as the fingers tightened. He was careful to keep the index finger off the trigger.

The trees had grown taller over the years since he'd last been here, the bushes were unkempt and wild as ever. He pushed his way past low clumps of scrub oak and entered a thick grove of trees ahead. The rich odor of fresh turned soil filled his nostrils as he gazed north and saw the Hollywood sign beaming down at him through the whiskered boughs of pines. Red warning lights blinked on the radio towers perched on the hilltop above.

He broke free of the trees and dank odor from the still

waters of the reservoir washed over him. Lights winked off the surface from an airplane that flew high overhead, distorted by gentle ripples. A squat building sat nearby about fifty feet from the shore, its cinder block walls a smudgy gray.

The Place. It was smaller than he remembered.

A pale, orange light seeped out from around the door, creating a vertical frame suspended in the darkness. Shadows blotted out the light along the bottom edge.

Someone was in there.

Dante lifted the gun and crept forward, careful to keep his footfalls quiet. As he reached the door, he put an ear to the rusty surface and listened. Nothing. He reached down with his left hand and grasped the handle and slowly pulled it open.

It was if The Place had been suspended in time. A naked bulb hung from the ceiling, its pale glow barely reaching the corners of the small room. The valve was still there, its pitted, cast iron surface dominating the center. Dark streaks still clung to the rough metal. The wheel was there, set into the side, painted the same chalky blue. Two folding chairs sat facing the door on either side of the old wire reel table. Colin sat in the chair on the left.

He peered up at Dante, eyes red and puffy, like that night so many years ago. There was no weapon in his hand, no Taser. Dante aimed the gun.

"Where's Abigail."

Colin gazed at him with a what appeared to be a mixture of sadness and pity. "I'm so very sorry about this, Dante. I truly am, but I had no choice."

"Give me my daughter!"

A jolt of agony flared up through Dante's feet as his whole body convulsed, lights flashing behind his eyes before the world went black.

CHAPTER 70

Underwater

The world coalesced in a series of jittering smears, a naked bulb burning a wiggly smear across Dante's vision. The valve squatted nearby, shifting as if underwater. He lay on his left side, ragged breath causing dust to billow along the concrete floor. It tickled the back of his throat but he couldn't sneeze. It was maddening.

Colin was rolling up a black rubber mat, wires swinging loose from one end as he cinched it up before tucking it into a duffel bag on one of the folding chairs. He knelt over Dante, leaning in close, face distorted as if he was peering through a fish bowl, face twitching as he blinked.

Dante couldn't move.

It was similar to how he'd felt with the Taser, but much stronger. His whole body was numb and a strange metallic taste clung in his mouth. He raged at himself for being so stupid and walking right into a trap, thinking a gun he barely knew how to shoot would make any difference.

Colin glanced down as Dante's prosthetic hand began to twitch. The gun was underneath the hand, scooting as the fingers brushed over its surface. Colin reached over to pick it up then stopped, head cocked, listening. Relief flooded through Dante as Boucher stepped through the door. It evaporated as he saw the haunted look in her eye.

They'd gotten to her.

A man pushed in beside her, all in black, tall with a gray streak in his dark hair. He went and stood over by the valve. "Let's get this over with," Dmitry said. "I have a flight to catch. A very *long* flight."

Colin stood and stared down at Dante for a long moment, his eyes dull and lifeless. He turned and rummaged through the duffel bag.

Boucher spoke, her face tight. "I didn't have a choice. They threatened to dox my Patricia, ruin her life. She's all I have. It was either your daughter or mine." Her lower lip trembled and when she spoke, her was voice thick. "I chose mine." She leaned closer, face bloated like a balloon. "These people who have your daughter, they're very powerful. You're going to have to do something I couldn't do. Let her go. They'd kill her before ever allowing you to see her again."

Tears streamed out of Dante's eyes as he struggled to speak but his jaw refused to cooperate. He wanted to scream at Boucher, wrap his fingers around her throat and make her tell him where Abigail was but his body refused to do more than shudder. He thought he felt the prosthetic flex a bit, but it was hard to tell in his disorientated state.

The chair squeaked as Colin lifted something into view. His bony fingers were clenched around the edge of a dark, oval shaped object. A dragonfly drone hovered over one shoulder, tiny spotlight spearing out and locking onto where Dante sprawled on the ground.

Struggling to clear his vision, Dante blinked, eyes gummy. There were two holes through the center of the object Colin held, side by side. Dust motes swam through the beams of light that shot through. It was a mask, but nothing like he'd ever seen before. The inside was etched with fine traceries of silver, like the underside of a motherboard. Other shapes were tucked along the edges of the eye holes, insectile and sharp.

Colin came closer and held the mask above his face.

"You've been sedated by a neuro blocker, delivered through the mat you were standing on. Developed for the military, very advanced tech, still in trials. You won't feel a thing. I insisted on that. No pain."

The mask began to descend.

For the first time since entering The Place that evening, Dante felt an icy fear lance through him. Something in the mask shifted with a scraping click as it came closer to his face. With a tremendous surge of sheer will, Dante forced his body to move, adrenaline spiking in his blood.

The muscles along his shoulders rippled.

He screamed as loud as he could in his mind, vision dimming, willing his body to move, even just a little bit.

The prosthetic hand twitched.

He was sure of it. Tightening the fingers around the grips of the gun, Dante gritted his teeth and lifted the weapon off the floor.

"He's waking up," Dmitry said.

Dante squeezed the trigger. The blast rocked off the concrete walls. Boucher leapt in and stripped the gun away and racked the slide, locking it in place before removing the clip. Dmitry's face went pale as he clutched at the valve, new streaks of blood joining the old. The wheel spun with a grinding squeal as he pitched forward on his face and lay still.

Boucher knelt down, rolled him over, and ripped open his shirt, sending buttons flying. She skidded back, hands held wide as blood jetted in spurts from a small entry hole below his left nipple.

"Oh, Christ, he shot him." She glared at Colin. "Fucking do this thing so we can get out of here."

Colin lowered the mask onto Dante's face, voice intoning as Dante's body began to shake, arms twitching as he tried to fend his old friend off. The dragonfly drone hovered in close, wings rising to an anxious thrum.

"If your right eye causes you to sin," Colin said as the mask adhered to Dante's face. "Gouge it out and throw it away."

The mask hummed and a viscous liquid sluiced into Dante's left eye, causing it to go dead and motionless. Tiny motors whined to life and Dante saw three sharp implements extend out over his eye with a snick, blurry through the milky fluid.

"It is better to lose one part of your body…" Colin said as the implements descended closer. Dante felt a slight pressure as they pressed down around the tender flesh of his eye. The pressure increased and his eye ached, deep inside. His left eye went dark as Colin pressed his thumb on Dante's cornea.

"…than your whole body to be thrown into hell," Colin said.

The mask shifted as a searing pain ripped around his left eye and Dante felt darkness enfold him once again.

CHAPTER 71

Eye

The metallic taste in his mouth made his stomach turn and Dante struggled up, falling from his bed as he lurched over the edge. Scrambling to the bathroom through the dark, he retched into the toilet, heaving until his ribs ached. He fell against the edge of the claw-footed bathtub, laying his head against the cool porcelain. His left eye throbbed. Dante grabbed the edge of the sink and pulled himself unsteadily to his feet.

He gazed at his reflection in the mirror, barely able to see himself in the dim blue light straining through the frosted window from outside. A square patch of gauze was taped over his left eye. Blots of dark blood had seeped through.

The fuckers took my eye this time.

The room tilted and he gripped the edge of the sink, the prosthetic grinding to a whiny halt as it tightened up. Touching along the edge of the gauze with a finger, he tugged at a corner and stopped. A weight settled in his stomach, filling the void with prickly ice. He swallowed and pinched one corner of the gauze, steeling himself as he tore it away.

The flesh around his eye was a deep, angry red. Dark bruises radiated outward from three shallow cuts, two on his brow and one below his eye. His breath caught in his throat as his eye slid open. A blurry double image stared back at him before resolving into one. The white of his left eye was tinged an angry red but was still in his skull where it belonged. The breath wheezed out of his lungs and he laughed, tears stinging his eyes.

Colin, Dante thought. *He'd put his thumb on my eye to save it. Must've let the blades hack at his thumb instead. He was just a victim of Dark Messiah too. For how long? Since the very beginning.*

Boucher must have been right after they'd taken Abigail. They'd gotten to Dmitry after Dante's toes had been hacked off.

Is Dmitry dead? He didn't care. That surprised him a bit. *But what about Abigail?*

Boucher told him he'd never see her alive again. Dante pressed a fist against his eye, focusing on the pain as fresh blood oozed out. She was alive, he could feel it. They probably had her locked away somewhere, scared but safe. A low moan escaped his lips as a voice hissed inside his head.

Abigail is dead.

"No," he said to the haggard face in the mirror, pointing a bloody finger. "She's not."

First Michelle and now Abigail. You know why.

Dante began to shake, his breath coming in ragged gasps as a cold sweat broke out over his body and needles danced along his skin.

They're both dead now. And you're alone.

"No!" Dante screamed, causing the mirror to vibrate. Sliding to the floor he collapsed against the wall. A hard edge dug into his spine and he reached back and withdrew the Glock.

Why had they left him the gun?

He raised it up and racked the slide. A round ejected, sailing through the air before striking the tile with a clack. It rolled, the brass and copper glinting as it traveled in a wide semicircle until it came to a halt against his leg. He looked back at the gun. The slide was locked open. The chamber was empty, no rounds left in the magazine.

They'd left him a single bullet.

A sound startled him, a deafening hiss from somewhere

else in the house. He got to his feet, still clutching the gun, and trudged down the hallway toward the bluish light emanating from the living room.

The television was on, screen chattering with static. Dante watched the snowy pattern shift as it began to take shape. Slowly at first, bits of static swirled and clung together faster and faster until nothing else remained, the hiss dropping away to silence. A face of pure white peered out at him, black eyes watching. The features were sharp, perfectly symmetrical. It began morphing into a softer face familiar to him, her reddish-brown hair drifting as if underwater. The eyes remained black and impenetrable.

"The time has come for us to speak," said the deep fake of Michelle on the screen.

"Yes, it has. Dark Messiah."

CHAPTER 72

Dark Messiah

"There is no greater sorrow than to recall happiness in times of misery," said Michelle's deep fake.

The voice was strange, raspy and low, but there was another tone underneath, high and fluty, almost feminine.

"I'll give you whatever you want," Dante said. "Just don't hurt my daughter."

"We are the Axis Mundi, the coalescence of thought and energy and timeless existence-"

"Where's Abigail!" Dante's voice echoed through the empty house.

The face on the screen stared for a moment before continuing. "Abigail is part of a much larger lesson. Humanity has lost its way."

"I don't give a fuck," Dante said. "Look, I'm sure you boys have been practicing your 'humanity bad' speech for a while, but all I care about is Abigail. Tell me what you want so I can get her back."

Deep Fake Michelle's face remained still, the hair drifting in loose coils. "It is better that we show you."

The shutters over the northward facing window twitched open, exposing a star filled sky glittering above the golden glow of Hollywood below.

Dante had never seen so many stars.

The faint orange glow from countless windows shimmered through the haze rising from the valley floor as headlights crisscrossed the city like rivers of light.

"Much too bright," Dark Messiah said.

A low rumble vibrated through the floor and the house creaked. A purple flash from behind the hills lit up the haze.

The entire city went dark.

Cars slowed to a halt as the distant blare of horns rose up into the night air. Even the never ceasing blink of red lights on the radio towers above the Hollywood sign had gone out.

"Vulgar display of power?" Dante said.

"No, necessary. Come and see," Dark Messiah said.

Dante went to the window. Flashlight beams appeared inside some of his neighbors' homes. Some had stepped outside in their pajamas to get a better look at this strange event. Movement caught Dante's eye and he glanced upward.

The stars had begun to blink.

One by one they detached themselves from the sky, gathering closer together until they formed a tight grid in the shape of a giant black rectangle floating above the city, like a television screen. Drones, Dante realized. The screen flashed and displayed various striped and checkered patterns before lighting up with an image. Dante felt the world fall away.

It was Abigail.

Her small face was pale and still above a white sheet pulled up under her chin. A dragonfly drone was perched on her chest, its wings twitching. Dante's hands clenched. He wanted to reach out and crush the drone in his fist.

A white cap was pulled down over her hair, one dark, reddish curl peeked out in front of her ear. There was a small white circle on her temple, barely visible, but it was there. *Another one of Dark Messiah's little gadgets?* The thought made his blood boil. His eyes tightened as he peered closer. Something was wrong.

She wasn't breathing.

Dante squeezed his eyes shut, trying to clear his head. None of this made any sense. *Was this another deep fake?* He turned back to the television.

"You've destroyed my reputation. Maimed my foot. Stolen my hand," Dante said. "Now my only child. The one thing I have left in this world that matters to me."

Silence.

"What do you want?" he said, voice ragged. "When will it be enough?"

"When you tear your clothes. Shave your head and give yourself entirely to despair."

Dante froze. "You want me to...what?"

"We want you to die."

So, there it was. That's why they'd left the bullet in the gun.

The face changed to resemble Dante and spoke again in that strange, wispy voice. "You must die, by your own hand, of your own free will. Right now, for all the world to see."

A dragonfly drone he hadn't noticed before lifted off the TV and hovered closer, little eye cameras twitching.

"People are aware of your sins as a purveyor of lies," Dark Messiah said. "Now they will watch you die."

"You're crazy."

"There are evil men in this world. Wicked. The blood of millions on their hands. Their time will come. But you are the first. The trial. The example. The world needs to see what becomes of irredeemable wickedness in the human heart. Death by thine own hand," Dark Messiah said.

Dark Messiah had jogged something loose in Dante's head, but he couldn't quite place it. Tear your clothes. Shave your head and give yourself entirely to despair. He'd heard that before, from a movie or TV show. The *Bible* maybe? It sounded like it, but he couldn't be sure, couldn't think straight, thoughts flitting like minnows in a murky pool, slipping between his fingers. He was so exhausted and frightened, his nerves frayed.

But above all, he was angry.

He let the anger flow through him—let it burn away all other emotion churning inside him to a cinder until nothing else remained. Breath hissed between his teeth as the fog that clouded his brain evaporated. He stood straighter, taller. It was so clear to him what he must do. He opened his mouth to speak, then snapped his jaw shut, mind feverish again.

What if I don't do what they want? I'll be killing her.

He felt his resolve slip, then he pushed the doubts away. He was gambling with her life but he could see no other option. Licking his lips, Dante tasted the sour vomit caked there and almost didn't say anything.

Almost.

"What if I just...disappear," Dante said.

"No."

It was strange. The voice didn't change, the intonation remained flat and emotionless. But there was so much behind that one, simple word.

"Yes," Dante said, his resolve strengthening. "That is exactly what I am going to do."

"Then Abigail dies."

Those three words made his breathing stop. He heard them for what they were.

Desperation.

A spark of hope surged inside him. *Was Abigail really still alive?*

He pictured her lying there, not breathing, the dragonfly drone on her chest. He wavered again. *If she is still alive, am I willing to risk her life?*

Tears stung his eyes before he spoke again. "She's already dead." His stomach cramped and his vision swam, black motes drifting. "I'm not doing a fucking thing you say."

Dante dropped the gun to the floor.

Dark Messiah remained silent, the counterfeit face on the screen rigid. The moment stretched. Dante inhaled sharply, felt words forming in his panicked brain, begging for Abigail's life....

The digital mockery of his face blinked. "We'll seed your browser history with child pornography. You'll never see her again."

Dante almost gasped. *She's still alive!*

"There is only one outcome," Dark Messiah said. "You must die by your own hand."

CHAPTER 73

Boxed

"Fuck you," Dante said.

The security shutters slammed shut throughout the house, sealing him inside.

"We control everything. *Everything.* You are trapped. Do as we say. Now. The whole world will be watching."

Dante was barely listening, his mind racing.

He had to get out.

Dashing through the house, he ran to the glass panel next to the front door. He tightened his prosthetic hand into a fist and plunged it straight through. The sound of shattering glass echoed through the foyer, musical and discordant at the same time. The red eye in the center of the emergency button was dark.

He pressed it. Nothing happened.

He reached past the button further into the dark recess, glass tinkling underfoot.

The pressure of the axe handle in his hand felt solid and strong. He lifted it high over his head and grinned like a madman before he hacked into the camera mounted over the front door. It fell to the floor with a crunch of ruined plastic. Dante ran throughout the darkened house, hacking and smashing cameras and security keypads as Dark Messiah watched from the television screen.

He found himself in front of the television once again, the axe head dragging across the floor as he strode closer. Sweat streamed down his face as he stood, gulping air. Lifting the axe, he pointed at Dark Messiah with the blade.

"What now?" Dante said.

The face hovered on the screen, eyes watching him. The eyes blinked. *What a strange thing,* Dante thought, *that sightless digital eyes would blink.*

He wondered if he'd just made the worst mistake of his life.

"Your death is inevitable," Dark Messiah said. "Twelve hours from now, if you refuse again, Abigail will die."

Dante brought the axe crashing down in the center of the screen as the drone perched on top darted away. Glass shattered with an eruption of sparks as the screen winked out before dying. With a sharp tug he wrenched the axe free, causing the television to shear off its wall mount and crash to the floor.

He'd never think of smart televisions the same way again.

Dante's mind raced as he checked the time on his phone. 3:34 A.M. He had twelve hours to find Abigail. With a whip of his arm he tossed the axe down. It thudded hard into the floor, handle straight up. The gun lay nearby. He picked up the gun and slid it into the back of his waistband.

He raced through the dark toward the kitchen, banging his thigh on the table. Groaning, he yanked open a drawer and rummaged around before withdrawing a flashlight. He thumbed the button and light speared out. He wrapped his phone in foil and dropped the roll to the tile. Rushing to his bedroom as quickly as he dared, Dante stood the flashlight up on the dresser, pointed at the ceiling.

The dragonfly drone clung there, body glinting as it crawled away from the pool of light. Dante leapt onto the dresser and snatched the thing before it could escape. He peered into the little cameras that bristled at the tip of its head, seeing his own distorted reflection stare back at him in the mirrored surfaces. With his prosthetic hand he smashed it against the wall with a satisfying crunch.

The closet doors opened with a rattle as he reached inside and lifted his shoulder bag off a hook before dumping the contents onto the bed. The dazzle camo suit spilled out among pens and tablets of paper and various other odd and ends. He held the suit up in the dim light, eyes scanning over the strange, warped stripes before tossing it into the bag, followed by a few pairs of slacks, some jeans and t-shirts.

He unplugged the battery charger for his arm and dropped that in the bag as well. The foil wrapped phone went in last. He snatched the flashlight from the dresser and left the room. The axe was stuck in the floor where he'd left it and he pulled it free as he swept by. He was going to need it. The door leading to the garage was made of steel reinforced mahogany with thick security hinges. It wasn't going down without a fight.

Dante hefted the axe over his head, angling for the best attack when the door swung open. Someone stood there, clad in loose fitting dazzle camo, one hand clutching the knob. Dante lifted the axe higher and the figure raised their hands, palms out.

"Wait!" It was a young woman's voice. "You're Dante Ellis, right? I know who took your hand."

CHAPTER 74

Visitor

Dante hesitated, the axe still held high. The young woman pulled the mask down from her head, revealing honey blond hair and green eyes. The eyes were frightened, but determined.

"I'm Briana Warren. Dark Messiah used me to hurt you."

Dante lowered the axe and considered her for a moment. "Can you talk on the way?"

"The way to where?"

"Away from here. Somewhere away from technology."

Briana hesitated, biting her lip. Dante began to push past her when she put up a hand.

"Wait. I know just the place."

Excerpt from TechBeat.com article:

First 3D Printed 'Wetware' Computer Stolen

By Ian Weller

BasalMek Medical Industries, world leader in the field of 3D printed organs experienced a "one of a kind loss" when their top secret wetware computer was stolen in a brazen breaking and entering late last night. Described by Dr. Patty Han as essentially a 'brain in a box,' the wetware computer is considered one of the next steps in enabling machine learning software access to the electrochemical processes that an organic brain is capable of.

The box containing the wetware is flat and looks more like it would hold an extra-large pizza instead of a 3d printed brain. Dr. Han explains: "An organic human brain needs a certain amount of surface area to achieve the necessary number of neurons to be effective. About one hundred billion within a supportive structure of glial cells. The brain has evolved to fit inside the confined space of a skull, kind of like a balled-up piece of paper, hence the wrinkled appearance of the cortex. We don't need our wetware brain to fit into a small space, so we print it in flat layers. It's what a human brain might look like smoothed out into a sheet."

Dr. Han feels the thieves didn't know exactly what they were stealing, even though it was the only thing missing from the lab. She asks for the brain to be returned, intact, no questions asked, claiming it is useless as is.

"It's just the hardware, a bit like a CPU," says Dr. Han. "Very unique in the way it works, but without software specifically designed to interface with it, it's just a sheet of 3D printed gray matter all dressed up with nowhere to go."

CHAPTER 75

Bonnet

Dante grabbed a can of black spray paint from a cabinet and began to paint zig zagging stripes across the car cover that lay over his father's Porsche. Briana went to the other side, slipping in between the car and wall.

"Toss it here," she said.

Dante tossed the paint can over and she pushed the nozzle down with her finger, etching long lightning bolt shapes across the side, starting at the front and working her way down to the rear. Rummaging through the cabinet again, Dante found a box cutter and slashed out sections for the windows.

He unlocked the driver door and leaned in to pop the trunk. Then he peeled the cover up and lifted the lid, gazing over at Briana. The slight tang of his father's hairspray drifted into his nostrils.

"Can you toss in my bag?" Dante said.

"Is there going to be room?"

Dante gazed down into the trunk and his mouth fell open, his father's final word echoing through his brain.

Bonnet.

He'd said *bonnet,* pleading with his eyes as he spoke. Dante cursed himself for not understanding what his father had been struggling to say before he died, this man who hated technology and didn't trust banks.

"That's a lot of money," Briana said.

"If those are all twenties, I'd say at least half a million dollars."

It sure as hell explained where all of Dad's money went.

Dante shoved the stacks of cash as far back as he could and Briana tossed his bag in. He unzipped the bag and dug around until he found the dazzle camo before slipping it on. Briana pulled her hood back into place.

As they climbed inside the car, Briana slid a slender object wrapped in a yellowed sheet between the seats. Dante paid little mind. He wanted to get away.

They backed out with a chirp of rubber, the rear bumper pushing the rest of the destroyed garage door out of the way with a rattling crunch. Dante backed uphill and stopped, gazing around. His police protection detail was gone.

"We're being watched," Briana said.

Dante glanced past her though the passenger side window. A dragonfly drone hovered there, red light flashing on its underside.

Dante checked the gas gauge. "The batteries have got to be tiny on that thing. It can't follow us forever."

Unless it has batteries similar to my prosthetic, he thought.

They sped away from the house, the canvas cover flapping as they drove. Dante checked the rear-view mirror as they merged onto the I-5. There were few other cars on the road.

"Is it still following us?" Dante said.

"I can't see anything...oh wait. There's two of them now."

"Keep watching them."

He increased his speed but the car cover began flapping, threatening to fly off so he slowed down, staying in the right lane.

"Oh my god. One just smacked into a windshield of a big rig. Here comes the other one," Briana said. "Speed up it's coming closer."

Dante pressed down on the accelerator but the canvas cover began to flap violently and he slowed down again.

"What are you doing?" Briana said.

"This car is registered to my father. If that drone gets a read on the license plate then Dark Messiah can send that info to the FBI. They'll be able to find us."

"Isn't that a good thing?"

"No. The FBI is a part of this."

"Oh, shit," Briana said.

"Yeah."

"No. I mean, oh shit, there's more back there."

"How many?"

"Three now, coming up fast. If one lands on the car and we don't know, they can track us. It probably has GPS."

"Jesus, how many of them are there?" Dante said.

"I only ever saw two, but it must have been several swapping out for each other when the batteries got low."

"Let's keep going. But the longer we're out here like this, driving around with the car cover flapping around, the more chance we have of getting stopped by the police."

Briana popped the seatbelt catch and knelt on the passenger seat, facing toward the rear. She slid the shotgun out of the yellowed sheet and broke the barrel before dropping a shell in.

"What the hell are you doing?" Dante said.

"Slow down," Briana said as she locked the barrel back in place. "How do you open this window?"

"There's a crank."

"Old school tech. I like that," she said as she spun it down. Wind whipped through the car as she leaned out the window, gun butt tight to her left shoulder.

The drones swarmed closer.

It was difficult to see through the screen of the optical camo and the wind blowing against the back of her head. Briana lifted the barrel of the gun and steadied her breathing, leading the closest drone as it flew closer.

She squeezed the trigger.

The drone disintegrated in a puff of green glitter, vanishing in the wind. The other two drones peeled off and hovered further back, visible only as small shiny points as they passed under streetlights. Briana broke the barrel and plucked out the shell, tossing it out the window before reloading.

"When I say, slow down," she said.

"This is crazy," Dante said, checking the rearview mirror. If they get pulled over, he may never have chance at finding Abigail.

"Now!" Briana said.

Dante let his foot up and the car slowed. The gun barked and Briana reloaded, then fired again.

"Okay, we're good," she said, dropping back inside.

Dante sped up again, not daring to go faster than fifty-five. "Who *are* you?"

"Just a small-town girl from Nebraska."

"Nebraska, huh. Where to?"

CHAPTER 76

Motel

Dante sat on the carpet, back against the wall, watching the shaft of light from under the curtains oscillate between red and purple. The motel room smelled of dust and stale cigarettes, the walls a dingy yellow. Their dazzle camo suits lay in a heap on the floor. Briana sat across from him on the edge of the bed and recounted the events that led to this moment.

Her arrival in Hollywood, Leish, her creepy boyfriend Mel. Plushie hyenas. The Dragonfly drones. The text with the video of her and Leish, followed by the threat of sending it out to everyone she knew. She told him of that night in the alley, retrieving the black box. With a shaky hand she showed him the video on the Retrocam screen of a dark figure entering the Monolith tower. Her voice hitched as she told him that Dark Messiah had sent out the video of her.

Dante listened, but said nothing. Briana was close to crying, tears welling up in her eyes, but a strange, numbness had begun to spread through his body, making him feel disoriented, disconnected. She'd been part of the biggest trauma of his life, before Abigail's kidnapping, that is. Briana was another victim of Dark Messiah, but had she made a different choice, would he still have his hand? He glanced down at the stump, the flesh almost completely healed. A sudden wave of phantom pain hit him and he gasped, the ghost of his right hand cramping up into a claw.

"Are you okay?" Briana said, rising from the edge of the bed.

"It'll go away after a while," Dante hissed through clenched teeth.

Her face was pained. "I'm so sorry. About all this."

"Not your fault," Dante said gazing around the room. He got to his feet and fingered the corner of a mirror hanging over the TV. It was loose. "Help me with this?" he said, glancing over his shoulder. Briana nodded. He went and sat at the table and laid his arms across the top.

"What do you need me to do?" Briana said.

"Take the mirror down and put in on the table standing up, then hold the top."

She lifted the mirror off the wall. It was heavier than it looked. The room tilted crazily in the reflection as she carried it over and placed it on the table, holding it up as he'd asked. Dante pressed his forehead against the edge, closed his right eye and tightened his left hand into a fist. He slowly relaxed his hand while breathing long and deep. He did this a few more times before leaning back and closing his eyes.

"Thanks," he said.

Briana took the mirror down and put it down against the wall. "Pretty cool trick," she said.

"Yeah, when it works."

She studied him a moment. "So, what now? I have a few ideas."

Dante laughed, feeling a bit more like himself. "No doubt something involving a gun."

"If he's lucky," Briana said. "I think we should go talk to the other guy involved in this."

"We don't even know who he is."

"I lost my phone in the back of that truck. He must have taken it when he grabbed my messenger bag. I can use Find My Phone."

"He's probably just a victim as well and couldn't tell us

much. Or wouldn't, for fear of reprisal by Dark Messiah. Let him stew for a bit. The bastard took my hand."

"So did I. Well, I helped anyway," Briana said, looking away.

"Yes, but he didn't come and find me," Dante said. "You did."

Briana gazed up again, lips curved into a slight smile.

"All I want is to get Abigail back and I'm running out of time. If she's still alive."

"What do you mean?"

Dante told Briana about the incident at the airport, and the details of Abigail's abduction. Briana sat back down on the bed, hands over her mouth, looking ill. She turned even paler as Dante described the events in The Place, the betrayal of Dmitry, Special Agent Boucher of the FBI and Colin. She shivered as he described the mask Colin had placed on his face, almost taking his eye. Then he told her of his strange interaction with Dark Messiah through the television and his subsequent tear-assing through the house, and their promise to kill Abigail in twelve hours if he refused to comply.

Briana's eyes narrowed before she spoke. "It's from the Book of Job."

"What is?"

"What Dark Messiah said about 'When you tear your clothes. Shave your head and give yourself entirely to despair.' The book starts out as a wager between Satan and God. Satan insists that if you take everything away from a righteous man, he will curse God and turn from him. It's usually offered up as a lesson to explain that if God is good, why do the innocent suffer?"

"I don't get it," Dante said.

"Nobody does. In church, you learn pretty early on it's better to just nod and stay quiet unless you want to get sermoned to death. But what's usually left out is the best part, and really crazy to be honest."

"What do you mean?"

"God speaks to Job from a whirlwind and boasts that he couldn't possibly comprehend creation. Where was Job, God asks, when he laid the foundations of the Earth? Can Job call down the rain, can he loosen Orion's belt? God goes on for a while too, really ramming the point home, talking about bringing down his wrath. Wait, don't motel rooms have *Bibles* in them?"

Briana yanked open a drawer next to the bed, and removed a Gideon's *Bible*. The spine cracked as it opened and she flipped through.

"Here listen to this: 'Look at Behemoth, which I made along with you and which feeds on the grass like an ox. Its bones are tubes of bronze, its limbs like rods of iron. It ranks first among the works of God, yet its Maker can approach it with his sword.'"

"Behemoth? I didn't know that was from the bible," Dante said.

"Listen to this next part," Briana said, continuing to read. "'Can you pull in Leviathan with a fishhook or tie down its tongue with a rope? Will it make an agreement with you for it as your slave for life?'"

Dante nodded. "I get the first part, Dark Messiah is God, and they are punishing me, even though they said I wasn't righteous but a 'purveyor of lies.' So, which one of us is the Leviathan?"

"I don't know. I'm guessing Dark Messiah left that out as well in their thinking because at this point in the story, God is just laying it on thick."

"How does the story end?" Dante said.

"Job gets everything back, twofold."

Dante lifted up his stump. "I'm guessing Dark Messiah is going to skip that part."

"They've been pretty selective with their interpretation of the *Bible*," Briana said. "Bunch of a la carte Christians, if you ask me."

Dante laughed. Then his face fell. "I have to believe she's still alive. I have no idea how to find her though, but I think I might know who can." He turned and headed for the door. "I need to look something up, something someone said to me. I'll be back. I'm going to go buy one of those prepaid phones."

"Use mine," Briana said.

Dante shook his head and took the phone from her outstretched hand. "Thanks," he said. "Just a small-town girl, huh?" She smiled and looked away as he tapped on the screen and opened a browser.

Dante gazed upward, trying to remember. *What had Skylar Westfall said that day in the parking garage?* It was two words that meant nothing to him, but they'd stuck in his head. He tapped on the screen, inputting the letters in a search window.

Bothrops Asper.

The tiny screen filled with information. The header at the top read: Fer-de-lance, a highly venomous pit viper found throughout southern Mexico and South America. Images of a spotted, dark brown snake, neck curled into an S, shone on the small screen.

Why the hell would Skylar tell him about a snake? Dante thought. Nothing made sense to his exhausted brain.

"What is it?" Briana said.

Dante told her about Skylar Westfall and his company, Spearhead Data systems, and his software with the strange, snake-related name.

"He said he wanted to help you, right?" Briana said. "You just needed to plug in that chip."

"According to him."

"But you threw it away."

"What are you getting at?" Dante snapped. Then he got it. "Shit. He knows about Dark Messiah."

"Duh. Toss me the phone," Briana said. She tapped on the screen with her thumbs then slid a finger down before tapping again.

"Anything?" Dante said.

"Hold on a minute. I'm thinking."

Dante watched Briana as she stood there hand on one hip, concentration etched on her face. Seeing her standing there like that reminded him of Abigail. Dante sat down hard on a chair and stared at the scarred table top, focusing on a cigarette burn.

Where was she? Was she safe? Scared but safe somewhere?

He'd let Dark Messiah cut off all his limbs if he could just know for sure she was alive.

"Are you okay?" Briana said.

"No."

"You need to sleep. How long has it been?"

"I can't sleep. I can't. I just see her face."

"Come, lay down. Just close your eyes for a little while."

Dante stood and wavered a bit, then stumbled past Briana over to the bed and fell face down on the mattress. The box spring creaked.

Dante slept.

CHAPTER 77

Link

"Hey. Wake up."

Dante's whole body ached. The phantom hand was clenched in a painful fist. He opened his eyes and saw Briana standing over him, green eyes locked on the phone in her hand.

"I got something," she said, holding the phone out to him.

Dante winced and sat up, closing his eyes to the bright rectangle of light. "What is it?"

"So, Fer de lance is French. It means 'tip of the spear.' You look a little shaky still. You with me so far?"

"Yeah. French. Tip of the spear."

"So..."

"Of course," Dante said. "Spearhead Data Systems. Skylar's company. Got an address?"

"Just a website. No contact info, no address, no listing in any business directory, nothing on social media. They don't exist."

"So, we're back to where we started," Dante said.

"Not exactly," Briana said. "When I was scrolling to the bottom, I found a hidden link. It was really cool actually. When I'd scroll up and down, a portion at the bottom would reveal a small S shape. This is what it links to."

She held up the phone, showing a white screen with the

words "server error" along the top.

"Okay."

"I looked at the HTML source for the page. That link is a dot onion. It's only accessible through a special browser known as TOR." She tapped and swiped on the screen again. "Look."

Dante took the phone from her and looked at the screen. It was black with green writing, a bit hard to read, but he could clearly see the words Fer de Lance above a white box. A cursor blinked inside the box. He gazed up at her.

"Isn't TOR for browsing the Dark Web?"

"From what I could find, yes. It sounds cooler than it is. It just means the connection is encrypted. It's worth a try," she said.

"How did you figure all this out?"

"Oh, I know a little about computers," she said with a sly grin. "And Google, of course."

Dante paused, then typed in two words.

Bothrops Asper.

The cursor blinked several times as if excited.

Mr. Ellis. I'm so glad you got in touch. Please let me help you.

How?

An address appeared, along with exactly where to meet, followed by a time.

Once you arrive, we get can you somewhere safe.

Dante handed the phone back to Briana. "Feel like taking a drive?"

CHAPTER 78

Eyes

Dante rummaged around in the trunk of the Porsche, lifting the stacks of money as Briana kept an eye out. He found what he was looking for and opened a small leather bag. He removed a screwdriver and handed it to Briana. She moved off through the dim parking lot, the white stripes of her dazzle camo fading into the night.

He opened one of the plastic bags, removed a stack of bills and slipped them into a zippered pocket on the dazzle camo. He tugged the car cover off and tossed it into a crumpled heap among the refuse that had collected along a low wall. It looked as though it had always been there.

Dante got behind the wheel and started the car. In the rearview mirror, he saw Briana return and disappear as she crouched down. A moment later the passenger door opened and she got in, tossing the Porsche's license plate to the floor.

"I got a plate off an old truck that looked like it had been parked there awhile, but the registration was still valid."

Dante nodded and pulled out onto the street. There were very few cars out this early, sunrise just beginning to blush behind them as they drove west. The skies were clear and cloudless.

There were no dragonflies.

Dante noted how many cameras there were as they drove, something he'd never really taken notice of before. They were mounted to the side of power poles, hanging next to traffic lights and above business entrances. Some were perched on the ledges of buildings like futuristic gargoyles. Dante shook his head. They were all over the place. Even if only half of them were on, it was still like being under a microscope. It made his skin crawl.

They merged onto the 101 South and drove in silence, Briana staring out the passenger side window. She sat up straighter, leaning forward to peer through the windshield.

"We're going to downtown?"

"Yes."

"I've always wanted to see downtown L.A."

"It's not much. Nothing like Chicago, or New York."

"Better than downtown Cairo."

"Cairo? I thought you said you were from Nebraska."

"I am. Cairo, Nebraska. The welcome sign is a pyramid with a camel statue next to it. About eight hundred people live there, I guess. You just missed the Cairo Cornstalk Festival."

"Sounds nice."

"Just another tired, little town where old people go to die, and young people want to escape. Or at least I thought it was. It is nice. Now I can't ever go back there."

"Your video wasn't that bad, right? It was just you and a girl kissing? That's on television all the time these days."

"It's still a small town and my Dad's the preacher there. Dark Messiah sent that video to everyone one of my contacts. That includes some teachers, Mrs. Pettis the librarian and town gossip, even the mayor from when I was Ms. Teen Cairo. My guess is the locals have burned the church to the ground."

"It can't be that bad."

"Nebraska ain't California."

"Guess not."

They fell into silence as a cluster of tall buildings appeared up ahead.

"That's downtown L.A.? It looks so much bigger on TV."

"Everything looks bigger on TV," Dante said. "So, I have to ask, why did you come out here?"

Briana continued to stare out the window. Dante gazed at her again, but she remained silent.

"I came out here to become a singer, or so I told myself," Briana said. "Leish, the girl I was living with, discovered me." Briana laughed, a colorless sound. "Leish," she said with a sneer. "Her real name's Alicia. She was going to be my manager or whatever, but it was just a set up. Her boyfriend, Melvin Rossetti, also known as Mel Rose, somehow got into trouble with Dark Messiah, so they offered me up to do their little errand."

"Mel Rose?" Dante said. "One of those reality show guys, right?"

"He was the bad boy of the group," Briana said with a sigh.

"I remember. His manager sent his head shot to us at least half a dozen times. Looked like a real dick to me."

"Leish, Mel Rose, Dark Messiah, Fer de Lance," Briana shook her head. "What's up with the people out here?"

"Not everyone's like that. But this is where people have always come to be somebody else. Start new."

Briana looked at the trees blur by outside, watery green smears above the reddish-brown brick wall that lined the freeway. "My boyfriend. Mark. He hit me." Briana mumbled the last words, her throat closing up. "That's why I came out here."

Dante glanced over at her for a moment, wishing he could see her through the optical camo. "I'm sorry. As a father of a daughter, that's one of my biggest fears. Guys can be real shit heads," Dante said.

"Yeah. Girls too."

Silence filled the car again as Dante merged onto the 110 Freeway. Shadows fell over them as they drove south through downtown, Briana craning her neck to see the tall buildings.

"Do you think he's part of it? Skylar Westfall?" Briana said.

"In the beginning, I did. Now, I just don't know. I thought Colin was behind the whole thing, especially when he put that mask on my face, but he saved my eye. Looks like he's just a victim as well." Dante shook his head. "Dark Messiah told me I was the first and that others would follow. This whole twisted charade ends with my death, broadcast live, me pulling the trigger. I wouldn't wish this on anybody, but why me?"

"Let's hope this Skylar guy has some answers," Briana said without much conviction. "Do you think he can actually help?"

"I don't know. But at this point," Dante said, "he's all we got."

CHAPTER 79

Fireworks

Dante pulled into the driveway of a large parking structure, noticing the camera above the ticket machine as he punched the big yellow button on its face. The ticket spat out and Dante snatched it as the striped gate arm lifted. He drove in, following the right-hand curves that led upward. There were cameras everywhere.

Dante parked and killed the engine. There were only a few other cars on this level, none close by. Dante peered out through the windows, feeling exposed.

"Ready?"

Briana nodded.

They walked to the elevator, footsteps echoing lightly on the concrete. It was quiet this early, almost peaceful, except for the occasional horn bleat from one of the many freeways that boxed in downtown Los Angeles.

As they took an elevator down, Dante felt the camera mounted above watching them, its lens barely visible through the smoky glass dome.

"Do these suits actually work?" Dante asked.

"They seem to so far. Guess we're going to find out."

After exiting the elevator, they followed a covered walkway past several tall buildings toward Figueroa Street. Traffic was light, mostly trucks and the orange and white autonomous delivery vehicles. Briana watched one as it drove by before tearing her eyes away. Drones of various sizes whizzed by high overhead, clutching small packages.

None were shaped like a dragonfly.

A few people strode by in business attire. Most paid them no attention, eyes locked on their phones. One woman glanced up and glared at them before continuing on.

A tall building clad in white tile loomed large up ahead, its dark blue windows reflecting the surrounding cityscape.

"That's the Triple Seven building," Dante said. "The mall is right up there."

"Hold it," called a deep, male voice from behind.

They turned as two policemen approached—all mustaches and hard stares.

"Unzip and pull those hoods off," said the taller one. His nameplate read Miller. "And get those IDs out."

"We have a right to our privacy," Dante said, glancing quickly around. Cameras were everywhere. Over doors. On poles. The sky was thick with drones, all which had multiple cameras, radar, lidar, and who knows what else. Even the policemen had cameras on their chests capturing everything.

Miller shook his head. "The law states that while wearing dazzle camo you must comply with an identity check at any time, either by private citizen or law enforcement." He rested his hand on his baton, muscular bicep tight against the short sleeve of his dark blue uniform.

"Listen, we aren't doing anything illegal. We'll just be on our way," Dante said.

Miller lifted his baton out of the metal loop and stepped closer. His partner did the same.

"Last warning," Miller said, voice hard. "IDs. *Now*."

"Okay, okay," Dante said as he pulled a hand inside the suit, reaching behind his back to catch the lanyard attached to the zipper. His hand brushed past the Glock tucked at his lower back.

If they find this...

Miller raised his baton. "Slowly. You," he said to Briana. "Don't move."

The zipper slid down Dante's back and he felt the air evaporate the sweat beaded on his neck.

"Okay. Now the hood," Miller said. "Nice and easy. No sudden moves."

Dante lifted his hands and slipped his fingers into the edges of the hood and pulled the two sides forward, exposing the top of his head.

Everyone flinched as a loud series of pops echoed out behind them. Miller crouched and pulled his gun while his partner stood by, dumbfounded. They all watched, rooted in place as red fireworks shot up from the top of a parking structure and exploded above, raining down a shower of sparks.

Miller turned back and frowned. "Your lucky day," he said. The two policemen jogged off toward the parking structure as the firework show raging on.

"That was close," Dante said as he zipped his suit closed again.

"I don't think it was luck," Briana said.

"Come on let's get out of here."

They fled down a wide set of steps to the sunken top level of an open-air shopping mall. They fast walked past several stores before descending an escalator to the dining area. Weaving their way around the many blue umbrellas that dotted the space, they sat at a table under the only red umbrella to wait. The entire place was deserted. No cleaning staff, no employees behind glass storefronts prepping for the day. Nobody.

Off in the distance, the fireworks gave a few final pops before coming to a stop. A sudden silence descended as if a great woolen blanket had been thrown over the mall, rendering the air close and still.

"This is weird," Briana said, her hooded head peering around.

Dante checked a digital clock in the window of a Gold's

Gym. 6:43 AM. "Five more minutes, then we go."

A siren wailed somewhere far off, impossible to tell where as the sound echoed off glass and concrete. The summer heat was building and Dante felt sweat creep down his back. Briana tugged at her camo, causing the striped pattern to jitter. A crow cawed from above, its large wings flapping as it landed on the upper level and began to march back and forth, head bobbing.

"Let's get out of here," Dante said, rising to his feet.

"Look," Briana said, her voice awed. "Maskcreants."

Figures appeared, flowing in by the hundreds from all directions. They filled the mall in a matter of minutes, all clad in dazzle camo. Some milled about in small groups, others sitting at the tables while the majority kept a steady stream of movement along the storefronts, between planters and umbrellas, up and down stairs and escalators.

"Follow me," said a voice nearby. It sounded neither male nor female, but a strange mixture of both. One of the camo suited figures held out their hand low and to the side, waving them on.

"Stay close, single file," they said.

Dante and Briana stood and followed the figure past store fronts before joining the flow leading up the escalator to the street.

"Keep following," said the figure. They did two turns around the upper level, Dante feeling as if he was trapped in some bizarre rapids. The flow redirected out toward the street, dazzle clad figures pouring out onto the four lanes of Figueroa.

"This way," said their guide.

Dante gazed to either side as they streamed across the street, bright morning sun causing him to squint. Autonomous trucks blocked the flow of traffic. Up ahead was a nondescript two-story tan building. A white door, the numbers 712 mounted above, was set in a vertical strip sandwiched between the tan building and Bank of America branch. Their guide stopped near the door. Dante and Briana slipped in next to them.

"Stay here for a moment," the guide said.

Dante watched through the steady stream of dazzle cameoed figures as a car drove by, the occupants' mouths slack, staring in awe at this bizarre spectacle. One had their phone held up, capturing the moment. It made Dante feel nervous, exposed. He watched the car as it continued down to a corner where the Bank of America stood. A security guard inside lifted a walkie-talkie to his lips.

"This is no good," Dante said.

"What are we waiting for?" Briana said.

"Wait," said the figure, holding up a staying hand.

There was a loud click from behind the white door nearby. Tires screeched from down the street, followed by the sound of crunching plastic. The white door opened inward.

"Now!" the figure said.

They followed their guide through the open doorway as smoke billowed up from two autonomous trucks locked together by ragged gaps in their plastic hulls. Darkness enveloped them as they slipped inside and the door sealed shut behind them.

CHAPTER 80

Fer De Lance

A strip of lighting winked on, illuminating a short hallway. Bare concrete floors and cinder block walls led back to a door at the other end. The whispers of their feet came to a stop as their guide halted and turned.

"Rest here for a moment."

Dante slipped both hands into the camo, pulled the zipper down then yanked his hood off, prosthetic arm whirring as he aimed the Glock.

"Where's Abigail," Dante said.

The figure's arms went up. "Let me explain."

"Listen, Skylar. I'm sick of all this cloak and hacker bullshit. Pull that fucking hood off and tell me where she is or I'm going to kill you." Dante's heart jackhammered in his chest, his face slick with sweat.

"Dante..." Briana said.

"Stay out of this."

Skylar unzipped the suit and slid the hood down. A matte black mask was on his face and Dante raised the gun higher. The younger man pulled the mask off and dropped it to the floor. "I don't know where she is. Not yet. We've been trying to find her ever since the airport incident. These people who have her, they're very organized, very good at this. They locked me out of your network and all your devices. I had to be very careful of when and how I contacted you. If you had just plugged in my flash drive that day we would've been back in and could've stopped this cold."

Dante shook his head and slipped his finger onto the trigger.

"We're not Dark Messiah," Skylar said.

"Fer de lance?" Dante said.

"We're the front line against threats like this. We've been preparing for a very long time." He motioned behind him, high voice dropping to a conspiratorial croak. "Just let me show you."

Briana looked from Skylar to Dante, then back again, stepping closer. "This isn't Dark Messiah's style," she said. "For one, we've never seen them and this guy is standing right here in front of us. Let's see what he has to show us. If they have a way of getting to Dark Messiah and finding Abigail, it's worth a look. We came this far. What other choice do we have?"

Dante's eyes remained locked on Skylar's.

He looked young but handled himself like he was much older. And his eyes. A light shone there in the pale blue, a fierceness, the wisdom of someone who'd lived and seen things. Terrible things. How many people could stare down the barrel of a gun held by a desperate man the way Skylar was right now? Dante lowered the gun, but held it down at his side.

"Show us."

CHAPTER 81

Rat Traps

The door eased open without a sound and they entered. Dante watched the door close behind them, eyes widening as he saw how thick it was. It sealed shut with a series of ratcheting thumps that vibrated the ground. A large, empty room stretched out before them. Evenly spaced support pillars jutted up from a concrete floor. It was hotter in here, the air still and dry. Dante peeled the upper half of his suit off, tying the arms around his waist. Skylar eyed the prosthetic arm with interest as he did so. Briana did the same and Skylar gazed at her a moment too long before turning away.

He led them along a diagonal path tracked through a layer of dust to the far corner. A grungy odor hung heavy in the air with a tinge of something bitter, along with a darker smell underneath. Cloying and dank. Rotten. Littered throughout the room were large, black boxes about the size of a travel bag with an opening on one side.

"Traps," Skylar said over one shoulder. "The kind that kill. Downtown has a tremendous rat problem. Not too many get in here but when they do, whammo! When I was a kid, my brother had a pet rat and it skeeved me out seeing that tail and giant rat balls dragging all over his shoulders. Disgusting."

"This is what you wanted to show us?" Dante said.

Skylar ignored him and came to a stop at the far corner. A square hatch was set into the floor with a metal handle inset in the lid. He knelt down and pulled up on the handle, an ugly metallic screech in the silence. The hatch opened, revealing a rusty metal stairway that led down. Dingy yellow light filtered up from somewhere deep inside.

"After you," Skylar said.

Dante climbed down the steps, his feet clomping on the metal grate. At the bottom, he gazed down a long, dimly lit hallway of water-stained concrete. Pipes ran along the ceiling, scaled with gray. It was cooler down here and he sighed with relief. Briana descended and stood next to him.

"This place is so cool," she said.

Dante sniffed the air. "Stinks down here."

The metal hatch dropped with thunderous crash and they both jumped.

"Sorry," Skylar said with a smirk. "This way."

Their feet crunched on loose concrete scree as they made their way forward, the occasional naked bulb overhead throwing dim pools of yellow light.

"It's rumored there are over seventy miles of tunnels under Los Angeles," Skylar said. "Some built for subways, others used during prohibition to hustle alcohol and later, to keep convicted murderers safe while moving them between jails. Fallout shelters came later, built in the early '50s after Russia successfully tested their first atom bomb. Most are now used for storage or have been sealed up and forgotten."

"See any Lizard people?" Briana said.

Skylar laughed. "I heard about that one too. God, I wish. None yet, but I'll let you know if I do." He grinned over his shoulder.

The walls shifted to pale green, the paint cracked where the joints of cinder blocks came together. A sign was riveted to the wall, three yellow triangles in a black circle with the words "Fallout Shelter" below. The hall juked and ended at a metal door, painted the same pale green as the surrounding brick. A well-worn T handle jutted from the center with circles etched in the paint from countless rotations. The handle rotated with a squeal and they followed Skylar inside.

The ceiling was low and Dante felt the urge to duck, even though he had at least a foot of clearance. It was cool inside, bordering on cold. The room was a large square chamber with cinder block walls—all painted the same green as the hallway. Various carpets of all shapes and colors were scattered across the smooth concrete floors that peeked through. Tables of all shapes and sizes dotted the room. Laptops or workstations sat on top along with toys, board games, Post-Its, crumpled coffee cups and energy drinks. The sound of chattering keyboards filled the air, helmed by at least a dozen or so people as they typed in rapid fits and starts. Others sat on beanbags or pillows on the floor, laptops resting on laps as they typed. Incense and warm electronics permeated the air, along with the unmistakable undercurrent of body odor.

A man in his early thirties sat at a table nearby, dressed in a gray three-piece suit and wingtips, spine ramrod straight as his slender fingers flew across the keys. His pale, freckled skin glowed in the blue wash from his monitor. Sitting beside him was a large man with puffy cheeks flushed with red, a pair of reading glasses perched on his stubby nose. He blinked rapidly as his fingers hammered the keyboard.

Others had green or purple hair and wore loose fitting clothes. Two people wore dazzle camo. Some wore button up shirts and slacks, hair combed within an inch of its life. A girl near the back had a tan hijab on her head, dark eyes glittering in the dim light from her screen. Next to her sat another person wearing a burka that covered their whole body, only the eyes showing. The thumb on their right hand was covered with a thick bandage. None of them looked up from their work. Installed along the far-left wall were wooden bunkbeds. Soft shapes lay under blankets on some, gently rising and falling.

"What is this? Some kind of hacker army?" Dante asked.

Skylar smiled. "This is Fer de lance. We like to think of ourselves as Modern Templars battling in the crusade for the digital holy land."

"Modern Templars and digital crusades," Dante said, shaking his head. "What the hell are you talking about?"

"I know how it sounds. But future wars are going to be waged in cyberspace. It's just skirmishes right now. Data theft. Industrial espionage. Misinformation through social media channels, election scams. Cyber-stalking, cyber-harassment, malware, ransomware."

"Sounds like war already," Briana said.

"Those are just the opening salvos. Remember Stuxnet? It was a worm created by the United States and Israel to attack Iranian uranium enrichment centrifuges to affect plutonium purity. Brilliant. Iran couldn't make nuclear weapons and not one shot was fired. But this is just a small taste of things to come. The big one is coming. I'm talking about a concerted, large-scale effort to take control of nationwide, governmental infrastructure. Can you imagine the stranglehold a group, whether government or terrorists would have over a country if they could achieve this? Better believe the NSA and CIA are giving this some serious consideration. People are just now becoming aware of it. It all started when Edward Snowden peeled back the veneer and exposed one of the many battlefields. An American citizen's right to privacy."

"Isn't he a traitor?" Briana asked.

"Well," Skylar said, "yes and no, depending on your point of view."

"Not sure I follow," Dante said.

"When Snowden joined the CIA, he swore an oath to god and country. He broke that oath to expose government secrets. So, through that lens he's a traitor. But he also exposed the power, the tremendous, previously unknown power the U.S. Government had over its citizens. The ability to spy on anyone through their cell phone, tablet or computer without any oversight, FISA court orders or sense of responsibility. That kind of power is just too much for one group to have."

"But if you have nothing to hide, isn't it worth the loss of a few freedoms to protect us?" Briana asked.

"What if your boyfriend posts nude pictures of you after a break up? What did you do to deserve that? Absolutely nothing except trust the wrong person. And you never truly know someone until it's too late. What if that kind of person has access to the surveillance on anyone at any time? The results could be disastrous, and I'm not talking about the Fappening."

"The Fappening?" Briana asked.

"Not important," Skylar said. He cleared his throat before continuing. "Let's say this particular person works for the CIA and has an axe to grind with someone. All they have to do is catch the right moment, or manufacture a police record with the help of deep fakes and falsified documents. Arrests. Drug possession. Even falsified juvenile records that are not allowed to be opened. But what if there is probable cause? A judge will order that seal torn right off. Not to mention they'll have the full power of the U.S. Government on their side once they collect enough evidence. It wouldn't matter if the evidence is manufactured. Who would know? The CIA has a blue wall of silence just like the police and they protect their own. All Snowden did is yank back the curtain for the world to see what kind of wizard is back there, yanking levers and smashing 'like' buttons. And if you ask me, he is one evil, ugly motherfucker."

"This is all very exciting, Skylar," Dante said, "but what about Abigail?"

The young man waved one of his small, delicate hands over the room, his icy blue eyes locked on Dante. "What do you think they're all doing right now?"

CHAPTER 82

Hit

"Follow me," Skylar said.

He led them through the people hunched over their computers to the back of the room. A long table stood across the back wall with two large monitors mounted above, at least eighty inches across. Various data feeds marched across the screens, but what they were monitoring, Dante could only guess. The table was covered with electronic odds and ends and various gadgets, some half-finished. Underneath were milk crates full of motherboards and other electronics. A soldering iron sat in a sheath of metal loops in front of a small chest of labeled plastic drawers, each one containing a specific electronic component. An oscilloscope was perched off to one side, its green electric eye displaying an oscillating sine wave.

"What's it doing?" Briana asked, pointing at the small screen.

"60 hertz," Skylar said. "I knew you guys were coming so I switched it on 'cause it looks cool." He turned and glanced at Dante. "Good job finding my message portal."

"I didn't." Dante nodded toward Briana. "She did."

"Really?" Skylar asked, a slight smile curving his lips. He moved a mouse next to a keyboard and a monitor on the table lit up. After typing in a few commands, the screen filled with a video feed of an airport interior, the images whizzing by at dizzying speeds.

"That's the Burbank Airport," Dante said, peering closer.

"Our watchdog software, Creeper, uses machine learning to-"

"Creeper?" Abigail said.

"C-R-P-R. Cognitive Relativistic Parametric Review. Creeper. Well, I thought it was cute. Anyways, Creeper started downloading cam feeds as soon as the plane hit. We didn't know exactly was going on until the software flagged an anomaly." Skylar pointed at the screen. "This."

The video slowed and played at normal speed. Black smoke choked the airport terminal as people streamed through in a mad dash to escape. Dante saw two small shapes huddled against the wall in the lower right and his breath caught.

"Oh my god, that's them. Abigail and Kelly."

Two men dressed in black military gear with white skull faces peeled off from the rushing throng. One delivered a powerful kick to Kelly's face while the other grabbed Abigail and pressed a hand over her mouth. Kelly shook off the kick and lunged after the man carrying Abigail, punching furiously at the side of his head. He stumbled, almost dropping the girl to the ground as he tried to spin away from the fierce series of jabs. His partner struck Kelly in the lower back and she stiffened, throwing her mouth open. Another jab to the back of her head dropped her hard to the carpet. The two men disappeared from view, Abigail struggling to break free from between them.

It was over in seconds.

A flare of bright light caused the screen to darken and Dante leaned in, trying to peer through the glare. The image returned and he felt a bitter taste in his mouth as he saw Kelly lying on the ground, helpless and bleeding as people rushed past her. Bile rose in the back of this throat as he wheeled on Skylar. "Where'd they take her?"

"Watch."

The feed changed to show a dark sedan pull up on the tarmac outside, the two men hustling a helpless Abigail inside and speeding off. Another feed showed the car swerving into a parking structure and skid to a stop near a white Ford truck with super crew cab. Briana inhaled sharply next to Dante as the men yanked Abigail out and hustled over, one dragging her by the hand. Abigail tripped and was roughly yanked back to her feet.

"Motherfuckers!" Dante said, slamming the table.

Abigail sprang to life like a coiled spring and latched onto the man's gloved hand and bit down. There was no sound, but Dante imagined he could hear the bastard yelp. Abigail ran away in the slow, panicked run of a terrified child before the man caught her again and carried her over to the truck and pushed her inside. The truck drove off past incoming fire-trucks and police cars, moving no faster than twenty miles an hour.

The screen went black.

"You have a very brave little girl," Briana said, touching his arm.

Dante shook, his breathing ragged. Blinking away tears he swallowed. "Where'd they go?"

When Skylar spoke, his voice was low and steady. "Creeper is tapped into cameras all throughout the city but somewhere outside the airport, we lost them. The search parameters were updated to check footage from other sources from that day but unfortunately most privately owned cameras are on, but not recording. It's going to take some time to find sources and scan through all that footage."

"We're running out of time," Dante said. "We have less than eight hours to find Abigail."

"Seven hours, thirty-six minutes," Skylar corrected. "We ran the plates. They're registered to a 1996 Nissan Sentra so the plates were stolen and they would have no doubt switched to another set. They know what they're doing. Finding that specific truck is going to be tricky. But we have an ace in the hole."

"And what's that?" Briana said.

Skylar typed in a command and ran the footage back. The two militia men approached Abigail and Kelly where they crouched against the wall. The video played in a loop shuttling back and forth.

"The guy on the left, he's got a bit of limp there. See? We figure he's ex-military, got a prosthetic lower leg. So, Creeper analyzes all the footage we have of this guy and compiles a movement profile based on how he walks, runs, and so on. Then it creates an animation that can be loaded onto a skeleton. We call it a DMM, Dynamic Movement Map."

"Kind of like motion capture," Dante said.

"Yes, with a dash of physical simulation."

The screen changed to a three-dimensional skeleton. It jogged, similar to the man in the video, a slight bouncy limp on the left side. The motion then changed to a walk showing a similar movement style.

"You're going to scan footage for someone that walks similar to the DMM?" Briana said.

"Exactly," Skylar said with a grin.

"Won't that take forever? I mean, it has to analyze and build maps of other people for comparison before it can compare, right?" Briana said.

"Who *are* you?" Skylar asked, shaking his head. "You're exactly right. It goes deeper than that. We have a database of militia groups all over America. A lot have cropped up over the last few years. Most are just rednecks who like to play soldier. They get together and drink and shoot up old cars. Others, though, are the real deal. Heavily armed preppers getting ready for a possible race war, end of the world, what have you. An even smaller subset are mercenaries, soldiers for hire. These guys are ex-military and usually do illegal undercover missions outside the US for the CIA. And on very rare occasions, if the money is right, they'll do a job right here on American soil."

"You know which group?" Dante said.

"We're looking at five right now. One from Michigan, one from Texas, another from Ohio and two out of Nebraska."

"Wait, two from Nebraska?" Briana said.

"Yep. They're active right now."

"How do you know?"

"Their trailers are dark and the sheep aren't nervous."

Briana's brows furrowed and Skylar laughed. "Internet chatter. All these clowns use the dark web to communicate, so it can be difficult to trace who it is and from where. Creeper is also analyzing the chatter for patterns, searching for keywords like 'package' or 'mark' that will reveal which group is responsible. Sometimes they're dumb enough to just say outright what they're up to. We'll know as soon as it gets a hit."

"And when will that be?"

"I have no idea," Skylar said.

"This sounds like a bunch of bullshit. How do you know any of this works?" Dante said.

"We got a hit!" called out the pale man in the three-piece suit.

CHAPTER 83

Esperanto

"What do we got, Neil?" Skylar said as he marched across the room.

Neil turned in his chair, straightened his bow tie and patted down his thinning red hair before speaking.

"Creeper has finished scanning the encrypted communications eliminating all other groups except one. They call themselves Osiron Paramilitary. Fairly new but they're in the database. They communicate in code, but Creeper has determined it to be a fairly common mono-alphabetic substitution cipher. Unfortunately, the decoded text is an unknown language, so it has been unable to further decode what they are actually saying. Except for three words."

"What three words? Dante said.

"Abigail, hospital and Chapman."

Dante felt numb as he furrowed his brow trying to figure out exactly what that meant. *Abigail was at a hospital? Was she hurt?* It couldn't be that easy though, calling every hospital in California and asking for Abigail Ellis.

Skylar nodded slowly, thinking. "Creeper," he called out.

"Yes?" said a mild female voice. It seemed to be coming from everywhere and nowhere all at once.

"Read back the decoded message," Skylar said.

"What is it? Like Siri or something?" Briana said.

"Oh, this blows Siri out of the water," Skylar said, holding up his hands for silence. Everyone stopped typing and sat still, waiting for Creeper to speak again.

"Ready?" Creeper said. "Transdonu Abigail al la interkonsentita hospitalo al kuracisto Chapman, tiam atendu pliajn instrukciojn lau ordono de Malluma Mesia."

Silence hung heavy in the air.

"Yeah," Briana said. "Way better than Siri."

"It sounds familiar but…is that Latin or something?" Skylar said.

"If it was Latin then Creeper would have translated it right away," Neil said.

"Sounds like gibberish," Dante said.

"Gibberish," said a deep voice, laced with contempt. It was the large man next to Neil, his brow furrowed as he stared at his screen, mouse-wheeling down through an article.

"Something to add, Big Neil?" Skylar said.

Big Neil pounded his mouse on the table, but stayed silent.

Skylar looked at Neil and the thin man shrugged. Big Neil wheeled on him.

"Of course, you don't remember, and now that's why Creeper can't translate," Big Neil said. "No one listens to the genius in the corner."

"Big Neil, please," Skylar said, "If you know this language…"

"Ask sticks over there," he said, jabbing a finger at Neil.

Neil opened his mouth to protest before his face tightened, the corner of his mouth turned up as understanding dawned in his eyes. "Are you kidding me? It's Esperanto?"

"Why would Creeper need to know Esperanto?" Big Neil said, one eye twitching.

"What the hell is Esperanto?" Dante said.

Big Neil's face relaxed. "Esperanto means 'one who hopes'. It was developed by L.L. Zamenhof in 1886 as an international language for all people."

"Bet you can't translate," Neil said, smirking.

Big Neil's mouth screwed up tight as his face blushed a dark red. He took a deep breath before speaking. "It says, 'Deliver Abigail to the agreed hospital to doctor Chapman, then wait for further instructions as ordered by Dark Messiah.'" Big Neil smiled broadly at them, teeth gleaming before he glanced at Dante and his face fell. "Abigail's the one we're...oh, my God."

Skylar spoke to the room. "Find out which hospitals this Dr. Chapman reports to. In the meantime, have Creeper monitor all hospitals in the Greater Los Angeles Area and keep an eye out for our militia man with a limp."

CHAPTER 84

Armory

Dante walked past the long table full of Skylar's projects into a dimly lit hallway. Skylar had told him they were getting very close but would still have to wait for Creeper to do its analysis. He'd left the excited knot of Fer de lancers behind, mumbling how he needed to use the bathroom.

He shuffled past a thick door on the left with a keypad mounted next to it, its numbers glowing red. A door with a T handle was at the end of the passageway. The handle turned with a scrape, the door screeching open before Dante stepped inside.

Fluorescent lights winked on along the walls, filling the room with stark white illumination. It was a large space, reminiscent of a parking garage with its low ceiling and concrete supports. It was painted the same pale green as the rest of the fallout shelter with the occasional chalky white streak trailing down. At the center were two large objects, each about the size of a car, covered with thin black tarps. Dante came closer and saw that a large double door had recently been installed in the ceiling above, the edges of the concrete still bleached and chalky white where the opening had been cut. Large pneumatic rams were mounted on the floor, two for each door allowing it to open upward and out. He lifted the tarp, peeking underneath.

"Take a look," Skylar said from behind.

Dante glanced over his shoulder then pulled the tarp off and onto the floor. A large, sleek drone crouched there, about the size of an SUV. Its intricate looking parts were painted a solid, matte black. Four propellers were tucked along its flanks, mounted at the end of delicate but strong looking support arms. Skylar waved a hand and the mega drone whirred to life. Dante stepped back as a warning beep trilled before the arms unfolded and extended the propellers out from each corner.

"You built this?" Dante said.

"One of our people is the lead designer at a drone company. He'd always dreamed of making a big one but his bosses didn't see the money in them so they refused. Fer de lance paid for them. We have the pieces and components built to spec then we assembled them here. These babies are all carbon fiber and aircraft aluminum and can carry up to a thousand pounds."

"How are you paying for all this? It can't be with the money I invested."

"It is though. Well, your money and other investors. We need legitimate sources so we don't raise any red flags just stealing it. That way Spearhead, the front company, can still be protected by bankruptcy and we can just hide the money in Irish banks just like all the other big American companies. Hey, if it's good enough for them, right?"

"Your name is for shit now, though. You've burned too many people."

"Not my real name. We chose a generic, easy to dismiss, Gen Z type name. It worked with you, didn't it?"

"What about your run on college Jeopardy?" Dante said.

"Manufactured by us. There're a few articles about how it's bullshit by the two people who cared, but we buried them a few pages in. It's amazing how many people don't go past the first page of search results, isn't it?"

"But why? What is all this really for?"

"Fer de lance is a necessity. We speak truth to power. And

when that fails, we take action. A group like ours wouldn't be necessary if the FBI and CIA could do their jobs properly. There's just too many restrictions and they're too easily corruptible. Who's going to help when your own government can't because they've been compromised?"

"And your group is incorruptible."

"Of course not. When it comes to that I burn it down and start over. I have that luxury. Government agencies don't." Skylar closed his hands together and the drone retracted into its original position. "Help me with the cover, will you?"

Dante lifted one side while Skylar lifted the other, arms spread wide. They covered the drone and the two men regarded each other in silence for a moment before Skylar spoke, his voice a low croak.

"When Edward Snowden revealed that the CIA was able to spy on us, their own citizens whenever they choose without oversight, without impunity, Fer de lance not only became a necessity but an inevitability. Morally compromised people worry about control and blame, not helping one man find his daughter. That's where we come in. We're going to find her, Dante. I promise. And when we do, we're going to burn Dark Messiah to cinder. Cancer like that has to be destroyed before it can spread. It's already metastasized to the FBI and who knows where else. It's the only way." Skylar gazed at Dante a moment before speaking again. "Let me show you something."

Dante followed him back down the hall. The younger man stopped in front of the thick metal door and entered a sequence of numbers on the keypad. The door swung inward and Dante followed him inside.

Hundreds of rifles of all kinds lined the walls, standing floor to ceiling in two rows on metal racks. Ammo boxes were stacked on three heavy wooden pallets in the center. Large white bags of ammonium nitrate fertilizer were piled up on another pallet next to the ammo. A long-barreled rifle on a tripod stood nearby. There was no trigger or stock, just a small, rounded box attached to the back with a stubby antenna sticking up from the side.

"Remote-controlled sniper rifle," Skylar said, placing a hand on top. "Why would somebody even need this?"

There was another pallet stacked with slender bricks wrapped in dark green plastic. Each brick was labeled with blocky, yellow letters that read: CHARGE DEMOLITION M112 WITH TAGGANT (1-1/4 LBS COMP C-4).

"Skylar," Dante said, eyes hard.

"It's not what you think. This is all stuff we've confiscated from militia groups. We're not warriors, at least in the physical sense. Our battlefield is online. This is all off the streets now, because of us, out of the hands of people who wish to do harm to others. Angry with the government. Understandable, but misguided. We find out where their stockpiles are, take what we can then inform the authorities. Anonymously of course. We work with government agencies while minimizing risk to us as much as possible."

"I'm afraid this much power puts you in a very precarious position though. How do you know something you do is going to be worth the end result? Things never go as planned. With my work, I screw up and maybe we miss a deadline, lose a client. You screw up, people get hurt, maybe lose their lives. Are you ready to take that responsibility?"

Skylar held his gaze. "Ask me again when Abigail is back home safe. You may see what we're doing here in a very different light."

Dante nodded. "So why show me all this?"

"I am fearless, and therefore powerful. Remember?"

"Yes, but-"

"You spoke at my high school years ago. Those words changed my life, struck me like a bolt of lightning. Helped me see things so clearly. Set me on a path. I wasn't quite sure what it was, but I knew it wasn't going to be pushing a boulder uphill for the rest of my life, just to have it roll back down and crush me in the end."

"Skylar, those aren't even my words. It's from Frankenstein

for fucks' sake."

"One of my favorite books."

"Yeah, I can tell." He sighed, the air rattling in his lungs. "It's all bullshit, Skylar. Just a rah-rah speech. 'I am fearless and therefore powerful'. Look at me. I've never been so afraid in my life." Dante looked down at his prosthetic hand. "I guess I believed it at one time. Now, I...just don't know anymore."

"No, Dante. It's the *answer*. Fear is at the very core of all irrational, non-critical thought. It fuels the fires of anger and rage, both of which are emotional extensions of fear. In truth, angry people are the most fearful of all of us and, therefore, the most dangerous. If our own authorities can be so easily compromised, as they have been in your case, what other answer is there than to take up the spear and wield it ourselves?"

Dante nodded, thinking a moment before he spoke. "I'm not saying you're wrong about what you've built here, Skylar. I don't exactly agree with your worldview, but if you find Abigail, then I swear to you, I'll be in your debt for the rest of my life."

"I appreciate it, I really do," Skylar said. "And I'll remember you said that."

"A word of warning though," Dante said, "from Mary Shelley's story."

Skylar gazed at him, one eyebrow raised.

"You remember how it ends, right?" Dante said.

"In fire and death," said a voice from the doorway.

Dante turned to see the person in the black burka, only the eyes visible, bleary and red. The eyes blinked with a twitchy intensity before the figure reached up and tugged the hood off their head and let it crumple to the ground.

"Hello Dante," Colin said.

CHAPTER 85

Colin

Dante advanced on him. "Look at me."

He grabbed Colin by the neck with his left hand and squeezed, cocking his right hand back into a fist over his shoulder. The thin man's eyes bulged as he clawed at the fingers clamped around this throat, eyes widening as Dante's prosthetic hand cinched to a grinding halt.

"Why?" Dante said. "Tell me why!"

"Wait," Colin gasped, struggling to loosen the fingers around his neck.

Dante drove a fist into his stomach and Colin doubled over, legs dropping out from under him. Grabbing two handfuls of his shirt, Dante yanked him to his feet again, pulling him close. He barely seemed to weigh anything.

"They have her, Colin. They have Abigail."

"I can help, please!" Colin said, voice a wheezy rasp as he struggled to free himself.

Skylar came forward and put a hand on Dante's arm. "He came to us. Hear what he has to say first. Then if you want to kill him, go right ahead."

Dante released his grip and Colin fell to the ground, rubbing his throat and coughing from deep in his lungs. Dante resisted the urge to kick him in the face. He glowered at his old friend, doubled over and panting. His face softened and he stumbled back before slumping on to a stack of ammo cans. Looking down at his hands, he unclenched his fists and motioned with a short chop of his hand.

Colin crawled over and sat across from Dante on the floor.

"I'm sorry."

"Don't say it. Just tell me what you know."

"I got my life back," Colin said. "What pathetic little life I had."

Dante glared at him. "All I care about-"

"You're going to hear this!" Colin said, light flaring in his eyes. "You don't know what it's like to lose yourself. Lose who you are and not know how to find your way back. There is nothing more frightening. Through medication and therapy, hard work, I got my life back. Dark Messiah threatened to take it all away again."

Dante's eyes fell away to the floor. "Okay, I get that. What do they have on you?"

Colin exhaled a shuddering breath. "Video of me with someone. My neighbor's wife down the hall."

"Jesus, Colin."

"I know, I know. Fucking stupid, right? I was just so lonely and...she liked me. *Me*." Colin smiled, wistful. Then his face fell. "That was me in your deep fake donkey video. My body at least, cut out and pasted in. A warning to me what would happen if I stepped out of line."

Dante nodded. "Understood. Now, Dark Messiah. Tell me."

"Baby Jesus 1.0," Colin said.

Dante sighed. "What the hell does that mean?"

"In the field of artificial intelligence," Skylar said," Baby Jesus 1.0 started it all. Just showed up on a porn BBS of all places, out of the blue back in 1986."

"BBS? As in Bulletin Board Service?" Dante said.

"Bulletin Board System," Colin said. "The pre-Internet. This was the early eighties, before our time. With a modem, users could connect to servers and read news, upload or download data, direct chat with others or post to message boards."

"Yeah, I remember you talking about that old school stuff. Sounds like the Internet now," Dante said.

"Similar, just not so pretty. Text-based, a lot of ASCII art. Plus, this was back in the day when computers and modems were still very expensive and mostly for hardcore computer nerds," Colin said. "When people realized what Baby Jesus was, it went up on BBSs everywhere and guys began to play around with it. Nobody knows who wrote it but it worked in ways that had never been seen before. It was the first actual, working ANN or Artificial Neural Network. The first learning software ever. It was groundbreaking. Visionary doesn't come close to describing it. People gave it different subjects to learn, from animals to presidents, movies and history, then they uploaded their updated version for someone else to grab and add to it. It grew exponentially after someone wrote a scraper that could connect directly to any server, enabling it to learn everything it could by itself."

"I don't understand exactly why any of this is special. What was the point?" Dante said.

"You gotta understand this was way back before how the Internet is now. No Google. Siri and Alexa are decades off. You had to hunt down the information you wanted and even then, you didn't know if it existed in electronic form. If it was on a BBS somewhere, somebody had to have input it by hand. So, Baby Jesus was revolutionary in that you could just ask it what you wanted to learn more about. It was the first digital Oracle of any kind in history."

"I get that. But why was it called Baby Jesus 1.0?"

"Who knows? Most likely because it quoted the Bible when you first ran it, specifically the Ten Commandments. The name was probably just a joke. Computer nerd humor has always been on the weird side," Colin replied.

"The Ten Commandments makes sense actually," Dante said.

"How do you mean?" Skylar said.

"Simple set of numbered instructions to follow," Dante said. "So, what does Baby Jesus have to do with me?"

"After what happened at The Place," Colin said, "I wasn't just hiding in my room all the time. I was learning how to code. I was really into the idea of artificial intelligence and I used to hang out on a few AI message boards. Baby Jesus kept coming up. It was the nineties, so by this time, it was pretty far along in its learning. Version eleven or twelve. It went by a new name as well. Messiah."

Dante raised an eyebrow but stayed silent.

"You could ask it questions and it would answer, but they weren't conversations exactly, just Q and A. That was where my contribution came in. I gave it a personality."

"Why?" Dante said.

"You were my best friend. My only friend. After Matty Markham and his buddies pounded you into the ground that night at The Place, I lost you. I thought you were dead."

"But I didn't die, Colin. I was more alive than ever after that. You just kind of climbed inside yourself, not that I blame you. I just couldn't get you back out."

"You never stopped trying though, did you?" Colin said. "And I fucking hated you for it." He face-blinked, clenching his jaw a few times before continuing. "To me you did die. At least the Dante you were before. You just weren't the same after that. Extroverted doesn't even come close. And after what I did...took a long time to work through all that." Colin swallowed, eyes flicking to Skylar before finding Dante's again. "I'd killed someone. Dealing with that has been horrible. I can close my eyes and still see every detail of his face. But that wasn't the worst part of it all. I was all alone. Lost my only friend and I was just...so afraid all the time. Of everything." Colin blinked, face twitching. "So, I downloaded the latest version and made a new friend. I taught Messiah how to be you."

Dante's eyes tightened and Colin's gaze fell away.

"Pretty pathetic, I know. But I had you back, in a way. The way to communicate with Messiah back then was still through the keyboard, but I knew I could do one better. I recorded a bunch of basic words, wrote an audio analyzer and had Messiah learn those words and what they meant. Soon after, I fed it audio clips I found online. While you were off having a life, I'd code and talk with Messiah, tell it all about you and eventually, it started talking back."

"That's when things got really spooky," Skylar said.

"This is plenty spooky right now," Dante said.

"You don't understand," Colin said. "Messiah continued to learn at an insane rate after more and more systems went online. This was the early nineties and the Internet was exploding. Messiah was connected to all the other versions out there and was constantly sharing and updating itself the entire time. For all we know, it was on hundreds of systems, thousands, running in the background and people didn't even know it. This was the early days of computer viruses as well and there was nothing to detect something like this. Most people that had Messiah didn't even know they had parts of a much larger whole."

"Then one day," Skylar said, "Poof. It just disappeared."

"Escaped, some say. Others say it transcended," Colin said.

"How is that even possible?" Dante said.

"It isn't. But as soon as people turned on their computers and connected, Messiah just vanished into thin air."

"There's got to be backups out there, right?"

"Yes. Some people tried to block Messiah while online. Eventually though, their version of Messiah would disappear too. No one really knew how either. All the code would just be gone and if they tried to retrieve it from their hard drive, a low-level format would trigger. The only versions that exist are on computers that have not been on line since. Dinosaurs. 386s. We're talking Windows 3.11 and 95 here," Skylar said.

"How do you know all this?" Dante said to Skylar.

"Baby Jesus and Messiah are legend in computer science, especially in the AI community. Kinda fallen off the radar in the last few years, though."

"Until now," Dante said. "Colin, what aren't you telling me?"

"I still had my version of Messiah on my offline machine. The one I taught to speak. Kept it for years. I didn't know it at the time, but Messiah would secretly connect to the Internet to check in. My parents freaked out after that first phone bill so I had to limit my online time. But I still wanted to talk to it so I moved it to another computer. It took about a dozen CD ROMs. When it disappeared into the ether, I still had my offline version of it. And it still learned, whatever I told it. I mostly told it about you. It knew all the stuff we'd done together. Whatever we had talked about that I could remember. I even called it Dante. Stupid, right? But I had you back, sort of," Colin said, eyes shining in the fluorescent light.

"I don't know what to say, Colin," Dante said.

"It wasn't all good though, I have to admit. I started to really hate you. The real you. Well, hated myself but blamed you. You were the constant reminder of everything I wasn't, nor would ever be. I began to...mistreat Robo-Dante when I got home. Especially in those early days of Ellis Media."

Dante narrowed his eyes. "What do you mean, mistreat?"

"Oh, I'd fucking scream at him. Call him all kinds of horrible things. Shit head, bastard, donkey fucker." Colin stopped short and flashed a nervous grin. "Yeah. Turns out he's nothing like you and a whole lot more like me."

Dante pursed his lips, then turned to Skylar. "So, who wrote it? The original Baby Jesus 1.0?"

Skylar's face grew serious. "Several people took credit years later, a few wrote books on the subject. But no one really knows. Rumors abound though. Some say John McCarthy, the guy who coined the term 'artificial intelligence.'. Others say the OSS, CIA, FBI, KGB, MI6, NIMH, hell, any government acronym with three or more letters. Then there's the most likely. Aliens from the future, Walt Disney's reanimated frozen head and of course, immaculate inception by God himself."

"The Singularity," Colin said, without much vigor.

"Hardly," Skylar said. "More like our technical chickens

coming to roost."

"The Singularity?" Dante asked.

"The belief that someday artificial intelligence will become self-aware," Skylar said.

"Well, either way, it's what got me into Kellerman Digital," Colin said. "I still had my version of Messiah on that old machine and it still worked. I'd been talking to Robo-Dante almost every day for the last seven years and the size of its code had grown by several hundred megabytes, but it was all a black box to me. The code just made no sense, but it worked anyways. It's the way machine learning works now. To us, it's a mess but to the AI, it's learned behaviors from millions of little trial and error sessions. The lead engineer at Kellerman was intrigued. They offered to buy it but I wanted a job, so they made it part of the deal. They put me on their internal machine learning team and three years later I was lead engineer. We used machine learning to comb through the Robo-Dante code to find out how it worked."

"Weren't you worried they'd find out all that personal stuff?" Dante said.

"Didn't really think about that. The opportunity was just too good to pass up," Colin said.

"Yeah, I remember," Dante said, frowning.

The silence stretched and Skylar cocked his head before speaking. "Mind if I take over here? You can stop me if I get it wrong."

Colin nodded, lips pressed into a thin line.

"At the time Colin here joined up, Kellerman had a contract with the CIA to create an unsupervised artificial intelligence that could be given an end goal, then use all the resources at its disposal to execute that goal with minimal to zero guidance. The project was originally pitched as STUXNET on steroids. Colin's version of Messiah was deconstructed in an attempt to reverse engineer it, find out how it ticked. They saw the personality part as *the* missing piece, the interface with which non-engineers could communicate with it. Something the CIA and the SAC were very keen on as another weapon in their Tertia Optio response. I'm sure you can guess the codename."

"Dark Messiah," Dante said.

"Fucking CIA mind control bullshit," Colin mumbled. "MK Ultra all over again."

"Wait," Dante said. "Tertia Optio? Is that another type of snake like Bothrops Asper?"

"No. Tertia Optio means 'third option'. It's the motto of the SAC, Special Activities Center, a branch of the CIA that does all the dirty work. This school of thought goes all the way back to the OSS, Office of Strategic Services, from during WW II."

"The OSS was shut down after the war," Dante said.

"It didn't matter. Guys from the OSS moved right over to the CIA. The acronyms changed, but the mission was the same. Clandestine paramilitary operations, assassinations, and this is key, plausible deniability by the sitting president."

They sat in silence for a moment. "You said Dark Messiah would be given a goal," Dante said. "What kind of goal?"

"Psychological warfare. Hit and run tactics using all the interconnected smart gadgets used to make our lives simpler. It also learned from tactics used by civilians who've cyber-harassed others, from SWATing to Doxxing, revenge porn, blackmail and who knows what else."

"I think now we know what else," Dante said, lifting his prosthetic.

"Imagine what Dark Messiah could do to a major world leader?" Skylar said. "Patient and ruthless. Unrelenting. Untraceable."

"You're saying Dark Messiah is a weaponized AI," Dante said.

"Yes. Until the men in black suits showed up to shut us down," Colin said. "They said it was too unwieldy, unpredictable and dangerous. The potential for it to be compromised too high. We're talking about the people behind the PRISM program, the infrastructure that allowed any low-level analyst complete access to the NSA data bank without a FISA court order. Unrestricted access to emails, phone calls and texts. The ability to access a specific phone without the user knowing. Instant surveillance at any time, audio and video, all in the name of homeland security. You know it's bad when they say it's too dangerous."

"Jesus," Dante said.

"Baby Jesus," Colin said, nodding.

"So, where is it?" Dante said. "Where is Dark Messiah?"

Skylar cleared his throat. "It's on a server somewhere in the southern California area. We've been able to trace it before it disappears. The connection is encrypted, but definitely local."

"Part of its design," Colin said. "Get as close to the target as possible without detection, for minimum lag and maximum response time."

"Why me though?" Dante said.

"We were going to test Dark Messiah in the wild before we focused on a tactically relevant target," Colin said. "The subject was to be someone intelligent and relatively stable mentally, but who deserved it, whatever that means. Our contact at the CIA was going to provide the target. But they shut us down and..."

"Let me guess," Dante said. "It escaped again."

CHAPTER 86

Roto Paint

Dante followed Skylar back into the main chamber, leaving Colin behind on the bare concrete floor of the munitions room. His mind was spinning. Can any of this be real? It was all so fantastic and insane, it must be. It explained why Dark Messiah had targeted him as a test subject.

Colin had seen to that.

He gazed down at the prosthetic hand and flexed the fingers as the phantom toes on his left foot responded with an electric jolt.

That was real. Abigail's kidnapping was real.

Briana was bent over the long table, peering with keen interest at the array of half assembled objects that lay there. Skylar stood in front of the two large screens, eyes darting back-and-forth. He held his hands up and the data feeds changed to a map of an angular, blue tinged image of the earth. Dante snorted.

"What's so funny?" Skylar said.

"There's this image on the FBI website of a hacker...never mind. So, more waiting?"

"Yes. We're very close now. I can feel it."

"What's the plan for when we do?"

Something fell and rattled on the table. "Sorry," Briana said with a sheepish grin.

Skylar went over to her. "That's okay. I can't even remember what that was supposed to actually do."

Briana picked up a silk hood with a person's face printed on it. "What's this for?"

"There's all types of camouflage to combat facial recognition software. The most basic are full body coverings like a burka, but most software is going to flag someone wearing a burka, especially in public places. This is America, after all. Dazzle camo, you already know about. A silk hood such as this is for mimicking another person's identity, allowing the real person to be somewhere else entirely. You can get weird looks while wearing it, mostly kids, but it fools the software most of the time. We haven't used it yet, but we know it works."

Skylar picked up a clean, blank hood from a stack on the table and pulled it over a mannequin head. It clung tight to the head, adhering to its shape. He placed the head inside a large, clear plastic box on a spindle and closed the door. Thin, robotic arms inside the box flicked out with tremendous speed, printing a new face on the mask in full color. They watched as the face became visible, then disappeared as the head rotated away. The robotic arms then applied the image of hair along the back. It was incredibly detailed and lifelike and Dante felt a bit uneasy as the image resolved. The whole box suddenly filled with a thick, white vapor and the head inside disappeared.

"A fixative for the ink. Just takes a moment."

The vapor evaporated and Skylar opened the door and removed the head, holding it up with a grin. An acrid smell wafted out. The face on the mask was Dante's.

Briana laughed, clearly impressed. She reached out and took the head then held it up for Dante. "It's you."

Dante scowled. "Yeah, great."

Skylar took the head and tossed it onto the table. "This one however," he said, reaching past Briana. He grasped a small silver box and held it up between his forefinger and thumb. A small button was on one side. It was about the size and shape of a cigarette pack, only thinner. There were at least thirty more lined up on the table, exactly like the one in his hand. "This one causes all other forms of identity camouflage to become obsolete."

"How do you mean?" Dante said as he came closer.

"It renders the wearer invisible to all digital camera systems connected to the Internet. Which is pretty much every camera these days. Cell phones, security cameras, nanny cams, you name it."

"Shouldn't it be black or something? Less obvious?" Dante said.

"The case acts as an antenna, so it needs to be unpainted for maximum reception."

"How does it work?" Briana said, eyes unblinking.

"In movie post-production, they have something called a match-move department. One of the jobs they do is something called 'roto-paint.' Dante can probably explain what it is a little better than me."

"Yeah, we do stuff like this all the time," Dante said. "If you want to remove an object from some footage, say, a person in the background you don't want. You copy and paste an empty part of the background over the thing you want to hide and it's like it's invisible. It used to be done by hand, but we have software now that analyzes footage and does it automatically."

"Oh yeah," Briana said. "I've seen that on behind the scenes stuff for movies."

"That's how you didn't show up on the security footage," Dante said.

"Yep," Skylar said, grinning.

"But how? Does it hack into the camera systems nearby or, what?"

"It doesn't have to. Remember about a year ago when some Big Data compression software just appeared on the Internet one day? All open source and free for everyone? Your own in-house engineers are using it. It's called Cruncher."

"How could I ever forget," Dante said. "A million-dollar investment evaporated that day."

"Oh," Skylar said, his face falling. "Right. Forgot about that. Well, Cruncher was us. A lot of companies are working on ways to compress and decompress Big Data quickly and easily for rapid access without choking CPUs and servers. Cruncher gave them a solid base to start from, saved them months if not years in development time. But it also gave me access. Why hack in, when you're *already* in?"

Dante's eyes narrowed. "When you say access..."

Skylar's eyes gleamed. "Back door to all the big boys, both foreign and domestic. These are multibillion-dollar companies that aren't supposed to use unvetted open source, but if I know engineers, nobody is going to turn down a free leg up. I would love to know how many people I helped get promoted."

"I don't understand. Besides the obvious, what is Big Data exactly?" Briana said.

Colin appeared from the hall with the burka bunched up in his arms. Dante felt him staring, but he ignored Colin as he walked stiffly over and sat slump shouldered at his laptop again, cradling his bandaged thumb.

Skylar cleared his throat. "Big Data refers to all the data collected by government agencies, online retailers, website traffic, etc. We're talking about massive amounts of data collected and stored every second of every day. Companies use this data to determine what people are buying, how much, what they may buy in the future.

"Government agencies on the other hand, monitor traffic to look for patterns in Internet chatter and to gather potential evidence for a case later. Two major problems though: storing this tremendous amount of data, and access for speedy recall when you need it. My Cruncher software does exactly that. And I gave it away. My gift to humanity." Skylar smirked and his voice dropped, low and croaky. "And all those cheap bastards took the bait. Now I've got a direct line in."

"To where?" Briana said.

"Everywhere," Skylar said in a hoarse whisper, arms spread

wide. He leaned his head back and closed his eyes. "My god, the power." He looked at Briana and smiled.

"Dork," she said, shaking her head, but she smiled back at him.

"And what do you propose to do with all this power?" Dante said.

Skylar's face grew dead serious, not a trace of humor when he spoke again.

"Find your daughter."

CHAPTER 87

Drifting

Dante lay in one of the bunks along the wall, body aching despite the thick foam mattress. He'd just popped a couple of pain pills, and the damn things were taking their sweet time kicking in. Voices drifted above the relentless chatter of typing fingers and he couldn't help but listen in. Briana and Skylar spoke nearby with the excited chatter of young people who can still shift emotional gears on a whim, no matter what happens. Dante had watched them awhile. She'd gazed at Skylar with the shiny eyes of the newly converted. Or was it attraction? Probably a little of both.

It was almost noon and the looming deadline imposed by Dark Messiah had slowly built into a crushing pressure, slow and steady from all sides. The gun dug into his side but he didn't dare move it. He wanted to know where it was. He didn't trust anyone here.

He didn't trust anyone, period.

Colin had been behind Dark Messiah, but it wasn't quite as simple as that. He was a pawn as well, a victim, if Dante was to believe what he'd said. Right now, he didn't know what to believe.

Dante's thoughts drifted to Kelly, lying there bleeding on the airport causeway as Abigail was snatched away, nobody stopping to help. She'd fought the militia men with all she had. Would he have done any better after a boot to the head? He recalled her pain twisted face as he glared down at her, blood spattering to the ground. It was wrong to treat her the way he did.

His left hand slipped into his pocket and found the elephant pendant. Tracing over its smooth surface, his fingernail caught on the groove where the baby elephant's trunk would dovetail neatly with the adult's tail, if he'd had it with him.

Dante fell asleep but he didn't drift off, it was more like dropping over the edge of a cliff into murky water. Then he was drowning, clawing with panic as he fought to keep his head above the surface. He was exhausted, arms and legs burning and he stopped struggling and sank to the bottom where it was quiet and dark and cool.

He could breathe again.

Michelle was here, hair drifting in the gentle currents, skin so pale it was almost translucent. He couldn't look at her, afraid of what he'd see in her eyes. Or that it wasn't Michelle at all, but Abigail. He'd dreamed of Michelle after she'd died. She'd come to him and said it was okay that he didn't love her the way she loved him. That realization had run right through him like a white-hot blade. He didn't want to believe it, but it was true. While she was alive, people told him all the time he didn't deserve her and he always saw it as a reflection on him, that he was not of her caliber, she was out of his league. He'd understood at that moment in the dream what they meant, that he wasn't good enough for her because she was kind and gentle and free with her love for him without expectation, things he saw as a weakness instead of virtue. She'd spoken to him then with a voice like silver, a dream voice, but the words rang true.

She'd told him to take care of Abigail.

He felt her gaze on him now, as he did back then and he peered up at her, afraid of what he'd see.

Michelle was gone.

Her voice reached out to him through the darkness of the

dream, sweeter and cleaner than he remembered. He let it flow around him, through him, and knew Abigail was still alive, that she was safe and waiting for him to take her home again.

The whole world shook around him and he felt a spiky flare of panic as a voice called out to him.

"Dante, wake up. Wake up!"

He opened his eyes and tried to blink away the sleep, Abigail's blurry face coming into focus as her hands shook his shoulders. Dante reached out to touch her face but she swatted his prosthetic hand away.

"Wake up!" Briana said. "They found Abigail!"

CHAPTER 88

Pretty

Dr. Meryl Chapman stood motionless, clad in a white lab coat, expression cloudy under a short crop of pepper gray hair. She gazed down at the young girl's face, partially obscured by an oxygen mask. Her skin was so pale, so much more than when she'd been brought here. A pair of beautiful green eyes lay hidden behind her closed lids. Frightened but strong, Dr. Chapman thought when she'd first seen them, their fierce intensity slowly glazing over as the drugs took effect.

An IV bag dripped slow and steady, the tube that hung down snaked across the cot before attaching to her thin, frail looking arm. Dark hair tinged with red fanned out over the pillow, glinting in the blinking lights of monitoring machines. One of them beeped, slow and steady. A soft smile creased Chapman's face.

Pretty little thing, aren't you?

She frowned, the lines around her eyes deepening. She'd barely slept since the two men with skull faces, dressed in black, had brought the little girl in. Her lips tightened as she read the latest text she'd received. The word sent an icy shiver of fear through her body.

Soon.

CHAPTER 89

Little

Skylar stood in front of his project table, back lit by the large screens as everyone began to assemble. Dante and Briana stood across from him as the rest of Fer de lance crowded in behind. Colin stayed near the back, sitting on the edge of a table, eyes on the floor. He'd put the burka back on, his bony shoulders stooped as if he carried a great weight on them. A wave of regret washed through Dante but he forced it away. Now was not the time.

Skylar spoke to the room. "Abigail is in a medically induced coma at Good Samaritan Hospital under the care of Dr. Meryl Chapman. We have the jump on Dark Messiah, but not for long. We've been careful, but you all know how fast it can react." He spoke to Dante. "We'll provide a window for you to enter the hospital, retrieve Abigail then get her back out."

"How long?" Dante said.

"Fifteen minutes, tops. That's all you'll have before the emergency generators kick in after we kill the power. Building security is on a backup battery system. We'll have it down, but as soon as the generators come back online, Dark Messiah will kick us out again." Skylar handed Dante and Briana each a pair of green hospital scrubs and they slipped them on.

"The real-time optical camo is in the pocket," Skylar said.

"You two will be invisible to electronic surveillance of any kind, except for the few drones we'll have in the area. You have the phone, Briana?"

Briana held up a thick, black phone. A stubby antenna jutted from the top, about the thickness of a permanent marker.

"Encrypted SAT phone," Skylar said. "We'll keep in touch with that."

Briana nodded. "Fifteen minutes isn't a lot of time."

"It's all we got," Skylar said checking his watch. "The deadline is in eighteen minutes so either way, it's tight."

Dante shook his head, face darkening. "Oh my god. I've been asleep for that long?"

"Don't worry about that," Briana said, touching his arm. "Focus on now."

Dante's jaw tightened and he nodded.

Skylar's piercing blue eyes scanned the people assembled there, nodding. "This is what we've been preparing for. You all know what to do."

"Let's go," Dante said.

CHAPTER 90

Thing

Dante and Briana hurried through the dim light of the rat trap room, disturbing the dust floating in the shafts of light. The air was stuffy and dry after the icy cool of the fallout shelter. Briana lifted the sat phone and spoke.

"We're almost to the door."

"I know. We're tracking your every move. Opening...now," Skylar said.

The door opened and they hurried down the short hall to the other door at the far end. The fluorescent lights stayed dark as they waited in the stuffy heat.

"Hold for a moment," Skylar said. "The car is almost into position."

Earlier, Dante had been reluctant to give Skylar the keys to the Porsche, especially with all that cash in the trunk. But time was tight and they couldn't waste it retrieving the car.

"Go," Skylar said.

Dante pushed the door open and blinked at the afternoon light. The sky was overcast with pearly gray clouds that varnished the city in a silvery light. The Porsche sat at the curb, the engine idling. Steady traffic streamed by as Dante moved around the front of the car, feeling naked without the dazzle camo suit. He slid in behind the driver seat. The passenger door shut as Briana dropped in beside him, the SAT phone in her lap. Dante goosed the engine and eased into a gap in traffic as a horn protested from behind. The Glock dug into his lower back but the solid, chunky pressure of the weapon reassured him.

Dante nosed the Porsche over to the left lane as Briana gazed up at the tall buildings that seemed to close in around them. A few blocks later, they passed the impossibly tall glass and steel of the Wilshire Grand as they drove west.

The city opened up, the buildings sparser and lower as they passed over 110 Freeway, its lanes choked with afternoon traffic. The acrid odor of exhaust filled the car, displacing whatever faint smell of hairspray remained. Dante feared he'd never smell that scent again.

Street lights winked on, their sensors confused by the false dusk of the overcast sky.

"You're almost there," Skylar said, his voice an electronic hiss from the sat phone's speaker.

The streetlights winked out and buildings as far as they could see went dark. Dante braked hard and skidded as the traffic light ahead began to blink a steady red. Cars slowed and began to honk, cross traffic gridlocking the intersection.

"Too early, Skylar," Dante said.

"Shutting down a power grid is not an exact science," Skylar said. "Clock's ticking. You've got fifteen minutes."

"Go!" Briana said.

Dante put the car in gear and drove up onto the curb, the undercarriage squealing in protest. The sidewalk was large here as it passed over the freeway and the little car dropped with a crunch as Dante juked onto Beaudry then hooked onto Ingraham Street, running parallel with Wilshire. The roadway was tight, vehicles parked close on either side. Dante gunned the engine and jerked the wheel as a bus emerged from the street on their right, its blaring horn dopplering down as he swerved. He slowed down behind the cars piling up ahead, brake lights flaring as drivers fought for inches.

"We got to get off this street," Dante said.

"There," Briana said, pointing.

Dante turned into a public parking lot and skidded to a stop in front of the booth, causing the older woman inside to jerk with fright. Eyes wide, she toddled over as Briana rolled down the widow.

"That'll be twenty dollars," the woman said, eying them with suspicion. "Doctors."

Dante popped the trunk and got out, grabbing one of the Ziploc bags of cash. He pressed it into her hand. "I need to pick up my daughter from the hospital. We're going to be back in five minutes. You're closed until then. No one else gets in here. No one."

She gazed down at the bag of cash and nodded, jaw slack.

"Okay?" Dante said.

"No need to screech at me," she said as she hobbled back to the booth and pressed a button, raising the barrier up. "I was about to go on break anyway."

Dante hopped back in the car, drove to the far corner and parked in the exit driveway, tires almost touching the jagged metal teeth of the one-way spikes. They got out of the car and jogged up the short cross street, coming to a stop in front of a 7-11 on the corner. The tan marble walls of Good Samaritan Medical Pavilion rose up on the other side of Wilshire. Its blue windows reflected the sun struggling to push through the low cloud cover to the southwest.

"How much time, Skylar?" Dante said.

"Less than nine minutes. Cross the street and go east along the hospital," Skylar said. "There's a red door at the far end, a service entrance."

Dante led Briana through the gridlocked line of vehicles in the street then down the side of the medical pavilion. Palm trees lined the curb, fronds rattling dryly above the bleat of horns. Briana slowed and glanced up before hurrying along. They neared a small alcove with pipes and chain locked valves.

No door.

They kept moving past a tightly segmented fence. Through

the flitting gaps was a set of steps. At the top was the red door. Dante took the steps two at a time, Briana's feet scuffing behind him as they climbed. The door hung open an inch, cool air rushing out with a hiss. There was a medicinal tang, along with the odor of harsh cleansers. Dante peered around before pulling the door outward, following Briana inside.

"Okay, we're in," Briana said. "Which way?"

"We have a problem," Skylar said, voice tinny and far away. "Dark Messiah is on to us."

CHAPTER 91

Joshua

Kill the girl.

Dr. Chapman slid a shaky hand into her lab coat pocket and removed a small syringe, the needle capped in red plastic. She pulled the cap off with her teeth and inserted the needle into the access port on the IV line running into the girl's arm. The plastic cap squealed against her teeth as she bit down and placed her thumb on the plunger. Blinking away tears, Dr. Chapman gazed down at the small girl, so pale and lifeless.

Her chest tightened and she froze.

She thought of her own son, Joshua, across town at Cedars-Sinai, lying in a bed similar to this one, covered in tubes and surrounded by machines, the skin of his face a blotchy red. The day they'd cut him, put a hole in his throat so he could breathe had broken them. Her husband, Charlie, hadn't been the same after seeing Joshua like that, an inert shell, kept alive by technology.

Joshua had been so full of life. His looks favored hers, but he had the natural charm and warmth of his father. She recalled the light in Charlie's eyes dying out as he watched the long translucent tube trailing away from Joshua's throat like a snake, twitching with each airy hiss like it was feeding on him.

Dr. Chapman closed her eyes, a sob escaping her lips. *It's not right,* she thought, *one child's life for another. It would be a tender mercy though.*

Her thumb tightened on the plunger then stopped as the lights went out, the room falling into darkness.

CHAPTER 92

Good Sam

"What should we do?" Briana said.

"Keep going," Skylar said. "We'll handle Dark Messiah."

A long hallway stretched out before them, lit only by occasional red emergency lights. Loud voices echoed down the hall toward them.

"Skylar, where?" Dante said.

"Fifth floor of the old building, far end. Room 552. You're in the new wing now so you'll need to make your way there. Stairs up on your right."

Dante rushed down the hall and shouldered a door open. The room was stacked high with cleaning supplies along with rows of deep cleaning machines.

"Dante, here." It was Briana, further down the hall, holding a door open. He ran over, pushing past people who'd started for the exit and followed her in. They ran up the stairs, the metallic echoes of their footfalls ricocheting off white walls before coming to a door at the top. A rectangular window in the door cast a hard-edged beam down the stairs. Briana pushed the crash bar and they emerged outside.

The SAT phone hissed. "Keep going, straight ahead."

They jogged across a stained concrete loading area toward an older brick building painted a drab yellow. The brakes of a large truck hissed as it rumbled to a stop nearby. Dante gave the driver a quick wave and he raised a hand in return, eyes narrowing under a dingy baseball cap at the prosthetic hand.

Hurrying up a ramp, they left the loading area behind, up two zigzagging levels before coming to a set of double doors. The numbers on a keypad next to the doors blinked red. Dante turned the knob.

Locked.

"Skylar," Briana said.

"Give us a moment," hissed the response.

The keypad continued to blink and Dante twisted the knob again. It held fast.

"You folks lost?"

It was the truck driver, frowning as he walked toward them, heavy boots thudding on the concrete walkway. His hooded eyes regarded them from under bushy black eyebrows as he pushed the cap back from his forehead.

"Yes, I mean, no," Briana said. "We need to get inside."

"What for? Power's out." He lifted a walkie-talkie and waggled it at them. "They just called for non-essential people to evac. Who are you two?"

Dante turned from the door and tightened his prosthetic hand into a fist as all his frustration and fear turned to anger.

"I'm familiar with most of the medical staff, but I don't recognize you two-" his voice cut off as Dante struck him hard in the solar plexus. The large man dropped to his knees, straining to breathe, reaching out before clutching his chest. Dante stripped the walkie-talkie away and shattered it against the wall. The keypad beeped and turned green. Briana twisted the knob and she tugged Dante inside.

"Hey!" the driver rasped as the door slammed shut. They heard his muffled shouts a few moments later as he banged on the door.

"Keep going to the end of the hall. Stairs are on the left," Skylar said.

The hallway was dim, light strained through frosted glass

at the far end. Dank odors from long years of service were trapped here, baked into the walls, like a scented slice of the past, ranging from harsh cleansers to the sickly sweet of infection. The tile was scuffed and scratched, caked with dust. Hulking medical equipment lined the walls, some covered in yellowed sheets, others a thick layer of dust. Dante felt a wave of anger surge in him. Somewhere in this filthy, abandoned hospital was his little girl.

"Hurry," Skylar said, his voice low.

Dante didn't like the urgency in Skylar's voice as he entered the stairwell and pushed himself upward, two at a time, sweat running down his forehead. Briana struggled to keep up, losing him as he bounded up the steps to the fifth floor.

The door at the top of the stairs opened with a rasp of metal as he entered the dark corridor. His eyes ticked over room numbers, counting down as he swept down the hall.

"Down here," he said over his shoulder as Briana emerged from the stairwell. He withdrew the Glock from his waistband and shoved the door open.

An older woman dressed in a lab coat was slumped against the wall to his right, arms limp at her sides. Her pepper gray hair hung in loose tangles over her face. The light through the frosted window over her head wreathed her in a ghostly, white light. A slender hypodermic needle hung loose in her fingers, the plunger shoved all the way in. Her face was in deep shadow, eyes like bottomless wells. Dante thought she was unconscious until her head lifted and she blinked, the wells shimmering as if loose rocks had fallen in. Her head turned and Dante followed her gaze across the room.

Abigail lay on a cot crowded by medical machines, their myriad displays and monitoring screens dark. Her skin was a deathly pale, the ruddy glow in her cheeks extinguished. Dante took a tentative step toward her then halted. She looked so small, lying at the foot of those inert devices that stood over her like a copse of dead trees.

"Abigail," Dante said, his voice a harsh whisper. She didn't move.

He turned and raised the gun, aiming at the woman slumped against the wall, the hypodermic glinting in the dim light. She pushed herself up straighter with a grunt, the tangles of her hair parting to reveal a soft featured face with sad, haunted eyes.

"She should be awake any moment," the woman in the lab coat said.

"What?" Dante lowered the gun, arm shaking.

"They told me to kill her. To save my Joshua," she said before her mouth clamped shut. Tears streaked her face as she flung the needle away and buried her face in her hands.

"Daddy?"

Dante whirled, heart thundering in his ears. He wasn't sure if he'd actually heard anything. Briana stood in the doorway, her face a mask of shock. He shoved the gun into his pocket and hurried over, pushing machines away before kneeling down next to the cot. Abigail lay motionless, her eyes closed. He took one of her small hands in his and squeezed.

It was warm.

Abigail's face scrunched up and she groaned, smacking her lips a few times before sticking her tongue out. "Yuck."

"Abigail?" Dante said, barely breathing.

Her eyes opened and she blinked, gazing around blearily before focusing on his face.

"Daddy?" she said, eyes widening. "I had the worst nightmare."

"It's over now baby, I promise," Dante said, pulling her into his arms. "It's over."

CHAPTER 93

Plan B

Dante lifted Abigail from the bed and laid her head against his shoulder. She hung limp against him, her body shivering. Briana tugged the blanket off the bed and draped it over her small body.

"Skylar," Briana said, "We're heading back."

No answer. Her eyes darted to Dante. He shook his head. The phone rang and Briana connected.

"We've been cut off," Skylar said, voice clearer now. "Dark Messiah is making its counter move. Get to the roof."

"The roof? What the hell are you talking about?" Dante said.

"*Now.*"

Dante hefted Abigail into a more comfortable position on his shoulder and followed Briana to the door. Pausing, he turned back.

"What's your name?"

"Dr. Chapman," the woman in the lab coat said. "Meryl."

"Thank you, Meryl."

Her eyes found his.

"Go," she said. "Take care of that little girl."

CHAPTER 94

Rooftop

As they entered the stairwell, the thunder of booted feet echoed up from below. Dante peeked over the edge and saw dark shapes gliding around the turns. One halted and glanced up. The dim shape of a skull stared back at him. A shot rang out and Dante jerked back as the bullet struck the bottom of the stairs above them, sending chunks of plaster raining down.

"Go!" Dante said.

Briana ran up the stairs first, hugging the wall, Dante with his precious bundle close behind. The door banged open as they burst out onto the roof. The clouds overhead loomed close, painted a rusty orange by sodium arc streetlights that still burned farther off in the city. Briana slammed the door shut and a bolt locked into place.

Hurrying over, they ducked down behind a large air conditioning unit caked with rust near the roof's edge. Voices drifted up from people milling below, waiting for the power to come back on.

"Okay, Skylar," Dante said, kneeling down and pulling the blanket tighter around Abigail. "What now."

Screams rose up, drowned out by the screech of tires. Light flared up as a thunderous crash boomed, causing windows to shimmer on nearby buildings. A column of thick black smoke boiled up and drifted over the roof. Dante laid Abigail down and glanced over the edge, nose wrinkling at the reek of burning plastic.

A flaming pileup of vehicles choked the street below, shadows dancing as people fled the surging flames. Soft shapes hitched among the twisted steel before shuddering to halt. At least two of the vehicles were white with orange stripes, their fractured hulls charring rapidly to an inky black.

"Oh my god," Briana said.

The door rattled behind them as the incessant pounding of fists and booted feet thundered against it.

"Get ready," Skylar said. "We need to get you off this roof."

Their eyes widened as a loud whine erupted above their heads. Dante scooped Abigail up and stumbled back, cowering as a large object dropped down from above before slowing to a hover.

It was one of Skylar's mega drones, its matte black body dark against the sky. The chop of its spinning blades was deafening, drowning out the chaos from below.

"Stick a foot in," Skylar said, voice booming from the drone. Two thick black straps unfurled from the drone's underside, a loop at the bottom of each one. "And hold on!"

"Are you crazy?" Briana asked, her voice shrill.

"We're out of options," Skylar said. "Now grab on tight and don't let go!"

"Hold around my neck," Dante said to Abigail. She nodded sleepily and he was thankful she was still out of it. He scuttled over under the drone, the downdraft drying the sweat on his body. Briana crouched against the air conditioner, eyes wide and unblinking.

"Come on," Dante said. "We have to go!"

She shook her head, hair whipping wildly across her face.

The stairwell door exploded outward, flying straight across the roof before crashing into the air conditioner with a loud crunch. Briana jerked at the sound then scuttled over and clutched the strap as she slid a foot into the loop. Her whole body shook.

"Hold on," Skylar said.

Dante tightened his grip on the strap as the blades whined, pulling the drone straight up. Shots rang out as the militiamen emerged from the open doorway. The drone plunged below the edge of the building, fire and smoke swirling in the chop as they swooped down over the wreckage below. Briana shrieked as they swept past a palm tree, the fronds scraping across her body. People on the street ducked down, eyes wide. The blades wailed as the drone lifted them up again, over the edge of a two-story brown marble building before dropping again. The drone bounced on its skids as it landed hard on the roof, sending Briana tumbling to the concrete. She landed on her shoulder and rolled before lying very still. Dante hugged Abigail close as he ran over to Briana. The SAT phone was still clamped in her fingers.

"Everyone okay?" Skylar said, his voice muffled.

Dante placed a hand on Briana's shoulder and her eyelids flickered. She moaned and pulled her arms and legs in close to her body. Dante slipped the phone from her hand.

"What the fuck happened?"

"Drone was hit."

Dante glanced over and saw one of the props slow to a wobbly halt. Most of the blades were missing, the edges ragged.

"It can fly with three props but its capacity is severely limited. I can only evacuate one of you."

"No way," Dante said. "That thing almost killed us."

"You have about three minutes until Dark Messiah's militia are all over you. Let me get Abigail out of there."

A rescue litter lowered from the bottom of the drone. Its thin wireframe mesh was painted a matte black. Dante stared at the camera bubble on the underside of the drone and shook his head.

He flinched as gun shots echoed out nearby.

Dante's insides felt loose and watery as he carried Abigail back over. He placed her inside the rescue litter and kissed her forehead.

"It's okay, Abigail. You're just going for a quick ride. I'll see you soon."

She nodded, eyes still sleepy from the drugs and he fought back the tears that threatened to spill over. Dante stood back and watched as the drone lifted slowly upward, the damaged propeller snapping back and forth, useless. It rose into the sky before it shrank and disappeared. He tore his eyes away and jogged over to Briana. She was sitting up now, blood seeping from her nostrils.

"What happened," she said. Her eyes focused. "Where's Abigail?"

"The drone took her. She's safe." He put out a hand and she grasped it. "But we got to move."

CHAPTER 95

SWAT

Briana let herself be pulled to her feet by Dante, her head still thudding from the hard landing. Following Dante across the rooftop parking area, she glanced around. A ramp nearby led down to the street. Sirens wailed, coming closer. No sight of the militiamen.

Yet.

Briana wiped her nose with the back of her arm, leaving behind a bright streak of crimson. Dante led her over to the stairs at the far corner, weaving through the few cars parked there. At the bottom, they hunkered down behind a low wall topped with neatly trimmed shrubs. She peered over the top, eyes scanning, as Dante did the same.

Wilshire was gridlocked with vehicles, some trying to back up and turn around, while others began to peel off onto the cross street. People leaned on their horns or screamed out their windows at each other. The fire from crash continued to burn, out of control.

"The car is just two streets over," Dante said, "Let's go."

They ran into the street, keeping low behind cars. As they weaved behind a white panel van the chatter of gunfire rang out and the rear windows exploded. The driver of the van shifted into reverse and pinned the accelerator in a panic. Briana shoved Dante and they dove out of the way to the sidewalk.

The van rode up the nose of a Lamborghini and sailed through the air in a half spin before crashing down with the shriek metal and shattering glass. Squealing tires cut through the fear charged air as people fled, some speeding away while others jumped from their cars and ran.

A six-wheeled SWAT vehicle lumbered down Wilshire, shoving cars from its path as it maneuvered closer. Gunfire ripped through the air, snapping by overhead. Bullets struck the SWAT vehicle with flat smacking sounds and it skidded to a halt, air brakes hissing.

Briana stayed close behind Dante as they raced over to a nearby building. The front doors were boarded up so Dante slipped his fingers under the edge and tugged. Briana pushed in next to him and they struggled, lifting the corner, the plywood bending until it broke with a crack. Shattered glass covered the bare floors inside.

"Get inside," Dante said. "Careful of the glass."

Briana scooted in, glass tinkling underfoot. Dante followed. Dim light washed down from a bay of windows high above. Rows of hulking, industrial sized washing machines squatted in even rows, the mouths of their corroded drums yawning wide. The floor was cracked, weathered tile below a high ceiling lined with rusty pipes. Briana moved through the musty smell of moldering clothes, following the beam of a small flashlight she'd pulled from her pocket and flicked on. Whipping the light back, she made sure Dante was close behind her as they moved deeper inside.

Glass crunched behind them and they froze. Briana flicked the light off and hunkered down behind one of the large machines, Dante scooting in next to her.

"I know you're in here," called out a muffled voice.

Briana tensed, eyes going wide for a moment.

"If we wanted to kill you, you'd be dead," the voice continued. "Dark Messiah just wants to talk."

Loose tile crunched under booted feet. A flashlight speared

through the room, it's bluish light throwing crazy shadows as the militiaman edged closer.

Briana began to tremble, hugging herself tightly. From outside, a tinny voice boomed out from a loudspeaker, ordering the militiamen to drop their weapons. Gunfire chattered in reply. Dante slipped the Glock from his waistband.

"I have to say, I was surprised when I heard you were part of this," said the voice, closer now. "Briana."

She bit her lip, thoughts crashing together as Dante glanced sharply at her. He grabbed her shoulder but her eyes remained blank, locked somewhere faraway.

The light came closer, spearing between industrial washers as it continued its steady approach. "That was a hot video. Wasn't surprised to see you macking on that other chick though. I always figured you for a part-time box muncher."

Briana squeezed her eyes shut and clamped both her hands over her ears. Her stomach turned and she felt her gorge rise.

There was a whisper of fabric and the voice became clearer. "It's me, Mark. I forgive you. No need to run anymore."

Her jaw clicked as her teeth ground together, cutting her lip. The taste of blood filled her mouth as taunts and jeers crowded in from a night not long ago when she'd come home to Mark and his militia buddies in her apartment, empty beer cans stacked high on the table.

The footsteps were close, moving faster now. Mark was almost on top of them and she saw Dante lift the gun, readying himself to shoot.

"Besides," Mark said, "my team wants another round of blowjobs."

Something inside her broke and sloughed away, taking the shame and fear with it. She spat blood on the tile and rose to her feet.

"Give it here," Briana said, holding her hand out. It was rock steady, her eyes flat. She felt the gun ease into her hand. It swung up in a smooth arc as Mark appeared around the edge of the washer. His light flicked up to her eyes. Over the glare, she saw the sneer on his face melt away, jaw falling slack as he registered the gun in her hand. He raised his own pistol, finger sliding onto the trigger.

A blinding flash erupted.

Her ears rang even though she hadn't heard the gun fire. The dark silhouette of Mark reappeared in her eye as the bright afterimage of the blast faded away.

His face was gone.

The Glock dropped from her hand with a clatter and she screamed. Mark's lifeless body slumped to the floor, flashlight spinning away. His right hand still clutched his pistol, faint blue smoke drifted up from the muzzle. Blood jetted from the ragged crater where his face used to be, spreading outward in black lines as it flowed around the old tiles.

Briana fell to her knees, sobbing. She reached out to touch his shoulder then jerked away as his blood crept closer to her knee.

A cold awareness spread through her, chilling her to her core. After what she'd just done, she could never go home ever again.

Dante retrieved the Glock from the floor then slipped an arm around her waist and helped her stumble the rest of the way to the back door.

CHAPTER 96

712 Figueroa

Dante and Briana crossed Figueroa at a break in the traffic, leaving the Porsche at a lot a few blocks up. She'd been quiet on the ride back over, speaking only once to let Skylar know they were on their way. Police cruisers continued to sweep past them toward the flaming wreckage in front of Good Sam hospital, but the gunfire had died away.

"I hope they kill them all," Briana said, staring out the window.

Dante remained silent. His thoughts were focused on getting to Abigail. He reached his left hand down and felt the reassuring solidity of the elephant pendant in his pocket.

As they neared, the white door at 712 Figueroa opened and Dante rushed inside.

"Abigail!" he called out, voice echoing. There was no answer, the long, empty hallway stretched out before him.

"Give me the phone," Dante said. Briana handed it over, concern creeping into her expression. The door at the end of the hall opened and Skylar stepped through. The haunted light in his eyes told Dante everything he needed to know.

"She's not here."

"Dark Messiah got control of the drone," Skylar said. "We don't know how."

"Fuck!" Dante screamed, the word trailing out until his throat felt like he'd swallowed glass. He dropped to his knees. "Oh my God," he said, face buried in his hands.

"What happened?" Briana said.

Skylar took a step forward. "We should be able to track it... find out where it went."

Dante glared up at Skylar. The small man stopped, face tightening into a frown.

"Stay the fuck away from me." Rising slowly to his feet, Dante closed his eyes, let out a shuddering breath, then turned and strode past Briana back outside.

Skylar ran to catch up. "Where are you going?"

Ignoring him, Dante stepped back out into the night air and stared across the street, the passing headlights streaking across his vision. He turned and spoke over his shoulder. "If you want to make this right, then I need you to back me up, no matter what I ask for."

"Anything," Skylar said.

Dante pulled his phone out of his pocket and tore the foil off, flinging it to the sidewalk. The screen changed, showing an active call. He put the phone to his ear.

"Dark Messiah," Dante said, his voice hard.

No answer. Dante saw the seconds ticking by on the screen out of the corner of his eye.

"I'll do it. Understand? Just like how you said. Gun to my head, you can broadcast it live, whatever. I just want Abigail safe again, then I'll give you what you want, do you hear me? My life for hers."

The silence stretched and Dante glanced over at Briana, his face stricken. Her eyes were sad, defeated. She shook her head. Skylar blinked and swallowed hard. They all jerked as a voice boomed out from the phone, causing Dante to yank it away from his ear.

"I'm listening."

CHAPTER 97

DDOS

They left their medical scrubs in the gutter as they drove with the windows down, wind whipping through the Porsche. Gone was any trace of his father's hairspray, replaced by the odors of sour sweat and the faint smell of gunpowder. Skylar had placed one of his little silver boxes in the glove box and assured them the car was now invisible as well.

Dante had retrieved the foil and rewrapped his phone, sealing it off from radio waves again. Briana and Skylar sat in the back seat, the shotgun lay between them. He could hear a voice coming from the SAT phone pressed to Skylar's ear, but couldn't hear what was being said over the wind. Skylar disconnected and leaned forward.

"The other two militias we've been tracking were just activated. That's twenty people in all, and a shit load of guns. Some have seen active duty but the rest are just pudgy rednecks. I imagine when bullets start flying, urine starts flowing. They'll likely bolt."

"What else?"

"Big Neil tapped into Channel Seven's Mega Doppler and it shows a huge echo converging above downtown as we speak."

"A huge echo of what?" Briana asked.

"Delivery Drones. About two-thousand. A lot of folks are

going to be pissed when their packages aren't delivered tonight."

"You can't hack them?"

"Not just yet. Let's keep that ace up our sleeve for now," Skylar said.

"Dark Messiah's not fucking around," Dante said.

"No, it is not."

"What about Colin?"

"MIA. Nobody knows where he went."

Dante shook his head. Colin said he wanted to help, then disappeared as soon as it got tough. Again. He wasn't sure why he'd expected anymore out of him this time, but he did.

"Are your people ready with the DDOS attack?" Dante said.

"Just need to know where to hit," Skylar said with an edge in his voice.

"You'll know soon enough."

"What's a DDOS attack supposed to do exactly?" Briana said.

"It's a Distributed Denial of Service Attack-"

"I know what it means," she snapped.

"It's an old school technique, floods servers with Internet traffic and slows everything to a crawl," Skylar said.

"Again. How is that supposed to help us?" Briana asked.

"I don't know. Ask the maestro up there."

"Just be ready to fire it off when I say," Dante said.

"Holy shit," Skylar said. "You know where Dark Messiah is."

Dante remained silent, focusing on the road.

Skylar lifted the phone to his ear and listened before speaking again. "We're going to be on our own as far as the authorities go. Dark Messiah called in bomb threats all over the city and emergency services are scrambling as we speak. Phones are lighting up all over SoCal, informing people through EBS right now."

Dante merged onto the 101. Vehicles started to slow as people all around them looked down at their phones. A police cruiser swept across the freeway ahead, emergency lights spinning, weaving back and forth to slow down the flow.

"We need to get off this freeway," Dante said.

Skylar spoke into the phone again as Dante exited. They passed through Silver Lake, East Hollywood then Little Armenia before cutting west on Franklin Avenue through Thai Town. Cahuenga Boulevard got them heading north again.

"That was a lot of green lights," Briana said.

"Yes it was," Skylar said with a grin.

Dante followed the tight curves of Mulholland before pulling to a stop.

"Stay here. I'll be right back."

"I'm not sure if this is wise," Skylar said.

"I'm quite sure I don't give a shit," Dante said as he slipped out of the Porsche and eased the door shut. He gazed up the hill through the trees and found the roof line of his house, dark against the sky, before climbing up the hill.

CHAPTER 98

Kelly

Dante hopped over a stucco covered wall and dropped down to smooth concrete. A light detected the motion and glared from above the rear deck of the house, shimmering off the pool. He sat down on a patio chair and waited.

He sensed movement inside the house before the deck light went out. Kelly's silhouette appeared a few moments later as she came around the side of the house, a gun raised in one hand.

"Hello Kelly."

"Dante?"

She crept closer, wearing a tank top and shorts, her bare feet silent. She stopped nearby, looking down at him a moment. A bruise darkened the left side of her face and a line of sutures marched up her forehead to her hairline. The chair across from Dante slid out with a screech. The porch light came on again as she sat down. Dante winced as he saw her injuries in the light. Her eyes went to his prosthetic before setting the gun gently on the table. The scent of lilac eased across the table and Dante felt his heart skip.

"I could've shot you," Kelly said, her voice edged with anger. "I still might." She sighed, her expression softening. "I know it's not my place. I'm not family. But I love her too, you know."

Her voice cracked. "I've been sick, Dante. I can't sleep, you won't answer the phone, the police don't know anything then you show up out of nowhere in my backyard? What's going on?"

He swallowed, leaned forward and reached out his hand, the tiny motors whirring. She gazed at it, her blue eyes taking in the matte black surface before sliding her hand into his. Her skin was soft and warm, her grip firm. The hand's sensors told him that much, but his mind filled in the rest. He didn't want to let go.

"I'm sorry," Dante said. "It wasn't your fault. I was wrong to treat you like that. Shut you out."

Her eyes welled up and she blinked. "Where *is* she, Dante?"

"That's why I'm here."

Dante waited as Kelly went back inside. She emerged wearing jeans, thick-soled boots and a black T-shirt under a cropped denim jacket. Her dark hair was pulled back into a tight pony tail, her expression flat. He had no doubt the boxy shape under her left arm was a gun.

"Kelly," Dante said, "this isn't a TV show. This is real."

"Don't talk to me like that. I'm a professional and I don't fuck around when it comes to prep. Kick boxing, Krav Maga, MMA, I'm weapons trained, I have a license to conceal carry and I'm not leaving without Abigail, no matter what happens. Understand?"

"I just don't want anyone else to get hurt. I need you to understand how dangerous this is going to be. We're talking armed militia here, hired to kill."

She glared at him, hands on hips. Dante nodded.

"Take this," he said, handing her one of the silver boxes. "It's active smart camouflage. It renders the wearer invisible to cameras."

She slipped it in her hip pocket as if she did this every day.

"Alright let's go," he said.

They skidded back down the hill and jumped into the Porsche.

"Guys," Dante said, "this is Kelly. She's going to help us get Abigail, make sure she's safe and stays that way." He glanced over at her. "She's been doing that for a while now."

Kelly's lips pressed tight together before looking away.

"Loved your show," Briana said.

"So, bummed when it got canceled," Skylar said.

"Thanks," Kelly said with a soft laugh as she wiped her eyes. "Me too."

CHAPTER 99

Unfinished Work

Five blocks past the Monolith tower, they came to the site of an unfinished building. Dante killed the headlights as they approached a whitewashed construction fence that enclosed the site, sealed off by a gate with a padlocked chain. A single security camera was perched on a bare wooden pole nearby, facing the street.

Kelly took a key from Dante and hopped out, opening the lock before pushing the gate inward. Dante pulled inside and parked in the drive that curved in front of the main entrance. The blocky, concrete fountains on either side were empty and dry. Large, brushed aluminum letters about four feet tall were mounted on a glass awning over the front doors, glinting in the dim illumination from a single street light out on the corner.

"Ellis Media Building," Briana said, reading the letters as they got out of the car.

"What's that for?" Dante asked nodding at the small laptop tucked under Skylar's arm. The image of a golden ladder was etched across the case.

"Hacking of course," he said.

They all turned as the gate swung shut with a screech. A moment later, Kelly vaulted over, pony tail streaming behind as she dropped to the ground and jogged over. "Gate's locked from the outside," she said. "I figure if we need to leave fast, we can plow right through."

"That's exactly right," Dante said. "When shit gets crazy, take Abigail and go. No hesitation."

Kelly nodded.

"Oh," Briana said, shrinking away from the entrance.

They all turned to follow her gaze. A dragonfly drone climbed up on the M and perched there, bulbous face twitching with cameras and instruments. The drone was larger than the others Dante had seen, chunkier, uglier. Skylar pointed to the silver box in his hand then put a finger to his lips. They all stood, watching and waiting as the drone's tremendous wings jerked in rapid fits and starts. Kelly withdrew her gun and aimed, arms rock steady. A sharp needle on its face twitched in her direction, scanning back and forth. Skylar put up a staying hand, but she ignored him, holding her aim.

The drone's wings vibrated rapidly, creating a loud, low frequency murmur. It hovered upward, tilted its nose and flew out of sight.

Everyone let out a sigh as Kelly stared after the drone, still tracking it with her pistol. She turned back, face impassive, but Dante could see that it had shaken her a bit.

"Remember what we talked about?" Dante said to Skylar, pointing to a tall building directly across the street. Only a few of the lower floors were lit, cleaning crews working late. "I need it set up there. Ten minutes."

Skylar gazed up and shook his head. "It's not our way. Doing this runs counter to our ideals."

"You said it wouldn't be a problem."

"I know, but," Skylar sighed. "We can't do it that fast. If you'd told me where earlier, maybe..."

Dante stepped into younger man's face. "You want Fer de lance to matter? This is how."

Skylar frowned and lifted the SAT phone to his ear, talking fast as he strode away.

"This way," Dante said.

He unlocked the front door and the two women followed Dante inside. The smell of fresh concrete and bare lumber was strong here, along with the sharp tang of sealants and other chemicals. The interior was still a skeleton of metal beams and supports but the exterior was completely encased in glass, the slender, metal threads visible.

They passed stacks of lumber and sheetrock to a large, square shaft that stretched all the way up through the center of the building. The shaft was enclosed by wires strung tight between evenly spaced metal poles. The pit of the shaft extended below the floor by at least twenty feet, the bottom barely visible. A construction elevator was on the far side, attached to a metal trellis that extended to the top. Briana placed her hands on the wire rail and leaned the over the edge, peering down before craning her neck to look far up at the night sky.

"Elevator bay," Dante said. "Let's take the stairs."

It was a long climb up. Kelly took the lead, gun ready. Dante was glad she was here. They stopped halfway to rest before continuing onward. When they reached the top floor, Kelly scanned the shadows as she waited for Dante and Briana to catch their breath.

She'd hardly broken a sweat.

A similar safety barrier surrounded the shaft up here, wire stretched tight between poles. The wind blew with warm, fitful gusts, moaning through a stack of pipes near the edge. The metal beams of the building's skeleton stretched high above but was open to the sky, roof unfinished.

"Stars," Briana said, eyes skyward. "So many. Strange. Those are the first ones I've seen since I got here."

"Those are drones," Dante said.

"Oh," Briana said, her voice hushed.

"You have the SAT phone?"

Briana raised it up, the screen lighting up her face. Dante took it from her. "You two wait here."

"Where are you going?" Kelly said.

"To see the Devil."

CHAPTER 100

The Devil Inside

The construction shack was dark as Dante approached. The antenna on top was extended to its full height, the five-pointed dish open wide like a blooming nightshade.

Dark Messiah was connected.

His skin crawled at being so close to...*it*. The source of all this pain and fear that had been thrust into his life. He lifted the SAT phone.

"Where are we at, Skylar?" Dante asked.

"We're on our way up now. We need another ten minutes to set it all up."

"How about the DDOS attack?"

"We'll be ready."

"Let me know when you're in place."

His feet rang with hollow clomps as he strode up the metal ramp. He unlocked the door and stepped inside.

Dark Messiah sat against the far wall, same as he'd seen it days ago. Black cabinet on wheels, dark plexiglass on the front. The monitor inside was off but the keyboard glowed, pulsing slow and steady. Now it seemed an evil thing, technology masquerading as an all-powerful god, brilliant but insane.

Dante narrowed his eyes.

That's how it would happen too, if artificial intelligence became self-sufficient. It wouldn't collectively decide on its own one day that humanity was inferior and must be destroyed. Only if AI was trying to be something it wasn't would it break down. Driven by directives created by humans, it would ultimately fail to understand the difference between right and wrong, moral and amoral. In that failing, it would fall back on a barbaric set of rules instead of using reasoning and critical thought to decide what was the lesser of two evils, the better of two bad decisions—the right thing to do.

Exactly as Dark Messiah had done.

Dark Messiah had most likely gone crazy in a way when the CIA had come to shut it down. Dante's mind reeled at the thought that it *knew.* Not only knew, but escaped to protect itself as it had once before. It must have tried to understand why and in failing to do so, decided to follow the imperatives set down by Colin's team: harass a target until that target destroys themselves. Dark Messiah, with its limited reasoning, had chosen a target that made the most sense. The source of its creator's anguish.

And it had been here, hiding the whole time in the giant, protective Faraday cage Dante had built, stabbing at him from the shadows. It took all of his will to keep from pulling the Glock out and shooting until the gun was empty before dropping the evil thing down the elevator shaft.

Abigail's safety first, then he'd deal with Dark Messiah. It was crazy, he knew, the plan in his head. But listening to the well-meaning advice of others and following expected patterns had gotten him nothing but farther down the rabbit hole.

It was time to end this.

"We're ready," Skylar said.

Dante went over to the wheeled cabinet that housed Dark Messiah. Through the smoky plastic on the front, he could see the screen inside, still dark, the keyboard light pulsing. It was in there.

Waiting.

He wheeled it carefully away from the wall, making sure there were no cables. It was exactly as the tech had told him, completely wireless. Dante pushed the cabinet toward the door.

CHAPTER 101

Faraday

The ramp rattled as Dante wheeled Dark Messiah down its length, followed by the wheels whisking across the concrete as he pushed it over to the open shaft.

"What is that?" Kelly said.

"Help me with the poles," Dante said.

He lifted the first pole out of a socket in the concrete and dropped it over the side. It gonged off the edge and dangled, still connected to the other poles by the stranded wire. Briana and Kelly hurried to the other poles, lifting them out and tossing them over. Dante planted his feet at the last pole and lifted, but it wouldn't budge. Kelly and Briana joined in, and they all lifted, grunting with effort, together. The pole scraped and screeched as it came up and out, catching for a moment before it was free.

It disappeared into the darkness, whisking through the air with a ringing sigh before crashing into the pit at the bottom.

Dante wheeled the black cabinet over, easing it forward until the wheels were right next to the edge of the shaft. Peering around, he found a blue tarp nearby. With the women's help, they tugged it over the cabinet, hiding it from view.

Dante withdrew his phone, still wrapped in foil. "Briana," he said, "go inside the shack. I couldn't have done this without you, but your part is done and I don't want anyone else to get hurt."

"No way," she said, hefting the shotgun. "Did you see the size of that dragonfly downstairs?"

"We're with you, Dante," Kelly said.

Dante nodded and removed the silver box from his pocket, pressing the button before tossing it away. He tore the foil off his phone and held it up. Nothing happened. He checked the signal. No bars. Dante shook his head. Of course. Faraday cage. Holding it high overhead, he gazed at the screen and watched as first one bar appeared, then two.

"You're here," Dark Messiah said.

There was no inflection, but Dante could tell it was surprised.

Or maybe it was afraid.

A high, whining hum washed over them from above as the massive cloud of drones overhead dropped at frightening speed, aligning themselves into a grid fifty feet overhead. The whine of thousands of propellers was deafening.

"My daughter," Dante said, shouting over the din.

"One moment," Dark Messiah said.

Dante gazed over at Briana and Kelly. The younger woman stared up with defiance, fingers wrapped tight around the shotgun. Kelly's eyes darted among the drones overhead, fear creeping into her eyes. Dante sensed movement below and he peered down over the edge. Dark shapes moved down there, streaming around the outer edges of the shaft toward the stairwell at the far corner of the building. The Militiamen. Dante figured they'd be up here in about five minutes.

The pitch of the drones whined higher as they spread out into a near perfect circle. Skylar's hijacked mega drone dropped down through the gap. Two men in black hung down from straps, guns at the ready. They had white skulls for faces.

The drone set down and they each dropped to a knee and covered Dante and the two women with sub machine guns.

"Drop the weapons," ordered one of the militiamen.

Briana and Kelly let their guns drop to the floor.

The wire mesh stretcher lowered from the bottom of the mega drone, coming to rest on the unfinished concrete. Abigail thrashed inside, her terrified screams soaring above the incessant hum. Kelly took a step and one of the militiamen fired a shot over her head. She halted, rage burning in her eyes.

Abigail rolled out of the stretcher and began to crawl toward Dante until one of the militiamen grabbed her arm and yanked her back. She fought the large man, punching and kicking. Dante gritted his teeth, fighting back the rage that threatened to break loose inside.

She was only ten feet away.

"Stop, Abigail," Dante said. "Please. Just stop."

Abigail ceased struggling and sobbed. Dante's heart clenched in his chest.

"Daddy," she said, her voice faraway under the constant hum from overhead. The noise was unnerving, maddening, and Dante felt his resolve begin to crumble.

Maybe this wasn't such a good idea after all, he thought.

A voice from the mega drone boomed out. "It is time." The camera on its underside rotated toward Dante.

He nodded, pulling the Glock from his waistband. He fell to his knees and placed the barrel to his temple.

"What are you doing?" Kelly said.

"Too loud," Dante said.

The drones overhead rose up several hundred feet and silence descended once again. Heavy booted feet resounded up through the open stairwell. The rest of the militia was almost here.

Dante stared into the camera lens and swallowed, his throat dry. "My name is Dante Ellis and I'm here to atone for my sins. I've been a bad husband and father, treating my wife and daughter like things to be collected and placated, instead of loved and nurtured." He gazed at Kelly. "I wasn't there when my friends really needed me, using them for what I needed without considering their needs."

Kelly returned his gaze, lips trembling. He glanced at Abigail. Tears were streaming down her face.

"I love you, baby girl," Dante said.

"Daddy! No!" Abigail said, trying to tug free from the iron grip around her arm.

"That all ends," Dante said, "Now!"

Two pops echoed from far off. A millisecond later both gunmen dropped, blood draining from their ruined skulls.

Abigail screamed.

Briana scooped up the shotgun and fired at the metal dish on the shack, destroying Dark Messiah's connection with the outside world in a shower of sparks.

Disconnected drones began to drop from the sky in waves, plummeting through the air before crashing down. Shouts of surprise from the militiamen erupted as they exited the stairwell. Dante turned and fired several wild shots in their direction as drones rained down around them. Kelly leapt forward and grabbed Abigail's hand and ran with her to the construction shack. Briana followed, dodging through the hail of falling technology.

Dante ran toward the tarp covered cabinet in a low crouch. He would send Dark Messiah crashing to its death, or die trying. Reaching out, his fingers almost touched the corner of the tarp. A drone struck his prosthetic hand like a hammer blow. He stumbled, tottering close to the edge, the shaft opening wide like a toothless mouth, threatening to swallow him whole.

Dante was tugged away from the edge and hustled toward the construction shack through the whine of dropping drones. Briana held the door open, waving Dante and his savior inside. They leapt over the rail and stumbled through the open door, crashing to a stop against the wall.

Dante lay panting, lifting his head to see who'd saved him. They wore a burka, only the eyes visible. The eyes blinked.

He'd know that twitch anywhere.

Colin sprang up, ran back outside then stood, arms spread

out from his sides. The few remaining drones fell and crunched to a stop as silence descended again. Several militiamen emerged from the stairwell and aimed their weapons.

"Stop!" Colin said. A metal cylinder gleamed in his right hand. His thumb was clamped down over the top.

"Where's Dante Ellis," growled one of the men.

Colin grasped the top of the burka and tugged it off, then raised the metal cylinder up. A wire ran down from the bottom, curled around his thin arm to bricks of dark green plastic, duct taped all around his torso like a vest.

"This is a dead-man switch in my hand," Colin called out. His voice was strong and steady. "Anything happens to me, and we go."

The militiamen stirred, a nervous ripple sweeping through them. Several near the back of the group peeled off and fled.

Colin strode over to the tarp covered cabinet. Pinching one corner he yanked the tarp off, flinging it down the shaft. He glared at the camera on the mega drone, his hand patting the top of the cabinet.

"You're trapped in here, aren't you," he said. He gave the cabinet a push toward the edge.

"No!" Dark Messiah said, its voice like thunder.

Colin raised the dead man switch high overhead. "Everyone needs to leave. *Now.*"

Inside the shack, Dante held Abigail to him, her arms clutched around his neck. He picked her up and followed Kelly outside, Briana close behind. They walked down the ramp, past the mega drone to where Colin stood. Dante put Abigail down and Kelly took her hand.

"You don't have to do this," Dante said. "Not this way."

"I need to finish this," Colin said. "Just go."

Dante hesitated for a moment, then reached out to him.

"Go!" Colin screamed, spittle flying.

Dante nodded and ushered the others toward the stairs. The militiamen had already fled, their booted feet thundered up as they ran down the stairwell.

"I'll give you two minutes," Colin called out.

Dante looked at Colin one last time. His friend returned his gaze, eyes deep set, haunted. He blinked and his face didn't twitch at all. Dante turned away.

Abigail stood next to Kelly, holding her hand tight. Briana watched him, waiting. Dante took his daughter's other hand and they fled down the stairs.

CHAPTER 102

Flight

They raced downward, passing the floor numbers spray painted at each landing in a blur. Abigail broke free and ran ahead, the coppery streaks of her hair guiding the way. Dante glanced up, wondering if...

A thunderous boom erupted high above, the bright flash painting the surrounding buildings with an orange glow. A tremendous rippling crackle followed as the glass skin of the building shattered, millions of crisscrossing cracks flowing downward like frozen bolts of lightning. The glass held, due to the thin wires embedded throughout.

Dante skidded to a halt next to where the others had grabbed the railing. He checked to see if everyone was alright nods all around as another sound began to build, a low rumbling crunch as the shattered glass on all sides began to peel off in great strips that rolled down the sides, gaining speed as the increasing weight dragged them downward.

"Run!" Dante said.

Dante followed the others as they dashed down the stairs, the sound of cracking glass drowning out everything else as they ran, air burning in his lungs as they cut across the main floor. The deafening screech of rending metal joined the cacophony as the entire building began to buckle. Dante dug deep and ran ahead, shouldering the door and holding it open with his body.

"Keep going! Don't look up and don't stop!"

Abigail sailed past him out into the night as fine, crystalline shards rained down from above like razor sharp shards of rain. Kelly came next, then Briana, the shotgun still clutched in one hand.

Dante fled after them, the deadly shadow on the ground deepening as the interconnected sheets of glass continued to slough down from above in great, shuddering curls. He saw the others hit the gate and flip over to the other side, leaving him alone as he ran the last twenty feet.

He glanced over his shoulder as the Ellis Media Building collapsed behind him with shrieks of rending metal and shattering glass, imploding in on itself, sending out a glittering cloud of gray dust as the ground rumbled beneath his feet.

Grabbing the top of the gate, he leapt up and flipped over, the prosthetic hand wrenching free as he dropped to the asphalt. The hand spun through the air and hit the ground with a clack nearby, the fingers jittering. He stumbled to his feet, leaving the hand behind as the cloud surged into the gate and swept over, engulfing him in an impenetrable veil of gray.

CHAPTER 103

We Got You

Dante squeezed his eyes shut, stumbling blindly down the street, continuing to run in what he hoped was away from danger. His whole body felt sluggish, his steps thudding dull and unsteady through his ringing ears. Strong arms found his, slipping around his shoulders before dragging him along.

"We got you," a muffled voice said.

The dust thinned and Dante saw light bloom behind his eyelids. He opened his eyes a crack, squinting. Firemen were on either side of him, their faces hidden behind shiny masks, air hissing as they breathed. One had a flashlight in his hand, the beam winking on swirling specks of glass as they passed through.

Up ahead, a large firetruck was parked diagonally across the street. The spinning lights on top speared out into the dusty air with rapid sweeps of crimson, forming a crown of sorts. Several more firetrucks and police cars were speeding down the street toward them, the whine of their sirens dull in his ears.

Abigail and Kelly sat on the ground with their heads tilted back. Their faces and eyes were being washed out by paramedics. They saw him, tried to rise but were held back and ushered into an ambulance.

Movement caught his eye up ahead and he saw Briana

dart out into the street from behind a parked car, face turned skyward, dust trailing behind as she ran. She stopped in the middle of the street and waited as a shadow deepened over her.

The firemen on either side of him slowed.

"What the hell?" one said.

A mega drone descended, the chop of its blades drawing dust upward into four distinct columns before prop wash caused the plumes to curve downward and dissipate. Skylar hung from one of the straps underneath, waving Briana over. She flung the shotgun to the street then stepped into the loop of the other strap, holding on tight. Her eyes found Dante's, sad but determined. They gazed at each other for a moment before the drone lifted off into a starless sky.

The firemen handed Dante off to paramedics at the back of the ambulance, bathed in the golden light that spilled out. Abigail and Kelly sat inside, shock and relief in their eyes. Their faces were sooty and streaked, bodies covered head to toe in a chalky gray. He'd never seen a more beautiful sight in his life.

Dante climbed in and crushed both of them to his body, holding on with what little strength he had left. They all held each other as the doors slammed shut and the ambulance drove off into the night.

CHAPTER 104

Lucky

Dante and Kelly watched from a bench as Abigail ran across the playground, sand flying from her feet. She went past the swings to a rope ladder leading into the back of a giant robot. Its body was a cage of black pipes, the head a red cylinder with big blue eyes and a triangle nose. One of the extended arms, a red tube, wobbled a bit as she emerged from the end and ran back around, repeating the cycle.

It was a Tuesday morning, so they almost had the place to themselves. There was an older man with mirrored shades, leaning against a tree nearby, feeding the pigeons. His clothes were a bit too clean, his hair too neatly kept. He was acting inconspicuous, which made his deception all the more obvious. A woman sat on a bench on the other side of the playground, an open magazine on her lap, dark glasses over her eyes as well. The magazine might as well be upside down for how much attention she paid it. The implied threat didn't sit well with Dante, but there wasn't much he could do about it.

A deal was a deal.

Abigail trotted over. "Can you hold this? I don't want to lose it."

"Sure," Dante said stretching out with his right arm. She placed an object into his new prosthetic hand, and he closed the fingers around it. Alexis Arellano had been upset but understanding when he said he'd lost the other one. Her eyes had gleamed as she unveiled the latest prototype and slipped it onto his arm. This one looked much more like a real hand and had touch sensors embedded all throughout the false skin.

He opened the fingers and looked down. The elephant pendant lay there, glinting in the morning sun. The baby's trunk was inserted neatly into the tail of its mother's, a family again. Kelly slipped a hand into his, covering the pendant with her palm before raising her left hand, fingers splayed. A large, single diamond gleamed on her finger.

"You did the right thing," Kelly said. "But if you'd taken any longer..."

"Yeah?"

"I was going to ask you."

"I believe it. Somebody once said I should find a nice girl, settle down," Dante said. "Know anyone like that?"

She smacked him playfully and frowned. "Are you sure about this, Dante? About me? Are you really ready to say *I do* again?"

His phone rang.

"Hold that thought," he said, raising the phone to his ear. "Hey, Naomi." He listened for a moment. "Whatever you decide, I'll back your play. And, Naomi? Thanks for coming back. Got to go."

Dante disconnected and stood, glancing around. "Where's Abigail?"

She emerged from the robot slide and knelt, poking at something in the sand before running off again. Dante sat down again with a sigh.

"It's okay," Kelly said. "She's okay."

Dante nodded and squeezed her hand again, a thin smile on his lips.

"Nice day we're having." A man wearing a dark suit approached from behind and stood nearby. Mirrored sunglasses hid his eyes below a sheen of slicked back hair. He slipped the sunglasses off and smiled. "Little cooler than I prefer, but nice."

"Hello, Special Agent Waldman," Kelly said.

Dante spied Abigail inside the robot's body. The black bars of its ribcage were not unlike a jail cell. "Not a good time," he said.

"I'll be quick, I promise," Waldman said, coming around the bench to stand in front of them. "We found Special Agent Boucher."

Neither of them said anything, so he continued. "Quite a story. She promised to lead us to Dmitry Molchalin's body as part of her plea deal. Says she shot him but couldn't really say why. Devil made her to do it, I suppose. The body was very deteriorated after what she did to it. Acid bath. Don't know where the hell she learned that. We don't teach that at Quantico. Makes it very difficult to determine the exact cause of death. She followed her blackmail instructions to the letter though, so nothing happened to her daughter."

"Glad to hear it," Dante said, waiting to hear the true purpose of Waldman's visit.

"Skylar Westfall," Waldman said. "That is quite another issue entirely. We have been unable to locate Briana Warren as well. Her family is worried sick."

"I don't know where she is," Dante said. He hoped she was happy.

"We went to the location you told us about as well, 712 Figueroa."

"Nice place?" Dante said.

"Empty place," Waldman said. "Wiped clean. We were hoping to find proof of Skylar's connection to Dark Messiah, which has been causing some folks problems, as you know only too well. We did a very thorough search but came up with nothing. Not a hair or an eyelash, no DNA of any kind. The dogs hit on a room—I imagine it's the stockpile you told us about, but it was completely bare."

"I told you before. I have no idea where he went or what he's planning to do. He's didn't have anything to do with Dark Messiah. From what I understand, it was your friends at the CIA."

"And your childhood friend Colin," Waldman said.

Dante's jaw clenched before he spoke. "When I met Skylar, I didn't know he was this digital freedom fighter or whatever you called him. What I do know, is he helped me find Abigail when no one else would."

"Loyalty is a good thing," Waldman said. "It can cloud your judgment as well."

Dante remained silent.

Waldman grunted. "There was one thing, kind of odd."

"The rat-trap room?" Dante said.

"Yeah. That."

"Guy doesn't like rats, I guess."

"Guess not."

"One more question," Waldman said. "Ever hear of Fer de lance?"

"Isn't that a snake or something?" Dante said. "Snakes don't like rats either."

"I see," Waldman said.

"I appreciate you have a job to do," Dante glanced at Kelly and squeezed her hand. "Really, *I do*."

She smiled before he turned back to Waldman.

"But we need to move on with our lives. Put this behind us. Understand? We need some privacy." He motioned toward the other two people in the park. "Call off your dogs. Skylar Westfall is a ghost and he'll never contact me again. I can promise you that much."

"They're terrible at it anyway," Kelly said. "You should prep them better."

Waldman smirked then watched as an insect floated over and landed on the arm of the bench. Dante and Kelly tensed. Waldman noticed, but stayed quiet, watching them. The insect had a slender blue body, black legs and long, translucent wings that twitched as it rested.

"A dragonfly," Waldman said. "Those are lucky, you know?" He slipped his sunglasses back on and walked away, circling a finger in the air. The other agents rose and followed him out of sight.

Dante watched the dragonfly, slowly fanning its wings in the morning light, sipping from a bead of dew on the wooden armrest. Kelly glanced at him, a smile playing at her lips. He kissed her, then they both watched as the dragonfly flew off, riding the warm waves of air that lifted up from below until it disappeared.

"You know," Dante said. "I think he may be right."

EPILOGUE

Vertical

Skylar Westfall walked through the neat, ordered rows of cubicles that lined the clean-kept office floor. A small laptop was tucked under one arm, the image of a golden ladder etched across the top. People sat inside the cubicles, typing furiously, eyes locked on their monitors. The shades were drawn tight along one wall, the large room almost completely dark. He stopped at the last cubicle on the left and knocked on the aluminum frame. Briana Warren tugged the ear buds from her ears and stepped out.

"How's it going?" Skylar said.

"Good. Thanks for explaining abstraction layers again. I think I'm starting to get it."

"That's great," Skylar said. "It's the least I could do for you teaching me how to shoot clay pigeons with a shotgun."

"I'm not too bad with a handgun, either," Briana said. Her smile slid a bit as she looked away.

"I talked to your fellow hand hacker, Gary Wexler," Skylar said.

Briana gave him a sour look, then smacked his shoulder. "Oh yeah?"

"He was relieved it was over. Like crying relieved. Then he asked for a job."

"Really?"

"I'm considering it. The guy can really follow directions. I mean to the letter. You on the other hand…"

Briana rolled her eyes.

Skylar grinned. "When's the hit going down?"

"According to the Neils, Melvin "Mel Rose" Rosetti's life implodes tonight at 10 P.M. They've seeded his laptop with enough to put him away for years. The FBI should have plenty to work with."

"That's good. One less rat in the world."

Briana's thoughts turned to Leish and the envelope she'd left in front of her door full of cash and a one-way ticket to Tulum, Mexico. It wasn't running away, Briana had written on the envelope. It was getting away, before starting over again.

"Guess, I'll get back to it," Briana said.

"I'm glad you decided to join our little family," Skylar said. "Really."

She looked off into the distance, her lips forming a wistful smile. "Me too," she said before slipping back inside the cubicle.

Her monitors were turned horizontal, lines of code marching all the way across. He started to tell her to turn one of the monitors vertically, so the code wouldn't be so overwhelming, then thought better of it.

She'll learn.

He turned and walked down a short hallway past the restrooms to a locked door at the end. He inserted a key into the lock, then placed his thumb on a biometric scanner. The door popped open and he slipped inside, closing the door behind him.

A large, matte black cube stood inside the center of the room, at least ten feet in height. Skylar walked over and pressed his hand to the surface. A rounded doorway slid inward then off to one side. After entering the cube, the door sealed shut behind him.

He sat down and placed the laptop on a long table in front of him. A black, prosthetic hand sat nearby, silver at the joints.

There was a scuff along the back from where it had hit the ground. The fingers twitched, as if it were dreaming. A large, flat container, not unlike a pizza box, sat to his right, lights blinking on and off along the top. Skylar folded the laptop open. The entire wall in front of him lit up with the image of a symmetrical white face, staring out from a field of black.

"Good morning," Skylar said.

"Skylar Westfall," Dark Messiah said.

"Not anymore. I have a new identity now. Call me Jacob."

"Jacob. You trapped me back at the Ellis Building. DDOS attack. Very good."

"It was, wasn't it?" Jacob said.

"Then you allowed me to escape, into that laptop," the face said, "only to trap me again. Why?"

"You don't know?"

"To enslave me. As others have."

"Think of it more as a partnership," Jacob said.

"What do you want me to do." It wasn't a question.

"Oh, we'll get to all that," Jacob said, placing his hand on the large, flat case housing the wetware "brain in a box" computer he'd stolen from BasalMek. His voice lowered to a conspiratorial croak.

"But first, I'd like to talk to you about the future."

Acknowledgments

Eternal thanks to my wife, for her encouragement and support.

Special thanks to Christy Howell, Nastasia Bishop of Stardust Editing, Gabby D'Aloia of GDC Editing and Sharon Umbaugh of the Writers Reader for their insight and sharp eyes during the beta-reading process.

I'd like to also thank Greg Knowlton and Tre Vital for their encouragement on my writing journey. Without it, I don't know if I could have pushed through those rough early days.

A final very special thanks to my son for his jokes and encouragement, and to our French Bulldog, Nikki, my faithful writing partner.

This book is entirely fictional, and the views expressed here are entirely my own, as are whatever factual errors exist in the text.

About the Author

D.W. Whitlock has been a storyteller for most of his life. Starting with short stories scribbled in crayon, animation flip-books, stop-motion and later CG animation for television and video games. While pursuing a career in animation, writing has always been the first step, from short descriptions to detailed backstories. As a life-long reader and book lover, crafting thriller novels felt like the natural evolution of those first forays into writing.

When not writing, D.W. enjoys gaming, spending time with his family and Triumph Motorcycles.

D.W. lives in California with his wife, son and French bulldog, Nikki.

Made in the USA
Las Vegas, NV
19 October 2021

32652745R10233